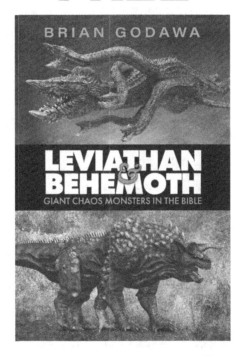

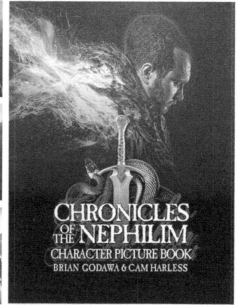

Abraham Allegiant

Chronicles of the Nephilim
Book Four

By Brian Godawa

ABRAHAM ALLEGIANT
5b Edition

Warrior Poet Publishing
www.warriorpoetpublishing.com

ISBN: 9798710828694 (hardcover)
ISBN: 978-0-9859309-8-1 (paperback)

Scripture quotations taken from *The Holy Bible: English Standard Version.*
Wheaton: Standard Bible Society, 2001.

Dedicated to
the fans of *Chronicles of the Nephilim*.
You helped me name most of the books,
including this one,
and you inspired me to work diligently
to satisfy your story hunger.

ACKNOWLEDGMENTS

Special thanks to the wife of my youth, Kimberly, and if you are a fan of the series, you should thank her too because without her there would be no *Chronicles of the Nephilim*. Thank you also to Amber Lary for her editing services, and Blake Samuels for his helpful content feedback in all things Mesopotamian. Special thanks to Sarah Beach for her fantastic editing of this new edition.

And thanks, Joe.

All gratitude to El Shaddai, God Almighty, who is El Elyon, God Most High.

NOTE TO THE READER:

The saga *Chronicles of the Nephilim* employs an ancient technique of changing names of both people and places from novel to novel and sometimes within the same novel. This peculiar technique was universally engaged in by all ancient Near Eastern writing including the Bible because in that world, names were not merely arbitrary sign references. Names reflected the essential purpose, meaning, or achievement of people or places. Thus, when people experienced significant changes in their lives, they might also change their name or the name of a location where it occurred. Or when one nation adopted another nation's deity, it would give it their own name. Even the God of the Bible uses different names for himself in different instances to communicate his different attributes. While this is not familiar to modern readers and can cause difficulty in keeping all the names and identities straight, I have chosen to employ that peculiar technique as a way of incarnating the ancient worldview and mindset. So reader be warned to watch names carefully and expect them to be changing on you even when you are not looking.

In the interest of aiding the reader in managing the name changes in the series up to this point, and including *Abraham Allegiant*, I have included the following charts that illustrate some of the more significant name changes.

	Creator	Semjaza	Azazel	Gadreel	Gilgamesh
Enoch Primordial (Sumer)	Elohim	Anu	Inanna	—	—
Noah Primeval (Sumer)	Elohim, Yahweh	—	Inanna	—	—
Gilgamesh Immortal (Sumer)	Elohim	—	Ishtar	Ninurta	Gilgamesh
Abraham Allegiant (Babylon)	El Shaddai	—	Ishtar	Marduk	Nimrod
Abraham Allegiant (Canaan)	El Elyon	—	Ashtart	Ba'al	Amraphel
Divine attribute	Creator Almighty Most High	High God of pantheon	Goddess of sex & war	God of vegetation & storm	A Nephilim

	Creator God	Nachash	Giants	Sons of God	Noah
Other Names	Yahweh Elohim	The Serpent	Nephilim	Bene ha Elohim	Utnaphishtim
	Yahweh	The satan Adversary	Rephaim	Watchers	Ziusudra
	Elohim	Mastema	Emim	gods	Chosen One
	El Shaddai	A Seraphim	Caphtorim	Heavenly Host	
	Angel of Yahweh	Shining One	Zamzummim	Divine Council	
	Son of Man	Accuser	Anakim	Shining Ones	
	El Elyon	Belial	Avvim	Holy Ones	
		Diablos	Horim	Anunnaki	

	True Heaven	Sumerian Pantheon Seven Gods Who Decree the Fates	Sumerian Pantheon Four High Gods	Mesopotamian Heavens and Earth
Hierarchy	Yahweh Elohim	Anu	Anu	Yahweh Elohim's throne
	Angel of Yahweh	Enlil	Enlil	The waters above the heavens
	Seraphim	Enki	Enki	The firmament
	Cherubim	Ninhursag	Ninhursag	The heavens
	Sons of God	Inanna	—	Earth
	M'alak (angels)	Utu	—	The Abyss
		Nana		Pillars of the earth
				Sheol

Could it have happened like this?

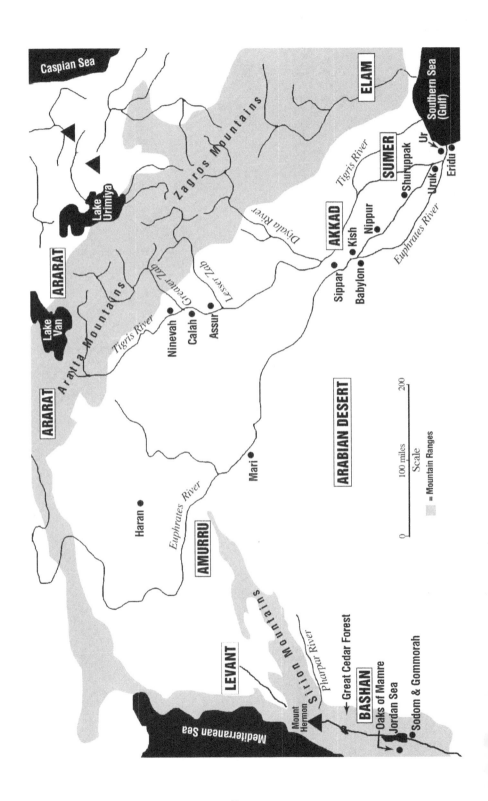

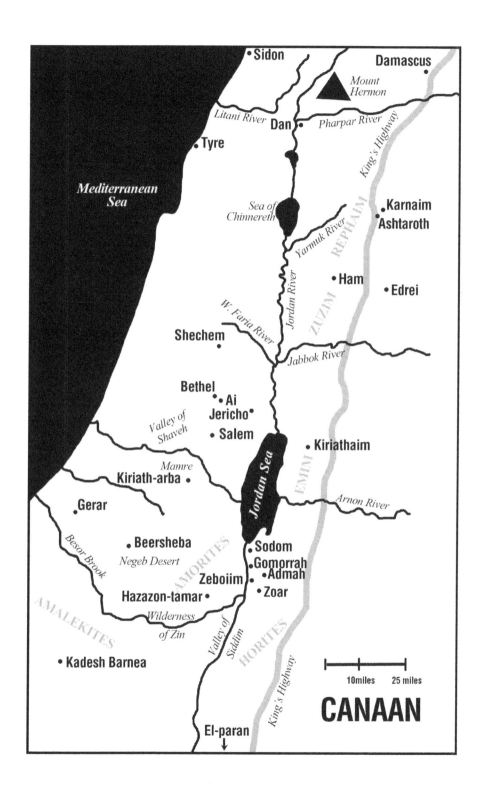

Sidon

Damascus

Mount
Hermon

Litani River   Dan   Pharpar River

Tyre

*Mediterranean
Sea*

King's Highway

Sea of
Chinnereth

Karnaim
Ashtaroth

Yarmuk River

REPHAIM

ZUZIM

Ham   •Edrei

Jordan River

W. Faria River

Shechem

Jabbok River

Bethel
•Ai
Jericho•
•Salem

*Valley of
Shaveh*

Jordan Sea

•Kiriathaim

Mamre
Kiriath-arba •

EMIM

•Gerar

Arnon River

Besor Brook

•Beersheba

Negeb Desert

AMORITES

Sodom
•Gomorrah
Zeboiim• •Admah
•Zoar

Hazazon-tamar•

*Wilderness
of Zin*

*Valley of
Siddim*

King's Highway

HORITES

AMALEKITES

• Kadesh Barnea

10miles   25 miles

CANAAN

El-paran
↓

CHAPTER 1

The mighty hunter, Nimrod, stepped off his four-wheeled chariot and looked into the thicket of reeds before him. He was the giant king of Sumer and Akkad, the land of Mesopotamia. At nine feet tall, with a closely cropped beard, piercing eyes, and hunter's armor, he was terrifying. He was a Naphil, one of the Nephilim, demigods born of the sexual union of god and human, which explained his towering height and massive strength.

A contingent of forty other huntsmen and trappers supported him. They waited on their chariots, equipped with nets, throwing sticks, clubs, and bolas. They did not carry their bows, swords, and javelins because they were not hunting to kill, but to trap. And they carried neck and hand bindings rather than cages, because they were not hunting animals. They were hunting humans.

"We spread out from here on foot," said Nimrod to his two captains. "Rendezvous at the target point at nightfall."

The captains nodded and took their squads of six men each into the thick forest of reeds before them.

The chariots were useless in the marshy wetlands. They were in the southernmost part of Mesopotamia, the marshes and waterways outside the huge city-state of Ur on the coast of the Southern Sea. It stood where the great Tigris and Euphrates rivers emptied into the Gulf after traversing the vast alluvial plains of Akkad and Sumer.

This delta area was quite different from the rest of Mesopotamia. Because of its location near the sea, it contained a myriad of shallow lakes and narrow waterways winding through dense thickets of reeds. The vegetation often grew taller than men, creating a natural maze of protection for the rustic inhabitants that lived in its midst. They were pastoralists who avoided urban life and sought independence, living off the land.

And that is why Nimrod wanted them as slaves.

He had left Uruk and moved to the central area of Mesopotamia to establish a new kingdom. He had to build a city to match his ambition. Such a massive undertaking required manpower, more than he had. So he built a slave force by conquering outlying rural tribes and transporting them upriver to his home base, now called Babylon.

In a very short time, he had controlled Mesopotamia by starting the communities of Akkad and Babylon. His mighty army consisted of hundreds of his own giant progeny. It quickly became feared and respected in the region. These were the giant offspring he had produced when he was king of Uruk and had claimed many of the city women as his own. He ultimately abandoned the practice because of the consequences of a populace that resented their king. He had sired hundreds of giant sons and daughters that he had brought with him to build his future.

Nimrod established a beneficent vassal kingdom through a treaty coalition with the tribes of the sons of Noah. Sippar, Nippur, and Kish were all allowed their own local rule without hostility under the condition of tribute and military support to Nimrod. He also started his northern expansion into the foothills of the Zagros with his newly established cities of Nineveh, Asshur, Rehoboth-Ir, Calah, and Resen.

In southern Sumeria, Nimrod's son Ur-Nungal ruled Uruk and helped him to consolidate his power over Eridu, Larsa, Lagash, and Ur. Ur overtook Uruk as the largest cosmopolitan metropolis in Mesopotamia. Its trading location on the Gulf and the surrounding vast agricultural regions of rich soil gave it the advantage. Hundreds of acres of villages, hamlets, farming land, and irrigation canals encircled Ur, all controlled by the government for the good of the people. At least, that is what they said to maintain the illusion of civilian participation in the collective. Beyond the city-state boundaries lay the marshlands where Nimrod now quietly stalked his human prey.

It was near dark.

The villagers of the marshland had settled down for their community meal. The food cooking on the fires consisted of boar and water buffalo, along with vegetables and some grains. They were a peaceful people who preferred to be left alone to care for themselves. They traded with the urban dwellers of Ur, but usually did so under the table to avoid the oppressive taxes of the city. Their village huddled beside a channel deep in the marshland. Their economy relied on the staple product of the perennial reeds all around them. They cut the strong flexible stalks down with sickles and used them for nearly everything, including fodder for livestock feeding and fuel for cooking. They even built their homes and boats out of reeds, covering them with a layer of pitch for waterproofing.

The reed houses went up in flames all around the village. Nimrod's hidden trappers, surrounding the village, set alight the pitch covering of the houses.

Some women screamed. It was too late to save the homes. They were burning to the ground.

Nimrod's men burst out of the shallows. They threw nets over whole families of villagers, pummeling the fighters, and chasing down stragglers.

Bolas and throwing sticks flew through the smoky chaos that enveloped the village. A woman bolted for the darkness of the marsh. A bola whirled through the air after her. The rope hit her legs, and the weighted iron balls whipped around, smacking hard. She tumbled face down into the soggy ground. A sturdy villager brought down a hunter with a large stone. He stood up, looking for another target, but became one himself. The flat, crescent moon shape of a hardened gopher wood throwing stick whacked his head. He crumbled to the ground. The hunters clubbed others into submission.

Men, women and children were chained up for transportation. The men who fought back with weapons were usually killed, if they could not be disarmed.

It took very little time before the entire village was captured, wrangled and bound for transport. Nimrod strode along the line of about seventy-five captives as he announced their destiny.

"People of the marshland, you are now slaves of my kingdom. I am the mighty Nimrod of Babylon. You will be brought to my region up north, to help build my city and temple for my name and glory. If you submit and obey, you will be treated fairly. If you do not, you will suffer and die. I will not tolerate insubordination."

One of Nimrod's warriors brought the chieftain of the village to him, bound, gagged and struggling defiantly.

Without pause, Nimrod drew his sword and cut off the head of the chieftain. The prisoners knew that their future would not be a hopeful one.

Nimrod said with deadpan frankness, "I am now your king. I am your god."

CHAPTER 2

As a port city with the prime location on the gulf of the Southern Sea, Ur became rich in transport taxes. All trade shipped in from abroad went through its harbor on the Euphrates to the other cities upriver. It would become known as "Ur of the Chaldees" because of the growing influx of Chaldean people in the region.

Ur already had a reputation for its elaborate funerals and the royal tombs of the deceased. The king, Urnanna, obsessed over bureaucracy and administration. He had constructed a voluminous library of laws and decrees in his perpetual quest for godlike control of the province. The urban landscape within Ur's walls could only be described as cramped and suffocating for its city dwellers. The city planners designed small and tightly-packed homes in order to create a dependent citizenry and minimize freedom of movement. Urnanna was Nimrod's vassal king; Ur, a tributary of his rule.

Nimrod rode his chariot at the head of the procession of newly captured slaves through the main street up to the temple district that stood at the height and heart of the city. He always performed triumphal entries with fanfare and grandiosity, in order to impress his subjects and reinforce his godlike authority. It helped that he was nine feet tall, a Naphil, born of Watcher god and human mother. He had discovered that the more theatrical and godlike his rhetoric and display, the more fear he garnered. His ultimate goal was deification.

The real deity rode beside Nimrod in his chariot as his personal bodyguard and emissary from the pantheon of gods. This was Marduk, a huge eight-foot muscle-bound hulk. He wore a hooded cloak and stood quietly in the shadow of Nimrod so as not to draw attention to himself. He was a fierce warrior, a master of many weapons. He had been waiting patiently for his moment to step out of the shadows and execute his own secret plan, a plan he kept hidden from even the assembly of gods.

But his time had not yet come.

The parade ended at the foot of the Great Ziggurat of Ur, a brick temple tower so large, it could be seen miles away, rising above the plains. It was named *Etemennigur*, which meant, "House Whose Foundation Creates Terror." It was about two hundred feet square and about one hundred feet high and was made of mud bricks that created a solid structure, the top of which was a shrine to the moon god Sin, the patron deity of the city.

Nimrod gazed upon the edifice with awe. The step pyramid, a man-made mountain, served in the minds of the people as a ceremonial staircase for the gods to descend from heaven. He knew the people believed the ziggurats connected heaven and earth. He thought to himself, *The temple I build for myself will dwarf this pile of bricks as a mountain dwarfs an anthill.*

He had been planning his temple structure for some time, along with the city he was building to house it in grandeur: Babylon. It would be more than the most glorious and mightiest temple. It had been commissioned by the assembly of gods to be a cosmic mountain to replace their current residence far in the west at Mount Hermon.

Their goal was that Nimrod would become the first world potentate, residing in Babylon. The gods would consolidate their heavenly power with his earthly rule, for an ultimate unity between heaven and earth. The Babylonian temple would be dedicated in an occultic ceremony of sorcery that would establish it as the new cosmic mountain of the gods. A portal would open to the heavens that would allow easy access for the gods to this "land between the rivers," the origins of civilization after the flood.

Nimrod had finally acquired the wealth and manpower to begin his building projects of both city and temple. He had only a few things left to take care of before returning to his home base upriver. The primary one was to have a private meeting with a sorcerer of Ur, an idol maker by the name of Terah.

CHAPTER 3

Terah ben Nahor's reputation extended from Sumer to Akkad. His fame grew from his innovative discoveries in astrology, and the art of divining the future and the will of the gods from signs in the heavens. He had started as a humble idol maker. His house idols, called *teraphim*, had become well known for their exquisite carvings. They were mostly small terra cotta statues of deities, both human and animal shaped, up to a foot tall. They were often lime-washed or painted in red and black. They were set in the doorways of homes or buried under the threshold to protect the inhabitants from malignant spirits. But they were also worshipped in private family chapels and buried with family member's bodies in graves as afterlife guardians.

Soon, the king commissioned him to craft larger-than-life idols out of imported stone for the royal palace and temple. His interest in deity expanded into divination, and so he studied texts on extispicy, hepatoscopy, and lecanomancy, the arts of divining from animal entrails, livers, and liquid movements respectively.

His interpretation of omens became legendary and he was appointed an official diviner, called a *baru*. But that was short lived as he began charting the heavens for horoscopic portents. It was believed that the heavens and earth were united in cosmic oneness and that celestial events were signs that foreshadowed earthly events of kings and kingdoms. Terah's study of the "heavenly host" carried a double meaning reference to both the stars in the heavens and the assembly of gods because they were considered interchangeable.

Urnanna had appointed Terah head sorcerer because of his vast knowledge of heavenly secrets. Terah was also a strong asset because he had been very amenable to the king's wishes. Terah sought to please Urnanna at all costs. This quality made Urnanna concerned as he led Nimrod and Marduk to meet Terah. The men marched up the long ramp of steps that approached the Great Ziggurat's temple of Sin at the top. Urnanna suspected that Nimrod wanted to build his own institution of magicians and sorcerers. Urnanna was sure he was about to lose his treasured Terah.

Either that or lose his head.

They entered the temple at the top. Pillars lined the white marble structure. An exquisite, black obsidian idol of the moon god stood before an altar in the center of the temple.

In a corner, Terah hunched over an astrolabe, a device that computed the mathematical text of astronomical observations and calculations. Nimrod and the others realized he had fallen asleep in his reading position. He snored away, oblivious to his new visitors.

Urnanna cleared his throat loudly.

Terah snapped awake. He noticed the king and stood with a bow. "My lord," Terah blurted.

"Terah, you need to go home and get some rest," said Urnanna. "You cannot live, eat, and sleep in the temple. You have a family and a life."

"Yes, your eminence," said Terah. Then he noticed the very large hooded muscleman, and the king looking closely at the statue of Sin.

Urnanna announced, "Terah, meet King Nimrod, your suzerain."

"Your high majesty," said Terah and bowed again.

Nimrod did not look down at Terah, but continued to examine the idol as he spoke.

"You have quite the reputation for a diversity of talents," said Nimrod.

"At your service, my king," said Terah.

Urnanna winced.

Nimrod said, "You may leave us, Urnanna."

Urnanna bowed and left the temple for the stairway descent. It humiliated him to be ordered around like a servant. But he knew that any show of pride or independence would result in punishment, if not instant death from the blade of Nimrod himself.

Nimrod returned to his examination of the idol once Urnanna had gone. He said, "You have crafted an amazing likeness out of this black obsidian."

"Thank you, my lord," said Terah.

Nimrod said, "Your terra cotta house idols are known all over Mesopotamia. One could say you have cornered the marketplace with your expertise."

"I pray my excellence honors the gods," Terah replied.

"How are your skills with coarse stone?" asked Nimrod. "Sedimentary or igneous rock."

"Competent, your majesty."

Nimrod said, "How would you like to have your own institute of astrologers, sorcerers and magi?"

Terah stuttered, "Well, I, uh – that would be – an undeserved honor, my lord."

Nimrod continued, "I want you to be my head sorcerer, Prince of the Heavenly Host. You would be fully supplied with everything you need and would answer only to me."

Terah could not think of what to say, so he repeated himself, "I am at your service, my king."

He paused and asked, "Shall I gather my wife and belongings to return with you to the north?"

"Not yet," said Nimrod. "Your first duty will be to accomplish a secret task for me down here and then travel up to Babylon at an arranged time in the near future."

"As you wish, my lord," said Terah.

"What would be the stone that has the largest deposit nearest Ur, and the best balance between hardness and speed for sculpting?" Nimrod asked him.

Terah thought for a moment. "I would have to say your best bet is limestone. It is the perfect medium between gypsum and granite. There is a significant region of it just west of here not too far into the desert."

Nimrod nodded. "Good. I want you to establish a guarded quarry there. Keep it out of sight of the cities. I have hired dozens of stonecutters from the Zagros and the Levant to provide you their services. They will arrive this week."

"I do not understand, my king," said Terah. "What would you like me to make out of the stone?"

Nimrod was looking again at the idol. "An army of limestone *golemim*. Stone Ones in the form of soldiers. Ten thousand strong."

Terah gulped. "Forgive me, my lord, but I still do not understand. Of what use will this 'army' of statues be to you? And how will I transport them all upriver?"

"You will not have to transport them," said Nimrod. "They will march up to Babylon for my command."

Shock kept Terah silent, leaving the obvious question unasked.

Nimrod moved close to him. He pulled a battered piece of parchment paper out of a pouch at his belt and handed it to Terah. The sculptor read it.

"This is highly sophisticated sorcery," said Terah.

"That is why I wanted the best sorcerer I could find," returned Nimrod.

"Its purpose is to animate the non-living. Where did you get it?"

"I stumbled across it on a journey I had long ago." Then Nimrod added, as an after thought, "In another life."

It was indeed another life. Nimrod had been the infamous Gilgamesh, king of Uruk, before he changed his identity and his life. He had stumbled upon the animated Stone Ones while seeking his great-great-grandfather, Noah the Faraway, remembered as Utnahpishtim. The written spell, placed into the mouth of a golem, brought it to life as a slave to do the bidding of its master. These Stone Ones had no life, no breath, just animation. So they could not be killed and were almost impossible to stop. Nimrod had almost been killed fighting several Stone Ones on his journey to Noah. He had commandeered the current spell from one of the mouths of the defeated golemim.

Nimrod explained, "You will keep the sculpted Stone Ones in the desert, hidden from the cities until you have completed their numbers. Then you will duplicate this spell on as many parchments, and place them in the mouths of the golemim. As you said, the spell will animate them to do your bidding. You will arm them with weapons and march them up to Babylon at a coordinated time. Then you may take residence in my city and begin your institute as you desire."

Nimrod obviously planned to have an invincible army to rule over all of Mesopotamia. It was also obvious why he wanted it done in secret in the desert. He needed the element of surprise to accomplish his purpose.

Better to be on the side of the conqueror, thought Terah, *than on the side of the conquered.*

"It will be my honor," said Terah.

Terah knew it was more like a lack of honor. But he was driven by self-preservation, not virtue. The pursuit of secret knowledge, of *any* knowledge, had created in him a fear of death. The more he learned, the more he realized how much more he had to learn. He suffered a dreadful awareness of how little time he would have left in his life to satisfy his craving. He would not live forever, so he sought to cram as much into his short life as he possibly could. Whatever maintained his survival would take precedent, so that he could continue his pursuit of more knowledge.

He served too many masters, all demanding his allegiance.

He did not have any children yet, so it would be relatively easy to pick up his minimal possessions, along with his wife Amthelo, and make the trek up to Babylon when necessary. Until then, she would be able to stay in Ur, while he accomplished his labor of mining and sculpting the sedimentary rock. He could make visits back home whenever he needed to.

"I will need the army two new moons from now," said Nimrod.

Terah gulped. He knew not to complain to this king. He could see there was no compassion in his eyes, only power. He could tell that hesitancy of any kind would provoke wrath. He would not see his wife for two full months after all. He would be working morning, noon, and night, carving an army of ten thousand soldiers and bringing them to life with the duplicates of the spell he held in his hand.

Terah said with bold confidence, "You will have your army of golemim in two new moons."

Nimrod grinned and slapped Terah's back.

"Now that is what I like to see, a willing attitude. You and I will work well together, Terah. As you can imagine, I have very big plans. And I want you to be a part of them."

"I am at your service," repeated Terah.

"Of course," said Nimrod, "if you reveal any of the details to anyone, I will torture and execute your entire family in front of your eyes, before I do the same to you."

"Of course, my lord," gasped Terah. "Of course."

CHAPTER 4

Nimrod had chosen the middle of Mesopotamia for his city of Babylon. The convenient location lay between the north and south where the Tigris and Euphrates bent their courses in close convergence. The location controlled the waterways of life that doubled as the main thoroughfare for trade. From Babylon, Nimrod had equal access to both his newly created northern cities as well as the conquered southern ones. He had found a plot of land well suited for his plans of a mighty city and had settled the area in preparation. He placed pillared boundary markers with serpent and scorpion curses engraved on them as guarantors of his oath to destroy trespassers.

Of the three clans of the sons of Noah, Nimrod had risen to become the leader of the Hamitic tribes. Joktan ruled the Shemites, and Phenech the Japhethites. As Nimrod extended his power, he did so through a beneficent suzerain treaty with Joktan and Phenech. They were allowed to engage in the local rule and administration of their cities, as well as their tribal traditions, so long as they paid tribute to Nimrod and supported the building of Babylon with some conscripted slave labor.

It was an uneasy alliance.

While Nimrod pursued his plans of building a city and temple, the goddess Ishtar had developed her own plans. The City of

Nineveh was being built up north, and it would be her very own city of patronage. She would be called "Ishtar of Nineveh." It was her spoils acquired by a secret deal with Nimrod back in Uruk.

Ishtar was the unruly and defiant goddess of sex and war. The pantheon of gods had rejected her for her megalomaniacal rebellion. She had a real problem with authority, unless *she* was the authority, so they ostracized her from their hierarchy. When she discovered their plans to unite with Nimrod in a scheme of global governance, she blackmailed them into giving her some territory and freedom, in exchange for her promise not to undermine their goals. Each party would agree to live and let live.

Ishtar did not like the idea of letting anyone live. She had no intention of being shipped up north to be out of the way of the action. She had other plans. She did not seek to overcome the assembly of gods, for that was not a likely possibility, even for the goddess of war. Rather, she would outdo them with a scheme so monumental, she thought it might even rival the originality of her previous idea for the War on Eden. At least in this postdiluvial world it would.

The heart of her plan was a person. A single person whose identity was crucial for accomplishing the long-term goal of Nachash, the Serpent of Eden, the Shining One whose attention she craved. Before she set off for Nineveh, she summoned the services of Sinleqiunninni, Nimrod's *ummanu*, or king's scholar.

As chief ummanu, Sinleqiunninni's responsibility covered the scribal and academic duties of Nimrod's kingdom. He was principal of the school of scribes and oversaw the accounting and library archives. Anything that had to do with writing on clay tablets and storing of information came under the ultimate authority of Sinleqiunninni. He was an introverted man who spent more time with tablets than with people. Thus, he possessed a lack of sociability and a poorly developed body. His obsession with details and correcting everyone in conversation drove Nimrod up a stone wall. Only one thing kept Nimrod from exiling or executing him. He was the only one who knew how and where to access the information needed for important decisions, from tax records to king's proclamations to ancient charts of stars. His memory was impeccable and useful for the king's control of his realm. His knowledge kept him alive.

While Nimrod had been down in the Ur province hunting humans for his slave force, Ishtar employed Sinleqi, as he was called for short, to scour the genealogical archives of the local cities. He was to look for a single person from the lineage of Noah's son Ham. Because the population had expanded rapidly after the Deluge, during the time she had been bound in the earth, it was quite a task to track down her target. Records were scattered and incomplete because it had taken some time for the early postdiluvian generations to become organized.

Sinleqi had begun his search in Shuruppak, Noah's city of origin. But he found what he was looking for in the labyrinth of chronicle archives at Kish, the first city of Cush, son of Ham.

Before the Flood, Noah's pregnant wife, Emzara, had been captured by the god Anu and the goddess Ishtar, who had been called Inanna back then in her Sumerian incarnation. Emzara had a son in that captivity whom she named Ham. Ham was seduced by the culture of his captors and was drawn into their idolatry. He became a priest of Inanna/Ishtar and had been initiated into the occultic secrets of the Watchers.

The Watchers were Sons of God, members of Elohim's divine council, or heavenly host. Two hundred of them rebelled and fell to earth during the ancient days of Jared. Led by the mightiest of the Watchers, Semjaza and Azazel, they had taken on new identities as gods of the Mesopotamian pantheon. They were referred to as gods, Watchers, or even Watcher gods. Semjaza had become Anu, the most high father god of the pantheon. Azazel had become his consort Inanna. Ishtar snorted in disgust at that memory.

They established a hierarchy of four High Gods over the rest of the pantheon, and Seven Who Decree the Fates. They had no idea that an insignificant scrapper, the Watcher called Gadreel, would bide his time, build his strength and perfect his fighting technique to become the mighty Ninurta of Uruk, and now Marduk of Babylon. Ishtar had to admit that he had been clever about it.

She stood before her tent, watching the puny humans labor on her fabulous temple, musing on the Plan of the Watchers. They had taken on the disguise of divinity in order to draw worship away from the Creator, who was known in antediluvian times as Elohim. He had other names, such as El Shaddai, which meant God Almighty; El Elyon, which meant God Most High; and the secret covenant name of Yahweh, the eternally self-existent one.

Ishtar smiled to herself. Drawing worship away from Elohim was not all the Watchers were after.

Following the Fall in the Garden of Eden, Elohim had promised he would one day provide a seed of royal kingship that would restore creation to its intended glory and humanity to its intended identity as the family of Elohim, true Sons and Daughters of God. The Watcher gods sought to corrupt that seedline by mating with humanity and violating the heavenly earthly divide. The result of their crossbreeding were the Nephilim, unholy hybrids of angel and human, giants who became known as the Seed of the Serpent at war with the Seed of the Woman, Eve.

When Ham was under the spell of Anu and Ishtar, they had secretly experimented on him through occultic sciences that were beyond the knowledge of mankind at the time. They had altered his body by splicing their own genetic makeup into his. But they also violated his wife, Neela, impregnating her with a newly developed genetic implantation. One that would carry the recessive genes of the Watchers without resulting in immediate gigantism. They hoped this would spread throughout the population with more efficient results.

When Elohim sent the Deluge as punishment for mankind's wickedness on the earth, part of that evil was this miscegenation or cross-breeding of human angelic hybrids. With those waters, archangels came from heaven and imprisoned many of the Watchers in the earth to await their final judgment. Seventy of the Watchers remained free.

And so did one of their abominable Nephilim offspring.

The eight family members of Noah who were saved on the ark included Ham and his pregnant wife.

Cush, the supposed son of Ham, carried the tainted bloodline of Neela. Nimrod sprang from this lineage.

But Nimrod was not Ishtar's interest. She had failed to persuade him to join forces with her. So Ishtar sought another child created by another abomination. After the Flood, Ham in his vile wickedness contested his father Noah's patriarchal authority by raping his own mother, Emzara. When Emzara gave birth to a son, he was hidden away out of shame and disgrace. Ishtar had heard that Noah cursed that son to be a servant of his other brothers. He was cut off from his inheritance. Of the three sons of Noah; Shem, Japheth, and Ham, the lineage of Ham would never be the Seedline of Eve. Shem's was the chosen line.

That abominable offspring of Ham was the man that Ishtar was after. As the cursed son of Ham, he would be the perfect vehicle through which to breed the Seedline of the Serpent in opposition to the Seedline of the Woman through the chosen son of Noah.

When Sinleqi was granted an audience with Ishtar, he approached her with trembling. She was known to kill servants in impatient fits of rage if she did not get what she wanted. She seemed particularly impatient as he drew near to her throne in the vast tent in the north section of the Babylon settlement.

"You had better be the bearer of good news, Sinleqi," snapped Ishtar, "for I have had a vexing hair day." Ishtar fancied herself a kind of divine fashion plate, who prided herself in a diverse wardrobe of beauty and pain. She would often combine exotic dresswear with accessories of violence in order to stress her ironic juxtaposition of identities as the goddess of both sex and war. Today, she had burned her hair trying to dye it white. It was frazzled and unruly. She simply could not do a thing with it. She decided to cut it all off and kill a few servants to use their hair for a wig.

Sinleqi bowed and said, "O Queen of Heaven, I have traveled far and wide and have borne the weight of many sleepless nights in genealogical research of the archives of the cities of man."

"Get on with it, hog nose," interrupted Ishtar. Sinleqi had an upturned nose that seemed to accentuate his pig-like endomorphic body.

Sinleqi turned and retrieved a tablet from one of the two servants who accompanied him. He handed it to Ishtar. She read it as he spoke.

"You are holding in your hands the tablet that I would argue contains the information you are looking for. I draw your attention to the colophon at the end of the tablet. It states the *toledoth* or genealogy, 'These are the generations of the sons of Noah, Shem, Ham, and Japheth. Sons were born to them after the flood. The sons of Ham were Cush, Egypt, Put, and Canaan.' Now by careful exegesis of the tablet text, I noticed that there was an unusual repetitive reference to 'Ham, the father of Canaan.' Hermeneutics, or the art of textual interpretation, would tell us that such repetition points toward an unusual identity of the object."

Ishtar interrupted again, "Get to the point, scholar!"

It always amazed Ishtar. This brilliant ummanu scholar had such a droning voice that she actually started to get sleepy. Watchers did not sleep, but they could fall into a hypnotic trancelike state that simulated sleep. She considered striking him dead, but then thought better of it. She realized there could be some utility in the future of multiplying these scholars and using their hypnotic effect, perhaps as a means to control the youth through mass indoctrination in schools of learning. The young were the most easily manipulated, because their minds were the least developed and, therefore, the most open to suggestion. She smiled. How deliciously ironic that something so apparently beneficial to the mind as education could be twisted into a tool of power to lull young minds into thoughtless adherence.

Sinleqi jumped to the conclusion with a faltering voice, "The text emphasizes Canaan's lineage from Ham because the patriarch Noah placed a curse on that son."

A fangy grin spread across Ishtar's face as she read the tablet. "So Canaan is my man. Where is he?"

"Actually, he is on our slave rolls," said Sinleqi, offering another tablet to Ishtar.

She ignored the offer and barked, "Well, go get him and bring him to me!"

Sinleqi cringed at the outburst. "Yes, your highness."

She added, "And Sinleqi, remember what I told you."

"Yes, your highness," he repeated.

Ishtar had commanded Sinleqi to maintain the utmost of secrecy in his pursuits. No one was to know what he was doing, not even Nimrod. In fact, she had ordered that he was to have everyone who helped him in the process clandestinely killed, including the two servants with him, obediently holding the tablets.

She wondered whether or not she should kill Sinleqi afterward as well. But she came to the conclusion that it would not be prudent to do so. It might draw too much attention, since he was the king's scholar.

Maybe I will just rape him instead, she thought.

CHAPTER 5

Canaan was a tall lanky man. As part of the slave force of Nimrod's growing kingdom, he did not receive any more rations than his fellow slaves, and thus he suffered, for the need of his larger frame which rose a head above the others exceeded that of the others. He entered Ishtar's tent behind Sinleqi, moving slowly and unresponsively. His malnourished body looked skeletal, with his eyes sunken in their sockets.

The voice of Ishtar boomed across the space, "Welcome, Canaan!"

Canaan hardly listened to the goddess' words. He stared at a table before him, overflowing with foodstuffs of all kinds. He began to drool. He could not help it. There were pomegranates, figs, and fruits bursting with juicy colors, crunchy vegetables piled so high that they fell on the floor, pitchers of milk and honey, bread cakes and beer. And at the apex of it all was a roasted boar, still steaming from being freshly cooked over a fire. The smell was unbearably delicious. Canaan wondered if it was a new form of torture that he was going to be put through, but for what reason he could not imagine.

Ishtar stood on the other side of the table of food. Sinleqi stepped out of the slave's way.

Ishtar watched Canaan like a master holding a bone over a dog. He trembled. She smiled and gestured to the table. "You may eat to your heart's content."

Now Canaan stared at her. But he did not move. He did not believe what he had heard. She could not be speaking to him.

She smiled and repeated with a soft, kind voice, "Go ahead, indulge yourself."

Canaan stepped forward slowly. He picked up some figs and cautiously ate them. He expected to be struck in mid-bite. This could not be real.

Ishtar did not smite him. She urged him on, "Enjoy." She turned and sat back in her portable throne to wait and watch him feast.

And feast, he did.

Canaan began to stuff vegetables and fruit in his mouth as if they were going to be taken away from him. He guzzled goat's milk, half of it splashing over his face onto the ground. He stopped, and looked at the boar beckoning to him on the large platter. After one more glance at Ishtar for approval, he tore into the meat like a ravenous jackal.

For the next quarter hour, Ishtar watched Canaan stuff his gullet with every bit of food he could. Unfortunately, it was a serious mistake on his part. His malnourished body could not handle the sudden intake of gluttonous amounts of flesh and produce.

Canaan stopped. Nausea swept over him. His gut started to spasm. He dropped the pig foot he had been gnawing on. He fell to his knees, bent over, and retched. Everything he had just gulped and eaten started to pour out of him in a stream of vomit.

When it was over, he noticed Ishtar standing over him, laughing. She laid an understanding hand on his back. "Do not worry," she said, "you will have plenty of food from now on, and time enough to digest it."

He looked up at her confused. What did she mean, plenty of food from now on?

As if she could read his mind, she peered deeply into his eyes and said, "Son of Ham, you have a destiny to fulfill."

Canaan stuttered, "I – I do not understand."

"Then I will put it simply for you," she said. "Would you like to stay here and die as a slave, or come with me and live as a king?"

Canaan could not answer.

Ishtar focused intently on her new little toy.

Sinleqi looked nervously at the tent entrance, sweating profusely, thankful that Ishtar did not notice him. He heard someone outside.

Ishtar stroked the confused Canaan's cheek, and clarified, "In your blood runs the future of a people who have the power to change the world. I am the god you will need to help you be able to do so."

"B-but I am cursed of Elohim," said Canaan, "to be a slave to the sons of Noah."

Ishtar bent down and whispered with a hiss, "When I am done with you, you will *rule* over the sons of Noah! And Elohim will choke on his curse as you choked on this food."

Canaan's eyes went wide with amazement.

Then Ishtar grinned.

It became contagious. Canaan grinned as if he understood her.

But he did not understand her. He only knew he had to choose between a living hell on earth as a slave and an unknown future of adventure with a goddess. It was not a difficult choice.

Ishtar suddenly realized they were not alone.

She jerked her head toward the tent entrance.

A huge bulky form, backlit from the bright sunlight pouring in from behind him, stood in the entrance of the tent.

Ishtar sighed, "Well if it is not my favorite Master of Farting Winds, the Almighty Artichoke." She topped it off with a fake curtsey.

Marduk growled and stepped into the tent.

He was, in fact, her rival, the divine bodyguard of Nimrod and ambassador of the pantheon of gods. Though he was opposite of her in temperament — quiet, reptilian, not easily provoked — she had found the one way to get under his skin: calling him sarcastic, derogatory nicknames of his true title as god of vegetation and storm.

Marduk brushed Sinleqi aside. To Sinleqi, it felt more like a shove. He crashed to the floor in a heap.

Marduk stepped up to Ishtar and placed a clay tablet on the table beside her. It was the toledoth tablet, the genealogy of the sons of Noah.

Ishtar continued in a stare down with Marduk. "Sinleqi," she muttered, "prepare your will and say your prayers."

Sinleqi quivered in fear. She was going to kill him for being found out.

"He will do nothing of the sort," said Marduk, eyes glaring into Ishtar's. "He is the king's scholar and he is under my protection."

Sinleqi got up and ran out of the tent.

Canaan continued to stare in open-mouthed wonder at the two titans facing off with each other.

Marduk and Ishtar had a history of antagonism that went all the way back to Uruk and the rule of King Gilgamesh. Marduk, whose name at that time had been Ninurta, became the protector of Gilgamesh and ambassador of the will of the gods. Before the Flood, Marduk had been a scrappy unimpressive deity. But in the intervening years, he had trained quite diligently. He rose to prominence in strength and accomplishment. He was the only divinity in the pantheon that could equal Ishtar in both cunning and battle skill. And he was the only one unafraid of her.

This last fact bothered Ishtar. She was not used to such competition since Semjaza, her only previous superior, had been bound in the earth. Marduk's silent, calm arrogance got under her skin as much as her insulting digs got under his. But they both knew that a face-off between them would be cataclysmic. A duel would, no doubt, result in one of them being bound into the earth until judgment, because that was the only way one could have victory over the other. Otherwise, it would be endless war with catastrophic consequences. When two gods battle, not much of the environment or humanity around them survives. Neither of them was willing to fight that battle until the moment was right, the moment each felt would be to their advantage.

So, the hostility continued to boil. One day, they would face each other in combat. That day was approaching fast.

She considered it. Perhaps it *was* today. After all, Marduk had just uncovered Ishtar's plot, so what other recourse would she have?

Marduk snorted, "Whore goddess, I care nothing for your pursuit of territory. As far as I am concerned, you can have it."

Ishtar hissed in reply, "Unfortunately, the assembly is not as apathetic as the Prince of Peas."

"The assembly need never know," said Marduk.

Ishtar could not believe what she just heard. She replied with skepticism, "And what is your price?" She was not about to allow this meathead the opportunity to control her through blackmail. But she thought she would at least see what con game he plotted.

Marduk continued, "I know you well enough to know that you will not abide an inferior position in a deal. So I propose a secret for a secret."

Now, *that* was the only thing that would tempt her. If Marduk was stupid enough to offer equal vulnerability in exchange, she might be very willing to oblige him.

"Pray tell," said Ishtar.

Marduk glanced at the cowering and curious Canaan, listening like a mouse.

Ishtar barked, "Canaan, take a hunk of meat and go wait for me outside the tent."

Canaan obeyed like a dog. He whisked himself out, leaving the two of them alone.

Marduk turned back to Ishtar. "I have my own territorial ambition," he said.

Ishtar raised her eyebrow in curiosity.

"I want to be the head of the pantheon," he declared.

"Surprise, surprise, big boy," she said, with just the right amount of sarcastic flirting. Ishtar's entire body became like a hypnotic cobra.

Marduk immediately felt himself attracted to the tramp goddess. She was good. She was very good.

He shook it off and said to her, "You have something I need."

Ishtar raised her brow again. His resistance genuinely caught her off guard. "You are just full of surprises now, are you not?" she said.

Marduk got to the point, not mincing words. "I will not reveal your intentions to the pantheon, if you do not reveal mine. But I have one other condition."

"Which is?" said Ishtar, eagerly.

Marduk spilled it, "You give me the containment spell you used before the Flood to capture Leviathan."

Ishtar and several other gods had used spells engraved on an underwater reef to hypnotize the enormous seven-headed sea dragon called Leviathan. They then placed the monster in a box of water in order to unleash him on the battlefield in the War of Gods and Men. It had been like unleashing chaos upon the enemy.

Marduk said in a speculative tone, "I assume you used a similar enchantment to get the Bull of Heaven to do your bidding back in Uruk."

He paused, and then added, "But I do not want to know about that one because it might anger me. And you do not want me to get angry."

During the reign of King Gilgamesh, she had indeed used the enchantment to draw the Bull of Heaven to attack the walls of Uruk. Her goal had been to kill the king and destroy his accomplishments. She had a vendetta against Gilgamesh. Marduk had been the king's divine guardian at the time. She agreed with his assessment that it would not be wise to drag that sore wound into the present. Some things were best left unaddressed.

"I certainly do not want you to get angry," said Ishtar. "But I also certainly appreciate the sensitivity of the issue. And I think that we may be of mutual benefit to each other."

She played coy and submissive. It was all part of her scheme to draw him in to her confidence.

It did not fool Marduk for a single moment.

Ishtar pried a little, "May I ask for what purpose you need this containment spell?"

Marduk replied, "You will know soon enough."

"Of course," she smiled and paused dramatically.

"Well, I think we have a deal, Marduk, king of the gods."

She did not say it with irony this time, but with flattery. It was the first time she used his name, and without the accompanying insulting title, such as Plum Prince or Gooseberry God.

Despite her calculated manipulative intent, he was still grateful for the momentary cessation of hostilities between them. He thought for a moment that if they could just put aside their differences, they might actually have the capability of thwarting the will of Elohim and replacing the earthly dominion of his pathetic clay humans with their own.

But for now he had his own goal to accomplish. Ishtar was going to travel up north to Nineveh, so he would probably not see her for an extended period of time. Let her try to breed her little clan of serpentine seed. Nineveh was one city and a vassal of Babylon. If she sought to foster rebellion against the pantheon, she would most likely fail, just as the Gigantomachy had failed and the Titanomachy had failed in the years before the Deluge.

But Ishtar was not going to Nineveh.

Or rather, she was not going to *stay* in Nineveh. She would certainly travel up the Tigris River, and make an appearance in the city. But it would only be just long enough to establish her presence and the temple cult around her personality. Then she and Canaan, son of Ham, would embark in a secret caravan for her true intended destination: Mount Hermon of Bashan in the far west, the home of the gods.

But she certainly was not going to tell Marduk that little key element of her plan.

CHAPTER 6

Nimrod examined the model plan for his royal city, sculpted in clay on an extremely large stone table sixteen feet square. His city engineers surrounded him. They had constructed the model and drew up the plans for building the eternal city, Babylon, Nimrod's glory.

The high gods of the pantheon had paid Nimrod a visit to approve the final plans and oversee the beginning of the construction. All four high gods were present: Anu, the overseer sky god of heaven; Enlil, the administrative head of the assembly and Lord of the Air; Enki, god of the waters; and Ninhursag, goddess of earth. Marduk was present at the gathering, but as usual, he remained silent as he shadowed Nimrod, his ward.

The gods were well pleased with the model plans they beheld. Babylon was indeed glorious. At roughly three square miles, the city proper would be bisected by the River Euphrates, creating efficient access for travel and trade. An outer wall around the square city would consist of two walls of kiln-fired brick and one inner wall of sun-dried brick. The space between the walls would be filled with rubble and stone. Nimrod wanted these to rival the great wall of Uruk, with the top of the walls wide enough to accommodate two four-horse chariots.

An inner double wall, surrounded by a moat and a military road, provided the next layer of fortification with multiple fortress towers and eight separate gates named after deities, including Marduk,

Ishtar, Shamash, Enlil and others. The city would ultimately be capable of housing about two hundred and fifty thousand citizens and slaves in mud houses and reed huts.

Ishtar had demanded a particularly ornamental gate for her northwestern sector of the city. It would have several towers through its long covered passageway and the walls would be covered in bright blue enamel brick and adorned with reliefs of red and white dragons and bulls and hundreds of other strange animals. She knew how to decorate with an eye toward the ostentatious.

Looking at the gate of Ishtar, Enlil mumbled with disdain, "Pompous and self-aggrandizing as usual."

"You should talk," countered Ninhursag. "You walk around the assembly like a peacock with the Tablet of Destinies."

The Tablet of Destinies was a talisman of authority for whomever guarded it. Enlil was the most recent to do so. It contained the pantheon's universal decrees of heaven and earth that involved godship, kingship, as well as magic, sorceries and occult mysteries.

Enki chimed in, "Do we really have to accept her flagrant showboating? It is distasteful and unbecoming the godhead."

Anu weighed in, "It is the price we pay for negotiated peace. We all know her volatility and what she is capable of. If excessive display and a patron city of Nineveh keeps her at bay from intruding on the plans of the pantheon, then I say it is worth it."

They knew he was right. Ishtar had vexed them all in one way or another in the past. She had previously flirted with Enki and stole the Tablet of Destinies to give to Enlil, whose authority she later undermined in a political coup. It was an eternal sore spot with Enlil. She had been an escort deity in his city of Nippur, and she had outperformed his glory and commandeered the devotion of the city's inhabitants, to the point that she had acted like the patroness deity of the city herself. It had taken her failed debacle of the Titanomachy to strip her of her political victories and reduce her to the position of an escort of Anu in the city of Uruk. But that was a long story and all so very long ago. Even a simple discussion of Ishtar provoked angry contentions in the assembly. She was like a magnet of animosity. She was the goddess of war.

They all gave their attention back to the clay model city. The royal palace would be housed in the north of the city, but the temple precinct would be in the city's center, right on the riverbanks. The processional road crossed the river as a bridge and split in half the walled temple area. The religious district would contain in the southern partition a series of temples, including one for Marduk, Babylon's patron deity. In the northern section, Nimrod had planned a mighty ziggurat entitled *Etemenanki*, which meant "Temple of the Foundation of Heaven and Earth." This was the most important point for the four high gods in attendance.

The temple tower would be three hundred feet square, and three hundred feet high, with seven progressively smaller tiers and a blue enameled shrine for the gods at the top. It would contain a golden table and a large altar for the Sacred Marriage rite. A vast courtyard would surround the temple for an assembly of citizens at special events such as the yearly Akitu Festival.

This huge tower would become the new cosmic mountain of the gods. They would engage in an occultic ceremony that would transform the ziggurat into a portal, a literal stairway to heaven that would enable the pantheon to recruit from the myriads of Elohim's heavenly host to join their revolution. The original two hundred had accomplished much since the days of Noah. They eagerly imagined what they could do with thousands or even millions.

With its head in the heavens, and its foundation in the Abyss, this tower would be the center of power for the pantheon of gods, uniting with the earthly potentate Nimrod. It would make them an unstoppable united force of heaven and earth.

The land was surveyed and the city was all laid out and ready to be built. There was but one thing that hampered the start of this splendorous majestic urban creation: a lake in the middle of the construction zone.

The small lake lay right where the Temple area was to be built. It stretched out into the eastern portion of the city. It would have to be drained before they could begin their construction. So the first task had been organized and implemented by the city engineers for draining the lake into the Euphrates River.

The situation annoyed Nimrod's impatient ambition, but it was fortuitous for Marduk and his secret plan.

The engineers had been at work for some time. Canal diggers had dug deep trenches that would connect the lake to the river. They broke through on both ends of the canal simultaneously and the waters of the lake flowed out and down into the Euphrates. But they discovered that the lake had a spring source from the Abyss.

The Abyss was the subterranean waters below the earth where the monstrous sea dragon Rahab and its seven-headed offspring, Leviathan dwelt. It was a mystical portal that connected the waters above the heavens with the waters below the earth, but it was also a passage-way to Sheol the underworld.

The Abyss-born spring would continue to supply the lake with an unending source of water. They would have to plug that source opening in order to complete their drainage of the lake. The overseers of the temple construction would send divers to find the source, and then create a landslide to cover the opening, like plugging a spout of water.

The night before the diving was to begin, Marduk secretly came to the shoreline of the lake around midnight with a line of six bound and gagged female slaves. It was quiet. No one else was around. The workers and other slaves were back in the camp, outside the city area. He left the girls on the shore, and took a large knife with him into the water.

Water greatly weakened the strength of the Watcher gods, Marduk included. But because he was immortal, he could swim underwater for as long as he needed without breathing. This skill proved particularly helpful because Marduk had taken with him the enchantment spells that Ishtar had given him in their deal. He swam around the entire lake, inscribing the spells on the bedrock below the waterline. It took him some time. The sun was not yet up when he finished the inscribing stage of his plan. He still had enough time to exit the lake and engage in an occultic ceremony to complete his plan.

The ceremony required virgin blood. He killed the six bound slave girls and poured their blood as a sacrifice into the lake. The bodies, he discarded in the feeding pen of the hogs.

The ceremony was for calling up a creature from the depths.

CHAPTER 7

The next day, the team of fifty divers rose with the sun, They made their way out to the lake. They practiced their breathing exercises for their deep dive. They expected the spring source of the water to lay far in the depths. They spread out all over the lake for reconnaissance and dove in.

Only one of them resurfaced.

"Tiamat! Tiamat!" he screamed, floundering. Tiamat was the Babylonian name for Rahab the sea dragon.

The great creature leapt out of the water, swallowing the diver whole. It landed with a huge tidal wave, splashing the entire shoreline.

Tiamat was huge and fearsome. It was the size of a ziggurat and covered with armored scales on its back and its belly. Pointed spikes protruded from its spine, and its teeth could crush battle ships under the pressure of its mighty jaws. Nothing human could stop it, let alone dream of vanquishing it.

Clan members refused to send more divers into the water.

The fearful slaves summoned Nimrod to the lake. He arrived with a large contingent of soldiers, for he saw the potential dangers of a mob uprising. He knew that once the superstitions of the commoners were excited, not even his own fearful and terrible punishments could procure obedience. Indeed, they might procure rebellion. To the people, Tiamat was the deified dragon of the primeval waters. No earthly ruler, no matter how mighty, could compete with that primal terror in the soul of the mob.

Nimrod wished that he had Terah with him. As prince of the heavenly host, Terah might know what to do to subdue such a monster of maelstrom. But Terah was busy with his task, creating the golem army down south. Nimrod had only his small usual group of sorcerers to do his bidding.

They performed spells of enchantment and sacrifices of atonement to the god of chaos. Nimrod then forced another ten reluctant divers into the water to see if their incantations had worked to appease the dragon.

None of the divers resurfaced.

None of the workers or slaves would continue their work of draining the lake. Nimrod knew that he could not arrest them all. If he began to punish them, he would have an insurrection on his hands, an unruly mob driven by religious devotion. He could not win this battle.

Nimrod convened an assembly of his advisors and requested the presence of the gods.

The assembly of counselors met in Nimrod's administrative tent. The high gods all came; Enlil, Anu, Enki and Ninhursag. Marduk stood by Nimrod as they sought a solution to their problem.

"Can we not move the city upriver?" asked Ninhursag.

"No," replied Enlil. "Rebuilding would take too much time and energy. But even so, this location is a spiritually aligned center point of the land. We must retain it."

Anu asked, "Enki, did you not develop enchantment spells to subdue the sea dragon for the War of Gods and Men?"

"No," lied Enki. "That was for Leviathan, a very different beast. And the spells were destroyed for protection from the hostile forces of Elohim."

Enki flashed a slight glance at Marduk, who watched him with falcon eyes. Enki had made a deal with Marduk to keep the spells from the council, in exchange for a united plan of overthrowing Enlil's leadership. Enki had, in fact, shared them with Ishtar for her use against the Bull of Heaven. She had in turn given them to Marduk.

"We have no power to defeat that monstrosity of chaos," said Ninhursag. "Water weakens us and the dragon is more than a creature. What can we do?"

The question rang with desperation. It hung in silence for a few moments before Marduk finally broke his silence and stepped forward.

"I will kill Tiamat," said Marduk.

Everyone looked at him with surprise. Even Nimrod. He was not privy to Marduk's secret plan.

"You are the mightiest of us all," said Anu. "But even you weaken under the power of water."

"No god has ever faced the mighty Tiamat," said Enki. "It is insane."

"I will kill Tiamat," repeated Marduk. "Under the condition that I become the king of the gods, head of the pantheon."

Enlil's eyes went wide with shock, and then anger.

"How dare you!" Enlil spit out. "So this is what you have been doing in your dark shadows of silence, conspiring to overthrow my authority!"

Marduk bowed submissively to Enlil and spoke with a tinge of irony in his words, "Lord of the Air, I have no mutinous intentions. I fully recognize your authority. And I will gladly step aside to allow you, as king of the gods, to slay the sea dragon."

Enlil glared at him with fury. Marduk knew full well Enlil would have no greater chance than any of them at vanquishing such a foe. And that chance was barely above zero.

Enki smirked. He enjoyed seeing his rival humiliated with such subtlety and finesse.

An idea occurred to Enlil. Marduk himself would have no more chance against Tiamat than any of them. So why not swallow his pride and let Marduk choke on his hubris in the bottom of the Abyss?

"Well, if you are that confident of your skill," said Enlil, "then who am I to get in the way of the will of the gods?"

Marduk said, "I will require the Tablet of Destinies as my guarantee of covenant."

"I will do no such thing," complained Enlil. "Prove yourself first."

Marduk countered, "If I fail in my task, you will have access to them again anyway."

Enlil steamed. He did not like the idea of letting the Tablet out of his hands for anything. But he had no choice. Everyone waited for him to respond.

"Fair enough," said Enlil. "I will give them to Anu for safekeeping." There was no way Enlil would allow the Tablet to be in Enki's treacherous hands or Ninhursag's incompetent ones. Anu had become a virtually ineffective figurehead of the gods, but as such, he was a rather impartial and trustworthy third party for such problems.

Enki piped up, "Are you sure you want to agree so quickly to a covenant so potentially devastating to your own reign?"

Enlil had no choice. He had been backed into a corner, and could now only hope that the odds were overwhelming against Marduk. If—no, *when* Marduk was taken by Tiamat and dragged to the bottom of the Abyss, Enlil's own status would be reaffirmed with the bravado he needed for his weakening reputation.

Enlil responded to Enki with his own jab, "One thing you may not understand about being king of the gods, Enki, is the leadership required in times of crisis."

Enki boiled. But he held back his own secret, knowing that he would have plenty of time to rub it in the face of Enlil later.

Marduk interrupted their sparring, "I agree to Anu as executor of the covenant. Now, if you will all excuse me, I need to take leave to prepare for my duty."

Marduk stopped before he left the tent and turned back to the assembly. "Just one more thing, I want my own temple dominant in the southern partition of the temple complex across from the ziggurat Etemenanki. I want it called, *Esagila*."

That drew raised eyebrows and smirks of scorn. Esagila meant "House of the Raised Head." Marduk meant to raise himself above the heads of all the gods. He wanted to rule in the heavens as Nimrod wanted to rule on earth. But there was no one else with the intestines to step forward and battle the sea dragon of chaos. So, what else could they do but acquiesce to his demands? Realistically, Marduk would be chomped and buried in the bottom of the Abyss by the jaws of the very sea monster that did so with Ishtar during the Flood. If the invincible goddess of war could not triumph over so deadly a foe, what chance could this ambitious stair-climbing upstart possibly have?

Nimrod had been conspicuously silent during this entire exchange. Even as a mighty earthly ruler, he was nothing but a slug easily squashed in the presence of the four high gods. He knew better than to join in as one of them. But one of them is what he wanted to be. They had promised him a living apotheosis, a deification. Apotheosis was usually performed on dead kings, as a means of raising them to godlike status in the stars. But such a ceremonial distinction was worthless to Nimrod. He did not want to be *considered* a god when he was dead. He wanted to *be* a living god here and now.

Marduk's victory and enthronement would be the path to Nimrod's own success.

CHAPTER 8

Marduk arose the next morning and arrived at the lake clad only in an animal skin loin cloth. He armed himself with a dagger strapped to his leg, a mighty bow, a battle mace, and a large axe of two hundred and twenty five pounds strapped to his back. Of what use arrows would be against the colossal armored sea dragon was anyone's guess. But everything had a purpose in Marduk's plan.

Two of the items were gifts from Nimrod. The loincloth was more than merely a minimal covering to allow Marduk free movement in the water. It was Nimrod's own magical garment that he had inherited from his mother. It was made from the skins worn by the first Man and Woman in the Garden of Eden. Those skins carried a magical enchantment that took away the fear of humans in animals. It was a hunter's advantage for animals to not fear him. And although Tiamat certainly had no fear of any creature, should Marduk begin to do some real damage to the dragon, its instincts would kick in. A healthy fear would empower it to surge to greater destruction in its fight. The lack of such a surge, caused by the Edenic skins, would surely make it vulnerable to strategic attack. Marduk was not certain the skins would have any real effect on the supernatural sea monster, but anything was worth the chance in this impossible task. He also received the battle-axe from Nimrod, who had himself used the mighty weapon in his campaign against the Rephaim giant, Humbaba the Terrible, in his Great Cedar Forest.

An additional weapon, that Marduk had commanded be created, was carried in by the hands of hundreds of slaves. It was a battle net large enough to entangle the serpent of the Abyss. It was rigged on a huge catapult for just the right moment, and the slaves had been instructed as to its use.

In addition to these hundreds of slaves, thousands of citizens came to watch the event, as one would a sporting contest. They brought blankets and food and drink for the day, so as not to miss any of the battle if it went on for long. Most expected it to be over quickly, with the bullying deity clamped in the jaws of chaos.

Nimrod and his royal entourage set up at a safe distance. The four high gods from the assembly were also there: Anu, Enlil, Enki, and Ninhursag. They were required as eyewitnesses on behalf of the assembly of the gods. They were the chief executors whose decisions were final. Should they declare Marduk as king, he would immediately ascend his throne with the authority of the pantheon behind him.

For the first time in his life that he could remember, Nimrod was truly afraid. If Marduk was not successful and was buried in the deep, Nimrod would lose his patron protector, as well as his co-conspirator in the plans they had drawn up. The assembly of gods would not be happy about those plans should they discover them. Nimrod wanted to pray to the gods for help, but he could not, because the gods he would pray to were right before him, and they were the ones from whom he was keeping his secret. So he kept his straight face on as a mask over the fears that boiled beneath.

Marduk knelt before the shore and engaged in a ritual incantation to call up the monster from below.

Its armored scales crested the waters.

Marduk raised his mighty bow and let loose an arrow made from meteorite iron. It was tied to a slender, yet strong cable of intertwined hemp and copper strands. The arrow found its mark underneath one of the monster's broken scales, digging deeply into the creature's flesh.

The purpose of the projectile was not to do damage. That would have been a ludicrous proposition. Its purpose lay at the other end of the cord, the end tied to Marduk's waist.

The beast dove deep into the lake waters.

The arrow's line snapped tight. It jerked Marduk from the shore like bait on the end of a fishing line.

He plunged into the cold waters, He grabbed the line, pulling himself toward the sea monster until he was able to grab onto its spiny back. He rode the beast like a bucking bronco in a water pen.

Usually, Tiamat was simply too mighty to withstand. Marduk would not have had a chance of riding out the fury of the beast. But this was not a usual occasion. The enchantment spells Marduk had inscribed into the surrounding seabed lulled Tiamat into a confused trance-like state. The spells turned the dragon's own chaos against it, and the beast swam without purpose or plan. It tried to get away, but from what, it just could not comprehend. It was being hemmed in by magic.

Marduk's animal skin loincloth had the effect of making him virtually invisible to the dragon. At a moment when it should have begun to fear, it did not. Confusion blinded it, compounded by the spells all around the lakebed. It dove deep, but could not find the opening of the Abyss because of its disorientation.

Frustrated, it went the only other direction it could imagine, to try and break free of the swirling confusion in its skull: upward, with a furious speed.

It broke the surface like a tremendous fountain. Its entire body came out of the water as if it were flying straight up into the heavens. On the way back down to the water, Marduk shouted a command.

The catapult released its load.

The battle net flew at the sea dragon. It enveloped Tiamat just before it hit the water with a huge wave that drenched the entire shoreline, dragging some slaves to drown in the depths.

The great serpent wriggled and writhed, trying to free itself, but it only wore itself out. The net entangled it like an underwater spider web of entrapment.

Though the water weakened Marduk, he was not incapacitated. He used most of his strength to ride out the beast's thrashing, until he could find his moment of maximum impact.

Then the great dragon found the lake bed and rolled around, trying to shake loose the netting. Its gigantic body smashed Marduk against the silt bottom.

He lost his grip. He twisted about in the murky turbulence, flailing for something, anything, to grab hold of. He prayed it would not be the mouth of the great beast.

The battle net kept him from being washed away into the tumultuous current. He found himself snagged on the sea dragon's upper back as the net tightened its tangled grip.

He held on for his immortal life. He could not be killed, but he could be trapped in a crevice of rock or a landslide of boulders from which he could not extricate himself. If that happened, he might be trapped there for millennia, losing his kingdom and awaiting the Judgment. And this enormous reptile had just the weight and force to accomplish that, should Marduk let go of his grip again.

They burst out of the murky turbulence. They were headed straight for the opening of the Abyss. The roof of the opening would crush him, if the dragon scraped its way through. There was nothing he could do. He held on, and awaited his demise. He thought he had at least done better than what any other god would have achieved. He had come so close.

Without warning, Tiamat altered its course ninety degrees and swam straight up toward the surface. The combination of the enchantment spells and the net had so thoroughly worn down the mighty gargantuan with confusion, blindness, and exhaustion that it did not see the portal to the Abyss.

Instead, it reached for land. It burst out of the water and landed on the shoreline. It then attempted to wriggle out of the net, using the ground as a surface to drag it off.

But Marduk was out of the water.

His full strength returned. He pulled himself through the rings of the net, his body naked. The loincloth had been ripped off in the midst of the battle. He pulled his huge battle-axe from his back, and swung it with all his force. The axe went deep into the soft exposed flesh where some scales had been ripped free.

Tiamat bellowed. The hideous sound pierced the souls of everyone still alive along the shoreline.

Marduk wrenched free his axe and swung again. The blade sank into the body. An artery of blood broke open like a geyser, drenching Marduk in thick red.

Tiamat had almost reached the water again.

The net was coming off.

Marduk swung one more time and the axe was lost in the sliced fat and muscle of the serpentine colossus.

Tiamat roared again. It shook the shoreline.

Marduk was out of the water and in his strength, but so was Tiamat. It was out of the water and therefore away from the spells that had restrained it. It had regained its wits.

And it was aware of Marduk, for the magic skins were gone from his body.

Just as Tiamat hit the water, regaining its bearings, Marduk hacked wider the wound he had made. He then dropped the axe, dove into the wound and burrowed his way into the body of the beast.

He drew his dagger and cut his way through the innards of the dragon.

The dragon desperately swam in circles. It could feel the parasite digging its way through its organs. The serpent could do nothing about it.

Marduk reached the heart of Tiamat. It was huge, the size of ten men. Marduk sliced its arteries off with his dagger, and then plunged the blade into the beating muscle, ripping downward with all his might.

Tiamat jerked and spasmed as its heart became a useless severed organ.

The enormous serpent died in a sea of its own blood, floating slowly to the bottom of the lake.

Its belly sliced open with Marduk's blade. He came out of the great beast and swam upward.

Marduk broke the surface. He crawled onto shore, exhausted. But he had an image to reinforce. So he quickly rose to his full eight-foot naked frame with a proud bravado. He lifted his chin toward the entourage of gods and king, and said simply, "Tiamat is dead. Long live Marduk, king of the gods." His voice of divinity easily carried across the distance to the assembly of Watchers and humans.

A rousing cheer blistered the shoreline, as hundreds of slaves and workers were relieved that their lives would be spared the terrors of the sea serpent. Marduk had suppressed chaos and established his kingdom.

Nimrod felt new determination fill him, for he now knew that he and Marduk would be unstoppable. No other god had ever come close to such a mighty feat of power. A fleeting thought of Ishtar's demise even accompanied the thrill of victory. His guardian was now king of the gods.

Anu walked up to Marduk with the Tablet of Destinies.

Before Anu could hand the Tablet to him, Enlil stepped out of the crowd. "I want to see the body," he complained.

Marduk looked Enlil up and down, and then replied, "Oh, I am not finished yet. You *will* see the body."

Marduk turned to Nimrod. "Command your slaves to dredge up the corpse for me with the battle net."

Nimrod obeyed. Marduk turned back to Enlil. "You are welcome to watch, if you still require satisfaction."

Enlil wondered just what exactly Marduk had planned.

Marduk smirked, and then added, "On second thought, I command you and the other gods, as obeisance to my new superiority, to stay and watch me filet this great fish."

The gods begrudgingly watched and waited. The company of slaves hauled the body of the great sea dragon onto land, using the battle net and five hundred strong arms.

Marduk strode over to the huge carcass. He retrieved his large battle-axe and proceeded to cut the body of Tiamat in half, from jaws to tail. He chopped and hacked, covered in gargantuan fish blood and guts, until he had two perfect halves of the great monster.

The brutishness with which Marduk operated disgusted Enlil. He thought there would be a new era of barbarism under this monster's rule. But he dared not speak what everyone else also thought.

After Marduk finished cutting the serpent's corpse in half, he looked to the heavens, saturated in blood and stench. He shouted, "I am Marduk, king of the gods! And I have split Tiamat like a shellfish. Thus I have created the heavens and the earth out of the body of the great sea dragon. I have established the stars and their paths, the moon and the sun, and the constellations in their course. The Anunnaki gods all bow before me!"

The four high gods bowed. "Annunaki" was another Sumerian word for the gods of the pantheon. It meant "Princely Seed."

Marduk made sure that his ceremonial ritual of crowning as king of the gods occurred immediately upon the completion of his corpse splitting. He wanted his enthronement to be as close to his victory as possible, for maximum symbolic impact.

His throne had yet to be built in his new temple. But a symbolic one worked just as well, made of wood, gilded with gold and laden with jewels. The royal house of Nimrod and the four high gods, representing the pantheon, all participated in the ritual of transferring the crown and the Tablet of Destinies from Enlil to Marduk.

It was all very humiliating for Enlil. But there was really no challenging the mighty strength of Marduk, who now took on a litany of fifty names of greatness. The list was read before the observing crowd of Nimrod's people by Sinleqi, the king's scholar and scribe.

Sinleqi droned on in his monotonous voice reading from the freshly engraved tablets, "*Marduk*, as Anu, his father called him from his birth, who with the flood-storm his weapon, vanquished the enemy; *Murukka*, creator of all, who rejoices the hearts of the Anunnaki; *Marutukku*, the refuge of his land, city, and people; *Barashakushu*, of wide heart and warm sympathy;

Lugaldimmerankia, the lord of all the gods of heaven and the underworld…"

Enlil started to feel drowsy. Sinleqi's prattling was dreadfully long and redundant. It went on for what seemed an eternity with names, epithets, and etymologies that all served to say the same thing over and over again. How great Marduk is, how glorious he is, what a wondrous and gracious god he is, blah, blah, blah. It reminded Enlil of the pretentious, self-aggrandizing Ishtar. These two were complimentary whores of power.

Not like him. He began to plan in his mind how he might manipulate them to face each other in a contest of megalomaniacal egos. Maybe they would destroy each other. The assembly would be better off when they did.

But what if by some strange twist of fate, they partnered up together? Then the very pantheon itself would be in jeopardy. Enlil tried to put that horror out of his mind as he concluded his participation in the vainglorious enthronement ceremony.

When they had concluded the official transfer of the Tablet of Destinies and the crown to Marduk, Anu led the assembly of gods and men in a vow of devotion.

"We pledge our fealty and worship to the gracious Marduk, king of the gods!"

Everyone, human and divine, repeated the words that would usher in a new era, ruled by a new chief deity.

When all was performed and done, Marduk concluded the ceremony with a simple pronouncement. "And now we shall build Babylon, the gateway of the gods."

CHAPTER 9

The process of creating bricks for the building of Babylon began even before the lake was fully drained. It would take some weeks to seal the entrance to the Abyss, finish the canals, and dredge and finally fill in the lakebed with rock and soil.

Nimrod conscripted the entire work and slave force of tens of thousands for the laborious task of making bricks. They would work on the city, the wall, and the temples simultaneously. There were two kinds of bricks; sun-dried bricks for most of the homes, shrines, and inner walled areas, and kiln-fired bricks for the outer walls and most importantly for the temple-tower, Etemenanki and Marduk's complimentary Esagila.

The ziggurat Etemenanki was the largest of its size in all of Sumer and Akkad. It would take a year of continuous day and night labor to build it. Since the structure would function as a cosmic mountain upon which the gods would descend from heaven, it was a solid edifice with the shrine of deity on top and a stairway down its front. The inner base was made of sun-dried bricks, but the outer layer was made of kiln-fired brick. Firing bricks took more time and effort, but created a more durable, hardened ceramic block that could withstand outside forces such as wind, rain, storm, battle, and most important of all, floodwaters.

This was a deliberate choice on Nimrod's part. He had seen the devastation of the legendary Deluge first hand. He had rebuilt cities and temples on the ruins of the old world. He had seen how the achievements of gods and men in the antediluvian world had been swept away. And he had visited his distant kin, Noah. There, he had been told of the Creator Elohim, and his vindictive judgment on mankind that was the origin of the Great Flood. Nimrod rejected this despotic deity and his obsession for controlling things from on high. How dare this supposed Creator make mankind and the angels, and then demand sniveling toe-licking slavery.

Against this monolithic tyranny stood the pantheon of gods, who watched over mankind from Mount Hermon. This divine assembly of Watchers was willing to share power, to elevate man above his mud-brick existence. If there was one thing the Watcher gods gave him hope for, it was the glorious potential of mankind to become as gods, to commingle heaven and earth in a unity of being.

He knew that what he and Marduk planned would more than likely provoke another vengeful response from Elohim. So his purpose was to create a temple of waterproof structure that would resist another Deluge, and would be high enough to rise above any new floodwaters.

The four high gods that had visited Nimrod for the commencement of the construction had approved it and returned to their holy Mount Hermon in the distant west. One day in the near future that distance would be eliminated and the two seats of power would become one in Babylon, the gateway of the gods.

Nimrod was ready for the next step in his plan. He was ready to reveal his queen.

CHAPTER 10

Shamhat was going crazy from confinement. She had been sequestered in a secluded encampment out near the edge of the massive desert to the west of Babylon for over a year. She was guarded by a well-armed contingent of a hundred warriors, who were under strictest orders of secrecy and protection to kill anyone who ventured near their posted site. They did not even know her name or who she was, only that she was the holy property of Nimrod, their lord and king. She was not allowed to travel anywhere or have any visitors except for Nimrod.

This confinement was not punishment. It was part of the plan, and she had agreed to it. She was to be Nimrod's queen. But in order to create an aura of power and mystery to their reign, she would have to be completely dissociated from her past. She would have to be forgotten as Shamhat, and then unveiled much later with a new name and a new identity.

In distant days, she had originally been a harlot of Uruk. She had fallen in love with the Wild-Born Enkidu. He had been the only man she had ever met that showed her true love was possible. Enkidu married her and became the Right Hand of Gilgamesh, the King of Uruk, Nimrod's previous identity. But Enkidu had died from a mysterious disease, and with him, Shamhat's belief in love and grace and anything true in this life. She had determined to never again be the tool of men and to climb her way up the stairway of power to achieve her own goals.

Of course, it would always be a man's world. So she would have to play the system in order to accomplish her ambition. She would have to use her feminine wiles to her advantage. And her feminine wiles were a highly tuned and cultivated set of skills in manipulation. It was about more than their simpleminded obsession with beauty in women; it also involved their ridiculously transparent slavery to their egos.

Women, on the other hand, needed men like a fish needed a chariot.

Nimrod had taken Shamhat to be his queen, partly because of her connection to Enkidu, and partly because he saw in her the experience and ambition required to negotiate the political machinations of a kingdom. She knew men better than they knew themselves. This would be an advantage for his rule.

He knew her soul was damaged beyond repair. His Naphil insight could tell she was capable of great treachery. But that also gave her the qualifications to be his queen. Because of his connection to Enkidu, he too had lost his faith in friendship, trust, and goodness. So no matter how bleak and destroyed their past, no matter how shriveled that small piece of humanity was, it was still a piece of them both that he would eventually be able to use to his benefit, should the time come.

But now was the time for queenship and marriage. And Nimrod had just found the perfect opportunity for the birth of that queen.

The very evening after Marduk slaughtered Tiamat the sea dragon of chaos, Nimrod had Shamhat secretly transported to the lake and had her prepare for a theatrical entrance. He had concocted the perfect way to create a new divine identity for Shamhat, with a new narrative that would forever erase her past.

The next morning, Nimrod brought a cabal of priests, sorcerers, and magi down to the lake to consecrate the waters of Marduk's triumph. The assembly of two hundred celebrants performed their rituals and ceremony on the shoreline to sanctify access to the Abyss over which the ziggurat temple was to be built. This was to be holy ground.

Unbeknownst to the religious participants, Shamhat had been hiding in the lake waters. She used an artificial breathing apparatus that consisted of a large pitch covered reed balloon full of air, submerged and tied to the bottom. Shamhat then sucked the air through a small pipe attached to the balloon. It allowed her to stay below for several hours.

During a crucial point in the ceremony of blessing, the priests threw several lambs and goats into the water as sacrifice. Large stones were tied to the animals to sink them to the bottom and their deaths.

This was Shamhat's signal to come up out of the water and walk up to the shore, as if born from the waters of sacrifice.

As she stepped up onto the sand, the entire religious procession stood in wonder.

She raised her hands and spoke to the crowd surrounding Nimrod's chariot throne. "I am born from the holy waters of the Abyss, from the victory over Tiamat by Marduk, king of the gods. Who is the king who can crown me queen?"

Nimrod stood and approached her. The whole extravagant display of theater excited him. He found himself breathing heavily and staring at her.

He stepped up to her, his nine feet of height casting a shadow over her. "I am Nimrod, ruler of Akkad and Sumer," he announced. "I will make you my queen, divine one."

Shamhat bowed to the ground before him, then looked up into his eyes with complete and utter submission.

Then she stood again.

Nimrod asked her, "What is your name, O daughter of the gods?"

"I am Semiramis," she said, "Maiden of the Waters."

He held out his hand to her and shouted for the ears of the crowd, "Come, be my queen!"

The musicians began playing music. A royal robe of Nimrod's covered Semiramis. Her beauty fired the attraction of all the men. She was not merely a specimen of physical beauty. She had an aura of power that would turn any man into putty in her hands.

Nimrod was the only putty she was interested in.

CHAPTER 11

The preparation for Nimrod's wedding to Semiramis ran a month long. They constructed a large temporary shelter for the actual ceremony, and cleared an area large enough to host the hundreds of thousands who would attend. Nimrod called for the other kings of Sumer and Akkad and their royal households to be present. The heads of the clans of the sons of Noah; Joktan, and Phenech, would also bring many of their tribes to witness the wedding.

Nimrod had become increasingly demanding of his vassal kings. He had raised his tribute taxes on them and called for more and more slave labor to finish his city and tower in an unprecedented period of time.

The workers had finished draining the lake and leveling it with landfill. The city was surveyed and laid out for the construction of the temple. Bricks were being hauled in and it was just too much to hold his wedding around such a busy mess. So the wedding would be a few miles to the west of the city, near the edge of the great desert.

The day of the wedding shone clear and sunny. The night of celebration would be arid but cool.

The rulers of Sumer arrived from the south with their royal households and encamped in the southern plains. They were Nimrod's puppet kings ruled through his son in Uruk.

The rulers of Akkad were less puppet-like, as Joktan and Phenech of the clans of Japheth and Shem brought some armed forces as a personal guard, in order to express some independence. Nimrod had heartily accepted their caution, in the interest of building a better relationship with these clans. This marriage marked the beginning of a new dynasty. Nimrod declared that he wanted it to be one of trust and support, not mistrust and hostility. He even allowed the several thousand or so guards of Joktan and Phenech to assemble on the desert side of the festivities, so that they too could see the ceremony and participate in the feast. It was a gesture of good will that did not go unnoticed by the tribal leaders.

Joktan was the more distrusting of the two. His notice of Nimrod's courtesy carried a whiff of sarcasm. "I noticed our armed forces were useful to Nimrod to create a barrier from the desert sand winds for the celebration, while his malformed, overgrown giants stand comfortably in the aisles of honor."

Nimrod's elite Nephilim warriors, his giant progeny, had followed Nimrod and Semiramis in a long train of pomp and circumstance down the aisle that led up to the sanctuary stage. The Nephilim had then taken positions lining the aisles all the way to the back of the huge crowd. They were dressed in expensive royal garments of silken robes, jeweled ornaments, and painted faces.

"Look at them," sniffed Joktan, "they are like a giant gauntlet of the vainglorious ego of their leader, or rather, their shared father."

"Really, Joktan," said Phenech, "You must stop sucking on green persimmons. They accentuate your sour face."

Phenech was only trying to make the best of a humiliating situation. Joktan smirked and the two of them sat down in their assigned seats at the front of the crowd.

The royal families were seated in the place of honor at the head of the festivities. The commoners were kept separated by partitions of soldiers in the distance. The king was kind enough to include all the people, but not so kind as to ignore the proper hierarchy of caste distinction between peasants and nobility.

The representatives of the city-states of Akkad in central Mesopotamia, were up front: Nippur, Sippar, Kish and the surrounding area. Behind them were the rulers of the southern cities of Sumer: Uruk, Ur, Eridu, Shuruppak. And behind them, were the representatives of the fledgling new northern city-states of Asshur, Nineveh, Rehoboth-Ir, Calah and Resen.

It was a microcosm of the known world. Two hundred thousand people from every tribe in the land had come to see the wedding of the mighty King Nimrod. And Nimrod delivered to them from his bounty. Ten thousand sheep, cattle, and boars were killed daily for meals. Uncounted bushels of grain and barrels of beer flowed into the masses.

But the moment of the great celebration had arrived. All food had been put away, all drink withheld, and all eyes were fixed on the ceremony of union being performed before the great congregation. Temple musicians played the lyre, flute, and tambourine. The high priestess of Marduk officiated next to the high priests of surrounding states. It was a celebration of fertility and hope.

Marduk stood statuesque at the back of the sanctuary display, bestowing a divine validation of the union.

Terah had arrived only a few days earlier from his work down near Uruk. He stood in the entourage of sorcerers and magi. He did his duty and obeyed god and king. That was all any ruler could ask of a man. That was all he could offer.

The High Priestess declared Nimrod and Semiramis husband and wife, king and queen of Babylon. They stood before the mass of people and smiled as the cheers rose like incense into the sky.

When it all calmed down, Nimrod got up on a platform. He looked out over the mass of humanity before him. He smiled to himself.

"Thank you all for coming to my wedding and celebrating the ascension of Queen Semiramis to her throne. And now I have but one more pronouncement to make, and that is that from this point forward and forever, I proclaim myself emperor and potentate of all the earth!"

The people murmured amongst themselves. They were not really sure what they had just heard. Did he say he was now potentate of all the earth? What did that mean for the other kings?

They looked at one another with shock. They started clucking with anger at the gall of this king. They were his vassals. As if that was not enough! His hubris knew no bounds! He would claim total supremacy? Insufferable!

Joktan and Phenech looked to their Guard, calculating their options.

Terah screamed out, "STONE ONES, ARISE!"

All around the Guard and behind them, the ground began to move. Large stone beings rose from the dirt as if the earth itself was coming alive.

They were the golemim. The army of ten thousand Stone Ones, created by Terah and animated by the sorcery of enchantment. They had traveled silently up from the south and had dug their way into the ground in camouflage the week before. Now they surrounded the armed forces.

Some of the Guard drew their weapons, some of them tried to fight. It was hopeless. Sword, javelin, and mace were useless against rock. They were enclosed, hemmed in by a wall of rock that tightened in on them. The Stone Ones were three times their number and carried their own weapons of swords, maces and battle-axes. Blade glanced off boulder; rock and mace crushed human flesh. The several thousand guards of Joktan and Phenech were swiftly defeated and crushed by the multitude of silent stone warriors of Nimrod.

Everyone watched in terror.

They finished their slaughter in minutes.

The blood-drenched Stone Ones lined up in silent military attention, ready for their next orders. They were an undefeatable brute force.

The royal families and high priests on the ceremonial platform did not know what to do. But the concealed assassins did. The priests of Marduk pulled out daggers from their retrieved clothes and killed the other priests.

The gauntlet of Nephilim warriors that lined the aisle had not been there for mere pomp and circumstance. They turned to their task — executing the royal families of the city-states.

They pulled their blades and blunt weapons to rain death upon the nobles. Joktan and Phenech, being the heads of the tribes of Noah, were first to die. These giant warriors were well trained and performed their task with cold efficiency.

In mere moments, the armed guards were dead, the nobles were dead, and all of Nimrod's potential rivals had been purged in a river of blood. In mere moments, Nimrod had consolidated and secured his absolute power through a swift and mighty show of force, sorcery and bloodshed.

He breathed a sigh of great accomplishment. Nimrod was indeed potentate of all the land. Semiramis was his queen.

But now, he must rally the mob or find himself overrun by a tsunami of humanity awash in fear and panic.

He was never one to let a crisis go to waste.

He pronounced with an amplified voice of authority, "My people, fear not! My children! You are safe! No more harm will come!"

It was amazing. The milling and cries of anxiety stilled. His delivery carried across the hundreds of acres of land as if it were the amplified voice of deity.

"I regret what I had to do to the rich and powerful, but it was necessary for your good! This privileged upper class, these fat aristocrats who exploit you for their own benefit will do so no longer!"

The crowd began to rumble agreeably.

Nimrod continued, "These were the one percent of wealthy pigs who ruled over the ninety-nine percent of people with their greed and their selfishness! But I swear to you by my very head and by the head of my queen Semiramis, that as our subjects you will never go hungry!"

The crowd burst out in applause.

He milked it, "You will never be without shelter in the great city of Babylon!"

More applause resounded.

"You will never be without health and welfare!"

The applause turned to jubilation.

Nimrod reeled them in like a fish on a line.

"You will be taken care of from birth to death under the mighty rule of Nimrod, emperor of the earth!"

The masses swarmed with worship and screams of praise.

Nimrod had secured their total dependency upon city-state and king. Nimrod had become their lord and savior.

CHAPTER 12

Six hundred miles away from Babylon, in the Great Cedar Forest of Bashan, deep in the bowels of Mount Hermon, the goddess Ishtar sought a clandestine audience with the creature she most sought to emulate in her quest for power. In the divine council of heaven, he was called the *satan*, Elohim's legal adversary. In the Garden, he was *Nachash*, the Serpent of Eden. In this postdiluvian world, he was known by other names, such as Belial and Diablos. But Prince Mastema was his personal preference. It had a certain ring of royalty and power that appealed to his pride.

Mastema was the only Watcher who refused to take on the name of a localized deity as the others had done. His status as the primal Tempter of mankind was political leverage, and he gloried in his elite status among the Watchers.

Ishtar had traveled covertly to Hermon with her human consort, Canaan, son of Ham. Now, they were alone in the vast cavernous belly of the assembly of gods, awaiting the arrival of her mighty role model.

The cavern was empty. The gods had vacated their headquarters at the request of Mastema. Behind Ishtar and Canaan, the black waters of the Abyss were perpetually alight with flame. The sparkling gem-laden stalactites and stalagmites gave an eerie glow to everything in Canaan's vision.

A deep bass tonal voice pierced the quiet. "Ishtar, this had better be important. It was no easy task to garner this empty assembly hall."

Mastema stepped out from the shadows.

He was an eight foot tall Seraph, one of the original reptilian beings that guarded the very throne chariot of Elohim. He had six wings and eyes that could entrance any unwitting soul with hypnotic power. He was gangly, without the muscle mass of someone like Marduk. But he remained influential on the assembly nonetheless, because he had borne the title distinction of being the "Accuser" or prosecutor in Elohim's heavenly court. The other Watcher gods feared him. Not as they feared Marduk for his brawn, but because Mastema's legal cunning could wreak as much devastation as ten marauding Marduks. Mastema had figured out the advantages of law-twisting over lawlessness.

Mastema's reptilian gaze penetrated Canaan's soul. Canaan shuddered.

"Do you fancy my little flesh-bag of bones?" said Ishtar. "Delectable, is he not?"

"Is he an offering?" asked Mastema, salivating.

Canaan stepped a little more behind Ishtar. The hairs on his neck stiffened. His breath shortened. Mastema could smell the fear.

"Unfortunately, no," said Ishtar. "But trust me, he has more far-reaching benefit than human sacrifice could ever provide."

"Pray tell," replied Mastema. All his senses tuned in on Ishtar.

Ishtar grinned. She had him in her grip. "I am reminded of a certain prophetic promise in a certain garden so long ago. 'I will put enmity between your seed and her seed,' I believe are the actual words, though I could be mistaken."

"Do not remind me," grumbled Mastema.

That prophecy hung over Mastema like an axe waiting to strike off his head. The Creator, Elohim, had cursed Mastema and engaged a war between the Seed of the Serpent and the Seed of Eve. For generations, the Watchers had tried to corrupt that seedline of the Woman's with their commingling of heavenly and earthly seed. They had sought out the bearers of that bloodline to hunt them down and exterminate them: Enoch the giant killer, then Noah ben Lamech. But they had failed. The Deluge had crushed their accomplishments under its cleansing waves and frightened them from ever mating with the daughters of men again. And they had lost track of the Chosen Seed in the many descendants of the sons of Noah.

Until now.

Ishtar grinned. "We may not have the Chosen Seed," she said. "But we do have the Cursed Seed."

She pulled Canaan forward and cuddled him with a dark playfulness.

Mastema began to understand.

"I introduce to you, Canaan ben Ham, son of Noah. Say hello to your master, Canaan."

Canaan croaked out a trembling response, "M-my Lord, I am y-your servant."

"Indeed?" said Mastema, stroking from Canaan's head with his finger.

Ishtar continued, "He is the fruit of the incestuous rape of Noah's wife by her son Ham. The Chosen One cursed him."

Mastema's scaly brows rose with greater interest. He knew of Anu and Ishtar's experiments before the Great Flood. He had even known of their test subject, Ham, who had been called Canaanu in Uruk. The irony of the name similarity did not escape him.

"So, this one is a carrier of the Nephilim blood?" asked Mastema.

Ishtar answered, "From within the bloodline of the Chosen Seed himself. I know. I performed genetic alteration on his father."

Mastema followed this well. "What better bloodline to create the Cursed Seed from than the line of the Chosen Seed."

Ishtar added, "And what better location to breed that seedline than here in the Levant? We could call it the land of Canaan after our own chosen one, as a slap in the supreme despot's face."

Mastema paused. "What about Elohim? The Watchers' original breeding program brought down the Deluge of judgment. If we pursue that agenda again, we risk another cataclysm that will surely imprison the rest of us."

"But Elohim promised to never flood the earth again with water," replied Ishtar.

"There is always fire," countered Mastema, "and other disasters."

Ishtar disagreed. "It makes the Creator look like an incompetent moron to be destroying and recreating his creation over and over again. He will not risk that kind of foolishness. He is a vainglorious peacock."

Mastema listened intently. Ishtar was on to something here.

Ishtar continued, "The problem with our antediluvian scheme was that the Watchers took control and sought to reign *outwardly*. Our breeding program was too bold a scheme. If we avoid fornication with the humans ourselves and simply breed the Nephilim strain through the humans already tainted, then we will not draw undue attention to ourselves. It will take a little longer, but our precious little Canaan here is the key."

Mastema's eyes brightened with interest.

Ishtar concluded, "It dawned on me that once Elohim prophesied something, it was sure to come to pass. So why fight it? Why not use it to our advantage? After all, *he is* the one who promised there would be two seedlines of enmity."

"You are cunning," said Mastema.

Ishtar crowed, "Instead of defying Elohim's prophecy, we will simply fulfill it as instruments of his own will."

Mastema grinned. "We will breed his seedline of opposition. We will give him his war."

Canaan's knees almost gave out. He realized he was in over his head. He was a puny pawn in a very dangerous game of gods and men.

Mastema noticed. He bent down and said with a calming voice, "Do not be fearful, human. You will be a patriarch, a king among men. You will be completely under the good graces of our protection. What more could you ask for?"

Maybe the protection of Elohim, thought Canaan. But that was too late. He had already been cursed of Elohim. So this giant divinity was right. He was in the most capable hands of power in the pantheon.

Mastema turned to Ishtar with an interrogating demeanor. Interrogation was his specialty.

He said, "And what exactly do you want as reward for hatching your brilliant scheme, Ishtar?"

"Why to oversee it, of course," she said like an innocent lamb.

"Of course," Mastema mimicked. "But you are correct. My position as the satan in the heavenly court is far too important and public. You are an outcast of the pantheon. You can pursue this without need of the pantheon's knowledge or approval."

"It would be our little secret," purred Ishtar.

Mastema said, "You should take on the identity of a local deity as disguise."

"I like who I am," said Ishtar stubbornly.

Mastema countered, "Do not worry, the goddess Ashtart fits you well. Same persona, new name, established authority as the Canaanite goddess of sex and war."

"Well, in that case, Ashtart, it is," said Ishtar. She had done this before. She liked the idea of being a moving target, too difficult for her enemies to keep track of amidst constantly changing identities.

"I will alert the Canaanite deities, so they will not rise up against you," said Mastema.

"Who are they?" she said.

"The high god El and his consort Asherah, Molech, god of the underworld, and Dagon, god of fertility and the sea."

"Will the high god's pride of place become a problem?"

"El is my puppet," said Mastema. "The old man will not be trouble. And he is stationed in the far northern regions."

"I defer to your brilliance," said Ishtar.

"Spare me the flattery, tramp goddess," said Mastema. "I have just the southern location for you to do it."

"I am at your command," said Ishtar. But she thought, *I could slice you in half, you pompous ingrate. If it were not for your devious legal hegemony.*

Oh, how she hated the power of law. She knew he would not hesitate to crush her with it, if she caused him any trouble.

Mastema said, "There is a confederation of five tribes in the southern Jordan valley of the Jordan Sea. It is the most fertile area in the Levant with rich resources, and the tribes are ripe for leadership to unite them into a pentapolis of five city-states. Go there and build those cities."

"What are the tribes?" asked Ishtar.

"Admah, Zeboiim, Zoar, Sodom and Gomorrah. They are a particularly debauched people whom I am sure will be open to your creative depravity."

Ishtar could not help but grin. This was going to be fun.

"Well, we had better get hopping, Canaan" said Ishtar. "We have a seedline to breed — and an army to build."

CHAPTER 13

Etemenanki, the holy temple-tower of Babylon, took a year to build. The city and its walls had not been completed. The temple area was given priority. Nimrod finished the temple-tower along with Marduk's Esagila complex on the other side of the Processional Way. There were other temples throughout the city for Ishtar, Enlil, Shamash and others, but their construction had been deferred to the main temple complex, as well as the royal palace of Nimrod in the northern sector.

Within that year, Semiramis gave birth to a son, who was named Mardon.

Also within that year, Nimrod commissioned Terah to establish a school of heavenly wisdom. The school would seek out and train those with sensitivity to the spiritual plane of reality. There were several different institutes within the school for specialized knowledge based on the varying talents of the students. A court of sorcerers and magicians concentrated on enchantments, spells, and other magic. A court of diviners sought interpretations of omens from all manner of sources to discover the future. There was extispicy that studied the position and conditions of eviscerated organs of animals, livers, entrails, hearts, and lungs; auspicy studied the patterns and flights of birds, lecanomancy, the movement of water. Dream interpreters aided the difficult task of understanding the meaning of the king's dreams. Nimrod was particularly enamored with dreams. When he was king of Uruk, his mother had instilled in him an obsession with dreams. They had presaged his very future.

But most important of all in Terah's school was the new court of astrologers. Astrology was relatively undeveloped, which is why the god Marduk focused much of his time and attention over this first year in revealing the occult secrets of the heavens to Terah and his court of astrologers.

First, Marduk enlisted the aid of Sinleqi to engrave star almanacs on clay tablets. The tablets included a multitude of charts of the heavens with their constellations and planetary movements. There were seven planets: The sun Shamash, the moon Sin, The Morningstar Ishtar, the red warrior Nergal, the small swift moving Nabu, Ninurta of the rings, and the largest, Marduk. Since the stars and planets were divinely interchangeable with the gods, they exerted influence on the course of history, so it was crucial to study their course in the heavens.

As a consequence of this need, Marduk spent countless hours with the scribal scholar Sinleqi, elaborating detailed explanations of omens — celestial phenomena and their meanings as signs for terrestrial events. Marduk would dictate and Sinleqi would engrave in cuneiform with his reed stylus.

These omens would take the form of something like, "When Nabu becomes visible in the east in the region of Virgo, its interpretation is: The harvest of the land will prosper;" or, "If Marduk remains in the sky in the morning, enemy kings will become reconciled." Since gods and kings ruled the land, and the commoners were relatively insignificant, these omens related only to royalty and their kingdoms, not to individual citizens.

Of particular importance in spiritual manifestation was the rare phenomenon of planetary alignment. Every few hundred years, all the planets would be lined up in a near eclipse that would exert unprecedented dramatic historical influence on the earth below. It was a celestial spectacle of great importance. Marduk had only recently calculated that the next alignment was due within a generation.

An additional factor magnified the significance of the alignment. That was the change of astrological ages that was currently taking place. Every two thousand one hundred and sixty years, the constellations above would move through the sky such that a new constellation would become dominant in its position and influence. In the same way that the sun would move through the signs of the zodiac over its yearly course, so the signs themselves would move through a "Great Year" of twenty-six thousand years, but in reverse order. The current age was of Taurus, the Bull. This was an age of earth, agriculture, and the Bull of Heaven, something Nimrod was very familiar with in his past experience. The next age to come was the Age of Aries, the Ram. This would be an age of fire and war, and was the portent of Marduk's own rule through Nimrod of Babylon. However, the ages did not stop and start on specific days or years. Instead, they blended into one another over decades or even hundreds of years. This was called the "cusp" of the age. Thus they were on the cusp of the age of Aries, and the apex of that cusp would occur at precisely the time of the next great planetary alignment.

Marduk knew that this combined cusp and alignment would be the zenith of compounded heavenly forces. The power would open the new temple-tower Etemenanki as a portal to heaven for their plans. Thus, he had told a disappointed Nimrod that the emperor would have to wait another generation before they could consecrate the temple, open the portal, and establish it as their new cosmic mountain of the gods. Their plans for world conquest would have to wait another generation.

Such a waiting period was insignificant for the likes of Marduk, whose supernatural being had experienced eons of time. He would simply use the time to labor over concealing all this astrological information behind elaborate religious myths and rituals. It was an ingenious way of embedding his knowledge into the very operations of ancient religion.

But for Nimrod, who was only half god and half man, a generation was like an eternity. Since he knew he could do nothing about it, he would have to focus on building his glorious city, which would take about as long to finish.

This anxious interim was to be the least of Nimrod's concerns. That very evening, an event would occur that would change the world forever. It would challenge Nimrod's imperial rule over a depraved world seemingly abandoned by its Creator.

Elohim was coming back to the land of Mesopotamia.

CHAPTER 14

Nimrod felt that one of the advantages of being the emperor of the world, with the king of the gods as his patron deity, was the supreme authority that he had over his subjects. He could do whatever he wanted with them. He could use them, abuse them, beat them, kill them, or eat them as he wished. He had absolute authority over humanity.

However, one of the disadvantages of being the emperor under the authority of the supreme deity was the deity's right to do whatever *he* wanted with Nimrod. Of course, it would be of no advantage to Marduk if he beat Nimrod too badly, or killed, or ate him.

But there was one thing that Marduk could do to assert his power, remind Nimrod of his station, and keep him in line: physical abuse. Because Nimrod was a Naphil, being part god, he could endure more abuse than normal human beings without breaking or dying in the god's hands. Though Marduk made certain to keep Nimrod always in a submissive role, Nimrod had actually begun to enjoy the debasement and hurt. It gave him a richer understanding, knowing by experience what his own victims went through when he abused them.

Nevertheless, Marduk required Nimrod to beg for mercy and cower in fear. It had its intended effect of instilling in Nimrod a dutiful and submissive loyalty in public as well as private.

The clanging of an emergency bell in the palace interrupted them.

"This had better be important," growled Marduk, "or I will slaughter whoever it is interrupting my satisfaction."

Nimrod hoped it was the case, since that would mean a reprieve for him, as Marduk would take out his wrath simultaneously on the messenger instead of Nimrod that evening.

The two of them made their way to the receiving hall.

When Nimrod and Marduk reached the receiving hall, an entire cadre of wise men from the school awaited them. Some sorcerers, enchanters and astrologers had apparently been celebrating, because most of them were inebriated. But the celebration seemed to have worn off and they swayed on their feet in unbalanced anxiety.

Marduk steamed with fury. Sinleqi stood in the forefront, so Nimrod addressed him.

"Where is Terah?" It was customary for any important such aggregation of wise men to be accompanied by Terah, the headmaster of the school of heavenly wisdom.

Sinleqi spoke up. He did not like wine because he did not treasure the idea of losing control of himself. He treasured control.

"Your majesty, we just came from Terah's house. We were celebrating the birth of his new child."

"Oh, right. Very well," said Nimrod. He did not care much for such things, so it had easily slipped his mind that Terah had taken some days off for just such a thing.

"So, why are you bothering me?"

"My lord," replied Sinleqi, "in the midst of our rejoicing, some of us went outdoors, those you see here." There were about twelve of them. Sinleqi's body shook. And it was not from drink. "Your highness, all of us saw it. All of us. We looked up into the sky and were astonished to see a very large bright star come from the east and travel the ends of the heavens. This single star swallowed up the four stars of the four sides of heaven. We assembled together and counseled ourselves as to what this celestial matter was a portent of. We consulted our astronomical diaries and star almanacs in order to discover the meaning of this frightening omen. Now, as you may know…"

"Stop!" yelled Nimrod. "I do not want to hear every single scholarly detail and astrological minutia of every single consultation you engage in! Just tell me what it means, Sinleqi." Nimrod had often thought he should have executed Sinleqi long ago. But the man's obsession with detail became so handy in managing the bureaucratic details of a kingdom.

Queen Semiramis suddenly interrupted them as if out of thin air. She was with her handmaiden who was carrying her year-old son Mardon.

Nimrod looked annoyed. "Woman, must you, at this hour?"

"Forgive me, my lord," hissed Semiramis, "but the volume of your exchange has awakened your son and beckoned us to your presence."

She looked at Nimrod and Marduk behind him with an accusing look. "Of course, you should not be bothered by such interruptions in your *secret affairs* of state."

Innuendo was her only way to express her disapproval, since she could not do so explicitly without being beaten.

The baby began to cry. Nimrod closed his eyes.

Semiramis grabbed the child from the handmaiden and opened her robe to feed the baby boy.

There was an unnatural connection between Semiramis and her son. Mardon was fast becoming a surrogate object of Semiramis' affections and intentions.

Sinleqi finished his message. "Imperial Lord, the celestial phenomenon means that a child is born, whose seed will slay great kings, possess their land, and inherit the earth."

"Are you talking of Mardon?" asked Semiramis.

"No, my queen," answered Sinleqi, "This portent is of a new born."

"Whose newborn?" she barked, anger rising in her throat.

Sinleqi glanced fearfully at the other wise men and sighed. He wanted to delay revealing the details.

"Terah, the captain of my heavenly host," said Nimrod. He had figured it out within moments.

Semiramis was dumbfounded.

"Send for Terah," said Nimrod.

"Yes, your majesty," said Sinleqi. The group of wise men began to leave.

Semiramis blurted out, "What is the child's name?"

Sinleqi turned and said, "Abram, your majesty."

CHAPTER 15

Nimrod sat brooding on his throne. He was angered that it had come to this. Terah had been a faithful servant of his heavenly host. He had built the school of heavenly wisdom and trained the courts of all of Nimrod's wise men. Just as importantly, he had created the army of golemim for the king. The Stone Ones had enabled him to assassinate all his rivals simultaneously and maintain a powerful terror throughout the land. Terah had been very loyal.

But he was also a bit of a toady. He would change his mind to suit the whim of the king. He always chose that which would ensure his survival by maintaining perpetual support of his lord, no matter the issue, no matter the cost.

But was that not preferable to a man with a conscience? A man with a moral conscience could not be trusted to do the will of the king when it conflicted with his petty conventional scruples. And the gods only knew what Terah's wife – what was her name again? – he could not remember. The gods only knew how she would respond to the king's demands.

In all of Nimrod's well worked out plans, he had made one little mistake that would haunt him for the rest of his life. That mistake was making this situation almost unworkable: *Terah had the command and control of the golemim.*

Nimrod had ordered Terah to create the army of ten thousand strong out of rock down in the desert outside Uruk. He had given

Terah the enchantment spell to animate the Stone Ones. But he had neglected to consider the ramifications of his actions. The spell that Terah had to reproduce for all the mouths of the golemim was written to enslave the army's obedience to the caster of the spell. But in order for Terah to get the army to secretly march up north to Babylon and hide in the sand and rocks in preparation for the wedding ceremony of Nimrod, *Terah had to be the caster.*

Once the casting was accomplished, it could not be withdrawn or authority transferred. The sorcery established Terah as the commander of the army and Nimrod could not take that over. So Terah would always be required as a proxy commander on behalf of Nimrod with the Stone Ones.

If Terah changed loyalties or questioned his station, he could command the army to rise up in a coup against Nimrod. And if Nimrod killed Terah, the army would become a useless collection of immovable rock statues, and much of Nimrod's military power would be drained. Not all of it, but enough to cause his empire to weaken.

Nimrod could not kill Terah without losing his kingdom, but he would lose it anyway, when this son of Terah's grew to fulfill the astrological prophecy.

There was only one thing Nimrod could do.

When Terah entered the throne room, Nimrod sighed. He had made sure that Semiramis would not be here to jeopardize the men's ability to negotiate more freely. They shared a connection through the experience of war and rule together that no woman could understand.

"Terah, my prince," said Nimrod.

"My lord and savior," said Terah, bowing cautiously. He knew full well what this was about.

"I will not play games with you, Terah. You have been loyal for too long, and you deserve honesty. The astrologers and wise men told me of the heavenly omen and its meaning. Your son is foretold to multiply his seed and overthrow my kingdom. What would you suggest I do with such a prophecy hostile to my reign and the reign of my son?"

Nimrod was proud of his clever move. Rather than lash out and make threats, he pretended to ask Terah to put himself in the king's place and admit his own decision would be the same. How could Terah deny such a dilemma to his king, his emperor?

"I would have any child who laid claim to my throne executed," said Terah with a resigned sadness.

"Exactly," said Nimrod. "So you can appreciate my decision as being not a personal one, but rather a royal one, devoted to a higher cause of dynastic integrity and devotion to the gods."

Terah said, "Yes, my lord."

Nimrod sat staring down at Terah. His distressed expression said he did not want to make this command that all the gods and the universe forced him to make.

Nimrod said, "Hand the child over to me, and I will grant you a house full of silver and gold in compensation for your dutiful sacrifice to your king and your gods."

Terah stood looking at the floor for what seemed like an eternity of decision. Then quietly, humbly, he said, "Yes, your majesty."

Nimrod sighed with relief. It was easy after all. This sandal-licking toady would give up his son as easy as he gave up his own soul.

Yes, he did prefer this to a man with a conscience.

Then Terah added, "I only ask to have three days with him before I release him to you and say goodbye."

"Of course, my prince," replied Nimrod. "You deserve it. You remain my most trusted servant. And this proves your character. I grant you your desire with all my heart."

"I beg your leave, lord," asked Terah.

"You may go," said Nimrod.

Terah turned to leave the room with his head held low. He took a couple of steps and then stopped. He turned back to the king. "There was one matter of economic detail I have been meaning to take care of with you," he said. "It would only take a moment of your time for a decision."

"Of course," said Nimrod. "Anything for you, my noble liege."

Terah explained, "Remember the royal stallion you bred and gave to me, my king?"

Nimrod nodded. It was a supremely majestic horse, fitting of the highest commander in the kingdom — beneath himself of course.

Terah continued, "Well, the other day, Ayon, son of Mored, approached me and offered some money and a percentage of his harvest in exchange for the stallion. Would you advise me to make the trade?"

"What?" exclaimed Nimrod. "Have you been enchanted or turned moronic? No, I do not approve of your exchange! That is the finest warhorse in the kingdom. Of what value is even a house full of money or crops compared to such an invaluable animal? There is none like him. You can never replace such a creature."

"You mean, like a son?" asked Terah.

It hit Nimrod hard. Terah had tricked him, had led him into a trap of his own making, just to throw it back in Nimrod's face. The thought of strangling Terah right now crossed Nimrod's mind, but he thought better.

"Terah, do not vex me," said Nimrod. "I will slay your family and extended relatives, your entire bloodline, if I so desire."

Terah immediately submitted. "My lord, all that I am and all that I have is in the king's power. Do with me what you will. I will give you my newborn, as well as my other two sons, for no exchange whatsoever."

"Your newborn is all I require, Terah," said Nimrod. "Go take your three days and return with him as an offering of loyalty to your king."

Nimrod was relieved that he would not have to muster up a house full of gold and silver after all. This fool would give him up with no recompense. Terah was a man without a conscience *or* a soul.

"Thank you, your grace," said Terah, and he sulked out of the room with bent over shoulders and a deep sadness that permeated his entire presence.

After the three days were up, Terah arrived with his newborn son wrapped in swaddling clothes and presented him to the king.

Nimrod saw a redness in Terah's wet eyes, no doubt from hours of weeping with his wife and children over their offering. But the king also saw a resignation in Terah that showed he knew his station in this kingdom and he knew what he had to do to survive.

Nimrod sighed in relief. He had triumphed in this most difficult situation. He had skirted the loss of his army, the danger of a coup, and he maintained the loyalty of a man whose use for his kingdom was not yet done.

Nimrod received the child and held him in his arms.

"What did you say his name was?" asked Nimrod.

"Abram," said Terah.

"Abram," repeated Nimrod.

He looked into the little child's eyes and tried to imagine how this helpless little babe could have the favor of the stars, to rise up and become a conqueror one day. How strange and incomprehensible were the ways of the heavens and their portents. Marduk had told him about the promised Seed of Eve that would be at war with the Seed of Nachash. He had explained that the prophecy had survived multiple generations before and after the great Deluge had swept over the land.

Nimrod wondered at how astounding it was that this little creature nestled in his arms was truly that Chosen Seed so prophesied. And now he had the power and might to crush that prophecy.

He thought, *How like the power of a god.*

"If it pleases my lord," said Terah with a bow.

Nimrod was lost in his thought. He looked up. "Oh, yes, it would be best for you to leave."

Terah turned to leave, but Nimrod stopped him suddenly.

"Terah, I will not forget this supreme act of sacrifice and love that you have offered this day."

"Yes my lord," whispered Terah painfully. He left the room.

As soon as the door closed behind Terah, Nimrod lifted the baby high and dashed his head against the marble floor with all his might.

CHAPTER 16

A few miles to the west of the city of Ur, there lay a freshwater lake surrounded by rocky shores. Large buttes interwove with each other, creating a small maze of cliffs and streams.

Two cloaked figures, carrying reed baggage on their backs, trod around the lake and into the maze of rock. They turned down trails and pathways with navigational precision, until they came to a secret cave within the labyrinth of sediment and sandstone.

At the cave entrance stood a very old man and his wife, evident residents of the cave, awaiting their visitors' arrival with much anticipation.

The cloaked figures came to the entrance and pulled back their hoods. It was Terah and his wife Amthelo. She was a beautiful woman of dark skin and black hair, about ten years younger than Terah.

Terah looked at the old man and his wife. They appeared ancient, though not decrepit. There was an otherworldly quality about them.

Terah asked haltingly, "Noah ben Lamech?"

"In the flesh. Not dead yet," Noah responded. "And neither is my wife Emzara. And you are Terah ben Nahor?"

Terah smiled. "And my wife Amthelo."

Terah walked up to Noah and embraced him. "Do you mind if I call you Grandpappy? There are too many "Greats" to put before

Grandfather." Terah had calculated about seven, but he was not sure anymore. All he knew was that he was in the direct lineage of this heavenly man and his angelic spouse.

"Only if you call her Grandmammy," teased Noah. Emzara slapped Noah playfully.

Terah had never met his distant forefather before this. He had heard the legends surrounding him. How they had settled after the great flood and how there had been some sort of terrible incident, and he and Emzara had left for some magical island on the distant sea. But he had only recently learned from his great-great-grandfather Peleg that Noah had returned to hide out in these caves. It was a family secret kept from the public, because they thought Noah was engaged in another enterprise called by a god.

"Are you building another ark?" asked Terah. Noah burst out laughing, which ended in a coughing fit.

Emzara said, "My dear, Elohim promised to never again flood the earth as he did the first time. We can be sure he keeps his promises."

She noticed Terah's look of confusion and realized what was going on.

"Oh dear, you are not very familiar with Elohim are you?" she concluded.

Terah said, "I am well acquainted with the pantheon of gods. I study the occult, astrology, divination, and all manners of the mysteries of the heavens. But I have never heard a mention of this god, Elohim. Who is he?"

Noah and Emzara glanced at each other. Sumer had been heavily fortified against the knowledge of Elohim. They were surprised at how quickly suppression of the truth happened after the flood. They had better deal with this later. Emzara changed the subject.

"Amthelo, you look so lovely."

"Thank you," said Amthelo.

"How old are you?" Terah asked Noah.

"Far into our nine hundreds. We stopped counting decades ago. But we are still alive and kicking."

Amthelo said to Emzara, "May I say you do not look a day over five hundred."

Emzara shooshed her with a wave of her hand.

They all chuckled and the four of them became aware of the need to immediately address the reason for their coming.

"Well, you have a precious little package for us?" said Noah.

Amthelo smiled and lifted her reed basket off her back. She opened it up and pulled out the squirming little baby boy who was cooing and drooling.

"Ohhhhhhh my!" exclaimed Emzara. "Come to Grandmammy, you little cuddly bear cub!"

Amthelo spoke to her infant as if he could understand, "Abram, meet your ark of refuge, Grandpappy Noah and Grandmammy Emzara."

Emzara held him with glee, and felt life returning to her old bones as the little infant stared at her in open-mouthed wonder.

When Terah brought the child to Nimrod for execution, he did not actually bring Abram, but rather another newborn child from one of their servants in the household. Nimrod never found out that the child he killed was not Abram. Fortunately, Marduk had not been with him on that day, as he usually was, because he would most likely have sniffed out the deception.

Terah said, "We want you to raise little Abram and teach him your wisdom. We could not keep him in our household without the truth eventually getting to Nimrod. The king would kill our entire family bloodline in revenge."

"He is the Chosen Seed," said Noah, looking into baby Abram's scrunched little face.

Then he added with a wry smile, "It takes one to know one."

Emzara said, "So this is why Elohim called us back to this infernal land of evil."

"You see, woman," said Noah. "And you accused me of having bad hearing."

"Yes, dear," said Emzara, rolling her eyes.

Noah mused to her, "I wonder if this means an old friend will be showing up. You know — of the guardian angel persuasion?"

Emzara smiled with fond memories. Noah was alluding to Uriel, the slightly smaller sarcastic archangel who had been the guardian of Noah before the Flood. He had been annoying to Noah, but eventually grew on him and the two became best of friends through a lifetime of adventure and danger.

Emzara shook herself out of their reminiscing, and said to Terah and Amthelo, "You two must be famished."

They shared a meal together as was the custom of hospitality. As they ate, Noah and Emzara tried to explain to Terah and Amthelo about the call of Elohim on their son Abram's life. They tried to explain that Elohim was the Creator God who required complete and exclusive loyalty to his kingship over all creation. They said that the gods were actually fallen Watchers, rebels from Elohim's divine council in heaven, playing roles of deception to accomplish a diabolical war against God's chosen seedline. And this little child was the seed through which an anointed king would one day come and achieve victory over the gods of the people, and bring back all the nations under the allotment of Elohim.

Terah stopped them. He did not want to hear such blasphemy. He was too entrenched in his world of the pantheon, sorcery, magic, astrology and the occult. He started to physically tremble at the talk of an anointed coming king of the seedline.

When Terah threatened to take Abram back with him if they continued in their proselytizing, they stopped.

Noah concluded by saying, "We only love you and want to see you on the right side of the war that is coming."

"Coming?" said Terah. "You have really been cut off from civilization out here in these caves! The war *is already here.* And if what you say about this War of the Seed is true, then the General of this Elohim's enemy is Nimrod of Babylon."

They finished their meal with some uncomfortable tension. But Terah and Amthelo filled their water skins for the secret journey back to Ur before returning to Babylon upriver. Terah had come down to the region under the pretense of spending a vacation in his old hometown of Ur. He had maintained his previous residence for such visits.

Terah and Amthelo spent a minute with their infant, hugging him and kissing him. They would probably never see him again.

Amthelo could not stop crying. Terah had to pull her away. She grasped the little blanket in her fingers.

Emzara empathized with Amthelo's pain, having lost her own family in the deep past. She assured the younger mother, "We will guard him with our lives and will raise him to be a mighty man of valor."

Amthelo whispered, "Thank you."

Terah led her out of the cave and back onto their pathway home and to a new life without their precious son.

CHAPTER 17

A generation passed.

Through these years, Nimrod used his mighty army of Stone Ones to strike terror into the hearts of the entire world. The city of Babylon became the center of that world. Everyone spoke one language and worshipped in one religion under the supreme empire of Nimrod the Mighty Hunter.

The time had finally come to consecrate the temple-tower as Marduk had planned. Soon, the planets would be aligned, the climactic cusp of the Age of Aries would have arrived, and the gods of the pantheon would all be present to open the portal of heaven and establish this as the new cosmic mountain of the gods.

They would perform the ceremonial ritual during the Akitu New Year Festival, the twelve-day extravaganza that celebrated the arrival of spring at the vernal equinox. This was the point at which the sun ascended through the constellation of Aries. On the final day, a great procession of the gods through the city would culminate in their ascension into the temple and its portal opening to connect heaven and earth.

So much had happened in a single generation. While Nimrod focused on military expansion abroad, Semiramis concentrated on the administration of the city of Babylon. It was a mammoth task to make the government of so vast a kingdom run smoothly. And Semiramis had done so with obsessive detail.

Nimrod did not want to be bothered with the minutia of bureaucracy. He was a man of action. He would leave the petty worries of controlling citizens through taxes, regulation, and dependency to his queen and their son Mardon. He busied himself with asserting his military prowess and kingly presence to maintain the fear and awe required to control so vast an empire. It was not easy being the world's first potentate.

While it was crucial for a ruler to maintain his status in the eyes of the people, Semiramis had come to see that the real power over the people lay in the mundane details of controlling every aspect of their daily lives. A king could evoke fear with his military display, but a queen could evoke devotion and dependency through control of shelter, food and income. These latter issues were more primal in human nature, and therefore of more importance to the exercise of true power.

Semiramis had schooled their son Mardon in the craft of government details and political diplomacy. He had become shrewd and cunning in manipulating the system to his advantage. Queen Mother and Prince had together turned the majority of their kingdom — the peasants, workers, and slaves — against the wealthy members of society. They encouraged hatred of the rich for their indulgent consumption —all the rich, that is, except for the royal family, whose wealth was needed to rule beneficently.

Then they confiscated most of the wealth of these "greedy" rich through excessive taxation, in the name of spreading the wealth around, so that "all would be equal." But the rich were ruined and could no longer afford to employ the poor commoners in their fields and storehouses. The government then had to confiscate the means of production and place all citizens in their care as wards of the state.

So commoners ended up not much different than slaves. They depended upon the government for their daily bread, their shelter, and even their health. The daily survival of the citizens was completely in the hands of Semiramis and Mardon.

Sometimes, the queen and prince would even go to the granary and oversee the handing out of daily grain to the citizens so as to be personally equated with their daily sustenance. They would withhold the purse strings from any sector that became belligerent in performing their duties to the state or late in their taxes. They controlled the funding of all governance, including the military, through a convoluted labyrinth of financial accounting that Nimrod could not begin to understand. More and more funds were siphoned from the military in order to "remodel" or build up broken-down sectors of the city, and provide food for the inhabitants. It seemed the plans of building a glorious city of Babylon would never be completed, as a perpetual stream of money poured into sinkholes of unending construction and remodeling. This caused Nimrod the most concern, because the power of armed forces was quenched through strangled funding. The queen had even manipulated Sinleqi away from Nimrod and to her favor by blackmailing him regarding his personal use of government funds for personal indulgences.

Nimrod was not ignorant. He knew Semiramis and his son Mardon had an unnatural relationship that would prove to be a tangled web of corruption. Mardon obviously a tool of Semiramis' ambition. But Nimrod felt foolish for not addressing it in the early years when he had turned away from his wife and child to accomplish his greater purposes of worldwide empire.

The worst of it was that queen and son had become deified by the people, she as queen of heaven, and he as divine son. It would not be advantageous to Nimrod's reign to eliminate them. Their demise could very well cause an uprising amidst the people who had become their loyal and slavish dependents. Nimrod counted on the anointing of Etemenanki as the new cosmic mountain and official establishment of Marduk's reign to bring things back into line where they ought to be.

He had contemplated having mother and son sacrificed on the altar of Marduk during the Akitu Festival climax. He would have to wait and see if he would have the political pull with the population to be able to perform such a bold and daring move. Time would tell.

Semiramis stomped into the torture room looking for Mardon. She knew she would find him there. He spent too many hours in what he called his "playrooms," a series of rooms for sorcery, drugs and torture. The torture rooms were specifically for experimenting with new means of extracting information or punishing insubordinate vassal rulers. The goal was to discover ways of keeping the victims alive as long as possible in order to inflict the most amount of pain humanly possible on another creature, for as long as possible before sending them off to Sheol.

The achievement of this goal required practice in order to perfect the techniques for maximum effect. But Mardon enjoyed torturing anyone, even without reason, so he had to find a source of disposable humans upon which to exercise his craft. The logical choice was slaves. He would tell them in a soothing tone that this would be their ultimate offering of service to the king and his kingdom before he subjected them to the most barbaric acts of cruelty.

Today, one of the rulers of a city—he could not remember which one now—had been deemed two days late in his delivery of harvest taxes to the king. Mardon put the vassal ruler "in the tub."

"Sitting in the tub" as they called it, was a gruesome torture. The vassal was placed in a wooden tub, covered over with only his head exposed. They would regularly feed him large amounts of gruel. But he was not allowed to leave the tub. He would soon be sitting in an increasing pool of his own excrement, until his flesh rotted from the exposure. It would take weeks before the sufferer expired.

Mardon watched over his victim with curious, emotionless eyes. He was like a reptile. He had no conscience, no sense of empathy for other human beings or their pain. He was as cold as stone. He did not even get pleasure from his practice. It was more of a pursuit of perfection that drove him. The perfect torture could accomplish the perfect royal objective, the maintenance of a healthy loathing, dread and horror from the subjects of the kingdom. This would ensure the royal reign that he planned to inherit.

Oh, the plans he had for when he took over his father Nimrod's rule! He smiled at the thought of it. Absolute power was an aphrodisiac to him. And it might come even sooner than he had thought. He had begun to suspect that his mother planned a possible assassination of the king.

"Mardon," said Semiramis, interrupting his pensive thoughts. "I told you we have an audience with your father. Have I taught you nothing? Never disappoint the king, it breeds distrust, you fool."

She walked into the room and saw the victim he was experimenting upon.

"Mother! I worked for hours on this frog!" complained Mardon.

He called the humans frogs, lambs and other animal names.

It disgusted Semiramis how twisted her son had become. The proverb came to her mind, *From the wicked goeth forth wickedness.* It was a more than an apt description of this vile offspring of Nimrod. She had wanted to raise a tyrant that she could control. But there was something darkly removed and sinister about this one. It made her wonder if she would lose that control when he ascended to the throne. Once he had absolute power, would he simply put her to death to take her out of the way? Would all her plans for the past generation be obliterated in an instant, because she failed to recognize the true essence of this perversion of nature? Well, she could not worry about that now. She would have to plan for it later.

She wiped blood off Mardon's cheek, like any nit-picking mother, and said, "Get cleaned up and meet your father and me in the throne room within the hour."

"Yes, mother," replied Mardon. He was subservient to her. He so appreciated the care with which she raised him to become an effective emperor. She had educated him about religion, politics and the craft of court intrigue. She had taught him the fine art of treachery through diplomacy and getting your way. She had taught him how to rule a people through fear. He actually enjoyed the overbearing and domineering personality she exerted over him. It was an opportunity to feel a bit of what his victims felt, which would give him greater pleasure in their pain. His mother had been his education. Now, he was her hope for the future.

It was a pity that she would have to be eliminated once he rose to power.

Oh well, he thought. *From the wicked goeth forth wickedness.*

Mardon arrived in the throne room dressed in his royal attire. Nimrod and Semiramis sat on their thrones, waiting for him.

Nimrod was impatient and annoyed. "So sorry to take you away from your garden of earthly delights, Mardon, but I have a kingdom to run, and you will accompany me and Terah on a tour of my cities."

Mardon glanced at Semiramis. She nodded, and he stepped forward to kneel on one knee. He said, "Yes, my father."

Nimrod held back his contempt. He could see that Mardon was more the son of the queen than the king. Of course, he had no one to blame but himself. He had neglected his son once he noticed that the boy was not right in the head. But there was nothing he could do about the past. He thought he would make the best of it now and try to exert some influence on the reprobate scoundrel before it was too late. Though Nimrod was a Naphil, half-human, half-god, he was not getting any younger. He was over a century old. Even Nephilim die. Becoming the first world potentate would not be of much value if he could not establish a dynasty of power that would last for generations.

Mardon was the heir to that dynasty.

Nimrod announced, "We will start at Elam in the south and from there travel to Ur, before coming up to the northern cities of Nineveh and her sisters."

"A wise course, father," said Mardon patronizingly.

Mardon knew that of all the vassal kingdoms that served Nimrod, Elam was the most restless. Its king, Chedorlaomer, had been a prince of Nimrod's host before being given the city-state of Elam to administer. Chedorlaomer had become very successful and comfortable with his new identity as monarch. Elam was becoming quite a powerful entity. The king started to show signs of independence and because Chedorlaomer had served so closely under Nimrod, he knew the emperor's ways intimately. That meant he could anticipate Nimrod's behavior should Nimrod decide to use force to bring Elam under more control. It had become a touchy situation. Nimrod knew that personal presence was always superior to representatives when it came to political diplomacy. So their first stop would be Elam.

"Will the high god Marduk join us?" asked Mardon.

"No," said Nimrod. He knew his son despised Marduk. He was too much what Mardon wanted to be, a god without human weakness. Of course, it was what Nimrod wanted as well, but he could only imagine the havoc that might be created on the earth if his son was able to procure the attributes of divinity.

Nimrod thought, *He would be a male version of Ishtar.*

Marduk had been spending more time in his temple, Esagila, and less time around Nimrod. He was preparing for the fast-arriving "Convergence," as they called it. The Convergence marked the alignment of the planets *converging* with the cusp of the Age of Aries. It also marked the convergence of heaven and earth, as the temple-tower would open a cosmic portal to the heavenlies. As king of the gods, Marduk would preside over the entire twelve day festival. So he had his preparation work cut out for him.

This would be one very important year in the history of gods and men.

CHAPTER 18

In the desert outside Ur, a lone figure stood before a fresh tomb in the rocky clefts of the lakeside area. In the tomb were two bodies. One was Emzara, who had died a few years earlier, and the more recent one was the body of Noah. The lone man gave thanks to Elohim for the couple who had raised him. It was Abram and he was now forty-eight years old.

He finished his prayer.

He laid a pack of his life's belongings on the back of a donkey. It would accompany him and his horse to the city of Ur. Abram had lived in seclusion with Noah and Emzara since he had been an infant. They had raised him to know the Creator Elohim as El Shaddai, God Almighty, protector of the chosen seedline. They had poured their lives into their descendant because they believed he was new life for their promised hope.

They had not foreseen the potential danger of a child raised in solitude seeing himself as God's Chosen One. That was the disadvantage of living as an only child. Abram had been pampered, given total attention, and told over and over again that he was God's special instrument. He had gotten the impression that he could do no wrong. He had developed an overconfidence that lacked humility and almost presumed invincibility. After all, if El Shaddai was his guard and protector, who could slay him?

If any human did try to take him on, Abram had been taught some secrets of fighting by Noah. The secrets went back to his distant ancestor, Enoch the giant slayer. They were called the "Way of the Karabu," a martial art that had been revealed by the archangel Gabriel. Abram had a romantic view of himself as some kind of future king and adventurer, with El Shaddai by his side clearing the way for his purposes.

It had been a lonely forty-eight years, although not entirely without human interaction. Noah and Emzara had kept Abram away from the main cities of Sumer, but they made sure to take trips to way stations in the desert. There, they encountered trade merchants from all over the world, traveling through with their wares. Abram learned many customs and languages and interacted with interesting people who told fabulous stories of their travels. He would have left the cave residence earlier, but he wanted to bury both of his beloved ancestors before striking out on his own.

Noah had given Abram the name of Abram's brothers, Nahor and Haran, in the city of Ur. He told Abram to go to them with a tablet Noah had inscribed with a toledoth of Abram's genealogy. The brothers would take Abram in and introduce him to his father Terah when they had the chance. It was a bit risky, but Noah had always been one for shaking things up, even in his ripe old age.

When Terah had been inducted as Nimrod's prince of the heavenly host, he had kept the family down in Ur, under the pretense of focusing on his duties in Babylon free of their distractions. He would visit them on a regular basis, using the excuse of reporting to Nimrod on the state of the Southern kingdom in Sumer. Terah had an ulterior motive as well. He had seen the danger of his situation and the soul trap that was Babylon. He wanted to spare his family as much as possible from the detrimental effects of close proximity to the emperor Nimrod and his ruling city. He knew the unpredictability of the tyrant and considered distance the best protection against the impulsive reactions of royalty. Terah was a man of many masters and he tried to juggle them all, with the intent of protecting his family at all costs.

The family of Terah ben Nahor of Ur knew nothing of their long lost relative Abram. They had been told a child had died a generation ago and they forgot about him entirely.

It was a cool and cloudy day. Nahor and Haran had finished cleaning up their stall of idols in the marketplace and were returning to their home. They carried on the family business of idol making after Terah had been drafted into Nimrod's service. It was a tireless business of unending demand. People were constantly breaking their little terra cotta figurines of household deities called *teraphim*. They were also constantly changing gods or just wanting more gods to ensure their happiness. It was becoming more popular now to have stone-carved life-sized statues in homes. These fetched a higher price for their craft. It was a business with a sure source of consistent income, because of the spiritual hunger of humanity.

When the brothers reached their home, they were almost too exhausted to notice the man waiting for them.

He asked, "Are you Nahor and Haran ben Terah?"

They stopped and looked at Abram. He was wiry, with a full beard, a bit unkempt, and most likely a middle-aged bachelor — not a good sign. And he looked as if he had traveled a great distance.

They sighed. They knew the custom of hospitality, that one should welcome strangers into one's home and feed them and provide shelter if need be. Provided of course, the stranger was not hostile, in which case you could kill them.

Abram held out a clay tablet. "This is a genealogy of mine authored by Noah ben Lamech," he said with great confidence. "I am your brother and the long forgotten son of Terah ben Nahor."

The brothers stood open mouthed with shock. Nahor took the tablet and looked at it. Haran read over his shoulder in disbelief.

They read through the tablet and saw the colophon, "These are the generations of Noah." It was the signature of their beloved ancestor. Was it a forgery? It had the family marking on it. Nahor handed it back to Abram.

"Well, then we have much to talk about," said Nahor. "Please, come and have dinner with us."

"No, I could not impose on you with such inconvenience," replied Abram.

"As you wish," said Haran. "God bless you on your way."

Nahor gave Haran a dirty look. It was custom to turn down an offer of hospitality as much as it was custom to reaffirm the offer right afterward. Haran was being inhospitable.

"My brother is a mule and sometimes a jackal," said Nahor. "Please ignore his rudeness and have dinner with us tonight."

"Very well," said Abram. "Thank you." And he winked at the embarrassed Haran.

The household of Terah was large and well furnished. Several generations lived under his roof. As a member of the royal household, his family had been given special treatment and they lived in the wealthy quarter. And because of their idol making business, they had money to spare.

Abram sat before a spread of lamb, fish, fruits and vegetables, with bread and some beer to wash it down. He had not eaten so extravagantly in his life.

His two brothers, Nahor and Haran, entertained him, along with several others of Abram's cousins.

"This is Lot, my son," said Haran, "my wife, Eliana, and my daughters, Milcah and Iscah."

Abram wryly greeted the adolescent children, "Hello, nephew and nieces."

Nahor took over. "Milcah is my wife." He then gestured to the woman serving Abram. "And this is Sarai, your half-sister."

She surprised Abram. He had thought she was one of the servants. At least, she acted like one. Finally, she sat down in the empty seat.

Sarai would not look Abram in the eye. Abram, on the other hand could not take his eyes off her. She was stunning, the most beautiful woman Abram had ever seen. Which, on the surface, was not saying much, because he had been raised in obscurity in the desert. But the women he had met were often foreigners in trading caravans. He had actually been exposed to some of the most exotic and attractive females in the land.

But Sarai was far and away more attractive than any of them. Though she tied her hair up in a modest bun, she could not hide its blonde sun-like glow. She wore no make-up, but her bright white eyes with light green pupils were more penetrating than those of any traveling harlot that had ever tempted him.

Her physical traits were unusual for the area. Her lips were full and her neck, ravishing. It was all Abram could do to keep from staring at her. She seemed to hide behind her plain wool robe.

But Sarai was clearly older than a typical maiden. It was not that she had the wrinkles or wear of age, rather, her presence emanated maturity beneath her comeliness.

"Where is your husband?" Abram asked Sarai directly.

Big brother Haran interrupted before she could answer, "That is another story. Sarai ruined every chance she ever got to catch a husband when she was of marrying age. Now, we expect her to end up an old maid forever in the household."

Sarai blushed with shame, continuing to look down painfully into her food.

Eliana gave Haran a dirty look for his rude comments.

Nahor jumped in, "Which is probably good for us anyway, because she seems to enjoy serving her family."

Abram could not believe it was possible. Sarai totally entranced him, and for the life of him, he could not possibly figure out what she could have done to remain unmarried with such astonishing loveliness. Her beauty caused Abram to want to bow down to the ground in worship of the majestic God who created such exquisite artistry. It was a beauty that caused a burning longing in him.

Nahor interrupted Abram's staring with an urgent concern. "Our father is coming down in a couple weeks for a visit."

Haran threw in, "Mother died a few years back. We do not see him much anymore."

Nahor asked, "What will he do when he meets you?"

"Well, he was the one who hid me," said Abram. "I doubt he will want to give me up to the king."

Abram had explained to them what Noah told him about Abram's birth prophesied in the stars and Terah's rescue of him from Nimrod's clutches. They heard of the endless war of seedlines that began in distant Eden and continued to this day. It was all so bizarre to Abram's relatives. They could not imagine what this seed thing was all about.

Haran countered Abram's doubts, "But if he gave you away to protect his family, then he would surely not want to face those consequences again."

"He has not bothered to keep in contact with you for almost fifty years," added Nahor. "That is pretty strong evidence that he does not want you back in his life, *or* in ours."

Sarai muttered something too low for the others to hear.

But Abram heard it.

"Excuse me, Sarai," said Abram, "did you say something?"

Everyone stopped talking.

It was an odd thing for Sarai to speak up – or rather as Nahor would say, to "squeak up."

"But Abram is family," she said a little more audibly, finally glancing up at Abram. It sent a shiver down his spine.

She looked at me, he thought. *She said my name*. It was more like she looked *into* him, into his soul. But how could this be? He had just met her. As lovely a specimen as she was, how could she have that kind of sway over him?

He thanked El Shaddai that she had a different mother; otherwise, his rising feelings would be shameful. They had the same father, but different mothers made them only half-siblings, which was more like cousins.

Abram took another bite of lamb. It was savory, full of herbs and spices. Probably the finest lamb he had ever eaten — while gazing upon the finest looking woman he had ever imagined. It was a heavenly combination.

Meanwhile, everyone else considered Sarai's statement in uncomfortable silence. Eliana blurted out, "She is right again, and you know it." Abram was family and as such could not be turned away, turned out, given up, or rejected. They were obligated to care for their brother, their uncle, their cousin.

Sarai got up and began to clear the table. Abram stared at her, watching her every move. She was grace in action. When she walked out of the room, he watched her like a hawk. She must have been unaware of her hypnotic power or she no doubt would have sought to suppress it.

Haran noticed Abram's fascination. "Nahor," he teased, "I think our brother is pleased with our half-sister's service to our family. Although, I am not sure why he is drooling."

Abram snapped back into the conversation. "I intend to earn my keep here. What is the family occupation?"

"Idol making," said Haran. "And we are quite good at it."

Uh oh, thought Abram, *That is going to be a problem.*

CHAPTER 19

That evening, Abram cornered Sarai as she swept the outside mat to the house entrance.

"The outside mat?" he teased.

She jumped in shock. Then she smiled when she saw who it was.

"Is there no end to the lengths which you will go to slavishly serve your family?" he asked.

"Do not praise me," she said. "It is not out of goodness that I do this. I truly enjoy cleaning. So, it is really rather selfish."

"Well, that is even worse," he chuckled. "Come for a walk with me, Sarai."

She hesitated. She did not know what to say.

"I promise you," he injected, "I will come up with some way for you to serve me. But in the meantime, let us just talk."

She smiled, and nodded humbly, and set the broom aside. She called in the house for Lot.

"What are you doing?" Abram asked.

"We will need a chaperone," she said.

"To go for a walk?"

"Did not Noah teach you propriety in relation to women?"

Lot barged out of the door, "Yes, auntie?"

"Would you mind chaperoning our walk this evening?"

"Sure!"

Abram studied the lean and wiry frame of his nephew. Abram liked his spunkiness. But even though Lot was fast approaching twenty years of age, Abram did not think the youth's presence would fit well with his attempt to court Sarai.

They started to walk. Sure enough, Lot was virtually on top of them. He might as well have joined in the conversation.

Abram turned and said to him, "Would you give us a little room? Some privacy, please."

"Sure, uncle," said Lot. He winked at Abram and backed off just enough to satisfy Abram and not disappoint Sarai.

They strolled through the cool evening of Ur. The streets were mostly empty. Families were settling down for the evening to sleep and entertain themselves with games and amusements.

"Sarai is a lovely name," said Abram.

"It means 'princess,'" she said.

Abram was about to say, "How appropriate." But before he could, she added, "And do not call me 'princess.' I get teased enough about it."

"I would not dream of it," said Abram. He thought, *You are not a princess; you are a queen of glory and honor.*

She continued, "It is the name of the wife of the moon god Sin, our patron deity in Ur."

That made sense, since Terah had always been deeply and devotedly religious.

"How old are you?" asked Abram.

"Forty," she said.

"Forgive me, Sarai, but I am utterly perplexed at how such a stunningly beautiful woman, with such a servant's heart, is not married. It does not make sense to me."

"You obviously do not know me, then," she said. "And please do not call me beautiful. I am not beautiful."

He stared at her, shocked. He could already tell, however, that there was no guile in this woman. She meant what she said, as bizarre as it sounded.

"Sarai, please. I appreciate your modesty, but it is an objective truth that you are perhaps the most gorgeous woman I have ever seen, even more than women half your age."

"Pshaaw!" she sniffed. "You obviously only saw sheep and goats out there in the wilderness. Now, please let us talk about something else. Are you nervous about your first meeting with father? Are you afraid he will reject you?"

Abram began to understand why Sarai was so undesirable to other men. She had such a low view of herself that she did not consider herself worthy of anyone. This negativity bled into everything she said. Maybe she loved serving others because she saw herself as an unworthy slave. He wondered if her illegitimate birth made her think she did not belong anywhere.

Well, she is not going to get rid of me, he thought.

"I do not care what father thinks of me," said Abram. "I am known and am loved by El Shaddai, and he has big plans for my life."

"Who is El Shaddai?" she asked.

"He is the god I serve, our Creator, God Almighty," he said.

"I have never heard of him before," she said. "Is he new to the pantheon?"

Abram chuckled. "He *created* the pantheon. And they rebelled against him, and united with mankind until every intention of the thought of mankind's heart is only evil continually. The gods are not who you think they are, Sarai."

"Well, this El Shaddai certainly gives you confidence," she said.

She felt drawn to this blunt and boisterous man. She had never met anyone like him before. He was someone who had little going for him by way of the normal cares of life, yet he had a certainty of vision and purpose.

"So, what are these big plans he has for you?" she asked.

"Well, I do not exactly know," he said. It was a bit embarrassing for him to admit. "But he is the god of Enoch and Noah, and Noah told me I am to wait upon El Shaddai and he will someday tell me what to do."

"Tell me more of your god," she said, amused with his passion.

Abram took the rest of the walk to explain to Sarai the story his Grandpappy Noah told him many times. The story of Eden, and the Seed of Eve versus the Seed of the Serpent, the Titanomachy, the Gigantomachy, the war on Eden, and the Great Flood. He told her of El Shaddai's way of providing a path for his people who worshipped him. How the gods of the pantheon were false gods who stole divine worship away from the Creator, and how El Shaddai was going to bring a seed into the world that would bring redemption, and defeat the Seed of Nachash, the Serpent. He told her of the curse on Ham and the blessing on Shem and Japheth, and how he was in the line of Shem.

They were near the end of their walk when she turned to him and said, "So, if what you say is true about this El Shaddai, then our entire livelihood is idolatry? The worship of false gods?"

"I am afraid so," he said. Abram did not want to make her feel bad, but he would not deny the truth.

"And that means we should all turn away from these gods to worship El Shaddai alone?"

"Yes," he said simply.

"That is quite extreme," she concluded. But he could see she was thinking it through with her righteous heart.

"I think we should say goodnight, Abram. We are more different than I first realized."

They were back at the house. But she sounded as if she was saying goodbye forever. He knew he should not have spoken so freely. He should have eased her into it. Now he had blurted out too much, too quickly, and pushed her away.

She rushed inside to get away from him. He stood before the doorway, dumbfounded and sad. He wished he was not so direct, so blunt. He remembered how Emzara used to ease him into the things he had a hard time accepting. She made the truth desirable. But he just seemed to make it distasteful and offensive.

Suddenly something jumped on his back and grabbed him around the neck. It was Lot. He had totally forgotten Lot following them.

"Hey, uncle, what would El Shaddai give me if I turned away from the gods and worshipped him?"

"You *were* listening to us!" Abram yelped. "You little squirrel."

Abram roughhoused with Lot and wrestled him to the ground, pinning him.

"I am serious!" shouted Lot. "I do not want to make stupid teraphim statues for the rest of my life. I want to get out of Ur, see the world, experience life. Can I travel with you?"

Abram looked at Lot with affection. The kid had passion.

"I do not know where El Shaddai is calling me," said Abram.

"So what?" said Lot. "Anywhere is better than here."

"On one condition," said Abram.

"What is that?" asked Lot.

"You must endure the spittle torture," said Abram.

Lot was still pinned under Abram. Now a long goober of spit began to hang out of Abram's mouth. Lot squirmed to get away from underneath him. Abram sucked up the spit before it would drop on Lot, and started the process all over again. Lot writhed, trying to get free before the spit would break loose from Abram's lips and hit him.

Abram was an expert. He could get the spittle almost touching Lot's face before he slurped it back up. He could keep doing this for some time.

They both laughed in unison until Abram let him go because he was laughing so hard. He could not hold on to Lot any longer.

But the matter of Sarai haunted him.

CHAPTER 20

The next day, when the men left for work, Abram stayed behind. He wanted to talk to Sarai. But during his breakfast of bread cakes and figs, she ignored him and cleaned up without giving him a look.

He watched her and waited until everyone else had left the dining area.

He decided not to say anything. He just wanted to see if she would even give him one glance.

She did not. She looked very bothered, even agitated by his presence. But she finished up and left him alone in the room.

Have I ruined my one chance for pure happiness? he wondered as a melancholy overcame him. *Was I a hardheaded pig, insensitive to her emotions? Did I give her the false impression that El Shaddai is a despotic deity? An arrogant self-important person who thinks the world revolves around him — like me?*

Later in the day, he walked past the women and girls washing clothes and hanging them to dry. Everyone said hello to Abram – except the one person he wanted to hear it from, Sarai. She just hung her clothes with a distant, disturbed look.

Abram went for a walk through the city to clear his head and pray. On his walk, he saw the idolatry of the city with its shrines to the various gods of the pantheon. The huge ziggurat temple, Etemennigur, at the center of the city, was awe-inspiring. He had never seen one before, but Noah and Emzara had told him all about them. As he stood gazing up at it, he thought it was indeed a terror, a stairway not to the true heaven, but to evil and slavery.

When he ate dinner that evening, Sarai was still quiet and avoided his gaze. To the others, it was normal. But for Abram, it was unbearably cruel. Why would she hate him so? If they worshipped so many gods, why would she be so offended that he worshipped yet another one? What could he have possibly said that would have disturbed the heart of such a sweet and sensitive woman as this? It had to be his fault, because he already believed her to be more pure than he could ever be. Or maybe she really was not. Maybe her devotion to these diabolical deities brought out the true evil of her heart when confronted by El Shaddai. Maybe her external beauty covered a heart full of rancid idolatry for this moon god consort she was named after.

Haran interrupted Abram's thoughts, "You should come with us to the market tomorrow, Abram. We could show you our idol-making shop."

"I do not think that would be a good idea," said Abram, still watching Sarai like a hawk. He could see her agitation growing as she got up to clean up the dishes.

"Why?" asked Nahor. "We could teach you the craft rather easily."

Abram sighed. He began to explain to them everything he had told Sarai the night before. As Sarai came in and out of the room, cleaning up after everyone, Abram tried his best to be fair and tolerant in his interaction with them, but the truth of it still stung like a hornet. The family fell silent. He was telling them that their entire life was a lie of worshipping a lie.

The silence became tense, but Lot finally broke it with his irreverent tone, "Grandfather Terah is not going to dance with joy when he hears this."

"To say the least," added Nahor.

"Maybe I should just go on my way," said Abram. "I can see I hurt Sarai last night, and now I have insulted your family idols while imbibing your hospitality."

For the very first time all day and night, Sarai looked straight at Abram. Her eyes were filled will angry tears. Abram froze in confusion. It seemed that any gesture from her could affect his very soul.

She threw down the plates in her hands and ran out.

"What is wrong with her?" asked Haran.

Abram jumped up and ran after her.

"Leave them be," said Eliana. She had an idea of what was going on. The women always did.

Abram found Sarai in the small garden at the back of their walled-in property. She wept softly into her hands.

Abram approached her. He did not know what to say.

So he said what he was thinking. "What is wrong, Sarai? What have I done to offend you? I am sorry for being so aggressive about El Shaddai. I should have just…"

"It is not you, you blockhead," she interrupted him.

"What is it?" he probed. He wanted nothing but to bring her solace, to calm her heart.

"You have done nothing wrong. You have done everything right."

"I have?" he asked.

"The moment I heard you tell the story of El Shaddai, I knew in my soul it was the truth that I had been looking for my whole life."

"But why were you angry?" he said.

"I was angry at my family for raising me with lies. And I was angry at you because... because..." She was afraid to tell him.

"Why?" he reiterated, "Why were you angry with me?"

"Because something inside me changed, and you made it so difficult to know if I was changing my mind for the truth, or because..."

Again, she was too afraid to admit it.

Abram knew exactly what it was. This pure heart before him was so virtuous that she embraced the truth as soon as she heard it. But even then she questioned her own motives because...

"Because of me," he said finishing her sentence. "Because you did not want your devotion to the Creator to be based on the selfish motive of attraction to the man that is going to marry you."

She looked at him with shock. It took her a second to make sure she heard what she thought she heard.

Even Abram was a bit surprised he said it. He was certainly thinking it. But he would normally not be so hasty or impulsive. It was as if El Shaddai himself was hurrying them along.

Then she burst out in new tears. But this time, they were tears of joy.

Abram held her and they cried together.

"What in Sheol?" barked Haran. "You have been here two days and you want to marry your half-sister? Are you two crazy?"

Abram and Sarai had gone back to the dinner table. They stood before the family with their news.

Sarai complained, "Most of the marriages in this family are arranged anyway, and spouses do not know each other until they are betrothed. So why are you barking so loud?"

Haran's eyes went wide with astonishment. Everyone's eyes did. She never talked back like that before.

Nahor butted in, "Well, you certainly have had an immediate effect on our sister with your bare-faced brazenness, Abram."

"Consider it an arranged marriage," said Abram, "only the arranger is our Creator, instead of you rock-heads."

Abram had a big grin at the last words. His humor disarmed them. Haran and Nahor tried to suppress a smile.

Nahor tried to speak through a breakout chuckle, "Very well, so you are telling us, Sarai, that you have converted to this god El Shaddai, and now you want to leave us high and dry?"

Nahor's wife Milcah finally spoke up. "You are just concerned about your own welfare. No longer being served by your sister, Nahor. Grow up."

Nahor could not deny it.

"Do not worry," said Abram, "I intend to do everything properly. We will have the customary betrothal for negotiations of bride price and dowry."

"For Sin's sake," said Haran, "She is not a twelve year old. She carries her own weight in this household, *and* the weight of the rest of us."

Nahor jumped in again, "She is past child bearing age, Abram."

Milcah scolded him, "Nahor." He shut up with a shrug.

"I do not care," said Abram. "I am no spring quail, myself, you know. El Shaddai will provide."

Haran quipped, "El Shaddai is providing you with the best cooking, cleaning, and hygiene in the kingdom of Ur!"

Everyone laughed, especially Sarai. She could not wait to clean up Abram's scruffy and unkempt appearance. *Underneath that gruff was quite a handsome man*, she thought.

Haran lifted up a cup of wine to Abram. "Here is a toast and a prayer to, what is his name again?"

"El Shaddai," answered Abram.

"El Shaddai it is," said Haran. "I only hope father is as willing to give his blessing as your god is."

Everyone agreed, and drank the wine.

CHAPTER 21

Terah arrived in Ur ahead of Nimrod by several days. They were coming from Elam in the East, and Nimrod had to tie up some loose ends before joining Terah in Ur. Terah became thankful for this providential delay. He almost had a heart attack when he discovered Abram at his house.

"If Nimrod discovers you, we will all be put to death!" yelled Terah.

"I am happy to see you, too, father," said Abram with a bite.

They faced each other in the family courtyard that opened up to all the entrances of the house. The family gathered around them. Sarai stood next to Abram.

"That is – not – fair," said Terah. "I gave you to Noah to save your life. And now the entire family is in jeopardy! What would you have me do?"

"How about give me a hug?" said Abram with his arms outstretched.

"Awwwwww," exclaimed Terah and he embraced Abram with weepy eyes. "My son."

"Father," Abram whispered in his ear.

Abram held his father at arm's length and said, "No one need know I am a relative. I am a Bedouin desert wanderer. With your approval, I will marry Sarai before Nimrod arrives, and we will leave with no one knowing any better."

Sarai watched her father's face for approval like a hound watched its master for a morsel of food.

Terah sighed. "Come with me to the temple of Sin the moon god, and let us bring the petition before him."

"I am afraid I cannot do that," said Abram.

"Why not?"

"Because I worship El Shaddai, the god of Enoch and Noah, the true god and Creator."

Terah rolled his eyes. "I knew I should not have given you to that fanatic ancestor of mine! He has hypnotized you about his extremist intolerant solo god!"

Sarai tried to help out, "Father…"

Terah was not listening. "No daughter of mine is going to be caught up in a new cult of religion. We have always worshipped the pantheon."

"Father," interrupted Sarai, "It is too late. I am already caught up."

Dumbfounded silence struck Terah.

She continued, "I have given up the family idols and now worship El Shaddai."

Terah's jaw clenched in silent boiling anger.

He stared at Abram and shouted, "No!" and stomped out of the room.

Everyone stood there, embarrassed for Abram and Sarai. They did not know what to say.

Sarai started to cry softly.

Abram went after Terah.

He found his father in the family shrine room. It was a room large enough to house twelve wood and stone images of deities, one for each month of the calendar. They were situated in a circle around the room, each with their own shrines. This allowed the worshippers to kneel or prostrate themselves in the center and face any image of their choosing, based on the current month or need of the worshipper.

The place disgusted Abram. He avoided this room. He could feel the presence of oppression, as if these demon gods knew he was there and hated him with all their spirits.

But Abram swallowed his contempt and entered the room with a conciliatory attitude. He knew that his God was the Creator of all, and these pathetic imitators had no power over him.

"I can see you have infected the entire household as well," said Terah.

"Father, I am not seeking to undermine you. I am simply fulfilling my destiny, a destiny that you saw in the stars and saved me for."

Terah remembered that night when the star came and swallowed up the other stars. But if what Abram said was true, then everything Terah believed and lived was a cruel joke. He had spent close to two hundred years of life on the earth studying astrology, sorcery, and omen reading. He had engaged in countless hours worshipping a multitude of gods who were more present than this absent, invisible El Shaddai he had heard Noah boast about. And now Abram brought the same tales.

He gazed up at the exquisitely carved and crafted images that seemed to look at him with longing. He could almost hear them hissing in his ears, "Get rid of him, get rid of him." His was a world of too many masters. A king whose megalomania was only surpassed by the king of gods he served. A wicked queen and her evil son who would set the world in flames as soon as they got the chance. Gods who required so much detail and so many rituals, just to sort out their opposing wills. A family legacy that he had dedicated his life to protect.

But he had survived. He had managed to navigate all those masters demanding his allegiance. He managed to negotiate his way into becoming the prince of the heavenly host. He had worked so hard and for so long to master survival in the system. It was too much to give up. He would be a complete failure and most certainly lose his life and the lives of his family. It was too devastating to consider. He just wanted it to all go away.

"You have my blessing," said Terah with resignation. "Marry Sarai and go away. Far away from this family."

Abram did not say a word. He turned to leave, and saw that Sarai had been right behind him. Her eyes were red with tears. She heard it all. It had sounded like the eulogy of her own funeral. But it was not a eulogy. It was more like a curse.

She grabbed Abram's hand and would not let it go.

They walked quietly away.

CHAPTER 22

The wedding was two days later. Considering the circumstances, they decided to have a small family ceremony, so as not to draw attention. Terah did not require a bride price, since there was no betrothal period. But he did offer a generous dowry to Sarai, probably out of guilt for her illegitimate birth through another mother.

They had only one day, instead of the usual several days of festivities. They performed a ritual and had a banquet dinner for the family members alone. Terah was forced to officiate the wedding ceremony against his better judgment. They could not allow a priest or priestess of the local pantheon to officiate, for fear of discovery. Also, Abram wanted it to take place before El Shaddai, not the gods of the pantheon.

Terah bit his lip and officiated the ceremony under the condition that he only mention El Shaddai once. He had been so used to bending the rules for so many gods over so many years, he figured he could do it one more time, even for a god he had no more taste for than Ishtar. What was one more hollow performance of ritual duties among his thousands of hollow performances?

He was surprised to discover a sense of peace that came over the whole family. He had never seen it before. He had never experienced it either. It seemed to pervade the whole rite with a sacred holiness that everyone sensed and no one was courageous enough to talk about.

Abram allowed himself to be cleaned up by Sarai for the wedding. She cut his hair and shaved his beard to be more Sumerian. But in return, he had asked her to wear make-up under her veil and have her hair done up nicely.

She found it difficult to do so. She had avoided beautification for so many years that it felt foreign to her, like playing the harlot. She usually wore the plainest of robes that covered her figure like a big tent. Now, she wore a Sumerian white linen wedding gown that made her feel uncomfortable for its immodesty. She just did not consider herself pretty. But if her husband wanted it, she would do it to please him.

When Abram saw her walking through the courtyard up to the marriage tent in her wedding gown and veil, his knees went weak. He started to feel faint.

Why am I so blessed? He thought. *I do not deserve this woman of such goodness of heart and heavenly beauty.*

She watched him staring at her like a hungry wolf as she approached. But when she stood before him, they gazed into each other's eyes. She could see he was a complete lamb at her disposal. She could see into his soul and somehow knew that he was completely and totally hers.

How could this be? She thought. *Who would want me with such desire?*

She is a goddess, he thought. *I am a goat.*

They did not notice the astonishment of everyone else in the room. The family all knew Sarai had a natural beauty, but she kept it so well hidden they had forgotten it. Now, they felt an almost spiritual quality to her, as if she were an angel from heaven.

Even Terah's heart melted as he read through the proclamations. She was still his daughter, and he would always have a special place in his heart for the little "orphaned" girl of such grace and elegance.

She is too good for this boorish husband, Terah thought. She is too good for this family. Shades of Sheol! She is too good for me!

Terah began to cry as Abram poured the customary perfume over Sarai's head. He gave his precious daughter away and wondered what was in store for her with this man who followed a strange god, this stranger in a strange land.

As they ate their dinner feast of lamb, fish, figs, pomegranates and much drink, Sarai watched her new bridegroom's every move. He was so handsome and so strong. As he looked back at her, she noticed he was fidgeting in his chair. Adjusting his robe around his legs, and changing his seating posture as if bothered.

She leaned in and whispered, "What is wrong, my love?"

He looked at her surprised. "You really do not know?" he asked.

She felt a failure. How could she not understand his every response?

"Well, my wonderfully innocent bride," he said. "You have much to learn in the school of male nature. So let us start our class immediately. Lesson one, when a man is smitten with a heavenly beauty such as yours, there is only one thing he can think of, and he is thinking of nothing else."

She thought, *Love?*

He continued, adjusting his robe uncomfortably. "And those thoughts transfer down to a certain nether region, thus causing discomfort until such desires are consummated."

She stared with a white face. "Oh, I am sorry. I should have known better."

Milcah and Eliana had spoken to her a little about the way of a man with a woman. But obviously not enough.

She fluttered, "Is there anything I can do to help you?"

"Oh, you will, my flower petal. You will help me very soon, and *very* often."

She felt a shiver and thought, *His words are so comely and poetic. I could cuddle in his arms all night.*

For the first few days, the family planned on leaving them in Terah's large master bedroom. They had even cleared out the nearby bedrooms for further privacy. Family members would sleep in the courtyard under the moon, or in the case of Nahor, in the kitchen near the food.

When Abram and Sarai entered the chamber, they saw a bath drawn in a tub in the corner. Mandrake plants decorated the room, for the roots were famed for aiding in sexual arousal and conception. The aroma of love potion spices filled the entire room. Myrrh, aloes, cinnamon and frankincense, all wafted in the air currents. Aphrodisiac raisin cakes were beside the bed.

They walked to the tub.

Abram slowly pulled the strings on her robe and slid her linen vestments off. They fell to the floor.

He stepped back and helped her take off her undergarments until she was naked before him.

She felt embarrassed at first. No man had ever seen her so. But this was right. This was what she had saved herself for. She was naked and unashamed. She calmed.

He stared with wide eyes, and began to breathe heavily.

"Are you alright?" she asked.

"I am dizzy," he said. "I will sit down while you bathe."

He sat on the bed and watched her pour water over her body. Her silken skin glittered as the water flowed over her skin.

He was enraptured. She moved with such grace.

He removed his robe and joined her.

She said, "Now I understand why you were so uncomfortable at dinner."

They shared a smile.

He let her clean him. He returned the favor with ritual-like purity. They shivered at each other's touch.

They got up and dried themselves off.

He reached up to her hair and pulled off her headband. It had kept her hair up for the ceremony.

Her tresses fell down around her neck. She shook her head slightly to let it all lay down. She heard him gasp with more desire.

She ran her hands through her hair to scratch her head, sweaty from the bothersome headband. But he stopped her, and ran his hands through her flowing blonde locks with delicate sensuous scratching.

He thought, *Nothing compares with this golden garden. Thank you, El Shaddai.*

She moaned with delight.

Which made him moan.

They kissed.

Deeply.

Her lips were so soft to him, like the petals of silken flowers.

He grasped her with such firmness, she felt all her fears fall away. Whatever she would experience this evening, she knew she was completely safe inside his love.

He picked her up and laid her on the bed.

His eyes consumed her body. She was not used to the attention of being adored. He could see it in her face.

He said, "Sarai, as your husband, I command you to never utter the words 'I am not beautiful' again. It is a slap in the face of your Creator."

She shivered. She wanted to obey. She would do *anything* he told her.

She lay on her side so that her body created a flowing of curves she had no idea would drive Abram wild.

"You are, in fact, more beautiful than anything in all of creation. More beautiful than the mountains of God, more than the gardens and forests of Eden. More than the depths of the ocean."

Her form was more comely than a younger woman. She was voluptuous. *And she did not even know it.*

"I feel like a harlot with all this make up on," she said.

"No, no, no," he said. "It is all part of accentuating the magnificence of your form, my love. I do not see a harlot. I see a goddess."

He kissed her belly, and moved upward.

She giggled. "That tickles."

"You are a feast for my senses," he said.

Her smell was like incense of the gods. Her taste was like spice. The touch of her skin was silk. Her breathing and her sounds were music. Beneath his trembling fingers and lips was a fury of passion that would ravish her at any moment.

But he wanted it to last. And he wanted to help bring her into her awakening.

Which is why he focused on her pleasure.

She gasped with surprise.

A glorious surprise.

He was bringing her alive. Opening the door to another world she thought only existed in heaven and in romantic stories.

Soon, she was caught up into a delirious stream of rapture. She completely lost herself in abandon.

Then she felt him unite with her.

She came back to earth in a moment of pain. But she knew it was only because of her virginal innocence. She had learned that much from her sister-in-law.

As he looked into her eyes, the pain withered away and was replaced by his firm and assuring security. It was all right. Everything was all right.

Then she saw in his eyes his own enraptured release.

And the two were one.

They shared bodies. They shared souls.

They shared God.

CHAPTER 23

Abram and Sarai walked and played and enjoyed the Garden of Eden for three days straight.

They never got dressed.

They never left their room.

And they kept some family members awake at night.

But certain other married family members were inspired and rekindled their dried-out passion, learning a lesson or two from the inexperienced virginal lovers.

CHAPTER 24

The Jordan Valley was a resource-rich river valley that traversed the land of Canaan from the foot of Mount Hermon in the north through the Jordan Sea to the Red Sea in the south. The hills and mountains on the east and west side of the valley rose as high as three thousand feet and enclosed the winding river in a year-round temperate climate that made it among the most desirable locations in the land.

Thick forests grew in the north and some desert in the south, but nothing like Sumer and Akkad. Whereas Mesopotamia was a desert civilization that thrived on the banks of the Tigris and Euphrates, Canaan was a land of diverse conditions that relied upon rain from the heavens to bring it to life. It was hemmed in by the Great Sea on its west coast and the desert on its eastern edge. It was a different world, a different cosmos.

Along the Jordan's western plateau ran the King's Highway, a main travel route for trading caravans and military expeditions between Egypt in the south and the Amurru and Mitanni region in the north. Whoever controlled access to the King's Highway would be a formidable influence on commercial and political interests for Mesopotamia as well as Egypt and Amurru. It was the lifeline and spine of Canaan.

In the southern region of the valley was the Jordan Sea, a vast rich lake teeming with life. There were five great cities in this region that were built around the southern shores of the sea. Each one sat along a freshwater tributary that poured into the sea. Their names were Sodom and Gomorrah, Admah, Zeboiim, and Zoar. These cities had become a mighty center of wealth and power in the land of Canaan because they were situated in an area of rich natural resources, which they exploited with great success.

They were called the "cities of the plain" because they surrounded the Valley of Siddim, a vast flat plain of bitumen pits. The pits had became a mining resource of asphalt and pitch for the inhabitants. The five cities united in controlling the area for its bitumen extraction as well as other exports from the sea, and copper mining just south of the plains.

The aggregation of natural resources had created massive economic wealth. But that wealth was fast degenerating into poverty. The coalition of five cities had become a pentapolis of wickedness, where the virtues of hard work were being replaced by the vice of indulgence and entitlement.

A generation earlier, the area had been secured by the goddess Ashtart, with the approval of the local deities, under Mastema's influence. Most of Canaan was loose tribes and confederations of clans with a few towns and villages, but few cities like Jericho. Ashtart crafted her new urban landscape by raising up puppet rulers that she could manipulate. If you wanted to control a people, she believed, it could only happen through cities. People who lived in rural areas were too independent and family-reliant to be indoctrinated into one way of thinking. They therefore would be difficult to be centrally controlled. A city could breed and fester that singular mentality which replaced family and community reliance with government reliance. The more closely and tightly a population lived and worked, the more hive-like it became, and therefore more controllable by a queen bee — in this case, Ashtart.

But herein lay her problem. She needed wealth to build her pentapolis of power. But the profit incentive required to build that wealth was diametrically opposed to the hegemony of power needed to control the populace. So she crafted a new, advanced version of a strategy she had attempted before the Deluge.

First, she advised the kings to build mining businesses for the copper, bitumen, and other sea resources in their area and place them in the hands of owners. This allowed the owners and workers to make a profit for themselves, which inspired hard work, innovation, and rapid expansion of the business and the riches of the entire city. Everyone benefited. Those who were leaders and took risk were rewarded, and in return they were able to hire more of the poor, which elevated everyone's status.

The unfortunate effect of wealth creation in the workers and owners was a spirit of independence and a love of freedom. This would not do for Ashtart. So she had the kings enforce laws that abolished the carrying of all weapons within the city limits. Only the government soldiers could carry them. They conditioned the people to accept this outrageous infringement through a propaganda campaign labeling the pentapolis as the "Cities of Love." This slogan would come in handy later for her ultimate goal, but it served the moment to label those with weapons as violent haters. The populace had no idea the law's actual intent was to keep them indefensible against the tyranny of the city-state rulers and their god.

Once the area had built up a vast amount of wealth, the cities grew exponentially in population, and Ashtart had what she needed for her plan. She had the kings continue to increase taxes on the citizens, in the name of public services provided by the royal palace and holy temple. She found she could tax the wealthy business owners at higher percentage rates than others, if the kings would tell the commoners that it was only fair since the rich had more money.

And it worked. Nobody saw the obvious unfairness of such a scheme, because their personal greed and envy of those above them blinded them to it. The genius of feeding self-righteous hatred of "external oppressors" lay in its ability to take the eyes off the individual's own vices. This set the stage for unprecedented domination. Ashtart knew human nature well and knew how to exploit its essentially selfish character.

Of course, the royal rulers were not considered part of this "wealthy elite," they were the exception. Someone had to rule and it required a lot of money to do so.

Once the taxes became as high as ninety percent of the income of the businesses, it was a simple act to justify the city-state taking over the mining operations in the interest of "the people." In reality, it was in the interest of Ashtart. After all, the mining operations were brutal on the workers. They were also ruining the sea, the plains and the beauty of the Valley of Siddim. The kings promised that they would redistribute all the wealth from the businesses to the workers who deserved it. Then, everyone would be equal.

What actually happened was that the royal confiscation of wealth flowed into the government coffers. The money funded an ever-increasing government the size of Leviathan, with a royal government security force to match. Everyone was indeed equal – equally dependent on the city-state for every aspect of their lives, while the rulers were more equal than others. As Ashtart would often say, "Someone had to engage in the difficult task of administrative bureaucracy and protection of the people from themselves."

The five kings pooled their armed resources to control the King's Highway just to the east of the plains. This gave them extra wealth from trade import and export taxes. Since the Highway was the dominant trade route from north to south, their wealth grew even stronger.

Thirteen years previously, Nimrod had sent King Chedorlaomer of Elam to conquer the region and extract his own taxes from the pentapolis. He also took a cut of their natural resources of bitumen and copper. Ashtart stayed out of it. She knew better than to defy this earthly potentate, because it might bring Marduk and the entire pantheon down on her head if she did. She decided to allow the emperor his due, as long as it did not interfere with the second phase of her own diabolical scheme.

That second phase was to fill the land with giants — the Nephilim. She had brought Canaan to the land, the cursed son of Ham, whose blood had been altered to carry the Nephilim genes essential for her infiltration. Canaan's seedline would be the quintessential enemy of the blessed seedline that was even now being nurtured somewhere on the earth.

But this time, her plan would be more inconspicuous. Breeding would not be achieved through angelic mating with humans. And it would not be done all over the earth, because that approach brought the Deluge last time. This time, she would use artificial selection to breed giants through the bloodline of Canaan, and so spread their offspring throughout the land. She found several women with the blood of Nephilim in them to sire Canaan's growing clans. Within the first generation, he had already fathered the fledgling clans of Girgashites, Canaanites, Perizzites, Hivites, Arkites, Sinites, and Jebusites. But Canaan was also interbreeding with the Hittites and Amorites. Their territories reached from Sidon and Mount Hermon in the north all the way down to Gaza and the Valley of Siddim in the south.

Ashtart was no upstart strategist. She knew that it was not enough to breed clans of giants. She had to propagate a religious belief system that would drive them to hate their Creator. Her goal was to violate all boundaries of distinction between things, because distinction and separation was the natural order of Elohim's creation.

She had the kings pass laws abolishing all distinctions as oppressive and illegal. There was to be no rich and poor, for all were equal; no male and female for all were human; no human and animal for we were all one chain of being; no moral right and wrong, for all was freedom.

Next, she returned to the slogan of the pentapolis, the "Cities of Love." The phrase used to mean a culture of compassion and equality. But language was malleable, and language was also a means of controlling the minds of the populace. So "Cities of Love" was twisted to mean the ability to copulate with anyone and anything that one could imagine, without moral condemnation.

Rather than abolish marriage, which could cause too much a stir in their small minds, Ashtart made the king pass laws that legalized marriage between any two or more beings in love. First was polygamy, for those who loved many women; then there was marriage between consenting men or consenting women, since there was no difference between the sexes; then came marriage between family members who loved each other; then logically between adults and children; and finally, marriage between humans and animals.

Of course, marriage was not a necessity. In fact, it was discouraged. Fornication between all objects and things was encouraged as a pastime of amusement. There was even a holy partition of the temple with small holes dug into the ground so that some could have sex with the earth to display their love of the mother earth goddess.

Ashtart's secondary purpose was to debase the image of Elohim in mankind through everything unnatural. It would bring humanity down from its lofty heights of dominion over creation and suck them into the muck and slime. She so hated the Creator and wanted to spit in his face, that she inspired the hatred of all that was good and humanly beautiful in the name of "love." The delicious irony was that she had created cities of hate masquerading as "Cities of Love."

At the apex of all this immoral freedom was the ultimate goal of Ashtart: interbreeding humans with the gods. She wanted to eliminate all separation between gods and men. She invited select gods of Canaan – Molech, Dagon and Asherah – to join her in the covert activity of breeding with the daughters of men. But they were unwilling, out of fear of reprisal from Elohim. The Deluge judgment was still too vivid in their memories. So Ashtart cursed them and pursued her agenda alone, as she felt she always had to.

She would impregnate the women as a holy honor of the gods. And when her giant progeny were born, she would send them to tribes around Canaan, to rise as mighty warriors and rulers. It would take many generations for Ashtart's plan to bear the fruit she wanted, but she was patient. She had learned much about patience through the failure of her past exploits: the wars of the antediluvian age that were all consummate failures because the pantheon overreached and were too aggressive in their goals.

This time, she would be the fulfillment of the prophecy, instead of its object of judgment. This time, she would breed the Seed of the Serpent that was prophesied to war with the Seed of Eve, and she would do so subtly, without drawing attention through fanfare and flaunting. Elohim had allowed too much freedom in his creation, and he would one day regret it, as he regretted making man the first time. But this time, he could not flood the earth to wipe away his mistakes, because he had made a promise, and he could not break his promises.

All this, Ashtart had accomplished in a mere fifty years. She liked to imagine what she could accomplish in five hundred.

CHAPTER 25

Great fanfare greeted the arrival of Nimrod in his vassal city of Ur. Its local king met Nimrod at the gate with a marching band of musicians and a chorus of dancing temple virgins, many of whom would be abused by Nimrod that evening, and probably lose their lives as well, since Mardon accompanied Nimrod's retinue. They traveled the Processional Way amidst the crowd of cheering Urukeans, and took up residence in the royal palace in the temple precinct.

Abram and Sarai did not join the rest of the family at the triumphal entry. Lot was allowed to stay behind with them. Abram found him endearing. He thought Lot had much potential because of his ambition. But he also thought Lot had a weakness in that ambition. His passionate yearning for a life of adventure and experience came from a desire to be free from the constraints of his life. The institutions of society — his family, his community, norms of propriety — all made him feel constricted. He felt that boundaries were meant to control him, to keep him from happiness, rather than to protect him by keeping him within the safe parameters of the Creator's intent for his life.

Lot also had a fascination with darkness that seemed unhealthy to Abram. The music he enjoyed was the erotic deliberately off-key music played in the brothel precincts of the city. Abram had the distinct sense that Lot was not innocent. He had too much of a familiarity with the temple prostitutes, who seemed to wink and wave at him whenever he passed by, as if they knew him well. In the short time Abram had been with the family, he had more than once pulled Lot out of one of the theaters that performed bizarre disgusting plays that had little to do with drama and nothing to do with moral character.

Abram was alone in his room praying over how he might be an example of godliness for Lot when the thought occurred to him that his father would be returning soon from the triumphal entry to prepare for the arrival feast with the king.

He thought, *I had better get ready.*

Terah prepared to meet the king that night during the feast. It was to be a celebration at the ziggurat and an announcement of the next Akitu Festival in Babylon, a month away. Terah genuflected before his family teraphim in the shrine room and performed ritual incantations in honor of their zodiac involvement.

Terah suddenly noticed Abram watching him from the shadows.

"Abram?" he called out.

Abram stepped out of the darkness.

"Leaving no stone unturned?" quipped Abram. "One idol for each month. Twelve months in the year."

"Twelve days in the Akitu Festival," added Terah.

"Of course, the exaltation of that blowhard Marduk," said Abram.

"Watch your mouth," snapped Terah. "I expect you to leave quietly without King Nimrod's knowledge. You will at least grant me that much respect."

Abram looked sadly into Terah's eyes. "Father, it is so hard to respect you when you have sold your soul into spiritual slavery."

It angered Terah. "I should never have given you to Noah ben Lamech. He turned you into an intolerant, hateful zealot of this El Shaddai deity."

A tear slid down Abram's cheek, his heart breaking.

"I have my gods, and you have yours," said Terah. "Please just leave me alone, Abram. Go."

Abram left the room and Terah returned to his worship.

After Terah left for the royal feast, Abram went to Eliana and Sarai and asked them to take a kid from the flock and make a savory meat dish for him. He told them he wanted to put an offering before the gods of the household so that he might become more acceptable to them.

Sarai stared at him with shock. What did he think he was doing? Had he compromised his god because of his desire to be loved by his father? Had she been wrong in her judge of his virtuous character?

They prepared the kid and gave Abram the meal.

He then divided it up into twelve plates, one for each of the gods. He placed them in position in the shrine, and then sat before them, waiting.

After an hour, Sarai came to him. "Abram, my love, what are you doing?"

Abram turned to her and said, "Proving a point."

"What point is that?" she inquired.

"That these idols of stone and wood have mouths that cannot speak, eyes that cannot see, ears that cannot hear, hands that cannot feel, and legs which cannot move."

"Have we not believed as much?" she said.

Abram stood up from his seated position. She saw that he held a strong axe in his hand.

"Abram, what are you going to do?"

"Sarai, please leave," he said. "And close the door."

She went out and closed the door. She hesitated by it, before leaving. She heard Abram pound his axe away on the idols, chopping and pummeling. She ran to her bedroom.

An hour later, Terah returned home and made his way to the shrine room. A ghastly sight met him. All the idols save one were demolished; broken or chopped into pieces. The plates of savory meat were still arrayed on the floor, and the one largest stone idol had a hatchet in its hand. Terah could see it was Abram's hatchet.

He ran out of the room and stomped around the house until he found Abram, sitting peacefully in the courtyard.

His voice trembled with anger. "What is this you have done with my images, Abram?"

"Nothing," he replied. "I merely made an offering of savory meat that I placed before them all. But when all of the idols reached out before the largest one to eat, his anger was kindled and he went and took my axe and smote the other idols for their lack of etiquette. It was horrible."

Terah stared at Abram with incredulity.

"You speak such lies to me? I made those idols with my own hands. I carved them and I know full well they have no power to do what you have claimed."

Abram looked up at his father. "Then why do you serve such idols in whom there is no power to do anything? Why do you trust them to deliver you? Why do you pray to ears that cannot hear you, to eyes that cannot see you, and to arms and legs that cannot move? Why do you serve wood and stone, when you are *their* maker and they are not yours? This is the very reason El Shaddai brought the Great Flood on our ancestors."

Terah's jaw clenched in fury. He thought, *How could this be my son? How could I lay claim to this depraved and arrogant atheist who mocks my gods with such contempt?*

He turned to Abram and blurted out, "You are not my son." He stomped his way back into the house.

Abram knew this was the end. He had gone too far. He had pushed too much. He should have wooed his father with persuasion, but instead, he pummeled him into humiliation. He had ruined his chances of ever restoring a relationship, let alone converting Terah to El Shaddai's path.

He quietly walked back to his bedroom, where Sarai waited for him. He told her it was time for them to leave. They began to pack their things.

They said goodbye to family members. Sadness filled the air. The family would miss Sarai's sacrificial giving, and Abram's hearty self-confidence. Abram and Sarai would miss Eliana's and Milcah's supportiveness, Haran and Nahor's competitive natures, Iscah's precious smile, and Lot's eager playfulness.

They were almost done packing, stacking their bags in the courtyard, where the family watched them. Then Abram noticed someone missing.

"Where is Lot?" he asked.

Everyone looked around.

Lot came barging into the courtyard with a reed basket on his back, loaded with his belongings.

"Here I am!" said Lot. "I am going with you."

"You will do no such thing," said Haran. "You are staying right here with your family."

"But Abram *is* family," countered Lot.

Abram said, "Lot, listen to your father."

"No!" Lot cried out. "I am tired of being cooped up here, making stupid idols. I want to see the world. I want to experience the world."

Eliana began to cry.

"Mother," Lot whined.

"Do you not love us anymore?" Eliana cried.

"Of course. I will always love you," Lot replied. "I just feel like I was made for more than this."

"So we are just wasting our lives, is that what you think?" said Haran.

"No! I mean, it is okay for you, but I want more."

Haran protested, "Uruk is one of the largest cities and the most cosmopolitan in the entire land. What more do you think you will find anywhere else?"

"You just do not understand," complained Lot.

"Oh, right, we are just parents," countered Haran. "We do not know *anything*. We were *never* your age."

"I am not saying that," said Lot.

"Then what are you saying, Mr. Know It All?" said Haran.

Lot blurted out, "I want to follow Abram's god, El Shaddai."

Suddenly, everyone went quiet, a nervous quiet that they all wanted to escape.

The moment broke when a contingent of royal guards burst through the front door and into the courtyard. They grabbed Abram.

Sarai screamed. Lot held her back for her safety.

The main guard declared, "Abram ben Terah, you are arrested in the name of Mighty Nimrod, king of Sumer and of Akkad." The family were all surprised.

The guards shackled Abram and carried him away, past an angry Terah at the front door.

CHAPTER 26

Abram sat chained to a brick wall in the house of confinement. He had been there for only an hour or so before he heard approaching footsteps.

The door opened. Terah entered, followed by wise men, princes, sages, and astrologers. And lastly, Nimrod and his son Mardon stepped into the room, surrounded by guards.

Nimrod stared at Abram with narrowed eyes. Terah stood next to Nimrod, but he could not look at Abram.

This is not my son, Terah told himself again. He had to keep telling himself, or everything he knew would come crashing down to Sheol.

Nimrod mused out loud with a sarcastic bite, "So this is the one 'whose seed will slay great kings, possess their land, and inherit the earth.'"

Nimrod continued to gaze down upon the prisoner like a cobra would regard its prey.

"What have you to say for yourself, king slayer?"

Abram coughed and spit some blood. He had been beaten when first chained up. Then he said, "I am a servant of El Shaddai. He raises up kings and overthrows them. He owns all the earth, and gives it to whom he wishes."

Nimrod's eyes widened with humor. "Oh, he does, does he? Well, I am Nimrod the Mighty Hunter. Show me the face of this 'El Shaddai.'"

"He is the unseen Creator of all things. He serves no man's bidding."

"And this is why you attacked Terah's images and blasphemed the gods of the land?"

Abram remained silent.

Mardon leaned toward the king and said, "Father, can I flay him alive?" Mardon particularly enjoyed the peeling of a man's skin from his body with surgical instruments.

One of the sages cautiously countered Mardon's wish, "The sentence for blasphemy is hanging, my lord."

Nimrod ignored them. He continued staring at Abram as he addressed Terah. "Terah, I am going to ask you a question, and I want you to know that your answer will determine the fate of not only your son, but of you."

"Yes, my lord," said Terah, already shaking with alarm.

"When I asked for the infant Abram fifty years ago, why did you give me another baby in his place?"

Terah answered with withered humility, hiding nothing.

"He was my son, as Mardon is your son. My heart welled up inside of me."

Nimrod felt he could easily kill his despicable son Mardon, but he remembered when the child was first born, how he too had been moved by the frailty and hope of his little baby boy.

"Whose idea was it to give your maidservant's son?"

Terah hesitated. He did not want to say. Nimrod saw his hesitation.

"Whose idea was it?" he repeated, more as a command than a question.

"Your highness, it was my son Haran who came up with the idea. He was only a child at the time."

Nimrod said, "And evidently a cunning child."

Nimrod turned to face Terah. He could not kill the prince of his host without losing his army of Stone Ones. But he had to punish him. And the punishment he planned would be enough.

"Guards," ordered Nimrod. "Arrest Haran ben Terah, and prepare the brick fire kilns for these sons of Terah."

"Your grace," pleaded Terah, "Haran has changed since then. He has become a devoted follower of yours in this city."

Nimrod barked, "Have you changed as well?"

Terah's knees felt weak.

Nimrod softened. He spoke to Terah in a reasonable voice. "Terah, you have been faithful in discharging your duty to me. But remember the parable of you and the horse you told me all those years ago? You wanted me to see your own love and duty to your son. Well, I have a greater duty to justice."

He paused thoughtfully, then added with calculated seriousness, "Tell me, Terah. If you were king, how would you address such defiance?"

Terah sighed with defeat. "I would punish all defiance. in order to maintain the authority of the throne."

Nimrod whispered to him, "It breaks my heart to have to do this. But you agree, it is justice."

Nimrod knew he uttered a complete and total lie. He did not care one whit for Terah and his sons or for "justice." But it was political genius. Nimrod had to enforce his authority and punish all defiance, yet he had to keep Terah alive in order to maintain his army of Stone Ones. He had to maintain Terah's fear and respect, along with his obedience and loyalty. It was a tricky balance of conflicting interests, but Nimrod had done it.

For his part, Mardon could not wait until he had the throne. He would kill them all, Terah and his entire family. After he raped the women, boys and girls in front of the men.

The royal guard arrested Haran. They ripped him away from his weeping family to imprison him with Abram.

Nimrod then called upon the entire city to meet at the brick kilns that evening to witness a burning.

· · · · ·

The city's huge central kiln was large enough to load thousands of bricks at one time to fire them for building materials. The workers stoked the flames extra white hot for the execution.

Tens of thousands of people surrounded the area with the hopes of seeing enough of the execution to make their time worthwhile.

Nimrod came out to the kiln in full regal display, followed by Mardon and Terah, his prince.

Abram and Haran were brought out before the crowd, bound and beaten. Their clothes were ripped off, leaving only their undergarments. It was not enough to execute them; they had to be humiliated. They were, after all, rebels against the Emperor, the sole ruler over all the earth in his splendor and majesty.

The crowds cheered with blood lust.

Nimrod quieted them down. "People of Uruk," he announced, "people of my empire, we have before you two men who sought to create an uprising against my majesty and against the majesty of the gods!"

Nimrod turned to Abram and said, "Renounce your claim to future kingship, bend your knee to me now, and plead for mercy."

Abram would not.

The crowd broke out in chanting, "Kill them! Kill them! Kill them!"

Nimrod waited for the chanting to die down.

A lone woman broke out of the crowd and ran toward Abram.

"Abram!" she screamed.

It was Sarai.

Abram jerked around to see her.

"Sarai!" Abram yelled. "Go back!"

A guard scooped her up. He was about to take her back, when Nimrod ordered him.

"Halt! Bring that wench here!"

The guard obeyed. Nimrod looked her over with hunger.

He said, "And who might you be, fetching little damsel?"

She jerked her arms away from the guards.

"Or, shall I say, sassy little spitfire?"

Mardon was scheming malicious evil for this beautiful one.

"I am Sarai, Abram's wife, my lord," she said.

Even better, thought both Nimrod and Mardon.

Mardon licked his lips.

Nimrod said, "And you have come to plead for your husband's life?"

"No, your majesty," she said, surprising him.

It surprised Abram, too.

"I know justice requires the payment of the penalty. I am here to offer myself in his place."

Nimrod's eyes opened wider with understanding.

Abram yelled, "Sarai, No!"

"Offer me to the flames as payment for Abram's crime."

Abram yelled again, "Sarai, NO!"

Nimrod smirked. "What a precious picture of eternal love and self-sacrifice. Whatsoever shall I do with them, my son?"

Mardon grinned like an alligator. "Cook him and eat him. But can I have the woman when you are done with her?"

Nimrod turned back to Abram. "It is a pity she is not merely your sister, Abram. She might have survived."

"What if I survive?" said Abram.

Nimrod looked at him curiously. "What do you mean?"

"What if I survive the flames? What will you do then?"

Nimrod looked at the flames, being stoked ever hotter.

He said, "You are a confident one." Then he said for fun, "If you survive the flames, then you can have her back. How's that?"

Mardon could not hold in the laugh. He could not stop.

Haran had watched it all. He saw the challenge, an impossible one on Abram's part. But then again, it was typical of Abram's confidence. But Haran did believe Abram had special protection. And he was a righteous man. Haran thought to himself that if Abram survived this, Haran would serve El Shaddai, who would then most likely save him as well. But, of course, if Nimrod prevailed and Abram perished, then Haran would renounce, bend the knee, and serve Nimrod and his god. That was the safest bet. Surely, his family would understand.

Nimrod said to the guards, "Cast them both into the fire!"

The crowd chanted, "Kill them! Kill them! Kill them!"

"No, no, wait," said Haran.

Terah looked away. He could not bear to see the consequences of his rash actions. He wished now that he had never had Abram arrested.

I started this, thought Terah. *It was my own selfish, depraved guilt over my own cowardice. And now my two sons will die. What have I wrought?*

Nimrod grasped Sarai firmly so she could not escape. His giant nine-foot frame dwarfed her. He whispered to her, "You would give yourself up for this man and his god?"

She nodded nervously.

"Well, then," said Nimrod, "I will give you a front row seat to his execution. You will appreciate it more than most."

Sarai squirmed and tried to get loose, but it was impossible. Nimrod was a Naphil with a grip like iron shackles.

The guards dragged Abram and Haran to the opening of the kiln.

Haran continued to plead more desperately, "King Nimrod, I renounce! I renounce! Please let me go."

The guards put the pair on the large sliders that were used to slide hundreds of bricks at a time into the flames for hardening.

Abram looked sadly at Haran as the two were rolled into the flames by the mechanism controlled by the guards.

Sarai, screamed, "Abram!"

A strange thing happened when they entered the furnace.

A large burst of flames leapt out and killed the dozen guards who had cast them into the fire.

Haran screamed in torment as the fire consumed him. It only lasted a few seconds. The heat was so hot, it burned his bones into ashes in minutes.

But Abram did not burn.

His rope bindings burnt to ashes on his hands and feet. But his loincloth remained, and his flesh was unsinged. A supernatural protection enveloped him, shielding him from the flames.

Outside the kiln, Nimrod, Mardon, Terah, and Sarai could see Abram walking around in the fire unscathed.

Nimrod's heart fainted within him. He knew that the god who protected Abram was not to be trifled with. His only chance was to hope Abram's god could be bargained with.

Inside the flames, Abram thought he heard his name spoken. He looked around and saw a figure in the flames. It was not Haran; Haran had been burned up. It was one like a son of man. The flames obscured him. Abram could not see much more than a dark figure.

It spoke with a voice he could almost hear inside his head, "Abram."

Abram stepped back in shock.

He heard it again. "Abram, I am El Shaddai, your creator and God."

Abram went down to his knees in awe, and whispered, "My Lord. You have met me in the fire. Have you finally come to tell me my destiny?"

The figure said, "Go out from your land and from your kindred and go into the land that I will show you."

"Yes, my Lord. What land is that?" asked Abram

"I will show you," El Shaddai repeated. And then the figure disappeared.

Abram looked around. Nothing but fire surrounded him.

Well, that was brief, he thought, *and rather anti-climactic, to be honest.*

He spoke out to the flames, "Lord, what land? Will you tell me later? Where shall I go in the meantime?"

He heard no answer. He only remembered the words in his head, "I will show you."

He thought, *Well, until you do, I guess I will just do the best I can.*

He saw the ashes of Haran. His heart broke for his brother. He knew his father was double minded and had hoped for the future.

But Terah had made his decision and paid the consequences. Nevertheless, Abram's eyes teared up with his loss.

Then a strange thought came to him, *There is a city up north called Haran, with the same name as my brother.* He did not know why he remembered that or why he would think it at such a moment as this, but he turned away and tried to think of something else.

Nimrod called out to his guards to roll the flat back out of the fire with Abram on it.

But when another eight guards approached the mechanism to roll it out, the fire was so hot that another burst of heat scorched the eight guards to death.

Nimrod could not care less. He concentrated on Abram in the fire.

Nimrod called out to Abram, "Abram, come forth from the fire and stand before me!"

Abram walked out of the fire.

Gasps and the rippling of gossip from tens of thousands of people who could not believe their eyes filled the air. Women fainted. Many were speechless. But all those who saw it, knew that the world was changed because a man defied King Nimrod and lived.

Abram walked respectfully up to Nimrod and stood before him.

The king of Ur and his princes and royalty came out of the crowd, moving reverently toward Abram.

Sarai wept tears of joy – and faith.

Terah wept tears of repentance.

Under his royal garments, where no one could see, Nimrod sweated in fear. A cold shiver ran down his spine and he tried to hold down the panic that was rising.

He maintained his kingly posture. "How is it you are not burned by the flames?" he said.

Abram said, "Because El Shaddai, the God of heaven and earth in whom I trust and who has all power, he delivered me."

The royalty bowed down before Abram.

That horrified Abram. "Get up! Do not bow to me. Bow to El Shaddai, the God who created the heavens and the earth and the bodies and souls of mankind."

"Very impressive magic," said Nimrod. "Who was that in there with you? I saw a second figure talking to you."

"It was El Shaddai, the Creator."

Another shiver of terror went through Nimrod.

"What did he say?" said Nimrod.

"I should leave here."

Nimrod looked to his trumpeters and nodded He turned to the noisy crowd, still aghast about what they had seen. He had to say something or things were going to go very bad for him very quickly.

The trumpeters announced their king's speech. The crowd calmed down.

Nimrod's voice boomed and echoed over the masses, "Abram has paid the price of justice! He went into the fire. He was purged of his crimes! The gods have birthed him anew from the flames! This court of justice is adjourned!"

The crowd went wild with cheers. It was good entertainment. They wanted more, but the guards already pressed them to disperse.

It was all a performance by Nimrod. This miracle had blindsided him. The deity El Shaddai had protected Abram. Nimrod knew it would jeopardize his authority before the people if he lost another confrontation with this deity. It would be foolish to engage an enemy about whom he knew nothing, unprotected by his guardian, Marduk. Instead, he used rhetoric to spin a narrative of legal technicalities.

Technically, Abram *had* paid for his crime by entering the fire. The fact that he survived was irrelevant to justice, because the sentence was served. Therefore, Nimrod was *not* giving in or admitting failure, but rather judging wisely. It was brilliant. He was rather proud of himself.

But now, he must get this Chosen One out of sight of the masses, lest he cause an uprising. The Akitu Festival was a month away and once the cosmic portal was open, this El Shaddai would have a real battle on his hands, a battle with the pantheon of gods and their king, Marduk. That would be a fight Nimrod would love to watch.

He released Sarai, who ran to Abram and embraced him.

Mardon's face went sour with disappointment. He had planned so much for the little whore. But it would have to wait. He would track her down later.

Terah looked at the fire, still stoked hot in the kiln. He thought of breaking away from his position in this gathering and jumping into the flames as punishment for his own foolishness.

Nimrod said to Abram, "You will have the gift of three hundred of my servants to join you and your household. But I want you away from the major cities."

Abram bowed. "I would like to go north to Haran, mighty king." He was not even sure why he said it. It was the first thing that came to his mind. But it was good enough anyway. If El Shaddai was not going to tell him where, then he would just have to go wherever, until he did.

"So shall it be," said Nimrod. Haran was a small enough town, hundreds of miles out of the way up north. It would cause no stir in his kingdom.

That just saved me the work of hunting her down, thought Mardon as he continued to stare at Sarai.

Then Abram added, "May my father Terah accompany us for protection?"

Terah looked at Abram with shock. *How could he suggest such a thing? After what I had done to him? Was he going to kill me?*

Terah shook visibly.

Nimrod mused over the request. "Hmmm. Yes, I like that. Terah shall accompany you, to settle his family in their new quarters, and be back to Babylon in time for the Akitu Festival."

"Yes, your majesty," said Terah. Inside, he felt full of shame. He could not look at his son.

Nimrod said, "Terah will bring you the servants in the morning. Go, say your goodbyes this evening."

CHAPTER 27

The next morning, Abram was ready to leave. Sarai, Milcah and Iscah all wept and hugged each other, knowing they would probably never see each other again. Nahor helped gather the mules and camels laden with their necessities, food and tents.

Lot came bounding out, with his own camel packed with belongings.

Nahor stopped him, "Where do you think you are going, young man?"

"With Abram" said Lot.

"Oh, no, you are not," said Nahor.

"Not again," complained Lot.

"Nahor," interrupted Abram. "His father is dead. His sister is taken care of as your wife. Let him come with us. I will watch over him and raise him up as my own."

Nahor's eyes narrowed. He realized it would be good to get rid of his lazy, troublemaking rear end.

"Very well," he said. "He is your responsibility now."

Lot yelped with joy.

Milcah screamed with tears, ran and grabbed her brother and would not let him go.

Lot eventually calmed her down. Nahor pulled her away.

Lot got on his camel.

Abram was setting up his camel when he looked up and saw Terah arriving alone on a horse.

He stopped, dismounted his steed and walked, trembling, to Abram, who stood and watched his father with pity.

Terah fell at Abram's feet weeping. Tears flowed like a flood.

"My son. My son. I am unworthy to be your father."

Abram reached down and touched his father's garment. He pulled the older man to his feet. He looked into Terah's eyes with compassion.

Abram said to him, "Father, you are forgiven."

Terah replied, "How could you forgive me after what I have done?"

Terah did not understand this grace. It went against everything he ever knew. His religion had no such notions. Though the gods did reign above, everything came down to a person's own ability to perform the right ritual or engage in the correct magic, or accurately discern the omens. There was a sacrificial means of atonement for sins, but such things were mere formalities, temporary appeasement. True forgiveness was not a reality. The only response for such things as betrayal or treason was death. That was why Terah harbored in his heart the fear that one day he would turn his back and Abram would get his revenge.

Abram said to Terah, "I have been forgiven of my debt. How could I not forgive you yours? Come, take us to Haran."

They met the three hundred servants and livestock offered by Nimrod outside the walls of the city. They paid for passage on some trade barges to begin their journey of six hundred miles, north up the Euphrates river.

• • • • •

The trip upriver was relatively uneventful. The barge they traveled on was a commercial one that carried barley, figs, and jars of wine, beer, and vegetable oil. It was about a hundred and fifty feet long with the trade products stored below in the tar-covered pontoons. Animals and humans shared the upper deck, and slaves rowed in the middle. The barge could travel about twenty miles a day. A bit slower than the caravan on land, but it saved them energy.

One thing happened that filled Abram with great curiosity. At one of the minor stops a hundred miles outside of Babylon, three strangers boarded the barge. They kept to themselves, but they stood out. One of them was very large, about seven feet tall, and muscular, like Marduk. The hooded cloak could not hide his physique. Abram thought they looked like bounty hunters or maybe spies.

One of them looked at him and a chill went down his spine. It was as if the stranger was looking *for* Abram and found him in his sights.

Then it struck him.

Assassins. Sent by Nimrod to finish off what his furnace of fire could not. It made perfect sense. Why did he not think of it sooner?

His mind started racing. Of course. Send Terah along with him and kill two birds with one stone. Nimrod could not abide the double-minded man that Terah was, a man torn between loyalties of family and king, submission and survival.

Where was Terah? Abram had to warn him. But he could not see him. His new head servant, Eliezer, a kind but gangly man, stood near Abram. But Eliezer would be of no use in a fight.

Where were Terah's guards?

The stranger started walking toward Abram.

He was all alone and unguarded. It was some kind of a set up.

Abram stiffened. He put his hand on the hilt of his sword in anticipation.

Suddenly, Eliezer stood in front of Abram. He whispered, "Master, I can be a diversion for you."

Abram could not believe it. This servant was already loyal to him? Who had such moral character these days?

Abram got his answer when Eliezer whispered, "Master, remember me when El Shaddai gives you the kingdom."

Eliezer was a convert to his faith. Abram's heart soared.

He moved Eliezer aside and said, "Alert the others."

Eliezer dutifully obeyed. He went to the men of the company to warn them.

Abram had one advantage, one thing these assassins did not know. He did not need guards to defend him. He was very capable in arms. He had been trained by Noah in the way of the Karabu, the ancient fighting technique of archangels. He shifted into a stance of preparedness. He was ready to call out.

The stranger was upon him. He was tall with a dark complexion inside his hood.

The stranger noticed Abram's stance. "Karabu," he said. "Well done. Trained by a master." He smiled.

Abram was confused. *How did he know?* The advantage was lost. Was this one a Karabu fighter himself?

"Who might you be, stranger?" said Abram.

The stranger looked around him. People were too close.

He raised his hand slightly and gestured for Abram to follow him away from the crowd to the edge of the boat.

Abram followed cautiously, giving a glance to the stranger's companions, who watched them.

Abram thought, Separate and divide. I am walking into a deeper trap.

"I am not separating you to divide you from your forces, Abram," said the stranger. "I just do not want anyone to hear us."

Abram blurted out, "How do you know my name?" His hand tightened on his sword blade, and drew it out half way.

"Put that away," said the stranger. "You will draw attention. I am not here to harm you."

"Then tell me who you are," snapped Abram.

"I am Mikael, the archangel."

Abram's face flushed.

Mikael took his hood off so Abram could see his face more clearly. He was handsome, his hair dark, full, and wavy. His eyes sparkled with penetrating blue hues.

"I take it Noah told you about me. What I looked like, about our exploits together in the War of Gods and Men?"

Abram nodded, mesmerized. This was the man Noah had described to him.

Mikael continued, "You and I will be seeing more of each other in the future. But for now, I and my companions have a task to accomplish."

"Who are they?" asked Abram.

"See the big one," Mikael replied. "That is the Destroyer. An angel of mass destruction. He kills entire populations. He is not pretty."

Abram gulped. The smaller one looked familiar in the way he held his shoulders.

"And the other is the Angel of Yahweh."

"Who is Yahweh?" asked Abram.

Mikael caught himself. The Creator had only revealed himself to Abram as El Shaddai, God Almighty, not as Yahweh, the covenant name he would later reveal to the children of Abram.

"You know him as El Shaddai," said Mikael.

Abram gulped. He felt a chill go down his spine. His knees went weak with the desire to kneel in worship. He said, "He is the God El Shaddai in earthly form?"

Mikael nodded with a smile.

Now Abram knew why his form was familiar. He was the one who met Abram in the fire. But now Abram had his wits about him.

"Why on earth would he do such a thing?" said Abram. It was beyond his comprehension that the Creator of the heavens and the earth, the Maker of all things visible and invisible, would condescend to such a humiliating form as that of a man. It reminded him too much of those pretenders to the throne, those Watcher gods of the earth.

Mikael could see the distaste in Abram's face. He said, "There is much that El Shaddai does that is beyond the understanding of even the divine council who surround him. But it does not surprise me that he accommodates to our finiteness. The gods of men are broken images of the truth reshaped into a monstrous lie."

"Then why does he not make himself more visible?"

"Trust me, if you were to see him in all his glory, you would not survive it. You would be consumed."

"Can I talk to him?" asked Abram.

"Not yet," said Mikael.

Abram said, "But he talked to me in the fire."

"It is not time," said Mikael more firmly.

"Where are you going?" said Abram.

Mikael looked upriver, a sad distant gaze in his eyes, and said, "Babylon."

CHAPTER 28

The strangers kept to themselves the rest of the journey. They disembarked at Babylon. Abram watched Mikael look back and give a subtle wave as they walked into the gateway of the eternal city.

As the barge passed through the harbor, Abram could see the ziggurat Etemenanki, and its complement temple Esagila, towering behind the kiln-fired brick walls. It was a stunning sight even from the river. There was good reason it was called "the eternal city," with its grandiose, painted arched gateways and huge statues of gods guarding its walls. He had been told much by Noah and Emzara about the spiritual reality behind the ziggurat step pyramids. He felt a dark oppression come over his soul, as if evil spirits hissed at him. He could not wait to get moving on.

At the next stop upriver, they got off the barges. They rode their caravan the rest of the four hundred miles up to Haran. This cut their travel time in half, to about ten days. Terah needed to get back to Babylon in time for the Akitu Festival.

Harran was a small city of only about ten thousand people, noted by trade merchants for its tapestries and carpet weaving. Because of its location, it had a significant population of settled Amorites, a nomadic people from the northwestern hill country of Amurru. The Amorites engaged in animal husbandry, selling their herds across the land. As they became more settled, they also became efficient in agricultural produce. They were an adaptive culture that worshipped Martu, the storm god, another name for Marduk. They had established trade routes from Haran all the way into the Jordan Valley of Canaan.

With the help of Terah, as Nimrod's prince of host, they were able to find a well-positioned home far enough away from the main temple of Sin the moon god, the patron deity of the city.

Abram settled his servants in the agricultural region around the city to work the land and raise herds.

It was time for Terah to get back. He had a mere ten days to return to Babylon.

"I am going with you," said Abram, as Terah prepared for his journey.

"Why?" said Terah. "You are needed here. The Festival will only anger you."

"I want to understand," said Abram.

"What do you want to understand?"

"The reason for God's wrath."

Abram thought about the angels he had met on the barge. He wanted to see what they were going to do.

Terah shook his head.

"Abram, if Nimrod discovers your presence, he will have you hung and quartered."

"Or thrown in a furnace?" said Abram with a smirk.

"You should not test your god."

"Do not worry, father, I have no intention of causing trouble this time. I will stay out of sight. I just want to observe."

"Who will oversee the family household?" said Terah.

Abram had already made plans. "Eliezer is already like a brother to me. And Lot can learn from him." Eliezer had proven dependable during their course upriver. Eliezer had moved to protect Abram against the strangers. He had also saved Abram's life once, keeping him from falling off the barge into the churning waters.

Abram added, "Most of the people of this city will be down in Babylon anyway, so trade and public institutions have shut down for the next couple weeks."

"I will not slow down for you," said Terah.

"You will not need to," said Abram.

"All right. Get your horse and let us go."

Abram said his goodbyes. He left with Terah and his personal guard of about twenty soldiers. They rode to Babylon.

CHAPTER 29

Babylon bustled with excitement and festivities. Hundreds of thousands of pilgrims from all the cities of Sumer and Akkad had traveled into Babylon to participate in the event. Many even came from distant lands like Elam in the east, the Levant in the west, and Egypt in the south, including royalty and political dignitaries. All the lodgings were full around the city, and tens of thousands spread their tents in the surrounding plains.

All the world was at Babylon. Babylon was all the world.

Abram and Terah made it back in time for Terah to perform his duties. Abram hid out in the massive crowds, looking for Mikael and his two companions.

It was the month of Nisannu, the spring new year, and the Akitu Festival would take twelve days to bring that new year into full fruition. During each day, the populace would engage in celebration in their homes and during public gatherings. But they would not necessarily be involved inside the temple areas during the priestly activities.

• • • • •

The first day, the *mubannu*, or high priest cook, brought a wooden key and opened the Exalted Gate of the Esagila, Marduk's temple area.

Abram wandered around the city of Babylon, trying to find the archangels in their disguises. He looked for any figure or stance that struck him as familiar. The crowds were jam-packed all over the city. His chances were near impossible. It was like wading through a myriad of ants in an anthill. There were just too many people.

• • • • •

On the second day, a *sesgallu* priest bathed in the river, and prayed a prayer to Marduk in his temple, before opening the doors to the public. The prayer exalted the supremacy of Marduk and Babylon, and offered a contractual agreement for Marduk to protect the city and establish his greatness.

As Abram strained to see the Esagila temple through the throngs of multitudes, he thought he heard his name called out.

"Abram."

Strange. The voice was in his head, not in the crowd around him. But he looked around anyway. He spotted Mikael, already upon him.

"What on earth are you doing here?" hissed Mikael. It startled Abram, who was not expecting such rejection.

"I wanted to see what you were going to do."

Mikael was incredulous. "And you were going to watch God's wrath standing right in the midst of it all, were you?"

"I guess I had not thought of it that way," said Abram.

He saw the huge form of the Destroyer standing in the distance, scanning the masses. He suddenly realized what a completely stupid, mule-headed thing he had done. If the Destroyer was the instrument of mass destruction, of course that would mean a kind of leveling that would not be selective in a crowd. Once again, Abram's overconfidence in his protected status dulled his thinking.

"I am sorry," said Abram. "Have I thwarted any of El Shaddai's plans?"

"Of course not," said Mikael. "But that does not justify your moronic irresponsibility. Follow me."

Mikael led him away, through the pulsating masses of idol worshippers.

They came to a small inn. Mikael took him back to the stalls of animals.

Mikael had a small blanket for sleeping.

"Where is the Angel of Yahweh?" asked Abram.

"In the heavenlies." Mikael considered how much he should tell Abram. "There has been a slight change of plans, and the divine council is in deliberation about what to do right now."

"Did I...?" Abram was horrified.

"I told you, it was not you," interrupted Mikael. He was a bit impatient with Abram.

"Is the Destroyer coming back here?"

"No," said Mikael.

"So it is just you. Why are you still here?"

Mikael looked at him like a parent scolding a child. "To protect you from hurting yourself."

Abram felt foolish. He was like a child being watched by a babysitter.

· · · · ·

On the third day of the festival, after the daily rituals, a carpenter, a metal worker, and a goldsmith worked together to create two small figurines of tamarisk and cedar, overlaid with gold and gemstones. These represented mankind, and in the hands of the figurines were a scorpion and a serpent, which represented the dangerous threats to their existence.

That day, Semiramis and Mardon had planned to assassinate the Mighty Hunter before the end ceremonies. That way, Mardon would ascend to the throne just as the new age dawned and the cosmic mountain was established for the gods.

But the assassination had to look like an insurrection, a reaction against tyranny. What authority would they have over a populace that knew they were seeking personal ambition and power?

•••••

The start of the New Year began on the fourth day. After the daily rituals, a priest recited the *Enuma Elish* before Marduk. The *Enuma Elish* was the Babylonian creation epic. It told the story of Marduk's victory over Tiamat, of his splitting of the great sea dragon's body in half to establish the new heavens and the earth with Babylon, and of Marduk's ascension to supremacy in the pantheon as king of the gods. It told of his receiving the Tablet of Destinies, and it ended with a recitation of the fifty names of Marduk.

During the recitation of the epic, the crown of Anu and the seat of Enlil were veiled in humility before Marduk's might and glory.

In the divine council of heaven, a different story was being unveiled. Ten thousand times ten thousand of Yahweh Elohim's holy ones, the Sons of God, surrounded his throne chariot in the heavenly courtroom of the temple above the waters. On earth, the forefathers Enoch and Noah knew the Creator only as Elohim, and Abram knew him as El Shaddai. But in the heavenlies, he was always Yahweh Elohim.

In this courtroom, the legal and providential decisions were deliberated by Yahweh Elohim. A particularly hostile lawsuit had been recently initiated. The prosecuting adversary, the satan Mastema, had sued for peace and had delayed the total annihilation of the city of Babylon. It was clear that the earth was once again unified in rebellion under the totalitarian regime of the imperial King Nimrod. But since Yahweh Elohim would never again flood the land as punishment, another means was necessary for justice to preside.

Yahweh Elohim cleared the courtroom of the myriad Sons of God. Yahweh Elohim sat alone with the satan. The judgment would not be revealed until the proper moment, because the satan had a gag order placed on him. He could not make public the court ruling until the sentence was carried out.

But Yahweh Elohim had changed his mind. That sentence would not involve the Destroyer.

• • • • •

The climax of the festival came on the fifth day. It was full of ceremonies, purifications, and rituals, including intercessory prayers, the building of a shrine, and an exorcism of evil spirits from the temple. But the most important event was the ritual humiliation of the king before Marduk.

The humiliation of the king consisted of a *sesgallu* priest stripping the king of the symbols of his power, his mace, his scepter and crown. These elements were placed before Marduk in his throne room. Then the priest went back and slapped the king across the cheek, yanked his ears, and led him before the presence of Marduk, to kneel in supplication and prayer. It was indeed humiliating for Nimrod; a mere reflection of the domination Marduk imposed on Nimrod in private. It publicly reinforced the hierarchy of power. It represented a reversion to chaos followed by the renewal of order, a reiteration of the very fertility rite of the entire festival.

Marduk then returned the emblems and insignia of kingship to Nimrod for one more year. The king dreaded the brutal debasement he knew he would have to suffer at the hands of Marduk that evening as payment for this honor.

• • • • •

On day six, the other gods of the pantheon arrived on boats to join in the festivities. They gathered in the shrine on the top of Etemenanki as sacrifices were offered. Then the little clay figurines of mankind were struck by priests and purified in fire for the atonement of the people.

Abram was allowed to stay in the city under the protection of Mikael. He wondered what God's remedy was to be for this obscene fulcrum of corruption and depravity. Why was mass destruction ruled out? What could possibly be enough? It was not just the city that was malignant; it was the entire earth that had come to be "one" under this maleficent tyrant. They all spoke one language, had one religion, and served one god king and pantheon.

Abram watched the royal representatives from the cities: Nippur, Sippar, Borsippa, Lagash, Uruk, Ur, Eridu, Nineveh. They had come from all corners of the earth to participate in this massive ritual of idolatry. What could El Shaddai possibly have in mind that could bring justice upon this festering boil of villainy and spiritual rebellion?

The thought passed through Abram's mind that maybe God had given up.

• • • • •

On the seventh day, the human statues were bathed and redressed in new garments to rejoin as new humanity.

On the eighth day, the gods aligned according to rank in the temple of Marduk. A pig was ritually slaughtered, the blood strewn around the base of the temple. Then came the decreeing of the destinies. Marduk carried out the Tablet of Destinies and was proclaimed all powerful and then was invested with supreme authority over the pantheon. The gods retired to the temple and there Marduk announced the decrees for the king and his people of that year, for the ears of the gods and priests alone. The scribe Sinleqi recorded them for the archives.

Semiramis had a destiny she secretly decreed for Nimrod, and it was not a long life. She had previously had Sinleqi do another archives search for any living members of the tribes of Joktan or Phenech, the descendants of Noah. Nimrod had had their immediate royal families executed at his wedding to Semiramis fifty years earlier, when he first took power as world potentate. But such matters were never cut and dry. There was always a family member who could not make it to the festivities, whether for sickness or for being abroad. Whatever the case, she felt certain there had to be some who did not make it to the wedding that day, and thus were spared their lives. But any known survivors, including household servants, had been immediately inducted into the slave force.

Sinleqi found them. There were two males from Joktan's family line who had been babes at the time and did not meet their intended fate. Their names were Ophir and Uzal. They had ended up as brick makers. They had been slaves for fifty years, building the city upon the blood of their fathers. That promised plenty of pent-up bitterness to exploit.

She arranged for their escape on the eighth day of the celebrations and made it look like they were alone in their conspiracy. It was quite easy, as there was not much security over the slave force other than a handful of wranglers and organizers. Where could a fugitive go?

She met with them. They were both strong, agile and practiced in weapons. As it turned out, they actually had hoped to escape one day and kill Nimrod in revenge. Perfect. It could never be traced to her. No doubt, they had leaked their intentions to other slaves who would corroborate the evidence in an investigation.

She and Mardon conspired with them about Nimrod's weaknesses and his ability to sense danger. It would be a difficult task, because he was a giant Gibborim warrior. But he had become flabby and unpracticed over the years, as he spent more time in his regal duties and less on the battlefield. There was no need for battle, for the entire world had peace under his absolute reign. They were all de facto slaves, but Nimrod's kingdom was at peace.

Should these two disgruntled assassins be successful, they would be hailed as the liberators of the people. Semiramis promised them a hefty financial reward and royal titles upon Mardon's succession to the throne.

In reality, she planned for them to be hanged immediately as traitors.

• • • • •

On the ninth day of the festival, Abram and Mikael positioned themselves to watch the grand parade of the gods. It proceeded down the Processional Way from Esagila all the way past the temple of Ishtar in the north of the city. A large flock of white doves, the bird of the goddess, was released from Ishtar's temple as they passed, creating a spectacle of peaceful liberation.

The parade continued out through the vainglorious Ishtar Gate on to another temple by the river, where they held a banquet of the gods. This was the most public of events. Throngs of people crowded the lanes of the Processional Way, trying to get a glimpse of the gods in their glorious chariots covered with dazzling jewels. Cultic musicians, dancers, and singers accompanied the parade through the city. Priests, royalty and visiting dignitaries received front row seats to the spectacle.

Terah had stationed the golemim stone soldiers along the Processional Way as a kind of rock fence of protection. It worked as he expected. The Stone Ones cast a presence of strength and power over the entire parade. Nimrod gloried in it.

It encouraged Ophir and Uzal to regroup and strategize about their target. They had only two days left of the actual festival. The twelfth day was a day of departures.

· · · · ·

The banquet of the gods was a gluttonous affair that lasted the entire tenth day. They ate from the finest of the flocks and the cream of the crops of produce in the kingdom. Then they vomited it all up in order to eat more. They saved the vomit to offer the pigs, goats, and slaves as their gruel. Wine flowed like a river. It took a lot of alcohol to inebriate a Watcher god.

Abram became impatient. The idolatry entirely repulsed him. He wanted El Shaddai to hurry up and destroy this place. Mikael calmed him down.

"In El Shaddai's good time. All things in El Shaddai's good time."

Ophir and Uzal surveyed the Processional Way. They knew that the pageant of gods would return tomorrow with Nimrod in his own chariot. They would be ready. They had struck upon a plan that was very risky, but if they were lucky, they would finally get their revenge on the monster that had slaughtered their families.

CHAPTER 30

On the eleventh day of Akitu, Abram and Mikael crossed the river to observe from a distant ridge what would happen that day. Mikael said they would not want to be near the epicenter. They found a large flat parcel of land without any structures around.

Abram strained to get a look at the activities down in the city. Then he heard the words beside him, "Behold, they are one people, with one language and religion."

Abram snapped his head around. El Shaddai stood beside him as the Angel of Yahweh.

Abram dropped to his knees in worship. He trembled.

El Shaddai continued looking at Babylon's magnificent architecture and achievements. He mused out loud, "This is only the beginning of what they will do. They will stop at nothing to achieve the impossible."

Abram blurted out, "My Lord."

El Shaddai looked down at Abram. He put his hand on Abram's head with loving care and smiled.

Abram melted inside. It was the Lord. He could not describe the look of the face that on the surface was rather common looking.

But in his eyes, he saw the heavens and the earth.

El Shaddai turned his face back to Babylon and continued walking.

Abram got up to follow him, but Mikael held him back. He looked at him with a mere shaking of his head "no." Abram stood still.

They both watched the angelic figure travel down onto the plain and cross the bridge into the city, its anonymous herald of judgment.

The cloaked figure dissolved into the masses at the gate.

At the north end of the city, the gods reversed their Processional march back to the temple complex to mount the mighty Etemenanki ziggurat. They would congregate in the temple shrine at the top and temple priestesses would engage in *hieros gamos*, the ritual act of consumation with the gods.

Nimrod and Marduk had planned for this eleventh day celebration for over a generation. All seven planets were aligned in a heavenly convergence. The cusp of the Age of Aries had arrived. All the high gods of the pantheon were present, as well as a dozen others. Anu, the father god of heaven, Enlil, the Lord of the Air, Enki, god of water, Ninhursag, goddess of the earth, Sin the moon god, and Shamash the sun god.

The only one of the Seven Who Decree the Fates absent was Ishtar. *Thank the gods*, thought Nimrod. *She would have made a catastrophe out of it. with her lime-lighting for attention and her tendency to hijack such ceremonies for her own exaltation.* She might have ruined their bacchanalia with her violent extremes.

These thoughts occupied Nimrod's mind when the first arrow penetrated his throat.

His head jerked back. Blood spurted from his wound as he grasped his throat.

The second one hit in his upper shoulder, jutting out from under his collarbone.

Everyone's heads whipped around to see where the arrow came from. A tall building overlooked the Processional Way, but no one could see an archer.

It went exactly as planned. Ophir had become skilled with a bow and especially in rapid firing. He was able to nock, aim, and release two arrows in a blink. He fired from a dark room on one of the upper levels.

They had planned to target Nimrod from behind because everyone would be focused forward in the parade, and would quite literally not see it coming. Ophir's hits drew the straining attention of most people whose complete focus would be on trying to see where the arrows came from.

Meanwhile, Uzal, secreted in the crowd with a pig-butchering blade, leapt out into the street. He raced toward Nimrod to cut off his head. His arms were strong, and his legs were built from slave labor. They carried him fleet-footed to Nimrod before any of the slow Stone Ones could catch him.

But while everyone, including Nimrod, looked backward, Terah did not. He saw Uzal coming and he drew his sword.

Uzal launched himself from the chariot wheel at Nimrod. Terah exploded and hit the flying Uzal midair with his blade. He stopped the assassin's momentum. The two of them tumbled to the floor of the chariot.

Uzal was dead, the sword buried in his chest.

The crowd that swarmed the building were certain to find Ophir in minutes. But he would not be caught alive. He slit his own wrists, rather than face the hideous torture that would surely follow his capture.

It had all happened so fast.

Semiramis was in the chariot next to Nimrod. She pretended to lose her mind with fear. She started to climb out of the four-wheeled boxy chariot, screaming. The ever-cool Mardon pulled her back, and held her with comfort — another theatrical pretention, as there was not a sliver of compassion or comfort in Mardon's soul.

Terah grabbed the reins of Nimrod's chariot and raced ahead to the Esagila. The healing priests might save his life.

The gods had drawn their weapons and scanned the horizon for enemies. None were forthcoming. It was a conspiracy against the king alone. It was common in this world, and to be expected. There were always rebels with revolutionary intentions. The goal was to smoke them out and kill them before they could organize. These two had evidently worked alone.

The Stone Ones held back the excitable crowds, keeping them from becoming a rampaging mob of fear. The crowd of flesh and blood was no match for their weighty unmoving rock.

A herald blew his trumpet.

Marduk took a position to speak.

The crowd finally calmed down.

Marduk bellowed to the masses, "Your king is alive and well! He will be healed by the magi and shamans of my temple! He is in good hands! Let us string up the bodies of these traitors. BUT the ceremony must go on!"

The masses roared in approval.

There was no way in Sheol that Marduk would let anything interrupt the opening of the portal to the heavens. Already, a funnel cloud was forming over the ziggurat Etemenanki. He could see the Convergence was almost upon them. The four winds had kicked up and the sky was getting dark. The time was at hand.

Marduk was not sure that Nimrod was actually alive. He did not care. Nimrod was dispensable. The pantheon was not.

Ophir's and Uzal's bodies were tied to the chariots of Marduk and dragged down the street to the entrance of Etemenanki.

The gods made it inside the temple complex and shut the gates on the public.

They made their way up the stairway to heaven to engage in their *hieros gamos* ritual with the hierodules of the temple.

The people outside hung what was left of the bodies of the conspirators on poles.

Deep in the temple of Esagila, the healing priests cared for Nimrod. He would have permanent scars. But he would not die. It was not even close. He bore countless scars from countless battles. These would merely be two more. The shoulder wound was minor. The archer assassin must have been aiming for the head and missed. The throat wound was a bit more complicated. The arrow missed his carotid artery, but nicked his vocal chord on its way out. For now, he could not talk. When he healed, he would have a raspy edge to his voice that he would carry with him to the grave.

Terah entered the chamber. He had stayed outside after he brought the king and queen to the temple. He returned now with the two heads of the conspirators. He showed them to Nimrod.

"They are slaves," he said. "I saw the brand marks on their bodies."

Semiramis blurted out, "Get eyewitnesses to identify them. Find out their motives and who they are connected to."

"Yes, my queen."

Nimrod reached out and grasped Terah's arm. He gurgled and gasped trying to say something. Terah figured he was thanking him for saving his life.

Terah said, "I guess even Naphil kings are mortal," and left them.

The phrase stung Nimrod. His memory flooded with his past journeys to Mount Hermon, the forest of Humbaba the Terrible, through the underworld, and to the mystical island of Dilmun — all in search of the ever-elusive immortality — only to conclude that he would die. All the old bitterness and anger raged up in him.

That will all be behind me shortly, he thought. *The gods have promised me immortality and full godhood when this day is done.*

Semiramis approached Nimrod and touched him with affection. "Leave the inquisition to me, my love. I will track down anyone who has a connection to the assassins. And will deal with them appropriately."

Nimrod noted her eagerness, not a characteristic he would connect to her affections for him. He glanced at Mardon, who was soulless as always, probably daydreaming of nefarious deeds.

Mardon was actually thinking how he might get away to Haran to find that succulent little lamb, Sarai.

A healer shaman finished bandaging the neck. Nimrod commanded with a scratchy voice through painful words, "When… Terah returns… assemble the… Stone Ones… at ziggurat base. I… meet… there."

Nimrod left for the ziggurat.

Since the gods meant to be glorified in a transformational shift of worldwide proportions, they decided to conclude their ceremony in the Etemenanki shrine with a sacrifice of the human priests and priestesses.

At the chosen moment in the carousing, Marduk announced, "Let us join the feast!"

All the gods took the throats or femur arteries of humans near them and sunk their fangs into them with abandon.

They had received plenty of animal blood from the daily sacrifices of the festival, but they found something delectable about human plasma. They drank their fill until the corpses were pale skeletal versions of their former selves. The scaled bodies of the Watcher gods shone with the glittering of full-orbed emotional release, the sign of their flared passions. They were the Shining Ones, and the pupils of their unblinking reptilian eyes widened to take it all in with relish.

A large gong sounded.

The earth rumbled. The noise brought Marduk out of his delirium of excess.

He stumbled to the edge of the shrine to see what was going on below.

A crack of thunder resounded overhead. The funnel cloud swirled above the shrine.

Below, in the huge courtyard of Etemenanki, the entire army of ten thousand Stone Ones assembled and stood to attention at the command of Terah. Nimrod, with bandaged throat, stood beside Terah. The king oversaw the complete entourage of every magician, every sorcerer, every astrologer and omen diviner in Babylon surround the ziggurat with ritual incantations.

The temple towered over them, standing three hundred feet high. It was a small mountain, a cosmic mountain. Soon it would be the new home of the gods, and an occultic portal through which they might storm heaven.

It was time.

The other gods joined Marduk in sympathetic magic with the sorcery below and began their own incantations and spells.

Across the river, Abram and Mikael watched the spout of the funnel cloud reach down to touch the shrine. A flurry of winds surrounded the entire complex. Loose animals around them brayed, barked, and bleated as if to warn everyone of something terrifying.

The spout came closer and closer to the congregation of the gods. The transformation of the ages was about to begin.

The voices of the gods grew louder. Their arms reached high toward the consummation of the opening. The spout touched down on the shrine. Contact was made between heaven and earth.

But instead of the portal opening up for more Watchers to come down, the assembly of the gods felt the horrifying pull of the whirlwind *upward*.

This was not the plan.

Abram saw all the gods in the shrine sucked up into the whirlwind.

He looked at Mikael, who laughed heartily.

It was the opposite of what the gods had expected.

Before Abram could grasp what he had seen, the earth rumbled beneath their feet. The land before them rose up like a rug being shaken.

The ripple of earth traveled speedily toward Babylon.

The outer walls of the city were hit first. They disintegrated under the impact of the quake. Abram could hear the screams of terror from the multitude of people across the river inside the city gates.

Then the earthquake hit the ziggurat Etemenanki and split it almost in two. The top half of the structure crumbled and fell upon the Stone Ones below, burying them in an avalanche of rubble. The bulk of the temple remained intact with a huge crack through its core.

The golemim that were not pulverized by the falling brickwork became victims of the concussive shock wave. They collapsed into piles of rubble.

A pathway of destruction and carnage made its way through the city and devastated the palace and the Ishtar Gate. The structures crumbled to mounds of painted bricks and broken bodies.

Then as quickly as the destruction had fallen upon them it was gone. The funnel cloud retracted to the sky and the storm vanished.

And everything was eerily still.

Then cries of pain and misery from human victims echoed throughout the city. Countless thousands lay dead, half again as many injured. They were bruised, cut, maimed and crushed by the debris of mud brick and stone that now lay across the city.

The bridge crossing the river to the Processional Way had collapsed into the river. Some survivors swam across the water to get away from the cursed city.

Abram and Mikael ran down from the ridge. They helped the dozen or so fleeing refugees to safety on land.

Abram noticed something strange.

One of the refugees spoke to him, but it was meaningless babbling. Abram thought the poor fellow was in shock and speaking nonsense. Then he heard another refugee cry out and yell more nonsense into the air. This one sounded different from the first.

As they walked, helping calm the refugees, he noticed that they all spoke in strange words he had never heard before.

"What is going on?" Abram asked Mikael.

"El Shaddai has confused their language so that they may not understand each other's speech," he said.

"Why would he do that?"

"To divide their unity and disperse them over the face of the earth."

Then it came clear to Abram what El Shaddai had done. He would not destroy the world again with water. But he would protect his plan against a world of unified rebellion. All across the ruins of Babylon, survivors from various cities tried to communicate with one another. But they had miraculously been given different languages. They could not understand one another and could barely help one another.

Mankind was supposed to multiply and fill the earth. But instead they had congregated in this city of Babylon to become one in evil. But the separation of languages would create a dispersion, a massive separation between peoples. It would divide them and spread them abroad over the face of the earth. Diversity would bring chaos and separation. But in a strange way, it would save the world from spiraling into a singularity of unstoppable evil.

Abram thought of a play on words. He said to Mikael, "It is no longer Babylon the great, the eternal city, but *Babel*, because there El Shaddai confused the language of all the earth. And from there El Shaddai dispersed them over the face of all the earth."

CHAPTER 31

In the heavens above the waters, in the very divine council of Yahweh Elohim, the *Bene ha Elohim*, the Sons of God, had returned to surround his chariot again with glory and praise.

The trisagion echoed forth, "Holy, holy, holy, is Yahweh Elohim Almighty. Who was and is and is to come!" Their voices were like the sound of many waters. The Cherubim that upheld the throne chariot extended their many wings and Yahweh Elohim took his seat as the Ancient of Days.

The rebel Watchers stood before the council, still awash in human blood, their shame dripping from their bodies. The satan took his position as their defense attorney, across from the enigmatic Son of Man. Normally, Mastema in his role as the satan, was a prosecuting attorney. But in this case, he had become the collective bargainer for this despicable union of corrupt hoodlums.

There would be no testimony or cross-examination. Today was a summary judgment from on high.

The Son of Man addressed the Watchers on trial, "This day, Yahweh Elohim has given over the peoples of the earth to their depravity. He has divided mankind and has given the nations their inheritance. He has fixed the borders of the people according to the number of the Sons of God, those Watchers who have remained on earth. All of humanity has incorrigibly worshipped false gods, so false gods will be their inheritance."

Marduk thought to himself, *Is he actually giving us the nations to rule over? What is the fine print? What is he not telling us?*

The Son of Man continued, "Yahweh Elohim has allotted the fallen host of heaven to all the peoples under the whole heaven. Mastema, the satan will be designated executor of the inheritance. The nations are your allotment. Divide them amongst yourselves."

The Watchers were shocked at the concession.

Marduk whispered to the satan, "There are seventy of us, plus some of our fallen angels. I want first choice."

"Do not worry," snapped the satan, "You will get yours, Mr. 'King of the Gods.'"

He uttered that title with sarcastic exaggeration. Marduk could physically crush him, but the satan had all the legal power to cast Marduk into Tartarus if he made a wrong move. Tartarus was the lowest most impenetrable region of Sheol the underworld.

Then the Son of Man said, "But Yahweh Elohim's portion will be his people. Jacob will be his heritage. He will have a people of his own inheritance."

There it is, thought Marduk. The qualification. The tiny little print at the bottom of the covenant tablet that indicated Yahweh Elohim's selfish grab for glory. But wait a minute. He only gets one nation of people?

The satan articulated what Marduk and everyone else was thinking, "Who exactly is Jacob? And what will be his people's allotted heritage of land?"

The Son of Man said, "That will be revealed in due time. They will be a people of my choosing, a remnant who will inherit the land that they will ultimately conquer."

"That is not fair!" squealed the satan. "You are going to give out an entitlement of land and then just take it away when you want it? That is not a fair share!"

The Seraphim bellowed out with their many-faceted voices, "The earth is the Lord's, and the fullness thereof, the world and those who dwell within!"

"Oh, please," griped the satan. "Now you are contradicting yourself. First, you allot to us peoples and lands, and then you claim ownership over it all?" He knew full well that was not a contradiction. Their inheritance was no more than a temporary loan.

"And why will you not tell us who this Jacob is? What are you trying to hide? Do you have some dirty little secret you are afraid we will find out and use to discredit you?"

The Seraphim had the last word, "Thus saith the Lord."

Mastema and the entire group of fallen Watchers were instantly sucked back down into a new funnel cloud. It deposited them, not back in Babylon, but on their Mount Hermon in Canaan. It was here they would begin the arduous task of parceling out their allotted seventy nations under the authority of the seventy Sons of God.

• • • • •

Nimrod picked himself out of the debris of the fallen tower. All around him he saw smashed piles of rock that were the remains of the golem army of Stone Ones which had secured his power over the earth. Their spells were forever useless now, locked up in the jaws of lifeless boulders.

Most of his astrologers, sorcerers and magicians were dead in the fallout. Everyone around him now spoke in different languages. He could not command those to whom he could not speak or whom he could not understand. There were dozens of different dialects and none of them could understand each other. They would disperse to start a new life all over the earth. There were a mere few hundred citizens whose language he could understand.

Babylon would not be transforming into anything, and not any time soon. It was decimated; not just structurally and in human lives, but more importantly in essence. It was no longer the center of the world. There would be no mountain of the gods, no golem army.

No more empire.

Nimrod's cosmos lay shattered into a million pieces.

He knew the Creator had cursed him. Nimrod had sought to make a name for himself as a Mighty Hunter, flaunting his prowess in the face of El Shaddai himself. He sought to make a tower that reached to the sky, linking heaven and earth. That tower had collapsed. The city would take decades to repopulate and rebuild the ruins.

But it was cursed. He would not be rebuilding anything.

His queen Semiramis and son Mardon were still alive, which felt more like punishment to Nimrod than relief.

Even Marduk had abandoned him. He was nowhere to be found. The mightiest king of the gods no longer protected Nimrod.

He had lost everything but his life.

There was nothing worse for a great ruler than being demoted in rank. If he had died in the disaster, he would be remembered as a great ruler who went out in a blaze of glory. To be killed at the height of one's power would forever burn that reputation into history like a kiln-fired brick. But to lose everything and go from world potentate to petty victim was the cruelest of all humiliations.

This El Shaddai knew what he was doing.

Nimrod would not give El Shaddai the pleasure of seeing him commit suicide. Nimrod would fight back. He would rebuild his forces. Then he would set his heart upon one and only one goal for the rest of his life: to hunt down and destroy El Shaddai's Chosen Seed, Abram. This despicable tool of a reprehensible divinity had escaped Nimrod's grasp when he was born, defied Nimrod's power and glory when he survived the furnace of fire, and had become the curse that brought the downfall of Nimrod's very own kingdom of Babylon.

Abram must die.

CHAPTER 32

Twenty-five years passed after the fall of the tower of Babel, with the confusion of tongues and dispersion of the peoples. The world changed drastically. The people of many tongues spread out over all the earth and returned to their communities of homogenous language. The tower of one world governance collapsed into seventy different nations whose divided tongues heralded a variety of diverse cultures, many of them at war with one another.

Unfortunately for Abram, twenty-five years had passed and nothing eventful had happened to him. His brother Nahor and the rest of his family eventually moved north to be with them. Haran became the family home, but nothing dramatic occurred. He waited for God's direction, but it never came. He felt he had been hung out to dry like a piece of laundry. *Why would El Shaddai do those fantastic, spectacular things in Babylon, and promise me he was going to tell me where to go, and then never contact me again? I thought I was his Chosen Seed!*

That title made the irony even worse, because in order to bear seed, one must be fertile. Unfortunately, that was not something El Shaddai saw fit to bestow upon Sarai.

She had been barren these twenty-five years. Abram was now seventy-five, and Sarai, sixty-five.

Had all of it been just an hallucination? Even the events of the past faded in his memory.

His overweening confidence was cracking.

Sarai told him that was probably the point of the waiting. That he needed to have less faith in himself and more faith in El Shaddai before he would accomplish his purpose.

But that was no comfort when you were already seventy-five years old, living an anonymous life in a small out-of-the-way town in the middle of nowhere, with no children and no inheritance.

His father Terah had found his way up to Haran after the Babel incident. When the earthquake had hit, Terah was right in the middle of the avalanche of brickwork from the Tower. He had survived it. But when he pulled himself from the rubble he discovered his entire army of Stone Ones had been destroyed. He knew the golemim were the main reason he had been protected from Nimrod's wrath all those years. They had been bound by the sorcery to obey Terah, not the king.

Now the Stone Ones were gone. Nothing would hold Nimrod back from punishing Terah for all his foolish errors through the years. He knew his future was not hopeful if he stayed in the city. So he immediately left, before Nimrod pulled himself from the rubble.

Nimrod assumed exactly as Terah had hoped, that he was dead and buried in the avalanche of earth from the Tower. There were many bodies missing from that day of terror.

Terah left for the desert with only the tattered clothes on his back and a sword in his hand. But it was freedom. Shackles fell from his soul. Terah was finally freed from slavery to Nimrod and Babylon.

When he found his son and family in Haran, he repented and converted to El Shaddai.

• • • • •

"Where is my beauty queen?" asked Abram as he pranced around the house. The family was in the fields working, Terah played with the children in the courtyard. Abram and Sarai had the house to themselves.

"My beauty beauteaous. Beautifulicious, beauticious."

He stopped to listen. He heard crying in their bedroom.

He opened the door, "What is wrong, beautiful?"

Sarai lay on the bed, softly crying again. "Must you constantly use that word? Can you not think of a different one to use?"

Even at sixty, she was a gorgeous woman who turned the heads of younger men. Abram thought she was quite possibly El Shaddai's greatest miracle. Her beauty absorbed him. He could not stop telling her that through the years. It would come blurting out of him as he watched her cook or clean, or play with the family's children.

"But you are beautilumptious," he said.

"Do not call me that! I am ugly!"

Abram's joyful countenance turned compassionate. He crossed the room and sat beside her, holding her.

She sobbed between her tears, "I have no children. I am useless!"

He held her tighter. "Do not say that, Sarai. You are my heart and soul. You are everything to me."

She had these episodes every once in a while. Her barrenness would overwhelm her and her feelings of inadequacy would rise up. When they did, Abram's use of the word "beautiful" became like a sick joke needling her, instead of a compliment encouraging her. She knew he meant nothing but admiration and love for her, but the tragic irony was too much to face in those moments. To her, beauty meant nothing. Children were what gave life meaning. She cared about family, not her looks. Was this El Shaddai taunting her?

"I am afraid," she whimpered.

"Of what?"

"That you will grow weary of me," she said, "and you will find a concubine to fulfill El Shaddai's promise of an heir."

Abram sat back, finally getting to the heart of the issue. It was customary law in Mesopotamia that if a woman was barren, a man could legally find a concubine to sire children to maintain the family lineage.

"So that is what this is about," he said. "You are worried that I might desire another woman."

"Well, do you?" she sniffled.

"Of course not," he said with a touch of anger. "Where is your faith, Sarai? El Shaddai has promised us a son."

"He promised *you* a son," she retorted. "He may have no use for me."

Abram said, "Are you saying that El Shaddai is a bad creator? That he created you useless?"

"No." She sounded like a scolded child.

"So you want me to take our future in my own hands and not trust that El Shaddai will provide as he promised?"

She stopped her crying. She sniffed wetly. It was almost instantaneous. She knew he was right.

His words became firm and adoring, "Even if your stunning beauty was all you had, you would not be useless. There is nothing in this world more valuable to me than you."

She so appreciated his solid strength in her change of life. She knew he had great patience with her dramatic mood swings and hot flashes. Some nights, she would completely kick off all the covers in bed because she was burning up. It would leave him freezing. He would wake up, politely cover himself, and give her a kiss on her cheek.

He was such a loving, strong man. She knew his overuse of the word "beautiful" came from genuine adoration of her. And it did encourage her every time she heard it.

She knew what was coming next.

"I know of some use you can be to your husband right now, for instance."

She giggled. He began kissing her face in a special way that amused her. He would press his lips against her cheek and give very speedy, tiny little kisses, so fast it made a funny little noise. He claimed he could give a hundred kisses in thirty seconds.

She smiled and turned to kiss him properly. Passionately.

When they first discovered Sarai was not getting pregnant in their early years, Abram would use that as an excuse to have more sex. "Well, honey, that is why we need to have sex every night," he would tease. "Sometimes, twice a night. God just wants us to try more often."

She did not really have the drive he had. In fact, she did not seem to have any drive at all, which bothered her because she loved him so truly and deeply. She thought maybe something was wrong with her. But she loved to make him happy, and she knew it took so little of her time and effort that it would be foolish to deprive him. It would be like kicking a dog. So instead, she drew comfort from the oneness she felt in their union. Thus, she had a happy little puppy that would do anything for her, and was always trying to lick her.

After a few years, when they realized she was barren, he tried to comfort her. "If we have more sex, it gives El Shaddai more chances to perform his miracle." That one was a little silly, but she accommodated him just the same.

He always had a way of surprising her. She would be completely without amorous interest. He would start wooing her. She would respond for his sake, and suddenly out of nowhere, his elegant, wonderful hands would sweep over her body, caress her, and before she knew it, she was flying above the heavens and the earth in delirious pleasure. He always thought of her first and would often tell her, "Half of my pleasure is your pleasure."

As the years went on, his drive decreased somewhat with age. Now, his desires were not as frequent. But eventually, she would see his beady little eyes gleaming at her like a hungry wolf. And she knew, *It is loving time*.

She knew it was his way of knowing he was loved. Men were so simple, so predictable, so basic. Which was why withholding it was cruelty and abuse. She never did. He always respected her wishes, when sick or truly too tired. He would never use her compliance for selfish gain.

She, on the other hand, was a woman, and had so many changing needs and particularities even she lost track of how complex she was. But she gave him kudos for his efforts at trying.

They held so tightly together because the only thing they had in the whole wide world was each other. True, they had El Shaddai, but even El Shaddai himself had said that he was not enough for their need for community. Humans needed each other. When Adam was without sin and with El Shaddai in the Garden, they walked in perfect communion. But even in that perfect pastoral paradise, El Shaddai had said, "It is not good for man to be alone." One would think that El Shaddai would not consider the man to be alone if he was with his Creator. But he did. And that is why he made the woman out of his side, to be his helper, equal to him.

"Uhhh," she groaned in surprised pleasure. He had done it again. Abram had brought her out of her melancholy thoughts into his sensual experience of love.

She held him tightly. They became one again before their Maker.

Suddenly, someone was standing above them.

"Abram."

Sarai screamed. Abram jumped off her. She pulled the sheets up to cover herself.

Abram looked up at the figure in the room and knew immediately who it was.

"Mal'ak Yahweh," he blurted out. The Angel of Yahweh. It was the same figure Abram had met in Babel. It was El Shaddai in earthly form.

Abram covered himself up.

El Shaddai chuckled. "You are not Adam and Eve, you know. No need to be 'naked and ashamed' before me. You think I have not seen everything you do in the bedroom? I created sex."

Abram's head tilted. *I guess he is right.*

Sarai calmed down. You cannot argue with your Maker.

"My Lord and God, forgive us," said Abram. "You just gave us a shock with your — unusual choice of timing."

"There is a closer link to sexuality and spirituality than you may realize," said El Shaddai. "But you are right, I have kept you in the dark a bit."

"Why are you here now, Lord?"

He said to Abram, "Go from your country and your kindred and your father's house, to the land that I will show you. And I will make of you a great nation, and I will bless you and make your name great, so that you will be a blessing. I will bless those who bless you, and him who dishonors you I will curse, and in you all the families of the earth shall be blessed."

Sarai stared, with her mouth agape and eyes of shock. A million things ran through her mind, not the least of which was how on earth a nation could come from her barren womb, especially since she was already entering her change of life for women.

"Forgive me, my Lord," said Abram, "but where would that land be?"

"The land of Canaan."

"But where in the land of Canaan? That is a big country."

"You will figure it out," said El Shaddai.

Abram and Sarai looked at each other, trying to figure it out. When they looked back, El Shaddai was gone.

They sat there in a moment of silence.

Then Abram announced like a victor in battle, "I have my calling!"

Sarai rolled her eyes and patted him patronizingly on the back. *Men, and their need to accomplish great tasks.*

She stopped and stared ponderously out into nowhere. "How do you think you will become a nation? I am still barren."

"Well, my nearest kin is Lot. I have treated him as my own. Maybe he will inherit."

Abram considered it further for a moment. Then he added, "I wish El Shaddai would give us more details. He keeps us guessing in confusion."

"You mean trusting in faith," said Sarai with a smirk.

The two of them began plotting in their heads their next four hundred and fifty mile trek into the distant and dangerous, exotic land of Canaan.

"You know," said Sarai, "the Amorites of our city have an established trade route to Canaan. We can join one of their caravans. And we speak their language easily enough."

Abram snapped his fingers. "Zimri-Sin, the tanner, has a cousin down there in the middle of the country. It is the perfect location. He is always boasting about Mamre and his brothers, Eshcol and Aner, and Mamre's mighty oak grove just outside Kiriath-Arba."

Zimri-Sin was a close friend of Abram. Like every relationship, it had its straining points. Zimri-Sin would often get on Abram's nerves with his boasting of other's achievements to make up for his own lack of initiative. And he boasted plenty about Mamre. He had a tendency to exaggerate to make the stories sound more adventurous and the land more exotic and perilous.

"Is not Kiriath-Arba a village of giants?" said Sarai fearfully. Mamre often spoke of the mighty Arba, a giant who had settled in that region.

"I am never too sure just what is fact and fiction with Zimri-Sin. But you can be sure he exaggerates everything, so do not fret yourself."

She scoffed, "You mean the giants are only ten feet tall, not twelve feet tall?"

"Sarai, we serve a living God a million feet tall."

"Yes, my lord," she said. "We better get packing, so we can be on our way to Giant Land."

Abram chuckled. She always had such a spry sense of humor.

He looked at her.

Looked at her lips.

His eyes narrowed like a predator again.

Uh oh, she thought. *He is back on the hunt. Mr. One Track Mind.*

He said, "I do believe we started something that requires finishing, my beauty queen."

She smiled. "I do believe you speak the will of El Shaddai, my lordly king."

"Let us give El Shaddai another opportunity for a miracle."

He kissed her.

And they performed a symphony of love for El Shaddai, their Creator.

CHAPTER 33

When Nimrod rose out of the debris of the Babel cataclysm twenty-five years earlier, he was a disgraced and demoralized creature. Fifty of his royal offspring, giants born of his union with the daughters of Uruk, survived with him. They traveled eleven miles southwest to Borsippa, to start anew.

He had lost an empire But he was determined to crawl back up out of the muck to become a mighty ruler again.

It would not be easy. It would take time. He had lost his sorcerers and magi, his invincible army was crushed into rubble, his indomitable guardian god abandoned him, and his kingdom of power and fear was demolished.

He had many enemies who had made several attempts on his life over the years. But he survived them all and began his obsessive pursuit of regaining dominion. He was driven by pure, undefiled revenge against the God who had cursed him and against the vile Chosen Seed, Abram of Haran.

But he had become a shriveled version of his former self, a skeletal soul of bitterness and rage. He did not eat or sleep, he seethed. His once bright blue eyes became darkened pools of deadness. His face was gaunt and his back stooped over so that he became physically shorter. Death threats made him paranoid. He surrounded himself with a personal guard of his finest warriors and would not be seen very often in the presence of his queen Semiramis.

Only one thing about his character grew stronger: his desire to kill.

After this many years, he finally felt that he had a hand on the region again. He had built up his army, and by pillaging and plundering the dispersed tribes, he regained some wealth and reputation as a marauder to be feared.

Nimrod sent a raiding party up to Haran to find Abram. When the hunters returned, their news infuriated him. Abram was gone, left for Canaan, and Terah was dead.

Lucky for Terah, thought Nimrod. *I would have skinned him alive and eaten his organs.*

Terah had been the source of both Nimrod's rise and fall, with his power over the golem army as well as his fathering of Abram, this "Chosen Seed." The bitter irony enraged Nimrod.

But he could not go after Abram now.

Canaan was wild and rough. Its environment was completely different from what Nimrod was familiar with. Allegedly, the land crawled with warring clans that had giants. He was not battle-ready for that kind of foray yet. Instead, he commissioned two pairs of bounty hunters to find Abram in Canaan and bring him back alive. That would give Nimrod time to reestablish himself as king of Shinar, his old land of Babylon.

The obvious choice for the hunters would have been to use his finest Gibborim warrior offspring. They were giants. Since such beings were a growing presence in Canaan, they would not stand out as much for their size. On the other hand, their foreign presence would be far too obvious, marking them as mercenaries. That would draw too much attention. Abram would most likely catch wind of their pursuit in advance.

Instead, Nimrod chose to use the opposite: female assassins. They were smaller and more agile, and could slip through entire locations without being noticed or leaving a trace. Also, they could be disarming. Disguised as hierodules of the cult of Ashtart, no one would ever suspect them of such a mercenary quest.

Their order was not to kill, but to capture. But their deadly skills would be useful. They could dispatch anyone who got in their way. Only if there was no way of capturing Abram and bringing him back were they allowed to kill him. Even then, Nimrod wanted his head as proof of his demise.

These were slender, feminine women, who did not wield swords, maces, or axes. Instead, they were trained to slash with daggers, hit moving persons with throwing blades, and pinpointing distant targets with bow and arrow.

These particular killers had an additional field advantage that Nimrod was anxious to try out. Before the confusion of tongues at Babel, Marduk had been working on a secret experiment tied to the antediluvian sorcery of Uruk under Anu. He had managed to recreate some of their strange occultic experiments that he called "transmutation." He explained it as fusing two different kinds of animals into one.

Elohim had created animals to reproduce after their kind. He had established the boundaries of separation within creation. The Watcher gods had sought to overthrow those boundaries with their unique kind of crossbreeding. Marduk had managed to splice some of the essence of animals into these women. They had each been enhanced with the essence drawn from different predator animals. Unlike the antediluvian mutations which had the body of a man and the head of a beast, these new creations still looked like normal human women, but certain senses and skills had been heightened to those of the animal predators with which they had been united.

Two had been enhanced with the essence of a steppe lioness, and two others with the essence of a peregrine falcon. The only indication one had that there was something unearthly about these women was their hypnotic eyes. The iris and pupils became like those of the feline and aviary kinds respectively. They formed two teams of a lion woman and falcon woman each and set out on their journey for Canaan.

• • • • •

It had not taken Semiramis long to reestablish herself as the administrative head of the government, while Nimrod focused on building his armed forces and man-hunting for slaves. But he also spent more time on animal hunts. He did not want to be at residence in the city for too long around his family.

That was just fine with Mardon. It allowed him to return to his human experimentation.

Nimrod never discovered the conspiracy of assassination led by his queen and son before the Dispersion. Intelligence revealed the two male assassins were surviving relatives of the sons of Noah who had escaped from slavery to enact their personal vengeance. It was a reasonable scenario that was not worthy of any more consideration, once the entire city fell apart into chaos.

Semiramis appreciated this good fortune. She had no intention of stopping her relentless pursuit of placing her son in the seat of power.

CHAPTER 34

The four hundred and fifty mile trek to the heart of Canaan took the Amorite trading caravan a couple weeks. They traveled through desert, forest, and mountain pass until they arrived at Shechem, in the center of Canaan, just forty-five miles north of Mamre.

Abram had heard of the famous Oak of Moreh, a divining place of the gods at Shechem. Oaks and terebinth trees were sacred locations of divination, where priests would perform rituals and the gods would grant revelation.

Abram admired the huge, gnarly tree. He wondered at the shade that lingered below the branches. El Shaddai visited Abram again, under the leaves of the tree, to tell him, "To your seed, I will give this land."

So Abram built an altar there to El Shaddai.

A famine came over the land, so Abram and his clan found refuge in Egypt. They stayed only through the duration of the famine, never comfortable there. As soon as possible, Abram returned to Canaan. Lot, ever restless, stayed in Egypt for a time. For many years there, Lot amassed many herds, flocks, and tents, driven by his ambitious pursuit of wealth, fueled by a competitive spirit. He had never been content with basic sustenance. He always wanted more. He always wanted the best. The exotic luxuriance of Egypt hypnotized him for a while. But he was trying to serve El Shaddai.

He rejoined Abram, to continue in his uncle's footsteps as his surrogate son. Abram had spoken often of adopting him as a son.

Lot had come to believe in El Shaddai and looked up to Abram's leadership. But he had a divided heart. He wanted El Shaddai's promises, but he also wanted wealth, luxury, and security. He could not stand the waiting or the vague and ambiguous nature of El Shaddai's communication. If Abram was to be king, what kind of kingdom would that be without his own children? And in a rugged land of such brutal people? There were few actual cities, because most of the people still lived in nomadic tribes or settled clans. These Canaanites were a barbaric lot and they had a growing population of giants in their midst to add to it.

He had seen that there were already some giant clans along the Transjordan valley. The northern towns of Ashteroth, Karnaim, and Edrei had giants called Rephaim that claimed ancient royal heritage. South of those communities were the Zuzim giants of the settlement of Ham, and further south still, near the Jordan Sea, were the large Emim of the plain of Kiriathaim and the gigantic Horites near the cities of the plain. It appeared to Lot that they were spreading from the Jordan Sea area outward to these other locations.

At the heart of the Jordan Sea region was the pentapolis, headed by Sodom and Gomorrah. He had heard some things about the urban confederation, but had never been there. They had rich natural resources of sea life, bitumen and copper mining. They were the wealthiest, most progressive and cultured of peoples in Canaan. It drove his curiosity wild with temptation.

All these years, he had so focused on building his wealth and influence that he neglected the pursuit of a wife. He was almost thirty years old and still not married. He had turned down the women Abram had arranged for him. They seemed too simpleminded, and without a vision bigger than their own tribe — like sheep in a flock.

He wondered if he could find a more cultured and sophisticated woman in the cities of the plain. After all, cities were centers of the best and brightest, the rich and powerful — the educated. Tent dwelling seemed more and more rustic to him. Rural existence felt unsophisticated and primitive, and could very well be the source of the violence that appeared to rule the land.

All his adult life he had dwelt in tents and shepherded flocks. He did it well and expanded his resources. One day, he would make the transition back to the city life he had been born in. He would sell his possessions to buy a house in a city and find a trade that would free him from the smell of goats, sheep and cattle.

He had done so well with his own herds that the land where he and Abram settled could not support both their growing households and herds. Abram had near two thousand members in his clan by now, and nearly seven hundred of them were under Lot's household authority. The tension between the households finally came to a head at the height of the grazing season.

Lot's herdsmen complained to him that Abram's livestock were getting the best grazing fields as well as imposing on Lot's livestock feed. This was no small thing, as it affected the health of Lot's herds, and therefore the wealth he sought to increase.

The time had come to part ways.

Lot met with Abram and explained the problem one afternoon. They sat together looking out on the rolling hills between Bethel and Ai.

"Are you mad?" exclaimed Abram. "We are a family! You are my inheritor. You want to just give all that up?"

"There is no more room for the both of us," said Lot. "This latest problem with our herds is only the smallest bud of the plant. You know that."

Abram shook his head sadly. He had been a fool to think that the young lad with a wandering eye that he had brought with him from Ur would be any more satisfied with Abram's clan than he had been with Nahor's. He was a restless heart and wanted more of the world than he should have.

But Abram would not give up too quickly. "Sarai and I will have no children and God promised this land to my seed. You are my nearest kin. I have always thought you would be the one to take on the family name. What if I adopt you now, and grant you firstborn privileges?"

Lot could not look at him. The offer was already too late. Lot had made up his mind. And he certainly did not want to live the life of livestock and agriculture as a nomad or villager. But he could not bring himself to say so.

Abram knew Lot's heart was drawn to city life, either of Ur or his more recent experiences in exotic and dangerous Egypt.

"Uncle, I have always respected and honored you. But I need room to grow my herds and build the life that I want to build, follow my heart, pursue *my* dreams — not yours."

Abram teared up. He loved his nephew deeply and had poured his heart into mentoring him into a man of El Shaddai. But now it seemed he had failed, and he was losing his only surrogate for a son. Was El Shaddai's promise being thwarted? Was it all a big jest?

Abram knew he had lost.

He sighed. "Let there be no strife between us. If you must go, then go. The whole land is before you. Choose your inheritance, and I will take the rest. If you go right, I will go left, if you go left, I will go right."

Lot could not believe it. Abram, the patriarch of the clan, was giving his lowly nephew the choice. It was yet another example of the love this man had given Lot all his life. Lot would not waste the opportunity. He already knew full well where he wanted to go; the

Jordan Valley, that Garden of Eden, that echo of Egypt, and in particular, the location of the five cities of the plain, his redemption.

He tried not to sound too excited or give away his strategy. He faked a casual observation. "Well, I suppose I will go east and you can stay here. You should not be the one to leave. I will cross the Jordan and find my way."

"Travel on the west side of the Jordan Sea," said Abram. "It is an easier trek to Sodom and Gomorrah."

Lot flinched. Abram knew exactly what he meant to do. He could not hide a thing from the man who had taken care of him all these years.

He could hear a soul wrenching pain in Abram's words.

Lot was breaking Abram's heart.

There was nothing he could do. He heard the cities calling him. It was his destiny. An exciting new world of unknown experiences.

Sarai suffered a bout of depression, or as she called it, a malady of sadness. She had married Abram and had followed him and his vision with her whole heart. She believed in him and he adored her. But it had been approximately five years since they had left Mesopotamia to become nomads in this unruly land. Even their stay in Egypt had not swayed her faith in El Shaddai and grace for her husband.

While Abram's clan had sojourned in Egypt to escape the famine in Canaan, the Pharaoh had noticed Sarai. He wanted her to be one of his concubines. Abram feared that if Pharaoh discovered she was his wife, he would have Abram killed to take her for himself. Then Abram remembered Nimrod's comments before the fiery furnace. He commanded Sarai to tell Pharaoh she was Abram's sister.

It was technically half-true. She was his half-sister.

She dutifully obeyed. Pharaoh took her into his court for marriage. As a bride price, Abram received from Pharaoh much of the wealth they now enjoyed: servants, animals, silver and gold. All of which, made Abram feel guilty. But he could not reveal the truth for fear of his life.

El Shaddai sent plagues upon the Pharaoh in return.

When Pharaoh discovered the real reason for the diseases, he returned Sarai into Abram's keeping, chastised him, and sent them back to Canaan.

Sarai knew her husband and his weaknesses, his sins, but loved him anyway. He was a man of confidence and faith, who still would have lapses of trust. He sometimes sought to control events for his own benefit. Even though El Shaddai had promised him his seed would inherit the land of Canaan, he occasionally felt he had to manage things on his own, because El Shaddai did not seem to be following through.

It only and always resulted in pain for them both.

But Sarai knew she had her own weaknesses and lapses of trust as well.

If El Shaddai had promised Abram a seedline, then why would he make Sarai barren?

Her childlessness continued to eat at her soul. She would see other mothers with their infants or playful children around them, and feel a deep pain of grief in her heart. She felt as if she was nothing. She had no purpose, no meaning to her life. Of course, she loved her husband with every part of her heart, liver, and intestines. He was all she had in this world, so she clung to him with a fierce devotion despite the uncertainties and suffering.

But those anxieties were only the half of what troubled her. The nomad lifestyle of tent dwelling and constant being on the move was wearing her down with loneliness and despair. She had been raised in a sophisticated life back in Ur. In a nomad camp there were no markets nearby to visit on a daily basis, no long-term close neighbors with whom to share her thoughts, no roots from which to draw stability.

Living in the tents was like living in poverty, compared to city houses. In the city, the mud brick homes kept a cool temperature in summer and warmth in the winter. Tents on the other hand were made of goatskins that barely provided a comfortable shade in summer and hardly kept the winds at bay in winter. They smelled atrocious in hot weather. There was little or no furniture. The only privacy she and Abram could manage came from hanging curtains to create separate rooms within the large tent. They slept on bedrolls laid out on the ground, and they ate seated on rugs.

It was not that she longed for the life of a princess. She just wanted a nest that was a refuge from the world outside. Their meager nomadic tent city was just another element of her increasing feeling of alienation.

So when Abram told her about Lot's departure from the clan, she broke down in bitter weeping. Lot was one of her few connections to her past life in Mesopotamia. Without his charming, energetic face around, she felt as if there was no hope. She did not want to be a burden to Abram, and she truly wanted to support him in every way she could, but this was too painful for her to hide.

"Sarai, what can I do?" asked Abram.

"How many are going with him?" she said.

"About four hundred of the clan."

"Where is he going?" she said.

"To Sodom and Gomorrah."

"That cesspool of evil?"

"We have never been there," he said. "We do not know how bad it is."

Sarai blurted out, "What are we going to do? Keep wandering aimlessly in the wilderness?"

Abram sighed. His stomach turned. He knew he had to tell her eventually. "We are going to settle down by the Oaks of Mamre, the Amorite. The one that Zimri-Sin told us about in Harran."

"It just keeps getting worse," she cried. "We are going to settle down by a clan of giants!"

"It is two miles north of the giants in Kiriath-Arba," said Abram. "Do not exaggerate, Sarai."

"I am sorry," she said. "We are only in striking distance of a clan of giants. That makes me feel safer."

"We will be in the midst of three Amorite tribes, the brothers Mamre, Eshcol, and Aner. And we come with the blessing of Zimri-Sin of Haran."

She snorted, "You are the one who is always talking about Zimri-Sin's penchant for tall tales. There is no telling what *that* is going to be like."

This time, Abram did not respond. Instead, he simply said to her, "Sarai, what is wrong, my love?"

She broke down into tears.

"I am sorry. I am so sorry. I have been a nagging wife and I have not supported you. I am so sorry, Abram. Please forgive me."

"There is nothing to forgive," he said. "My heart is broken that you have no children to raise. I cannot help but blame myself."

"No, my love," she said. "It is not your fault. It is mine."

"Listen to me, Sarai," he said. "You have sought to please people all your life with never a thought for yourself. You were born into a family as an outsider and you placed them over your own concerns. You married me, and you became a support to my calling from El Shaddai."

He knew her better than anyone. All her faults as well — and he loved her still.

"To be barren must feel like mockery to your soul."

She hugged him tight, and dried her tears in his shoulder.

"Maybe all this time, El Shaddai has been trying to get your attention. To show you that he cares about just you, and not how you can help other people to fulfill their purposes."

His words penetrated her heart. She had been so busy concerning herself with others that she had considered herself unworthy of El Shaddai's interest. It was an insult to her Creator.

She looked up into his eyes. "Thank you, my lord. You have led me with compassion, understanding and strength."

She smiled with irony, "You have made me feel more beautiful than I ever imagined I could be."

He smiled and kissed her. "You have given me more beauty than I could ever appreciate in a lifetime."

Uh oh. Here he comes again, she thought with amusement as she could feel him pressed against her.

Even at his age, every time he got around her, he could not keep his hands off her.

"I cannot get enough of you," he said wistfully.

"And I cannot get enough of you," she said in return, and kissed him passionately.

Eliezer walked by and remarked wryly, "Get a tent, you two."

They chuckled, realizing they were out in the open. A group of children had gathered, giggling at them.

So they got a tent.

CHAPTER 35

The Oaks of Mamre, standing a couple miles north of Kiriath-Arba, were a sacred grove of trees that were as ancient as the Great Flood. They rose to heaven like the pillars of the earth. As the caravan of Abram drew near to the spot, the mighty trees inspired awe in the clan. Mamre the Amorite owned the grove. Mamre's two brothers, Eshcol and Aner, had settled their tribes around the forest in a triune confederation. They now embraced Abram's tribe as a fourth member.

The Amorites were descended from Canaan, the cursed son of Noah. They inhabited the hill country around Kadesh-Barnea, west of the Jordan Sea. Some of them were giants, and all of them were warriors to be reckoned with.

When the confusion of tongues had occurred in Babel, Abram had been living among the Amorites. As a result, he had received the same language as his host people, which was another reason for choosing to live among their brethren in Canaan.

Mamre, a very big and fat fellow with a jovial temperament, greeted Abram when he arrived at the entrance to the forest. Mamre's brothers were leaner and more serious minded.

"Abram the Habiru!" yelled Mamre. "What took you so long? My brother Zimri-Sin has told me so much about you!"

Habiru was the term among the Amorites for rootless foreigners and invaders. Mamre used it in jest, for he always kept a light heart about everything. He loved to tease, but he loved the people he teased.

Eshcol and Aner greeted him as well. They grasped wrists and kissed each other's cheek.

Then the men saw Sarai. Eshcol gasped. Mamre said, "Abram, I see you are the luckiest man in the world, or I have just arrived in heaven."

Sarai blushed.

"Yes, I hear that often," said Abram. "This is Sarai, my wife."

"It means *princess*," said Mamre, "And what an apt name indeed. Welcome, princess with the undeserving husband."

They laughed.

Abram had always felt like he was a bedraggled cave bear next to a stunning sunrise when he was with her. He knew men looked at him and thought, How did *he* get *her*?

She was living proof that El Shaddai was good to him beyond his wildest dreams.

"Where are your children?" asked Mamre.

Abram sobered, "We do not have any, I am afraid."

"Oh, forgive me then," said Mamre. "May the gods grant you blessings without number." He leaned in, "But may they be mostly boys, because I can tell you my five girls are driving me up a tree."

Everyone chuckled again. Tragedy averted. Mamre was quite the host.

He noticed Sarai staring south to the plateau that rose above the valley. It was several thousand feet high with a thriving city on top.

"I see you have found our neighbors, the village of King Arba," said Mamre.

Sarai looked at Abram as a chill went down her spine.

"A giant clan. But do not worry, there are only a couple hundred of them."

"What are they like?" asked Sarai. "Are they hostile?"

"You can see for yourself," said Mamre with a smile. "We have invited them to your welcoming banquet."

Sarai fainted.

CHAPTER 36

When Sarai came to, she was resting on a large comfortable cushion. She looked around the room. Strange. It was not a tent; it was a wooden structure, made of oak, warm and pleasant. She sighed, stretched her arms, and lay there a moment taking it all in.

These Amorites were quite the cultured society. They seemed to have an eclectic interior design that reflected their wide-spread travels. Tapestries from Haran, golden lampstands from Egypt, an elaborate bed from Elam, and their own wooden, carved, life-sized idol of Amurru, god of the Amorites. He was a storm god who looked like an Amorite shepherd, created in their image. Sarai winced with disgust.

She got up and strode over to the doorway. She opened the door, and found a large porch with a railing on it. It was night. Exhaustion from the ride must have turned her faint into sleep. The glow of fires and lamps filled the air. She noticed the trees all around her. She stared at them in confusion for a moment, and then realized that what she saw were not the trunks and roots of trees close to the ground. She looked at the upper branches of the trees, high up in the air.

She walked to the edge of the porch and looked down. The ground lay seventy-five feet below her. Her stomach churned with butterflies. The home she rested in was part of an entire tree village, built into the forest, fifty or so feet above the ground.

She looked around. Though the night was dark, there was enough light from home lamps and bonfires below to allow her to see a vast interconnecting network of ladders, ropes and bridges joining all the homes clinging to their large trees. Some had spiral staircases going up higher into the branches to other homes. Because the trees were plentiful and quite close, many homes used several close trees as pillars around which to anchor a single home. Others were built around the trunks of older larger trees. All of them displayed solid well-crafted workmanship. The Amorites were a warrior culture, but they appreciated quality in their living space as well.

It took her breath away.

She had the impression that the village held a couple thousand people. She saw several large bonfires, around which a village feast seemed to be in process. She saw some dancing and heard the general murmur of party noises. Abram must have left her to recuperate while he joined them. He was always so thoughtful in allowing her the rest she needed.

She suddenly felt that she was missing out on the community because of her faint heart. She got angry with herself.

Next time, Sarai, she thought to herself, *have a stronger constitution, will you? In fact, I think I will start tonight.*

She rushed back into the tree house to get ready. They had brought her trunk of clothes up from the caravan to the home. She had everything she needed. Since these Amorites were so worldly wise, she wanted to be a bit colorful in her presentation. Sarai was a modest woman. But Abram had bought her many exotic clothes and cosmetics from his own experience with foreign traders. She decided to use the opportunity to take a risk and dress it up a bit.

She decided to go Egyptian. She wore Abram's favorite expensive tightly woven white linen dress with a slit over the right leg for walking. She put on her rings, earrings, necklace, and multiple bracelets, as well as another favorite of Abram's, a golden outer corset and belt.

She painted her eyes with black kohl eyeliner and used a green-hued eye shadow. She finished with henna dye on her lips and nails. She did not wear the black wig, but instead just wore a gorgeous headdress she had received from Pharaoh himself when she was in his keeping. She did not want to look like she was an Egyptian, just to wear it as a style, so her normal wavy blonde hair made that distinction clear.

She hurried as fast as she could and was ready within the hour.

She made her way out to the balcony. She found a roped elevator with a hand-drawn pulley system that she easily figured out. She let herself down to the ground to go find her husband. She got butterflies in her stomach, knowing she would surprise him with great pleasure.

His oft spoken words echoed in her mind and made her smile, *When I see you, I just cannot help myself. So I help myself.* She loved being a feast for his senses. She loved having her husband desiring her. She knew it would be difficult for him to enjoy the party, once he saw her. He would not be able to think about anything else but her.

She shivered again with excitement. The elevator reached the forest floor, and she got off it. She walked toward the feast to find her Abram.

As she approached the main body of people, she heard the music rise above the din. It was quite engaging.

She thought, *These people know how to enjoy themselves.*

She could not see through the large group of bodies pressing in to get a good view of the festivities. She recognized some from her own caravan. This would be where Abram as the guest of honor would be. She began to excuse herself as she tried to nudge her way through the crowd.

Suddenly, the men started to notice her. They stared. Others stepped back and let her through. They began to form a pathway for her, like some kind of gauntlet. It sent a chill down her spine to have so many men looking at her.

She hated the attention and thought to herself, *I knew I should not have dressed up like this. I thought it would be no big deal. I thought I would not stand out from the other women.*

In truth, the other women were dressed outrageously, and Sarai was very modest by comparison.

So why is everyone looking at me?

She kept on walking, hoping she would find Abram, so she could hide herself behind him.

Finally, the gauntlet opened up to a group of dancers performing before a dining table staffed with dignitaries. In the middle of the table sat Abram.

She saw him and instinctively went toward him.

She did not notice that the crowd had not merely parted for her. It quieted down, as more men and women saw Sarai approaching.

The music stopped. The dancers stopped. Sarai found herself in the middle of the dance floor, all alone in an unexpected silence, with everyone staring at her.

She started to panic. She trembled.

Then Abram saw her. At first, he stared at her as if he did not know her. He really had not expected to see her dressed as she was. It had taken him by surprise. She could see it in his eyes, an attraction she remembered from when he first saw her. It was like being noticed all over again.

Then the familiarity came to his eyes and he smiled.

And she felt safe again.

A giant strode out in front of the dinner table and bowed to her on one knee. He was adorned as a chieftain, a giant chieftain about ten feet tall. She suddenly remembered that they were to meet the Nephilim king Arba of Kiriath-Arba.

She filled with fright.

When the giant spoke, she could not understand him. A human translator accompanied him and announced for everyone, "What goddess has graced our presence this evening? Anat? Asherah, escort of the mighty El?"

She froze in terror. What was he talking about?

She looked around her to see if there was some goddess who had stepped in behind her. Maybe that was why everyone was acting so strangely.

But there was no one behind her.

She turned back to see Abram approaching her with arms open wide. His own translator echoed his words in a foreign tongue.

"Good King Arba, this is a woman far more glorious than any Queen of Heaven. This is my beautiful wife, Sarai!"

Everyone applauded.

Abram reached Sarai and whispered in her ear, "Fear not, my beautifulicious. Come with me."

He led her over to the worshipful King Arba, still on his knee on the ground. From behind him, came the voice of one very jealous wife, "Enough, Arba! Stop your gawking. She is no goddess."

Arba's wife appeared next to him as Abram introduced them.

"Sarai, this is King Arba, the founder of Kiriath-Arba, and his Queen, Naqiya."

His translators repeated his words for Arba.

Sarai bowed respectfully to the two giants. They towered over her, almost twice her size. They were large-boned people with fair skin and blonde hair like her own. They had thick, large necks that were disproportionately long, but extravagantly ornamented with huge gold and jeweled necklaces. She also noticed that they had the extra sixth digit on each hand, common to the Nephilim. They were at once both terrifying and regal. Sarai could not help herself from staring right back.

Arba was hypnotized by Sarai. Naqiya rolled her eyes. "You might want to stop drooling, my king. It might offend our visitors."

"My apologies," said Arba, wiping his mouth. "It is a pleasant surprise to meet you, Sarai. You are as lovely as your husband had warned us."

His human translated.

Sarai looked down embarrassed. "Thank you, King Arba."

Abram muttered under his breath to Sarai, "*More* lovely and beautiful."

Arba continued, "Dare I inquire if you are well from your fainting spell of earlier?"

"Yes, I am, thank you," she replied. "It was an exhausting journey." She tried to avoid the real reason for her passing out.

Mamre stepped up and said, "Come, Sarai, I have put out plenty of food and spirits to raise your countenance!" He pulled Abram and Sarai back to the table.

Arba stood watching Sarai as they walked back to the table.

Naqiya pulled Arba along, whispering in his ear, "She is not a meal to eat, husband. We have plenty of that on the dinner table."

Arba shook himself out of his trance and followed her back to their positions, to continue the feast.

The music resumed. The dancing continued. The feast was back on.

All through the dinner, Arba could not take his eyes off of Sarai. He was clearly smitten with her beauty and she could see the lust in his eyes. She found it creepy. She clung closer to Abram, who tried his best to divert the king's attention with exciting stories of Mesopotamia, wild tales of earthquakes, tumbling towers, confusion of tongues, and the fall of the Kingdom of Nimrod.

The feast was in Abram's honor, so he could not leave early. It would be disrespectful. Arba graciously accepted their new settlers to the forest without hostility. Though Mamre and his brothers were not subjects of Arba, it was good diplomacy to allow their Nephilim neighbors the friendly gesture of meeting the intended new residents. It helped communicate a lack of aggression on the part of the Amorites.

Finally, the night wound down. Many left. Arba pulled Abram aside, looking around to make sure his queen was not nearby. His translator shadowed him.

"Abram," said Arba, "I am a very rich king. I have gold, silver and jewels beyond measure. Just tell me what you want and I will give you your hearts' desire in exchange for your Sarai."

"She is my wife," said Abram, insulted by the impertinence.

"So?" said Arba. "Do you not have others to spare?"

"No. But even if I did, Sarai is the most glorious treasure I could ever have. She is beyond riches. She is not for sale, and I would die for her." Abram had determined he was never going to let another Egypt happen again. That had been the biggest mistake in his life. He was only too blessed to have a wife godlier than he, who forgave him for such a cowardly act. Yet here he was, faced with the same problem as before: a greedy ruler with an insatiable hunger for Sarai.

Not this time.

He was glad he had been practicing the way of the Karabu in late-night secrecy. His body was becoming wired and ready to spring into action, should this pompous oaf become aggressive.

Arba thought to himself, *One day you will die for her, little man.*

Finally, Arba backed down. "Well, I applaud your devotion and I welcome you and your priceless wife to our land in peace."

It was a complete switch. Arba dropped his pursuit like a child with a deficit of attention and moved on to the next item of interest. Now, he was all business.

"I only ask that you keep your flocks from grazing on the northern acreage of the plateau."

"I will respect your wishes," said Abram. "And I thank you for your understanding and gracious acceptance." He hoped he had dodged a dagger.

But Arba had not dropped Sarai from his mind at all. It was merely a ploy. No, he would never forget Sarai, the most beautiful object of desire he had seen in all of Canaan. The fact that she was a bit older than usual made it all the more unique and tasty to him. It would only benefit his cause for Abram to be lulled into a sense of safety and acceptance. He did not know how he might take this goddess of beauty for his own without all-out war. But he had time to think — and plan.

CHAPTER 37

A year passed. In Borsippa, Semiramis grew impatient. Nimrod's madness was increasing. She wanted to get Mardon on the throne as soon as possible. Nimrod would have fits of rage when things did not go his way. One time, he killed the royal chef and several servers when a meal of fowl was served with an arrow flint still stuck in the bird. It was an obvious oversight but Nimrod construed it as an attempt on his life.

Today, she planned to bring something up again. Nimrod had returned from a hunt on the steppe. She dressed in an alluring outfit reminiscent of her past life as a harlot. She entered Nimrod's bathhouse and stood before him. It had been months since they had shared a bed. He was becoming less and less interested in her and was taking to male servants. She had hoped to arouse his interest anew.

He watched her approach him. He sat comfortably in his bath. She brought two minstrels with her to play romantic music in the background. He stared at her as she moved her body in a hypnotic serpentine way, removing her outfit.

Nimrod watched her with lifeless eyes, daring her to keep going.

So she did. She entered the water and slid below the surface to pleasure him.

But he received no pleasure. He held her head below the water until she began to struggle.

He let her go and she burst from the water coughing and gasping for air.

Then, he assaulted her with blows to her face and body.

He could no longer have normal sexual relations. His descent into depravity had stolen any ability to enter into beauty, love, or normal sensuality. He had to treat his sexual partners as victims with force. He had to rape or he would not find satisfaction.

He nearly drowned her several times. Bringing her to the edge of death excited him the most. He considered killing her, but of course, she was the queen. He needed her to administer the kingdom, given his lack of interest in petty bureaucracy.

She had become devious and controlling in her ruling. He knew what she did, but he did not care. He knew she craved power and desperately wanted to put their son Mardon on the throne as her puppet. He had his spies. If he caught wind of a planned coup or assassination, he would immediately execute her. Until then, she was of use to him. He did not want to handle the day-to-day problems of ruling over people. And he certainly could not trust anyone else either.

If she thought Mardon would do her bidding, she was only fooling herself. Nimrod had decided that he would not kill Mardon. Should Nimrod fail to achieve his satisfaction against El Shaddai for taking away his kingdom, Mardon was his final dice to play. Nimrod would find some final pleasure in his own passing, knowing that he was unleashing hell on earth with the ascent of Mardon to the throne.

He lay in the bloody water, recovering his own breath.

Semiramis limped over to him and laid her head on his chest. He had blackened one of her eyes, making it swell up until she squinted. She raised her bruised arm and stroked the hair on his chest. She coughed up some of the water from her lungs. She knew she needed to get out of the water soon to bandage her wounds, or she would die from loss of blood. But for just this minute, she wanted to submit to her king, her husband.

Her silent tears blended with the water streaming down her purple-bruised cheeks. She wheezed with the pain of a couple of broken ribs.

Nimrod stared out into the distance. "If you are going to ask me to install Mardon as co-regent," he said, "you are going to be sorely displeased."

She pulled back and looked at him with surprise. He knew why she was there. It made her boil.

But she kept her cool.

"Nimrod, I cannot handle the administration of the kingdom by myself any longer. I am getting old and it is overwhelming me."

"You will have to make do," he said.

"You are never here," she protested.

"Precisely why I do not want him as co-regent," he said. "I do not trust him in my absence."

"Then why have you bothered to father him and train him all these years?"

"He will have his day. Right now, I am more concerned about building my armed forces. I have the numbers, but they are untrained. Mostly captured slaves and civilians."

She stood up and glared down on him. "Will you continue to your dying hour in this obsessive pursuit of the impossible?"

He glanced up at her, and said simply, "Yes."

"We are cursed of El Shaddai. What do you hope to achieve?"

He grabbed her small slender throat and drew her close to his giant frame.

He answered, "But one thing: To vanquish his Chosen Seed."

He shoved her away like an unwanted pet.

She stormed out of the bath, grabbing her clothes.

He watched her with cold, unfeeling eyes as she limped out of the bathhouse.

Semiramis gave up planning a coup. She knew that Nimrod was too paranoid and would see it coming. He had too many spies. There was only one way she would ever see him overthrown, and that would be in battle with a king mightier than he. Before the Dispersion, it would have been impossible. But now, he was just another king, in a world of kings fighting for dominance.

It gave her some satisfaction to know that he was descending into the rage of madness in the face of his humiliating loss of power.

In her private drawing room, Semiramis sat down and composed a letter on a clay tablet. She placed it in its protective enclosure and sealed it with the Queen's seal. Death awaited anyone who opened it other than its intended recipient.

The intended recipient was King Chedorlaomer of Elam, Nimrod's most feared nemesis.

CHAPTER 38

During the first year since he had parted from Abram, Lot had moved his tent near Sodom, learned the rudiments of their language, sold his entire stock and herd, and moved into the city. He released his household to find their own ways in their new urban lifestyle. He found a woman named Ado, who had no family, married her, and their first child was on its way.

He had moved quickly because he knew what he wanted. He had been dreaming of this for so long, he did not want to wait any longer.

At first, it had been exciting. Life in a big city was bustling and energetic. People seemed more progressive than in the rural areas. They were more open-minded about things. They did not judge you for being different, because everyone was different. Yet, everyone was united by a common vision: the city-state.

It was as if the city was itself one big family of communal existence, with the king as the father or midwife, taking care of children. This made real families less necessary. Everyone was equal with one another and all were citizens of the state. The state protected as many aspects of life as was possible, from the wages of the workers to the welfare of those who could not work. It took the pressure off immediate families to shoulder each other's burdens. The king would take care of them. They would simply ship their aged and infirm off to government communes, so they could get back to maximizing their service for the collective.

The city was something bigger than the individual, something higher than one's self to live for. The people found their meaning and purpose in that higher cause. The individual would die and go to Sheol, but the city that they had invested their lives in would go on forever.

After his initial excitement wore down, Lot began to see that all was not well in the "Cities of Love."

The government promoted tolerance of all religious devotion. They maintained shrines for gods from all over Canaan. Ashtart was the supreme goddess of the pentapolis and resided in Sodom, entertaining visiting deities like Molech, Asherah and Dagon.

There was tolerance for all the gods — except one: El Shaddai, the Creator God of all things, the god that Lot worshipped. El Shaddai was burned in effigy, mocked and criticized as being, ironically, an intolerant tyrant who demanded exclusive devotion and was thus unworthy of anything but ridicule. If anyone was discovered to have any kind of personal devotion to El Shaddai, they were imprisoned, tortured and made an example of.

Needless to say, Lot kept his faith to himself. He told no one of his family background, for fear of them discovering his religion. He never told anyone who he really was.

He also saw that the society that touted itself as the "Cities of Love" was actually quite inhospitable to strangers and visitors. Traveling merchants who came to sell their wares in the cities were usually beat up and run out of town, because they were considered greedy. In reality, it was because their prices were so cheap. But the local workers maintained a greedy control over the marketplace. The city took so much of the workers' income, they barely had enough to live on. So, they did not want anyone else to have what they could not.

There were no weapons in the city, because of the weapons control laws. Yet, Lot had seen more murders in this city than he had in any of the cities of Mesopotamia that had no such laws. He understood how some could believe that the implements of violence caused such strife. But he knew better. He knew evil was bound up in the heart of mankind. If you took away swords from good men, then only evil men would find a way to have swords, and they would end up killing the good.

But the depth of depravity that shook his soul most was the sexual perversity that saturated the cities. There was no respect for persons, animals or even things, as they engaged in rampant carnal excess. Regardless of the abortifacient herbs and potions, there was an explosion of births that the citizens had no desire to take responsibility for. This epidemic of unwanted infants became a source for human sacrifice to Molech, the underworld deity. Some just left their infants in the wilderness, to die of exposure to the elements and wild animals. It was called a "necessary evil." Everyone claimed it was a tragedy so many babies had to be sacrificed, but they fought for a mother's right to sacrifice her offspring or the gods would curse them with oppression. Ironically, oppression was what Lot constantly felt, living there as a citizen.

As an elder in the city gates, he had the undesirable privilege of knowing some of the darkest secrets behind the curtains of the ruling class of Ashtart. He discovered that she was breeding giants through the line of Canaan and sending them to different parts of the country. She was engaging in the Sacred Marriage rite with the daughters of men.

Such violation of the heavenly earthly divide had been a strictly forbidden behavior, since the Flood. Though Ashtart had made a commitment to Mastema to avoid these excesses that brought down such judgment, she could not help herself. She could not keep away from her taste for the strange flesh of humans. She was addicted to it, and she was getting more strident about her defiance. Word was getting out. Even humans like Lot were catching wind of her perilous behavior.

Lot was grieved to his soul. But he could not pack up and leave. He had released most of his servants and household and had sold everything. He was invested. He reasoned that the only way he might have a positive influence on his community was to be involved with the political process, to try to bring change from within. Maybe he could make a difference by becoming an elder of the city. These men acted as judges over the disputes of the people. They sat in the city gates and rendered decisions that became binding under the authority of the king.

So he continued to hide his religious devotion to El Shaddai, and joined the government to try to make a difference.

He had no idea what was coming.

CHAPTER 39

Good and Mighty King Chedorlaomer, I write this letter to you with a sad and grieved heart. Nimrod, the king of Shinar has gone mad. He is no longer competent to reign in this region. He is wantonly executing random citizens, he is causing starvation of his people, and he is planning to reconquer his lost territory to recreate a new slave empire.

But as of yet, his armed forces are weak and untrained. He is a prime target for victory over this region and I plead on behalf of the people of Shinar that you come and liberate us from this tyranny.

I can assure you that his son, Mardon, would be a fair ruler and obedient, devoted vassal of your lordship, if he should be allowed to ascend to the throne in your good graces.

Please make haste before Nimrod discovers my loyalty to you. And make sure to execute the bearer of this letter.

Forever in your debt,
Queen Semiramis of Shinar.

Chedorlaomer looked up from reading the clay tablet. He gazed at the messenger who waited for a command or reply to be sent. The king nodded to the guard behind the messenger, who promptly drew his dagger and killed the messenger.

Chedorlaomer grinned with satisfaction. He had been waiting for just this opportunity. In the past, he had been the fiercest of

Nimrod's vassal rulers. He had been used by the mighty hunter king to subdue Sodom and Gomorrah and the cities of the plain in Canaan and to secure the King's Highway for safe trade. He had done Nimrod's bidding with clenched teeth, just waiting for the fall of the cruel despot.

That fall had come with the Confusion of Tongues and the Great Dispersion. Babel was demolished and abandoned. But he had thought Nimrod was gone, vanished into Sheol. He had, after all, lost everything from his invincible golem army, to his mighty cosmic mountain, to his guardian storm god.

It was delightful just to remember the glorious downfall. And even more satisfying that Chedorlaomer had gained Nimrod's most valued advantage.

He considered it outrageous that Nimrod was on the rise again. Fallen kings were never so obstinate as to think they could regain their former glory. But then again, Nimrod was not the usual fallen king. He was a Naphil giant, born of exalted pride, and his obsession, blind to all reason.

He handed the tablet to his guardian counselor and asked, "What say you? Shall I muster my forces for the final slaughter of King Nimrod?"

The guardian counselor took the tablet and read it. He crushed it into dust in his huge muscular hands. "I have a better plan," he said.

Chedorlaomer smiled back at the mighty storm god Marduk, king of the gods.

CHAPTER 40

The village of Kiriath-Arba rested on the side of a large hill, overlooking a valley rich with springs and wells. It was a prime location for defense. They could see the valley all around them for miles. The backside of the hill was virtually inaccessible. They were a clan of only a few hundred giants, but were well-trained warriors between eight and eleven feet tall. They were a fair-skinned people, with blonde and red hair, a sixth finger and toe on each hand and foot, and unusually long, muscular necks that gave them a look of fierceness in battle. They seemed to be built for war.

King Arba had plans to expand his territory when he had the numbers. He actually had designs on the whole of Canaan. He was quite ambitious and Queen Naqiya would often tease him by calling him "King of Canaan."

They used regular humans as servants and lived in stone-built homes. They built a circular religious site at the top of the hill, with megalithic stones that were aligned with the stars to create an astronomical microcosm of the universe. They believed that by aligning themselves with the stars, they would be aligned with the gods.

In the center of the megalithic circles stood an upraised altar for excarnation, the practice of leaving the dead out to be de-fleshed by vultures before having the bones placed in ossuaries for burial.

A giant was out amongst the megaliths tending to a recently dead relative when he saw the approach of the caravan of donkeys in the distance. He ran and told the King, who came out to meet the caravan arriving at the village.

The caravan consisted of twenty mules, carrying loads of gold, silver, copper and gemstones. It had come from the Oaks of Mamre, or more accurately, was returning from the Oaks of Mamre.

When Arba saw the payload of precious metals and jewels, he screamed with anger at the top of his lungs. He stomped back to his stone palace and began demolishing things. He crushed two human servants before Queen Naqiya arrived to try to calm him down.

She was newly pregnant.

She was disgusted by the sight she found.

"You are pathetic," she said to him.

He wept tears of anger. He looked up at her, breathing hard. His eyes filled with hatred.

She did not stop.

"How dare you ransom our village wealth to satisfy your juvenile fantasies of that whore."

He stared at her. She was referring to Sarai of course and he did not hide it from her. Naqiya had what she wanted, carrying the royal seedline. But he was never satisfied with what he had. He always wanted was not his.

"Look at you," she continued. "You are like a little child throwing a tantrum, because Abram does not want your toys, but you want his. And he has more moral character than you. He sent back your bribe, which makes you look even more inferior and pathetic."

Arba had been obsessing over Sarai the entire year since he had first seen her at that feast in her Egyptian finery. He could not get her out of his mind. He would fantasize about her when he was with his wife or his concubines. He wanted her and he could not have her. He was going mad because of it. He sent spies to report to him her every movement. He was losing his focus on ruling and taking risks with the community.

This latest deed was the most foolhardy. He thought that by sending a caravan of half his riches with trust to Abram, it might impress him and tempt him to consider the offer as never before. These were riches accumulated from around the world. Exotic ornamentation and rare gems that would appeal to any man's greed. Or so Arba thought.

But he was wrong about Abram. It made him flush with rage.

Naqiya continued to berate him. "You have endangered this village with your piggish slavery to your lust. What kind of king would give away half his kingdom for a dried up old prune?"

Arba stood up and walked up to Naqiya — and punched her in the face with his fist. She grunted and fell down to the floor. Blood ran from her broken nose.

She was disoriented. She tried to get up.

He stomped down on her hand with his heel.

She screamed in pain.

He reached down and pulled her up by her hair, almost ripping it from her scalp. He lifted her up to his face. She was too dizzy to see straight. She started to pass out. He slapped her back to the present.

"The only reason I did not kill you is because you carry my son. Never speak to me that way again, or I shall cut my offspring from your belly and leave you behind."

He dropped her to the floor and turned to leave.

A silent servant with eyes wide open in fright accosted him.

"What is it?"

"M-my Lord," said the servant. "You have some visitors."

"Who?" he barked.

"Traveling hierodules of Ashtart."

Arba had wondered what hierodules of Ashtart would want with him. But he was commissioned by Ashtart in Sodom, so he knew it was not wise to keep her waiting or cross her in any way. He met with them out by his stone palace entrance.

When he arrived, his Naphil sixth sense made him pause. He saw before him small slender hierodules dressed in traveling robes. But he knew they were dangerous. They were tattooed appropriately for temple workers and were, as a matter of fact, quite attractive. Yet, there was something inhuman about them but he could not place it. Their eyes were the only visible giveaway. One had bright ochre irises and small pupils and the other had completely black eyes with no white at all. Then he realized what the second one reminded him of. He was a falconer himself and knew those eyes anywhere. They were the eyes of a peregrine falcon.

They were already accompanied by two of Arba's guards, so he thought he would not order more guards for security. It might alarm these strangers. Although they were quite small and manageable, he knew that such disadvantages could afford the element of surprise when combined with secret fighting skills or hidden sorcery.

They bowed and spoke in his tongue, "Your majesty."

"Please forgive my minimum guard," he said to the visitors. "It is royal protocol. Allow me to entertain you in my chambers."

The guards led the female visitors to a meeting hall in the stone palace. Once inside the room, Arba noticed how they moved with preternatural grace and elegance. He mused again how attractive they were. But he suspected that beneath that elegance and beauty was hidden danger.

He made a chirping whistle and servants brought some bread, fruit and wine.

"You must be tired from your journeys," said Arba. "You are not from around here?"

The feline one spoke. Her voice was soothing and sensuous.

"My name is Zula, and this is Laliya. We have been commissioned by Ashtart of Sodom to find a rogue individual who may have been in these parts. We request your kind help, good King Arba."

It made sense to him. Nothing seemed out of place.

"Do you have your commission from Ashtart?" he asked.

"Unfortunately, we do not," replied Zula. "We were robbed in the Negeb."

That sounded reasonable enough. The Negeb desert crawled with nomadic Amorites, who were notorious for their pirate activities. But for these two beautiful, slight women to be left unscathed? That did not seem right.

The falcon-eyed one interrupted Arba's inner questioning. She decided to be as bold and frank as possible to spare the doubts.

"We are looking for a man named Abram of Haran. We believe he has a wife named Sarai and a small clan. Our interest is private, but we do provide reward for any help that may lead us to him."

Her boldness worked. The honesty washed away all the previous questions.

Arba now knew Ashtart did not commission these two women. He understood why they had been able to travel unmolested in this brutal country. He knew why his sixth sense of danger alerted him in their presence. But their deception did not bother him anymore. He knew he was talking to a pair of assassins. And if a pair of assassins was looking for Abram of Haran, then he might finally get what he had been lusting after for too long.

He replied, "Rejoice this day, hierodules. For your search is over. I know the man of whom you speak."

They looked at each other with their otherworldly eyes.

"And I only ask for one small reward in return."

CHAPTER 41

The city of Borsippa lay about eleven miles southwest of the ruins of Babel. It was a sister city that Nimrod had turned into his new center of rule. Unlike Babel, it did not have protective walls. So when Nimrod received word of Chedorlaomer's approach with his armies of Elam, he knew he would have to muster every soldier from the surrounding cities of Kish, Akkad, and Sippar, as well as every civilian who had a pitchfork or tree ax to fight for their lives. Without walls to hide behind, they needed large numbers to face the trained armies of Elam.

Nimrod gathered seven hundred thousand soldiers and civilians on the plains of Shinar to meet Chedorlaomer's mere five thousand elite warriors. Nimrod had fourteen times the number of Elam's forces, but it would not be as easy as it seemed.

Nimrod's armies were not trained, so he knew he would have to pour myriads of souls into the slaughter with the hopes of wearying the king of Elam's fighting forces with too many to kill. Then Nimrod would ride his small guard of Nephilim into their exhausted ranks and seek to take out the king himself.

Nimrod cared not one whit for the lives of his subjects. He would sacrifice them all in order to achieve victory.

He would sacrifice his own family if he could.

It was time for Mardon to experience battle. He would lead a unit of the giants into battle. Nimrod hoped that Mardon would be killed in combat, so he could rid himself of his vile miscreant of an offspring. It might jeopardize his other plans for a legacy of destruction, but he would restrategize if that happened.

Mardon had been taught leadership and fighting skills by his father. He had the hardness of heart that would make him capable of handling the horrors of war. But torturing captive victims and beating servants was not the same as facing trained warriors. He carried some anxiety about combat, so he commissioned two of his best Nephilim warriors to guard him in the fight.

When Semiramis heard of the impending war, she called Mardon to her private chambers and sought to inspire him in the way she best knew how — sexual depravity.

In the throes of their unspeakable act, he bit a small piece of her ear off. When Semiramis slapped him and clutched her bleeding ear in pain, he claimed it as a means of absorbing some of her power into his own for the battle. It was like eating the flesh of deity he said. They finished their perverse tryst under the hidden, watchful eyes of Nimrod's spy.

As they lay on the sheets, Mardon told her, "The plans are set. I have spoken with my contingent of Gibborim warriors."

She looked at him with surprise. "They are loyal to you?"

He said, "They are just as dissatisfied with their father and king as we are — as all of Shinar is. They even believe the other Nephilim will join us when we carry it out."

Semiramis smiled. "We may yet have our day, dear son."

· · · · ·

Morning rose over the armies facing each other on the battlefield plains of Babel. Nimrod and Mardon each commanded two ranks of a hundred giant warriors, holding them to the rear of their seven hundred thousand-man army. The conscripted warriors were scattered without formation. They suffered a lack of proper combat gear and weapons. They were overworked and underfed, due to Semiramis' opulent demands on the king's treasury. They were rebuilding a kingdom after all.

Before them stood the warriors of Elam, led by Chedorlaomer. Five thousand of the best-trained men of the Eastern kingdoms. Their phalanxes of soldiers led, their square shields held tightly together, and their long spears thrust through openings. The formation created an impenetrable porcupine-type wall, used for attacking. Behind them waited the regiment of archers, carrying the newer developed composite bow made of horn, wood, and metal. It could launch arrows twice as far and with twice as much force as the normal bows.

Nimrod saw what was coming. It was going to be a massacre. But he had no other choice.

The horns of war bellowed.

Chedorlaomer raised his sword as a signal. The phalanxes began to inch forward. They were in no hurry.

The forces of Nimrod saw the attack and began to rush the field.

Behind the Elamite phalanxes, the archers drew their bows, a thousand of them, and released into the air a volley of death upon the advancing soldiers of Shinar. They quickly reloaded and fired, over and over again. It was a thunderstorm of lightning bolts piercing the armies of Nimrod by the thousands. They had to climb over their own dead just to keep advancing.

By the time the two forces met in the field, the phalanxes with their disciplined maneuvers were skewering the random untrained forces like shiskabobs. They pushed the army of Shinar back.

But then, all were stopped in their tracks.

Nimrod had been right. The dead bodies were too high for the phalanxes to climb without breaking ranks. That would leave them open to attack. So they backed off.

A hundred thousand had already been killed. It was the massacre Nimrod had foreseen. A bloodbath of carnage.

Then Nimrod made the mistake of angrily sallying out with his soldiers among the heaps of the dead.

Another volley of arrows from Elam's forces filled the sky.

Mardon had stayed safely behind the field of combat. Even so, two arrows pierced his body, one through his liver and the other through his lung, grazing his heart. He fell from his horse. He yelled out to his guard, "Go! Now! As we planned!"

The Nephilim guard left him and galloped toward Nimrod. Mardon cursed the gods and fate through wheezing breaths.

The giant warriors had been commanded by Mardon to kill Nimrod in the course of battle so that Mardon might rise to the throne and end the tyranny. They did not count on their brothers guarding Nimrod to still be loyal. When the Gibborim conspirators reached Nimrod, his Gibborim countered them. It created enough confusion for Nimrod to lose control of the battlefield.

His forces ran into a slaughter. By the time they surrendered, only a hundred thousand were still alive. Six hundred thousand soldiers had been wiped out.

The Nephilim had almost killed one another in the fight over Nimrod, but the survivors were captured along with their king.

The field lay saturated in blood. The cries of dying soldiers filled the air. The forces of Elam moved in on the city. Nimrod was chained and brought to the prison.

In the rear guard of the Shinarian army, Mardon had passed out. When he came to, he stared up into the sun at the face of a god.

It was the mighty warrior Marduk. He leaned down into the blood and mud and stroked Mardon's hair.

"You are the son of Nimrod," he said.

Mardon shivered with fear. "Have mercy."

"Mercy, I am afraid, is not a virtue I hold dear. But you are dying, human. And my plans are not for you, but for your father. I have no further use for you."

Marduk brandished his mace with a single mighty swing, and continued on his way.

Semiramis drew her bath with very warm, almost hot, water. She let her naked body down into the water of the ground pool. The steam penetrated her nostrils and the heat warmed the chill of her body. Two servants scrubbed her lightly with sponges.

She was cleaning herself for her meeting with Chedorlaomer, the conquering king of her city, of her kingdom.

She had always felt she deserved the kingdom far more than Nimrod, who was just a brutish boor trampling everything without discretion. But she had learned that her son Mardon was dead, so she would never see that specific dream fulfilled. She heard Nimrod was confined in the prison, probably to be dragged through the streets in triumph and hanged from the gallows before the watching world.

Another servant anointed her hair with oil. Some of it ran down her face and stung her bruised eye.

She dismissed her servants and relaxed beneath the cleansing waters.

She had fought so long and so hard to achieve her desire of power, and now she felt like it had all come crashing in on her. It was not fair. She was a woman. She had few advantages in a world of men. She was the useful tool of Nimrod, now she would probably become the useful tool of Chedorlaomer.

She had told herself long ago that she was never going to be the tool of any man again.

She pulled a dagger out of her bag to finish herself.

She put it to her wrists and opened her veins.

The blood poured out of her and into the pool in a spreading stain of red.

She became lightheaded, dizzy.

She slipped into unconsciousness, and then oblivion below the waters.

She was dead.

She had finally escaped her miserable life.

But she would not escape her Maker.

CHAPTER 42

A long, thin plume of reddish smoke drifted up from a bonfire in the center of Kiriath-Arba. The hierodules Zula and Laliya had given Arba some special powder to throw in the fire to create the strange colored smoke. They did it once a day for several days until the other two hierodules, Zakita and Kulla, finally arrived to meet them on the raised plateau.

The four of them were now together and briefed on Abram's location in the Oaks of Mamre. They planned their scheme. It would require complete surprise in order to kidnap Abram without being discovered by the clan.

Arba told them not to worry about the red smoke being a warning to the Amorites. Arba explained that they often did such things in their funerals so Mamre would consider it part of their rituals.

The assassins waited until evening to set out for Mamre.

It was a full moon, the optimum conditions for their feline and avian senses.

They bathed and donned dark clothes with their blades stored in scabbards and their bows and arrows on their backs.

They were virtually invisible, stealthy and lethal, and they were ready to capture their prey.

• • • • •

It was harvest time in the five cities of the plain. That meant it was time for the Festival of the Burning God.

It was the biggest event of the year, held in the Valley of Siddim, just south of the tar pits. It was a weeklong celebration, where everyone was free from their employment to engage in non-stop carnival of pleasures. A better term might be "circus of freaks," as the participants would clothe themselves in outrageous costumes. Men would dress as women, women as men, some would parade themselves naked through the streets. Others walked about in bizarre wardrobes that defied gender — and good taste. Everything was acceptable, nothing was forbidden.

It was all part of Ashtart's ongoing attack on El Shaddai, by degrading humanity created in his image. Grotesque replaced normal, freakishness replaced beauty, madness replaced reason, vice replaced virtue.

At the end of the festival, a huge effigy of El Shaddai "the unseen god" was built out of wood and pelted with their excrement before being set aflame in a delirious drug-induced ecstasy, courtesy of the city sorcerers. Sometimes, they would trap captured El Shaddai followers in the effigy to burn them alive.

As Lot walked through the festival, he felt the urge to vomit, it was so repulsive to him. He felt completely ineffectual in his campaign to instill a sense of righteousness in Sodom. He had tried to get citizens to boycott the event because of its wickedness, but to no avail. He had sought to pass laws that would protect traveling merchants from abuse, strangers in need of hospitality, the abandoned and sacrificed infants, and the followers of El Shaddai as victims of oppression, but the judges were all in league with the king and Ashtart. They had ruled that anyone who was not of the progressive Cities of Love and tolerance were to be treated with zero tolerance and deserved to be punished.

That progressive tolerance assaulted his senses as he made his way to the meeting he was to have with the king of Sodom. He passed by pens that contained people engaging in unspeakable acts.

The stench of refuse filled the air as he came upon a corridor of the arts. Another part of Ashtart's plan of debasing the image of Elohim in mankind was to inspire an obsession with excrement in their art. Urine and feces were celebrated in sculpture, wall and vase paintings, and public theatre, in a kind of fashionable cynicism. As the saying went, "In the end, we are all just excrement."

When Lot reached the king's tent, the Nephilim guards at the entrance admitted him, and ushered him to the throne where King Bera of Sodom sat. He was an obese blob of a man, whose god was his stomach. He must have weighed close to four hundred pounds and had to have everything widened or extended for him: doorways, chairs, bed, and chariot. He required a half dozen servants just to help him move from throne to chariot to dining table to bed.

He was a puppet of Ashtart, but she was not with him today. In her place stood another man, dressed in royal armor. He had a haughty look in his eye.

Bera said, "Lot! Welcome. You are familiar with our founding father, Canaan, son of Ham?"

Lot bowed toward Canaan, who did not respond.

"He it is who, under the patronage of the illustrious Ashtart, has built our mighty pentapolis and seeded the population of this land named after his legacy."

The legacy of the Seed of the Serpent, thought Lot.

Bera got right down to business. "Lot, you have been causing a stir again amidst our fine citizens. I cannot have an elder of the gates crowing about 'wickedness and judgment' and other mean-spirited condemnations. You are offending a lot of people with your hateful rhetoric. We are the Cities of Love. Can you not be more discreet and keep your private beliefs to yourself?"

"Your majesty," replied Lot. "My firstborn daughter died at the hands of these 'citizens of love' for helping a poor, starving man."

His young daughter, Paltith, simply gave food and water to a traveling merchant who had been beaten, stripped bare, and left for dead. When the mob that occupied Sodom's marketplace found out, they burned her at the stake. Sodomites hated merchants who made money because Sodomites were slaves of the government. They hated children of normal families because they were children of the city and of Ashtart.

Lot feared for the lives of his remaining twin daughters.

"Lot, I do not want to make light of your daughter, but you know the laws. The *government* is supposed to help the poor. Individual charity is forbidden."

"Forgive my impertinence, your majesty. I will seek to uphold the law and affirm your rule."

The fact of the matter was that Lot was not "crowing about wickedness and judgment," with "hateful rhetoric." That was all wicked rumors and hateful gossip. Lot had simply and quietly tried to petition for laws that protected the traditional family unit that had now been completely subverted by the legislation of the pentapolis. Every other form of marriage, from polygamous, to same sex, to other unions once unthinkable, had special rights and privileges not afforded to those who preferred one woman and one man, devoted to each other, with children. He only wanted normal families to be recognized as retaining the rights that all other legal unions and alternative couplings had been given by Ashtart.

He had failed to do so. As a result of the constant suppression of his efforts, he had became more withdrawn and kept his views to himself. The nature of the society seemed an inevitable, unstoppable juggernaut of evil. He just wanted some rest, some respite from the relentless hostility and hate foisted upon him. He was tired of the death threats, sabotage of his work, and vandalism of his home. He had stopped fighting for his "cause." He told himself he would just try to be a silent example of true love to his neighbors, hoping that they might eventually wonder what was different about him and ask him about his different god and different values.

But they never did.

So Lot had become a shell of the man he once was, defeated, depressed, and despairing. He had tried to change his society from within, but it had changed him. It had collared him with suppression, under the guise of "liberation from El Shaddai." He felt completely helpless. He was oppressed, hated, and treated with bigoted intolerance. The irony of it all was that *he* was the one being called oppressive, hateful, bigoted and intolerant.

Canaan watched Lot closely. His memory stirred. There was something about the accent of Lot's language and presence that reminded him of his past. He had studied the genealogies Ashtart had used to discover his own identity as the cursed son of Noah's Ham.

"Who is your father?" asked Canaan.

"Haran ben Terah," said Lot.

"Terah of Ur? The once past prince of Nimrod's host?"

Lot nodded his head weakly.

Canaan's interest piqued. *That was the line of Shem.* Canaan had once been a slave of Nimrod, before Ashtart liberated him and brought him to this new land. She named the land Canaan in his honor as the Seed of the Serpent, whom he had been told would be the warring bloodline against the Seed of Eve.

And that Seed of Eve came through Shem.

"Did your father have siblings?"

"Nahor, my uncle. He lives in Haran."

Canaan watched him like a hawk. He knew Lot was holding back information.

"Any others?" said Canaan, in a condescending singsong voice.

Lot hesitated, but he gave it up. He did not want the king to discover he had been dishonest to this visiting dignitary and punish him later.

"Abram of Haran."

"You are the nephew of Abram ben Terah," mused Canaan. "Where is he now?"

"I do not know," lied Lot. "I think back in Haran."

That was far enough away to warrant giving up any kind of spying on his uncle without great cost and planning.

Lot's status as an elder prevented Canaan from taking him away and torturing him to find out the information he wanted. Canaan did not have the authority to do that to an elder of Sodom. But he would take note of this and keep it tucked away in his mind for a more opportune moment.

For now, he dismissed Lot with a casual wave. "You may go. And please keep your prudish behavior and judgmental attitude to yourself. We are progressive, not primitive. We want to promote love not hate."

Lot bowed and left them.

Canaan smiled to himself with satisfaction. Today was indeed a profitable day. For now, it was time to go pour out his lusts on a four-legged beast.

CHAPTER 43

Nimrod had been working for hours, filing down a small piece of rock he had found in his prison cell. He was half delirious, chained to a large block of stone. The kiln-fired brick walls were not durable enough to secure prisoner's chains, so large stone blocks were imported. Nimrod did not know how long it had been since he had eaten anything. He was forced to sit in his own filth. He mumbled to himself absurd lyrics of poetic madness as he filed the rock down to a sharpened edge. His descent into the raging pit of blocked ambitions was about to be ended. He had lived a life of royalty and excess, becoming a world potentate, only to be demolished and dethroned, but kept alive for misery. He had begun to rebuild his kingdom but was once again drowned in the muck by the hand of a king who had once served him.

His only chance of escape was to take his life. The edge of the stone was now sharp enough to cut his flesh. He raised it with his manacled hands and pressed it to his throat. It was a difficult thing to cut one's own throat. It would have to be done quickly.

Just as he was about to use the primitive cutting edge, the sound of the dungeon door opening stopped him. He placed the rock knife beneath the edge of the large stone to which he was anchored.

Marduk entered the cell with a goatskin flask.

Nimrod thought he might be hallucinating. He had not seen Marduk in years, not since the fall of Babel. He had assumed that Marduk was somehow constrained in Tartarus for his rebellion.

Marduk held out the flask to him.

"It is wine," said the god. "You need your strength."

He handed Nimrod a loaf of freshly baked bread. Nimrod cautiously took the wine and bread and began consuming the loaf like a wild dog before it could be taken from him.

So it was not a hallucination.

Marduk said, "You were not the only one to suffer humiliation and loss at Babel. After the judgment, I sought to rehabilitate my status by joining the strongest ruler in the region who showed the most promise."

Now it all made sense to Nimrod. "Chedorlaomer," he said. "So that is how he knew all about my weakness and strategy."

"King Chedorlaomer is not going to execute you," said Marduk.

Nimrod stopped.

"I persuaded him to reinstall you as his vassal over Shinar, or Akkad, or whatever you are calling it these days."

"Why?" said Nimrod. He still seethed with hatred for Marduk and self-loathing at the prospect of more humiliation.

"Because you are of use to the both of us. Elam is drawing together a force of armies to raid Canaan. The five cities of the plain that Chedorlaomer originally subdued have not paid their taxes for thirteen years. He is going to punish them. The problem is that Ashtart, who was once Ishtar in our good land of Mesopotamia, controls the pentapolis."

Realization dawned on Nimrod. That slut goddess that caused him so much trouble in the past was also Marduk's arch nemesis. They had been at odds for many years. Nimrod knew there would be an eventual confrontation between the two that would split the earth open.

"So what do you need me for?" said Nimrod.

"You are still a mighty general, Nimrod. Chedorlaomer needs you. All you need are trained forces. He can give them to you if you swear allegiance to him."

More degradation and disgrace for Nimrod.

"Why would he trust me? He was my vassal for many years, and I did not treat him with trust."

Marduk leaned closer. "Because I persuaded him."

Nimrod looked into Marduk's powerful eyes. He was still the hypnotic and frighteningly powerful king of the gods, and he was still determined to achieve his plans.

Marduk whispered to him, "Ashtart has been breeding giants in Canaan. They are her minions in various clans and villages and they control the King's Highway. Chedorlaomer cannot afford to lose that trade route with its access to Egypt and up to Amurru. It is an economic lifeline. So he is creating a coalition of three kings to accompany him and wipe out the giant clans to secure the area. You will be one of them, along with Arioch of Ellasar, and Tidal, king of Goiim."

Nimrod was going mad, but he had not yet lost his reason. "Wiping out the giants will wipe out Ashtart's rise to power, securing your advantage."

Marduk grinned. "You and I have always had an understanding in our mutual pursuits. I never forgot that."

Nimrod was already planning on how he might commit suicide once he was freed. He did not want to be a tool of Marduk unless there was something in it for him. And there was nothing of interest to him in fighting other's battles.

"And I have never forgotten what you have always wanted," Marduk added.

Nimrod looked at him curiously. "What do you mean?"

"The source of all your misery and pain, the one born to bring your downfall, and to bear the chosen seedline of El Shaddai resides in Canaan: Abram of Haran."

Nimrod's eyes came alive with a fire within. He now had a reason to live, a reason to abandon his failed pursuit of power and submit himself to another king: revenge. He would be willing to debase himself as a servant to Chedorlaomer, if it allowed him the opportunity to hunt down Abram and kill him.

Nimrod grinned through his rotting teeth. "I give you my word, mighty Marduk, king of the gods," he said, "that I will be a loyal vassal king of Shinar for Chedorlaomer."

Marduk smiled. He knew it would work. Nimrod's obsessive desire to kill Abram would benefit all of them.

Nimrod interrupted Marduk's thoughts. "On one condition. I am allowed to change my name."

"To what?" said Marduk.

"To King Amraphel of Shinar. Nimrod and his family are dead now."

He had done it once before. He had changed his name when he was king of Uruk, to start over with a new identity to create Babylon. Now he would be reborn without the negative baggage of his utter defeat and shame as Nimrod.

Marduk smiled in agreement. "A wise choice, King Amraphel."

Chedorlaomer would have his renewed control of Canaan, Marduk would have his victory over Ashtart, Amraphel would have his revenge on Abram and El Shaddai, and the Seed of Eve would be choked to death for everyone.

CHAPTER 44

The full moon showered the fields outside of Mamre with a blue light. The Amorite night watchmen were lax because of the brightness of the evening. They were certain it was not the kind of night that any enemies would try to sneak up on them.

Four stealthy shadows slipped through the field brush, all the way up to the watchmen, without notice.

They made no noise, moved swiftly, and were upon their prey in mere moments. They were the four hierodule assassins from Nimrod.

Before the four night watchmen on the ground even knew what hit them, they were shredded by the retractable claws and talons of the genetically enhanced killers. The assassins saved their throwing blades for the two up in the trees, who plummeted silently to the ground.

Forests were like a playground for these four trained hunters. Their eyes were made to see in the darkest conditions. The falcon women could spot a mouse in the moonlight at a hundred yards, and though they could not fly, they could jump a full twenty feet and land on prey with talons gripping like vices.

The lioness women could crawl through any terrain in total silence, and climb trees with great ease, using the same claws that could rip through human flesh and even leather armor. Their small slender bodies disguised the powerful explosive strength that was hidden within. They had the strength of several men and the fangs of a lioness of the steppe.

And they were coming for Abram.

It was late. Families slept, with only the men and soldiers still stoking the fires and telling stories of exploits and adventures.

The female killers split up. They intended to listen in on several groups of men around the fires. They were not planning to kill these, because they did not want to draw the rest of the Amorite warriors down on their heads. They were listening to get any information about Abram's whereabouts.

One of the assassins finally overheard some men complaining about Abram's leadership. These must be his people. One of the men told the others to watch their mouths, the patriarch might be able to hear them. The lead assassin, Zula, saw him glance over his shoulder, at a tree house within their hearing range and she knew where their target was.

The four killers climbed the far side of the large oak the soldier had glanced at. They gripped the bark easily in their claws and talons and made it up the fifty or so feet in seconds.

The lights were out. Abram and Sarai were sleeping.

Getting into the tree house was the easy part. Getting out would be more difficult. In exchange for the intelligence from Arba on Abram's whereabouts, they were supposed to capture Sarai along with Abram and bring her back to Kiriath-Arba, before embarking on their return journey to Mesopotamia. But the kidnappers had no intention of fulfilling that agreement. They were going to kill the wife and place Abram unconscious in a carrying sack they brought with them.

Two prisoners were just too cumbersome and added too much danger to their undertaking. Two of the hybrid killers with their strength could carry Abram down the tree and out of the forest, but they would not have the stealth advantage they had coming in. Should they be discovered in their kidnapping, they would have a difficult time outrunning their pursuers. No, if they were discovered, they would have to kill him and cut off his head to bring back as a trophy of proof for Nimrod. They would have at least a two day jump on Arba should he try to go after them. They would take the backwoods instead of the King's Highway.

The tree home was built about fifty feet off the ground on the fanning outspread branches of an old growth oak tree.

The stealth kidnappers found the master bedroom, where the old man snored away next to his wife. They slipped in through the two windows.

The four shadows surrounded the bed.

Zula, the lioness, poured a sorcery potion into a rag and placed it over Abram's mouth. She made sure he never woke up before passing into a drugged unconsciousness. Her feline eyes tracked the forms of her comrades in the darkness.

The sleeping Sarai stirred. Kulla dragged her razor-sharp talon across her throat, cutting through her esophagus. Sarai managed a pitiful yelp before Kulla covered her mouth shut. The assassin held her until her struggling form quivered its last and died.

They placed Abram in the sack and moved to the door to leave.

Zula opened the door.

Outside the door, a stranger confronted her, holding two strange looking daggers in his hand. He punched her hard in the face. Her nose exploded in blood. She crashed to the floor unconscious.

Moonlight came through the door. It illuminated the dead form of Sarai in the bed. The fresh light allowed Kulla to see faint color. She realized the dead woman did not have blonde hair.

It was not Sarai.

The dead woman was Devorah, Eliezer's wife. They had mistaken the head servant, Eliezer, for Abram and had murdered his wife instead of Sarai.

Abram was the nemesis at the door. He had heard Eliezer's snoring stop and Devorah's cry of death.

The assailants dropped the sack with Eliezer in it and crouched to fight. Their animal senses heightened and their fangs, claws, and talons came out.

Abram faced three chimera killers with preternatural strength and animalistic skill in fighting.

They did not know that Abram had been trained in the way of the Karabu by his ancestor Noah ben Lamech, who had learned it from *his* ancestor, Methuselah ben Enoch. It was the ancient form of martial art practiced by archangels.

These cats and birds were in for a surprise.

He was a bit rusty from lack of practice, but he also had El Shaddai watching over him. He brandished his blades in sweeping gestures and moved into the room with a fluidity of dance that disconcerted the invaders.

It confused his first opponent, Laliya. Her talons were only able to block one motion of Abram's blades before he cut through her and she dropped to the ground.

The other two surrounded him with claws and talons raised and ready.

Zakita, the lioness hissed.

Abram remembered a tactic that Noah had taught him for such a situation. It had been a signature move of Noah's guardian angel, Uriel. He would extend his blades and twirl like a whirlwind, slicing through a circle of enemies surrounding him.

Abram held out his blades and spun.

But Abram was not an archangel. And he was much older now.

He became dizzy and fell off balance, crashing into a table and chairs.

Zakita instantly leapt on him.

Her claws slashed his chest and drew blood.

He kicked her like a mule, with both feet.

She flew back into the wall.

Kulla was on him before he could catch his breath.

She swung.

He ducked.

Her razor talons got stuck in the splintered table. She tried to jerk them free.

It was the moment Abram needed.

He drove both blades up and into her skull.

She fell backward in death, carrying his daggers with her to the floor.

Abram now stood weaponless before a very angry lioness, Zakita. She hissed at him and bared her fangs.

He reached for anything near him. Something met his fingers, and he grabbed it, raising it before him.

It was a shred of drapery torn from the window. It dangled from his hand like a limp wet rag. He sighed.

Zakita lunged.

Abram dodged with a Karabu spin that made him dizzy again, but saved him from a terrible slashing.

Zakita did not stop. She kept attacking.

Abram slid into a ballet of flowing moves to evade Zakita. He was a bit slow and unpracticed.

She scraped his arm, and then his leg.

But her multiple misses on this old, dancing geezer enraged her.

Her rage became a big mistake. She lost her strategic sense and got sloppy.

In a flash, Abram flipped over her. The drapery in his hand became a garrote around her neck. But he could not choke her. She would have her claws in him before he could pull it tight enough.

Instead, he used his momentary advantage to drag her to the window and throw her out.

There was no porch outside that window.

She fell to the ground fifty feet below.

But she was a feline hybrid.

She turned in the air and prepared to land on all fours to cushion the blow.

She did not make it to the ground. A broken branch about ten feet below the window stuck upwards.

It skewered her like a pike. She howled and woke up half the neighborhood. She died quickly.

In Eliezer's bedroom, Abram huffed, out of breath. He sank to his knees on the floor.

The death screech of Zakita drew Sarai from the real master bedroom. She ran to the scene of the fight.

"I am too old for this anymore," Abram wheezed. He grabbed the daggers out of the bird woman.

He looked up to see Sarai in the doorway. Then suddenly, Zula slid up behind Sarai, her claws at Sarai's throat. Zula's face still flowed with blood from her broken nose. Unconscious, she had been forgotten during the fight. She had come to, slipping out of the room while Abram was on his knees.

Now she had both hands in a death grip on Sarai.

Zula gurgled through her blood, "Life for life. If you submit to me, I will let her live. If not, she dies."

Abram gripped his blades. His only chance was to throw one and hit the lioness in the eye.

But she was too close to Sarai's head. She moved about, pulling Sarai in front of her as a human shield. He felt too old for such precision anymore. He was more likely to hit Sarai and lose her by his own hand.

On the other hand, he had seen what these creatures had done to Eliezer's wife, thinking she was Sarai. He knew Zula would kill Sarai anyway.

He hesitated. There was no way out of this. Either way, Sarai would die. If she died, all his happiness and purpose went with her.

He decided to do the one thing he had any sliver of a chance with. He would throw the dagger.

He prayed, "El Shaddai, help me."

He flipped the blade and raised it with trembling, bruised hands.

Suddenly, Zula's eyes rolled upward. She released her grip on Sarai and fell to the floor, unconscious.

It was an answer to prayer. Not a miraculous violation of nature, but a providential timing of nature.

Zula had fainted from loss of blood.

Abram leapt to Sarai, and moved her out of the way. He used his daggers to nail Zula's clawed hands to the floor.

The pain brought Zula back to consciousness.

"Who sent you?" demanded Abram angrily. "Was it Arba?"

Zula shook her head. She whispered weakly, "Arba only gave us information."

"Then who sent you?!" he yelled.

She refused to tell him.

He said, "It is your choice, to die slowly or quickly."

With labored breath, she whispered, "Nimrod."

Abram's eyes went wide with shock. So the mad king was never going to give up his obsession. He would hunt them down till his dying day.

He pulled one of the daggers from her hand and plunged it into Zula's heart, sending her straight to Sheol.

The sack stirred. Eliezer was coming to.

Abram opened the sack and pulled a groggy Eliezer from it.

"They mistook Eliezer for me," said Abram to Sarai. "They wanted to bring me back alive to Nimrod."

Sarai whispered ominously, "Now Arba knows who you are."

It had to be true. There was no way that Arba would provide intelligence such as this without procuring something for himself. If he knew Nimrod was after Abram, why would he not betray Abram for his benefit? He had evidently wanted Sarai murdered because, according to his reprobate mind, if he could not have her, then no one could.

Abram noticed Sarai's eyes drift to the door. He raised the dagger and turned.

Another warrior stood at the door, a muscular paladin with strange armor showing underneath an open cloak.

He was not an Amorite or one of Mamre's relatives, and he certainly was not one of Abram's warriors.

Abram threw the knife at him.

The stranger moved with lightning reflexes and caught it midair, before it could hit him.

Abram had no strength left to fight. He felt certain this one would kill them. He stepped in front of Sarai.

"Fear not," said the stranger. "I am not here to harm you."

"Who are you?" asked Abram.

"I am Uriel the archangel, and I am here for your protection."

"Well, you are a little late," said Abram. "It would have been nice if you had actually protected us."

Uriel smiled. This was not the first time he had done this kind of thing. "You were doing fine, crabby jaw. Besides, you needed the practice for what is coming."

"What is coming?" repeated Abram.

"Heaven knows," Uriel only hinted.

"A sarcastic archangel at that," said Abram.

"And quite attractive," kicked in Sarai.

Uriel was a handsome, young, muscular warrior. He had long blonde hair and a winsome smile.

He replied to Sarai, "And you, my lovely ward, have quite the reputation yourself for being the desire of many men."

Abram pulled Sarai back behind him.

"How do I know you are telling the truth?" said Abram.

"Well, for one thing, that whirlwind move you attempted with sorry results? I created it."

Uriel pulled out his two swords and held them close to him so as not to hit anything. Then he twirled in his signature move like a mini-cyclone and stopped on a shekel.

A gush of wind flowed over Abram's and Sarai's faces.

"And for another thing," Uriel smiled, "I could have waited to introduce myself to you in the same manner as El Shaddai has done, when you were kissing each other on your bed, but I figured that is his prerogative and none of my business."

Abram and Sarai never told anyone about the day and manner of Abram's calling.

"What do I need to know?" asked Abram.

"Only as much as you need at the moment you need it."

"We are getting used to that," quipped Sarai.

"You are telling me," said Uriel. "I get all the hand-me-down tasks at the last minute. In fact, I am only filling in for Mikael with you, until he has taken care of some other pressing tasks."

Abram and Sarai looked at each other with concern.

"You will find him more serious than me. And less fun."

Eliezer stirred again. He was coming to.

"But now is not the time for humor. You have a duty of grief, so I will leave you be."

With that, Uriel was gone.

Eliezer managed to croak out a question, "Where is Devorah?"

Outside Abram's home, a group of neighbors gathered in concern for the family. They had weapons. Some of them were already climbing the tree.

Then the sound of Eliezer's soul-wrenching scream echoed through the forest.

CHAPTER 45

The confederation of four kings from Mesopotamia traveled up the Euphrates then down through Amurru to the King's Highway. They were led by their suzerain, King Chedorlaomer of Elam, and included King Arioch of Ellasar, King Tidal of Goiim, and the newly installed King Amraphel of Shinar. His previous identity as Nimrod had been replaced with his new identity as vassal king under Chedorlaomer. Both Amraphel and Arioch were giants, and they had a few units of giants with their traveling army of eight hundred thousand strong.

They first faced and defeated the Rephaim giants in Ashteroth-Karnaim. It was a district of Bashan, near Edrei. The Rephaim worshipped Ashtart and were among the fiercest of the giants. They had elongated heads reminiscent of their divine seed as well as the twenty-four digits on their hands and feet, and two rows of teeth in their mouths.

The Rephaim fought in five organized defense units of fifty. They killed a good thousand soldiers before Chedorlaomer's forces overwhelmed them with sheer numbers and massacred them in a bloodbath of fury and revenge.

Chedorlaomer rightly observed that if they battled the strongest foes while their own forces were at their freshest and strongest, they would not only have a quicker, more certain victory, but word might spread ahead of them and create terror in others they planned to conquer.

Chedorlaomer impaled the fifty surviving Rephaim along with their fallen brothers on a small ridge just outside the town, all for sake of the terrorizing notoriety. It looked like a stripped forest of death. Vultures fed off the carrion for days.

The King of Elam had strategized correctly. By the time they traveled down to Ham and wiped out the Zamzummim giants in that township, their next target, the Emim in the Valley of Kiriathaim had decided to surrender without battle.

They sued for peace and acceptance as vassal township, which Chedorlaomer immediately accepted. But he knew that if he allowed these giants to live, he would eventually have to fight them later, if they grew in number and rose up in rebellion.

So during the ceremonial surrendering of arms by all the soldiers of Kiriathaim, instead of returning their weapons to the submissive giants with the suzerain blessing, Chedorlaomer had all two hundred of them slaughtered in a tidal wave of mayhem.

On their way south, near the cities of the plain, Amraphel wondered if the female hybrid assassins he had sent long before had been successful in their quest to capture Abram. Their paths did not cross on the King's Highway, but the professional killers would probably have avoided that main road for safety reasons.

Earlier, in Ashteroth-Karnaim, he had inquired of the priestesses of the temple of Ashtart that he hired. They confirmed that the women had passed through the town, looking for information leading to their quarry. As hierodules of Ashtart, the assassins would find sanctuary in the temple chambers for rest until they continued on their journey. So it was in their interests to use the town as a way station on the way back.

But they had never returned. They were most likely still searching or dead.

Amraphel did not look much better than he had when he was Nimrod the battered prisoner of Chedorlaomer at Borsippa. He was not eating well or sleeping. The malnutrition and insomnia took its toll on his body. He had shrunk a good six inches, and then lost another six due to his hunched shoulders. He avoided fraternizing with the other kings and kept to himself. He was often overheard mumbling arguments to himself, and even abusing his body with lashings with a whip and cuttings with a knife.

He was going mad, but he maintained a singular kernel of rationality deep down within. It was rooted in his obsessive hatred of Abram and his god El Shaddai. He would not allow himself to slide into utter oblivion, because he still had his final act of revenge to accomplish. That kernel of reason was the true controller of his madness. It dominated his every waking moment and provided him with cunning strategy for his every move.

He was not merely going insane, he was simply becoming totally and thoroughly evil. The difference between his current state and what he had been as a world potentate was merely the exercise of power. With power, he could satisfy his passion and anger immediately, and therefore maintain a semblance of sanity amidst his growing depravity. But without power, his frustrated and obstructed schemes of evil twisted and contorted his soul into a bitter rage that turned inward and ravished his nature like a consuming disease. As emperor, he had been an abomination of desolation. As demoted powerless vassal king, he was more like a shade of Sheol, a lost identity in a sea of insatiable unsatisfied hunger.

Amraphel stopped gnawing on his finger when he saw that he had chewed the flesh to the bone. He was in a required meeting with the other three kings. The pentapolis knew of the Mesopotamian army's approach. They had sent a messenger to Chedorlaomer to proclaim their defiance.

When the king demanded that the messenger be brought to his presence, they were surprised to see it was Ashtart herself, patron deity of the five cities, and the allotted authority over Canaan.

The goddess of sex and war was not to be trifled with.

When she entered, she approached the four kings, but stopped half way and sniffed the air.

Her eyes rose in anger and she seethed. "I should have known you'd be slithering in the shadows of this conspiracy! Come out and face me, you cowardly god of piss and farts!"

She had reverted to her irritating insulting again. She demeaned Marduk's storm domain of rain and wind into lowly human excretions.

All heads turned to Marduk.

He stepped out of the shadows behind the throne, into the firelight. He usually stayed out of the limelight, choosing to work more surreptitiously through human rulers since his humiliation at Babel. But he was no coward. His form bulged with obscene muscularity and his presence struck shock and awe into any created thing.

A confrontation had been brewing between them for years. Now Ashtart was calling Marduk out for a contest. He was not afraid of her. He was the only god in the pantheon who could defeat her, if it were possible. But over the years, Ashtart's power had grown over Canaan. The inevitable face off was becoming more probable.

The kings fell silent in the presence of these Watcher gods.

Ashtart hissed at Marduk, "I know what you are doing here, Marduk. You seek to annihilate my Nephilim children and stop my rise to power. But it is too late. The Seed of the Serpent has filled the land like a weed. You may cut off one root, but another will grow to replace it. I have been waiting for this moment for too long, and I think it's time we finished our quarrel."

Marduk remained silent. He was not one for wasted words. He considered talking too much to be a weakness.

Her attention fell upon Amraphel, who had been trying not to be noticed.

"Well, well, well, what have we here?" she sang.

She stepped up for a closer look at Amraphel. His degraded figure and countenance made him look completely different from when she had last seen him, but you cannot fool a Watcher. She knew who sat on that throne.

"Look who has been resurrected from the dead. Although, I have to say, you are looking less spritely and bubbly than I remember."

Amraphel said nothing. She could see he was a cowed vassal now. His past as the potentate Nimrod was distant legend.

"Apparently, our bad blood has been resolved decidedly in my favor. Thank El Shaddai." She made a mock gesture and bow to heaven. She shook her head with disgust. He had spurned her advances when he was the mighty hunter-king of Uruk, one-third man, two-thirds god. He had maneuvered her away from his worldwide empire in Babylon. And now, he was an unshaven, unkempt, demented slave of Chedorlaomer, sitting in his own unwashed stench.

She crinkled her nose and dismissed him.

She turned back to Chedorlaomer with boiling anger. "This is my land. The five cities of the plain will not bow to the petty dictates of your puny armies. If you want war, I will give you war, unlike any you have ever seen. You will plead for mercy, but you will receive none. And what I will do to you will be so heinous, it will not be spoken of for ten thousand years.

Chedorlaomer swallowed with a dry throat. All four kings looked simultaneously at Marduk.

When the god spoke, it was frighteningly malevolent and sure.

"I am going to bind you into the heart of the earth, bitch goddess! You will think on your failure for ten thousand years! And there will be no sea dragon to free you from your prison as before."

Ashtart grinned. She turned to leave, calling out over her shoulder with a chortle, "Bring it to the battlefield, Lord Lettuce Head!" That was her personal favorite when she could not think of a fresh insult.

She was gone.

Chedorlaomer looked at Marduk. "Can you defeat her?"

"I will break her in half," said Marduk.

"Good," said the king. "Because I have more giant clans to vanquish in the south at Seir, El-Paran, and Kadesh, before I finish up with these pentapolis ingrates and their princess of pouting."

Marduk smirked. It was a witty affirmation of the king to return Ashtart's wordplay on Marduk's behalf.

He offered his compliment, "A wise strategy, O king. Her pride will delude her into thinking we have run away. And arrogance is a most foolish blunder."

The King's Highway stretched out on the Transjordanian plateau, a good fifteen miles east of the Jordan Sea and the five cities of the plain with their preparing gods and kings. Chedorlaomer's forces simply passed them by. They resumed their trek down to the southern mountain range of Seir, where the Horites awaited their destruction.

CHAPTER 46

Devorah's funeral was a solemn affair. Eliezer had loved her dearly, as had Abram and Sarai. She would be sorely missed for her optimistic perspective on life and her dedication to Sarai. She had even been Sarai's confidante in troubled times. They buried her just outside the forest and placed some dolmens, large marker stones, over her resting place. Eliezer made Abram promise he would bury him with his wife when he died. There was much wailing and weeping, but life went on without her.

After the attack incident, Abram moved his family back out into tents amidst the flocks and in the open air of a clearing near the forest. He built an altar of unhewn stone to El Shaddai where his family worshipped by an oak tree. By living in Mamre's tree homes, he felt too obligated to the Amorite and his brothers. He also felt that their religion was offensive to El Shaddai. He wanted them as allies, but he knew he needed to be separate. Assimilation would not be healthy, if El Shaddai was yet to make a nation out of him. Though how that was going to happen became increasingly difficult for him to understand. He asked Uriel, but the angel was not privy to such details.

One day when Sarai and Abram were sitting down to eat dinner; they were interrupted by the arrival of Lot from Sodom. He was wearing his fanciest public service outfit as an elder of that city.

Abram and Sarai stared at him with mouths agape. They had thought they would never see him again.

Abram yelled out with joy, "Nephew!"

"Uncle," Lot replied. Abram's rushing hug almost toppled him to the ground.

"Where is your wife?" asked Sarai.

"She did not come with me. That is a long story," said Lot. "Better told with some drink in the belly."

Lot hugged and kissed them both. They invited him to eat with them.

Eliezer set out another place setting for Lot. They had plenty of boar with onions, radishes, and carrots to go around.

Abram smiled, looking at Lot's garish outfit. He wore an embroidered red robe over too many other cloaks. His hat was large and puffy as befitted the royal class. He wore jewelry and makeup that made him look a bit clownish.

Abram said, "I see your position in the city provides you with a wardrobe that matches your personality quite well."

Lot smiled back. "For once, uncle, you are appreciating my affluence and highfalutin intentions."

They had always tried to downplay their differences with subtle sarcasm.

Sarai could only shake her head. "You two." Nothing Lot wore would sway her from her optimistic love for her nephew. "So tell us about your wife, Lot."

Lot took a large gulp of beer before answering. "Her name is Ado. She would not come with me, or allow me to bring my daughters."

"How old are they now?" asked Sarai.

"Two years. Twins." He did not want to even mention Paltith and her sordid death in the city.

He continued, "The first born is Ishtar and the second, Gaia."

That made for a moment of awkward silence. Abram and Sarai knew those were the names of pagan deities, which showed just how compromised Lot had become.

Lot tried to dismiss his responsibility, "Ado cared more about the naming than I did."

It only made him look and feel less of a leader.

"What do you mean your wife will not allow you to bring her?" asked Abram.

Lot hung his head in shame.

"She has lived all her life in the city. She is afraid to leave it. Sodom is her extended family."

"How does that make her the head of *your* family?" said Sarai with contempt. "A wife obeys her husband, not the other way around."

"Sarai," interrupted Abram, "please be more respectful."

"My apologies," she said.

"You have to understand," Lot said. "I found Ado as a young orphan in Sodom. She has never had any family before marrying me. She is afraid of losing whatever family she has."

Sarai said, "Nephew, I think I do understand what it is like to be an orphan. And then to marry without the ability to have a family."

"Forgive me, Sarai," said Lot. "You have suffered much as well. But Ado is a good wife. She has a fierce devotion to her children, because she is afraid of losing them as we did our first born."

"Oh, I am so sorry," said Sarai.

Abram added, "Our sympathies go out to you, nephew."

"Thank you," he said. "Can we go for a walk, Abram? You and I?"

Abram and Lot took a stroll out under the moonlight and stars. Abram knew there was more going on than Lot let on.

"Why are you here, nephew?"

Lot took a big sigh. "A confederation of four kings led by Chedorlaomer is descending upon the pentapolis with eight hundred thousand men. He means to crush us."

Some information had reached even Abram. He knew that Chedorlaomer had been sweeping Canaan clean of giant clans along the King's Highway and in the southern regions. But this was news.

Abram said, "Those numbers seem exaggerated."

Lot replied, "They probably are, but they express the fearsomeness of Chedorlaomer's power, and that is no exaggeration."

"Why do you not get out before he attacks?"

"Ado will not leave. She says she would rather die at the hands of barbarians than leave her hometown. She will not listen to reason."

"Sarai is right," said Abram. "You have lost that leadership I have always known you to have. You seem dominated, brow beaten."

"It is not just that," sighed Lot. "I sold everything and released all my household to live in the city. I have put down roots and built all my wealth there. If I left Sodom, I would lose it all. I would have nothing. Where would I go?"

"You could come live with us," said Abram.

But they both knew Lot would not be able to place himself back under Abram's authority again.

"I was wrong, uncle. The city seduced me, and now I am a slave to it. I thought I might have an influence on the wickedness, but now I realize it was just a rationalization to justify my selfish ambition. Sodom is a cesspool of decadence and depravity. It has beaten me down with relentless oppression and has changed me more than I have changed it."

Lot paused after his self-revelation. Then he added, "But my family is everything to me. I will not leave without them."

Abram placed an understanding hand on Lot's back.

"What about the law?" asked Abram. "Are you not an elder in the gates?"

Lot said, "Law is a tool in the hands of power. And when the wicked rule, they make wicked laws. Every single judgment I make is overruled by a dozen judgments of others, or they just ignore it and refuse to enforce it. What is going on in the pentapolis is so dark and evil, I cannot even speak of it."

Abram mused, "Sodom's judgment draws near."

"Uncle, the reason I came to you is because I wanted to ask you a favor."

"Anything, nephew."

"If something should happen to me, if I am killed, would you see to it that my wife and daughters are taken care of? Ado would not want to leave the city to live with you, but if you could check in on them every once in a while, make sure they are all right."

Abram said, "I will do everything I can to make sure your wife and children are safe." He added with emphasis, "And you as well."

Lot took a deep breath of the cool, crisp night air. He chuckled to himself. "It is funny. I remember when I could not wait to get away from the smell of goats and cattle. Now, I miss it. It seems so fresh out here, so — natural and pure."

Abram thought of Arba and the assassins and the famine that razed the land. "I assure you, nephew, corruption and atrocity fills all this land; in city, village, mountain, and forest. But one day, El Shaddai will cleanse it, and set up his family among the nations."

Lot said, "It seems impossible."

Abram said, "With El Shaddai, all things are possible. Even to make a nation out of a barren couple."

"I have always been inspired by your confidence and faith, uncle. But I think sometimes it has gone to your head and made you a bit crazy."

They shared a laugh.

"Maybe so," said Abram. "Maybe so."

Their parting was bittersweet. Sarai hugged Lot, cried and would not let him go. She would always think of him as the spunky little child back in Ur, who would never stop getting into trouble with his curiosity and hunger for more.

She sniffled and pulled him back to gaze at him. "Look at you. I remember when you were only ten like it was yesterday. You tried to start your own teraphim business to compete with your father. Those little lumps of clay were so cute, and you had that beaming bright determination. Thank El Shaddai you could not sell them, or you might be a successful idol maker today."

"I am not sure you are entirely right, auntie," said Lot with a sad stare. "I am residing in a city of idolatry and I feel as if I am complicit."

Abram and Sarai knew there was nothing more they could say.

"Please pray for me, for my family," he said. Then he set off, back to Sodom.

CHAPTER 47

Ashtart paced back and forth in the king's chamber of Sodom. King Bera sat on the extended throne, made to accommodate his blubbery fat. He was eating a leg of mutton with his vomit pail next to his throne. A nervous messenger kept his gaze down to the ground, awaiting his instructions.

They had received word that Chedorlaomer had completed his campaign in the southern regions, from the gulf of Aqaba all the way back up to the wilderness of Zin. He had defeated the Horites and their giant clans from the hill country of Seir as far as El-paran on the border of the wilderness. Then he turned back and subdued all the country of the Amalekites, as well as the Amorites dwelling in Hazazon-tamar.

The messenger spoke with a fearful hush of voice. "Chedorlaomer's forces have wiped out all the giants he can find in the territories, Nephilim, Rephaim, Emim, Zamzummim."

Ashtart interrupted him, " Thousands of my children! That son of a whore and his muscle-bound moron Marduk have decimated my seedline!"

It would take generations to repopulate the land.

She swung in a furious rage and lopped off the messenger's head with the force of her hand alone. His decapitated body fell to the floor. Ashtart snapped her fingers to one of the servants standing by the king.

"Clean up this mess!"

The servant scrambled to obey.

"How close are they to our cities?" asked Ashtart.

"I do not know, mighty Queen of Heaven. The messenger had not told us yet."

Ashtart cursed herself for her impulsive outburst.

"Well, send a new scout to find out. And contact the kings of the pentapolis to muster their full forces."

Bera said, "Yes, mighty Ashtart. Where?"

"We will fight them on our turf, where we are the most experienced and they are not: the bitumen fields of the Valley of Siddim."

King Bera smiled. It was brilliant. An unanticipated belch took him by surprise. He felt a rise of vomit in his mouth, which he quickly swallowed so as not to distract the goddess.

She continued, "They will think us fools to face them on the plain, but they will be unprepared for the sludge and muck of the tar pits. We will drown half their forces in the trap, and fill their lungs with asphalt."

She thought to herself, *And that is where I will imprison Marduk, in the deepest darkness of black pitch.*

The coalition forces of Chedorlaomer arrived in the Valley of Siddim within five days. The warriors of Ashtart were ready for them, amassed in the northern valley. That would draw their enemies to them and into the bitumen pits.

The five monarchs of the pentapolis were Bera of Sodom, King Birsha of Gomorrah, who was a giant, King Shinab of Admah, Shemeber of Zeboiim, and Bela of Zoar. They each stood on a mounted chariot, behind their forces arranged across the field. Bera had a seat built onto his chariot and reinforced its four wheels and axels. It had to be pulled by six horses because of his weight. Even now Bera was munching on a sack of figs, as he found the sweetness comforting in stressful moments.

The forces of the pentapolis were arrayed in five units, one for each of the cities. They numbered about two hundred thousand to the Eastern Coalition's three hundred thousand. Chedorlaomer had let a number of the soldiers go home as they made their victorious way through the Wilderness of Zin. He was not worried about the humans he was facing; it was the gods that concerned him.

Though Chedorlaomer had Marduk, king of the gods, on his side, he knew Ashtart was long-experienced and cunning in the art of war, and she was fighting for her very freedom. Though these gods could not die, he had learned that they could be imprisoned in the earth until judgment day, which was a fate worse than death for an immortal being. To be alive and confined without movement under millions of tons of earth for thousands of years would be supernatural torture for supernatural beings. A titanic showdown was brewing on the horizon. No doubt it would dwarf any human battle he had ever been in or heard of.

He had sent scouts ahead to get a lay of the land. They returned with intelligence about the field of bitumen pits they were about to find themselves facing on the battlefield. It was a great disadvantage, but he was confident in his soldiers. And he had a few tricks up his armor.

The Valley of Siddim stretched out before Sodom and Gomorrah, the source of lifeblood for the wealth of the five cities. It was now about to become a bleeding artery of death in a battle of nine kings.

The bitumen pits covered the entire valley like a swamp of black pools. They gave off a foul and sour stench of sulfur, like that of rotting eggs and vegetation. Some pools were deep, others shallow. Some were not yet excavated, being invisible just below the surface sediment, ready to trap unsuspecting travelers. Some seeped up through cracks in the rock. There were also mining pits where a solid rock form of the bitumen was mined with pick axes, chisels, and sledgehammers.

The Canaanites had grown accustomed to the malodorous smell over the years, but the invaders were not prepared for it. When they lined up for attack, many of them got sick and vomited. Some of them passed out.

Chedorlaomer had his soldiers rip off lengths of their tunics and wrap them around their noses and mouths to filter the air.

The pentapolis heralds blew their war horns. The first wave of warriors took to the field. Because they knew the valley well, they were able to maneuver around the bitumen pits with ease.

The Eastern coalition soldiers marched out to meet them. Unfamiliar with the terrain, they lost their formation and many became stuck in pools of pitch.

Chedorlaomer saw what was happening. He ordered his archers to launch a volley of fire-tipped arrows before his infantry. He did not intend to inflict damage on the Canaanites, but rather to hit as many pools of pitch as possible. The fire lit the bitumen and created a maze of bonfires that struck fear into the hearts of the Canaanites. It created a clear pathway for the Mesopotamian forces to navigate. They had to avoid the fire, but they would not unknowingly fall into the pits.

The two forces met in the midst of the flaming pools and clashed with mace, sword, axe, and spear. The armies of Ashtart were well trained with swords split at their tips like a serpent's tongue. The armies of Marduk were masters of mace and pike.

Swords ripped into a few invaders, but pikes skewered more defenders at a distance before those swords could get close enough to cut.

Suddenly, from behind the Canaanite lines, an unearthly howl screeched over the valley like a hideous portent of doom. It was Ashtart's war cry.

A monstrous roar bellowed out in return from behind the Mesopotamian lines as a furious reply from Marduk.

The gods were at war.

Ashtart and Marduk both rushed into the mayhem of metal, flesh, and blood like dire wolves to a slaughter. They were racing for each other, both of them about eight feet tall, but unleashing a violent supernatural force as they bowled over their own soldiers in their pathway.

They had both stripped down to minimal garments and necessary weapons. Marduk carried his favorite weapons: a monstrous iron mace in one hand and a battle net in the other. He strapped a large sledgehammer to his naked back. He was barefoot and wore a simple loincloth beneath his leather belt. As a Watcher god, armor was more cumbersome than it was protective. There was something more primal and animalistic about fighting almost bare naked.

Ashtart felt the same way about simplicity in war. But she liked the idea of looking good even as she was slaughtering her enemies and wading through their blood. So she wore an outrageous outfit that showed her figure off and did her hair up in a tight but stylish fashion. She considered herself quite brilliant at effectively combining her fertility with her violence. And it worked to her tactical advantage to distract her enemies with the gorgeous body she worked so hard to maintain. Her only weapon: a scythe. Under the strength of a human, a scythe was cumbersome and slow, but under the grip of a Watcher god with the strength of a dozen mighty men, it was a whirling blade of death.

They met at the center of the battlefield. Ashtart spit out, "O mighty King Cumquat! I have been waiting for this for centuries!"

Marduk remained silent as they circled one another, waiting to see who would be the first to attack.

Ashtart struck first. She swung her scythe like a ballet move, which gave meaning to the phrase, "Ashtart's dance of death." If it connected with Marduk, it would cut him in half.

It sliced up nearby soldiers and soaked her clothes in gore.

The baptism of blood inspired her. She licked her lips and advanced on Marduk.

He was ready.

He used his iron mace to block her blade at every swipe, resulting in a shower of sparks that engulfed both of them and set nearby pools of pitch on fire.

The soldiers moved away from the battling titans and left them with plenty of room to finish what they started, unhindered by human obstacles.

Marduk waited for the right moment to make his move.

He saw it and threw his net on her.

She was ready for that move.

Her scythe cut the net into ribbons and it fell to the ground in pieces.

"That better not be your best shot, god of garbanzo beans," she said, "or this is going to be quite anti-climactic."

Her insults infuriated Marduk. He knew he had to keep his cool or he would suffer at the hands of her psychological strategy and make the one mistake that would cost him the fight.

The pentapolis army pushed the Eastern coalition back. They knew the geography better, and the fiery bitumen pits kept the Mesopotamians from engaging the phalanx strategy that had worked to their advantage throughout their campaign. It became a free-for-all.

The Eastern coalition were battle hardened with the recent experience of their Canaan campaign, but the cities of Ashtart were well trained by their goddess in her art of war. In fact, they fought with such wild ferocity that Chedorlaomer's soldiers felt they were battling demons.

They were. Ashtart had developed a way of harnessing the failures of the past into victories of the future. She had worked with her necromancers, conjurers, and exorcists to find a way to call up the spirits of the dead Nephilim from before the Flood. Because the Nephilim were hybrids between heaven and earth, they were neither fully angel nor fully human. So, when they died, they seemed to have the ability to wander the earth as demonic entities in search of habitation, trapped between those two realms of the above and the below.

There were many of them. Armies of Nephilim spirits.

Ashtart had achieved another miracle. She was able to engage entire regiments of her army with demonic possession by the Nephilim spirits. They were outnumbered, but they were infused with supernatural strength and viciousness.

That vicious strength began to fight back at Chedorlaomer's mighty warriors.

Ashtart made a serious mistake in her own fight. She backed Marduk up against a smashed chariot. She swung with all her might, downwards on his head, seeking to cleave him in two.

Marduk dodged the blow.

The scythe cut through the chariot metal and deep into the ground. She yanked on it. But it was jammed in the rock and metal.

Marduk made his move.

He clubbed her with his mace right in the temple. She slammed to the ground, losing her senses. She fought unconsciousness.

Marduk had her.

He threw his mace to the ground. He wanted to take her apart with his hands. It was more personal that way. He was much stronger than her. His bulging body mass outweighed her slender form by twice her weight.

He sat on her and pummeled her face with punches.

But looks were deceiving and arrogance was blinding.

Under Ashtart's wiry frame lay sinews of hidden reserves. And under her female persona lurked a masochistic tolerance of great pain.

As Marduk beat her, she feigned complete, disoriented weakness — until Marduk let down his guard, thinking he was triumphant.

Ashtart grabbed the dagger in his belt, and jammed it into his back.

He screamed in pain. He leapt off her, trying to reach back and pull out the blade. But his bulky frame was not flexible.

Ashtart took a running leap, tackling Marduk backwards.

He fell onto the broken chariot and scythe blade. The ground rumbled at the impact. The force nearly broke his back. The scythe handle shattered to pieces, leaving the blade to slice into his shoulder.

Now Marduk was angry.

He heaved Ashtart off of him.

She flew fifty feet backward. Her landing in a flaming bitumen pit sent a large splash of the black ooze blanketing the ground all around her.

Ashtart crawled out of the pit as angry as Marduk. Her hair and outfit were completely ruined by this disgusting sludge.

"This was my favorite battle skirt, Prince Potato Head. Now, you are going to pay."

But Marduk did not attack Ashtart. Instead, he pulled out the huge sledgehammer strapped on his back. He swung it down mightily and hit the earth with a thunderous strike. The Jordan Valley was a geological rift of earthquake activity. Marduk hit a fault line and a shockwave resounded outward from the epicenter of his hammer.

A huge tremor, followed by a quake, threw the human armies to the ground and some of them into the bitumen pits. A large crevice opened up underneath Ashtart and she fell deep into the earth.

Marduk jumped in after her.

Chedorlaomer finally found his break in the battle on the field. Ashtart's demonic hordes held the middle. But he noticed that the weakest forces were those of Admah, Zeboiim, and Zoar. So he concentrated his assault on them, in order to demoralize the others.

It worked. His forces decimated the left flank of the pentapolis army and drove a wedge into them on the right. The kings of Admah, Zeboiim, and Zoar fled on their chariots, into the hill country to get away. Their forces fell apart, leaving only Sodom and Gomorrah.

The Nephilim-possessed armies were strong, but not so strong as to take on Chedorlaomer's entire army hedging them in. It did not help the defenders that the spirits of possession were more chaotic than organized. Their advantage quickly dissolved in the face of organized, overwhelming attack.

Deep in the earth, Ashtart saw Marduk coming for her. The huge walls of rock rose above her like prison walls. She began to panic. She was his equal with a weapon, but not in strength, and certainly not without a weapon. She would to have to use cunning to overcome him now.

Marduk climbed down the rock and found her on a ledge, waiting for him.

He said, "Your mockery and abuse will do you no help down here, queenie. Prepare for your imprisonment."

He reached her and grabbed her by the throat. He took off his belt and tied both her hands together to stop her shenanigans.

He pummeled her again. Only this time, her disorientation was real.

Marduk had longed for such vengeance for years It now gave him great satisfaction to hurt her with impunity.

When King Bera of Sodom and King Birsha of Gomorrah realized they were only minutes away from total annihilation by the Eastern coalition, they commandeered their chariots for a retreat into the hills like the other kings.

They failed to issue any other commands to their forces, as they turned their chariots back around.

But Bera's chariot was so cumbersome, he could not make the turns quickly enough to avoid the bitumen pits. His chariot hit Birsha's chariot and both of their vehicles plunged into a pool of black pitch. It was not on fire, and it was not deep, so they would not die. But they were stuck, and would now be caught by the enemy who was almost upon them.

Bera looked up and saw Mesopotamians coming at them with pikes raised. He became so fearful, he lost his bowels and defecated all over himself. Unfortunately, he had been eating figs earlier, so it came out like a diarrhetic blast. All he could keep saying in his state of shock was, "Why me? Why me? Why me?"

The humiliation was appropriate. He was a pathetic ruler whose pompous bombast was only equaled by his sniveling self-obsession.

The Eastern forces surrounded Bera and Birsha with pikes at the ready. They prepared to die an ignominious death.

Down in the crevice, Marduk threw the limp form of Ashtart down another fifty feet of rock wall, where she hit the bottom. He ripped a boulder from the wall and raised it above his head. He meant to finish her off before he returned to the surface, to hammer the crevice closed.

But through her broken bloodied face, Ashtart shouted, "Wait!"

Marduk paused.

"You have bested me, Marduk," she said. "There is no doubt that you are the king of the gods, and I am your inferior."

He could not believe it. Was she really going to try to flatter him at this moment? Desperation at facing her imprisonment obviously made her willing to try anything.

"But I have an offer to make you."

Marduk scoffed, "You are in no position to bargain with me, quim."

"Please hear me out before you seal me in this tomb," she said.

He knew she was cunning, but he also knew she was brilliant when it came to strategic pursuits of power. He was not as smart as she was, so he would listen to what she had to say before he crushed her forever.

She saw him hesitate and took her chance to keep talking. "You are the Babylonian king of the gods, but Mesopotamia is falling apart. Canaan is the future. I was allotted this land and I have been developing it to breed the Seedline of the Serpent to rival the Seed of the Woman."

That appealed to Marduk's interests more than anything.

"It is true, you can simply chain me here and take over by yourself. But you need someone who knows this land to help you. Someone who is strong enough to be your right hand. Your subservient, submissive right hand."

"And you are that chosen one," he said with sarcasm.

"I would be your consort. I would submit to you as I did to Anu before the Flood. You know I was loyal, and I never usurped him. I knew my place."

She *had* obeyed Anu. She did what she needed to do to survive.

She said, "I not only have the ear of Mastema, I have his support."

This piqued his interest. If Mastema was behind her, it validated her claims to the seedline of the Serpent.

She continued, "I created the mythology here as well. You could change your identity to the local storm god and I would help you rise to power, choose a new holy mountain, and help you build a temple as king of these gods. Alone, you might accomplish some of this. But with my help, I can assure you supremacy over all, because I built this land."

"And you would do all this to my benefit," he said sarcastically.

"Mighty Marduk," she said, "I have lost our contest. You are decidedly my superior. I face eternal imprisonment or humiliating survival. Do you blame me for choosing the latter? As far as I am concerned, if benefitting you benefits me, then yes, I will do all this to your benefit. You will be the most high god, and I will be your consort. I will submit to your authority and obey your will. You will receive all the glory for my accomplishments here in Canaan. In return, I will avoid captivity, I will be your strategist, and I will continue to corrupt Elohim's land."

This was indeed a tempting offer. She would be the intellect behind his power.

Then she turned seductive. It was amazing how she could create an aura to her presence almost instantly.

"Do not forget," she said, "I am also the goddess of sex. I will satisfy you as no one else can. And I will submit to your abuse with cheer."

Her last statement finally convinced Marduk of his advantage.

He said, "If I sense you are betraying me in any way, I will cut you in pieces and cast you into the earth."

She said, "As you clearly have the power to do."

"What is this storm god's name?" he asked.

"Ba'al," she said. "It means lord or owner.'"

"I like it," he said. "It has a nice ring to it."

CHAPTER 48

The pentapolis forces laid down their arms and knelt before Chedorlaomer and his three other kings of Mesopotamia. The kings of Sodom and Gomorrah, Bera and Birsha, were retrieved from the bitumen pit and cleaned off as best as possible. They were not to be killed today. Chedorlaomer let them live at the request of Marduk and his new escort, Ashtart. They would remain subservient vassals of Elam.

Marduk told Chedorlaomer he was going to stay behind in Canaan and take on a new identity as Ba'al, the most high. It disappointed the king of Elam, but he knew he had no choice in the matter. He had been allowed these many years to build his own kingdom with Marduk, but he would have to continue on without him.

Chedorlaomer now paced before the royalty of the city. They were not sure if he intended to humiliate them all or execute them.

He gestured to Amraphel, who stood forward and pronounced through his scratchy, choking voice, "Dear people of the pentapolis, we are looking for a specific man. We have word that he is somewhere in Canaan. Should any of you have information as to his whereabouts, you will receive a large reward. This man goes by the name of Abram of Harran, or Abram ben Terah."

It amused Ashtart to watch this Amraphel, whom she had once known as the mighty hunter king, Nimrod of Babylon. Yet, now he had been degraded into a babbling, gaunt shell of man — a madman — with nervous tics in his eyes and body muscles. He seemed hardly fit for rule. She could smell his disgusting odor, for he had soiled his clothes without washing them.

Amraphel concluded his inquiry, "Is there anyone who knows of this man and where we can find him?"

Everyone looked at each other in ignorance. No one had heard of the name.

No one, except one man.

That man stepped forward.

It was Canaan. He had managed to stay out of the limelight, but now found his only possible chance of seeing that Chosen Seed of El Shaddai was captured and killed, forever thwarting the goals of the god who had cursed him.

"I do not know where he is, my lord, but I know one of our own esteemed citizens is his relative. He will surely have the information you seek."

Amraphel looked at Canaan curiously. Had he seen this man before? He could not remember.

"What is your name?" he asked.

"I am Canaan."

Amraphel's lack of response told Ashtart that Marduk, who was now Ba'al, had never told Amraphel about Ashtart's plans. Neither had Sinleqi, the scribe who helped her track down Canaan through the genealogy rolls. When Marduk made the deal with Ashtart to get her enchantment spell over the sea dragon, he had actually remained true to his promise of secrecy.

Ah, another weakness, she thought. *Marduk does not break his promises. I shall use that against him one day.*

"Who is the man you speak of?" said Amraphel.

"Lot, the nephew of Abram."

"Arrest this Lot and bring him to the torture chamber."

CHAPTER 49

Ba'al's first order of business was to brutally beat Ashtart in order to establish his alpha authority over her. Because she was divine, she could handle more violence and pain than any human could withstand and live. Ba'al made sure to stretch her endurance to the limit. He had pent up a lot of anger at this divine cross-dressing wench for many years, and now he would take it out on her full force. What he used to do to Nimrod was gentility compared to what he had planned for her. When he was through, she would need days to recover. But she would know her place after that.

Down in the torture dungeon of Sodom, Amraphel paced before the laying form of Lot. The prisoner could not be allowed to die, so they avoided the more gruesome tortures such as flaying, or staking, or sitting in the tub, in favor of simpler, old style torture.

First, they beat him bloody and senseless. Lot lost a few teeth, broke several ribs, and had to be brought back to consciousness with foul smelling herbs. Then they engaged in water torture, to wear him down into a blubbering fool gasping for mercy. Sometimes, the oldest and simplest techniques were the best. The simple dribbling of water on the forehead could reduce a man to insanity within a day.

Lot had held on as long as he possibly could, so that when he blurted out his lie, even *he* would believe he was telling the truth. He just kept telling himself over and over that Abram was hiding out in

Bashan near Damascus, some hundred and twenty miles north of Sodom, and that he was not going to tell them that.

But now, he was delirious. He was not sure what was the truth and what was the lie. But he trusted himself and kept telling himself that Abram was in Bashan near Damascus.

Amraphel leaned over and asked Lot for the fiftieth time, "Where is Abram of Harran?"

"I do not know," whimpered Lot. He was crying and delirious.

Amraphel spasmed with anger and flew into a rage. "I have no more patience for this fool! Start cutting off his fingers."

Lot was not even sure what he had heard, until the sharp pain of a blade cutting off his left pinkie finger cracked him out of his delirium.

He screamed.

Amraphel repeated, "Where is Abram?"

"I do not know."

The blade was put to another finger.

Lot screamed in pain again.

Amraphel gave a sickly grin. "You have twenty chances."

After Lot's fingers, Amraphel was going to cut off his toes.

The blade rested on his third finger.

Lot yelled, "Wait! Please do not! I will tell you! I will tell you where he is!" And then Lot burst out into remorseful tears.

He had been broken.

"Where is he?"

Lot said through sobbing tears, "In Bashan near Damascus! In Bashan near Damascus! Abram, I am sorry. I am so sorry."

It had worked. Even he had believed it for the moment, and his brokenness convinced Amraphel as well.

When Amraphel turned, he was surprised to find Chedorlaomer in the room having watched it all.

"Why your vengeance for this Abram?" said Chedorlaomer.

"He brought down my kingdom," said Amraphel.

"You are mad, Amraphel. I have never heard of this man, and I think I would have if he was powerful enough to take down the kingdom of Babel."

Amraphel did not want to reveal all his secrets. "It is on our way back to Mesopotamia, your highness. It is a mere inconvenience."

"No," said Chedorlaomer. "I have had enough of our campaign. I am weary and my soldiers want to go home. I forbid it."

Chedorlaomer left the room.

But Amraphel ran after him, spluttering.

"Wait, my lord!"

Chedorlaomer would not stop walking. He was done with this silliness.

"It is not my kingdom alone that is on the chopping block. It is your kingdom as well."

"Spare me your desperate lies," said Chedorlaomer.

"I am a liar, my lord. I am indeed. But I assure you, in this, I am not lying. There was a prophecy in the stars many years ago at the beginning of my kingdom, that all my diviners and astrologers agreed upon in their interpretation, which as you know, is next to impossible with those half wits."

Chedorlaomer kept walking, but his interest was piqued. He watched Amraphel, who continued to splutter and cough his way through his argument with his damaged voice.

"The prophecy was that this Abram's seed would slay great kings, possess their land, and inherit the earth."

Now Chedorlaomer stopped to look into Amraphel's bloodshot yellowing eyes. He could never tell with this sleazy, serpentine figure what was true or false. But Bashan was on the way, and if Amraphel was so bent on it, then let the crazy monster go after his phantom. Maybe Chedorlaomer would be lucky and Amraphel would be killed trying.

"Granted," said the king. "On one condition."

"Name anything, my lord. Anything."

"You take a bath and groom yourself. You are a despicable pig, and you reek like excrement."

"Yes, my lord," sniveled Amraphel, scratching his lice-ridden head. He did not think he smelled so bad. But he had better obey.

The king concluded, "Gather up the booty and captives from the cities. We leave for Mesopotamia by way of Bashan."

Amraphel bowed his eight-foot hunched frame to the floor, kissing Chedorlaomer's boots. "Thank you, your majesty. Thank you. You will not regret this."

"You had better hope not," said the king. He left Amraphel on the floor, still groveling.

CHAPTER 50

Abram watched over his personal squad of three hundred warriors, born under his household and trained in the art of war. They practiced every day for hours on end in a field with wooden substitutes for weapons.

They were an elite squad taught at Abram's request by Uriel some of the secrets of the way of the Karabu. He knew this fierce land would require fierce righteousness to stay alive. Though he had complete confidence in El Shaddai's promise to protect him, that did not eliminate their need to be prepared.

An ibex horn announced a visiting outsider to the camp. Abram and Uriel left the warriors and made their way to the meeting place near the outskirts. It announced an important visitor, requiring all the elders to show up, along with the patriarch.

When Abram arrived, a curious Sarai and Eliezer met him. They all knew what this was probably about: the war of the Eastern kings against the five cities of the plains. Lot had warned Abram about it. They suspected that this was the news of what happened.

Abram and Uriel entered the tent. The thirty or so elders surrounded a little table where a wearied messenger sat gulping water from a goatskin. Abram saw that he was quite beat up. He had a gash across his forehead and a bloodshot eye with bandaged hands.

The messenger looked up at Abram. They knew each other from past trading.

"The cities of the plain have been defeated," he said. "Your nephew Lot is one of the captives, and the armies of the east are already on their way back toward Mesopotamia by way of the Jordan through Bashan."

It was standard practice for victorious armies to take their spoils of war — men, women, and children — to be slaves, as well as gold, silver, and other wealth to compensate the soldiers.

This was too much for Abram to hear.

He marched out of the tent in anger.

Uriel followed him in a rush.

"Abram, do not do it," said Uriel. "Chedorlaomer's forces are several hundred thousand strong."

Abram said, "So they will be slow enough for us to catch up then."

"I am sure that will be encouraging to your three hundred warriors," said Uriel.

Abram said, "I will ask the Amorite brothers to aid us."

"Very well, that gives you a couple thousand — against *three hundred thousand* warriors."

"I guess you will have to make up the difference then, archangel."

Uriel got mad. "Here we go again. You are as hard-headed as your ancestor Noah was!"

"Runs in the seedline, I guess," said Abram smirking.

Come to think of it, thought Uriel, *Enoch and Methuselah too.*

"Abram," said Uriel, "Testing El Shaddai is not the same as having faith in him. Confidence is one thing, but pride goes before a fall."

Abram stopped and glared at Uriel. "What do you suggest I do then? Leave my nephew to rot in slavery in some foreign pagan city?"

Uriel said, "You mean, like Sodom?"

"That is not fair," said Abram. He kept walking.

Uriel knew he had lost the battle. Abram would not listen to reason.

Abram reached the training field and announced to the warriors, "Practice is over! Suit up! Prepare your weapons for battle!"

One of the captains approached Abram. "What are your orders, master?"

"We are going on a rescue mission."

Abram met with the brothers, Mamre, Eshcol, and Aner. They agreed to help Abram on his rescue mission. It was not in their village's best interest, but Abram had proven a vital part of their protective community. They would trust him with their lives.

Since the odds were great, all three brothers went along, in order to command the men in what could be a difficult strategy. They left a few of their number behind for basic protection of the villages.

Several thousand of them left the next day in the early morning, before any of the families arose. They had said their goodbyes the night before.

Sarai, however got up with Abram. She watched Eliezer help him saddle up his camel.

Sarai held Abram tight and whispered in his ear, "Come back with him or without him. I love my nephew, but you are my life."

"And you are mine," said Abram. "But if El Shaddai is to grant Lot my inheritance, then I must try to save him."

Sarai turned to Uriel and said sternly, "Do your job, guardian."

"I get that a lot," said Uriel. "Trust me, if I do not, you will be the least of my worries." He gave a quick glance heavenward and moved on.

Abram and Sarai kissed.

Then he left with his band of warriors for their long journey northward to catch the armies of the east.

CHAPTER 51

Abram traveled along the rich Jordan Valley at a fast pace with his regiment of two thousand soldiers. They did not know how far ahead Chedorlaomer was, but they were soon able to discern from the camp remains that they were getting closer.

Within four days they had caught up with their enemy targets, just outside Damascus in the area of Hobah.

Though the eastern armies outnumbered Abram's, it was not the entire armed forces that Abram would have to fight. Captives of war and booty were the last in line of the train of returning armies. Civilians and the baggage of spoils were too slow to keep up with the soldiers' march, so they were put at the back with a contingent of warriors to protect them. The main bulk of the army would then be far ahead in its journey.

Thus, there were only five thousand guards with the baggage train of several thousand captives when Abram and his forces drew near.

Because of his obsession with finding Abram, only King Amraphel stayed behind in the baggage train with Lot. Against Chedorlaomer's own orders to keep moving, Amraphel set up an extended camp in order to send forays into the area, looking for Abram or the hierodules who sought him.

He would not have to look for long.

Abram found him.

Abram split his forces into two divisions and attacked at night in a wedge formation. The eastern soldiers were blindsided and surrounded. Despite their superior numbers, confusion washed over them. They fell quickly to the spears and battle-axes of Abram's coalition forces.

As the battle raged, Abram hunted for his nephew. Uriel followed close behind, keeping watch over his human ward. Uriel became so busy blocking random soldiers' attacks, he did not hear the sound of the royal carriage wagon racing its way out of the melee, straight for them.

The wagon was a large enclosed cedar wood carriage, ornamented with gold and silver, which could only be carrying a king or other royalty. It was pulled by a six-horse team, whipped into a frenzy to get out of the battlefield.

Uriel yelled Abram's name only moments before the six-horse team trampled Uriel into the earth below their hoofs.

Abram heard him. He jumped out of the way, just in time to grab onto the back of the coach as it fled the scene.

He knew who was in that royal carriage. It had to be Nimrod, his old nemesis. He had recognized the hunter figure ensign on the wagon.

Uriel picked himself up from the muck. Archangels could not die, but it would take some time for Uriel to heal after saving Abram from a worse fate to the human body.

But Uriel was not interested in healing. He found the closest animal he could, to join the chase. It was a camel. He limped up to it, crawled on top and kicked his way after the runaway carriage.

Ten heavily armed paladin warriors of the East caught him by surprise. They came up from behind him, charging on their horses through the darkness after the royal carriage. They whisked past him in a whirlwind of dust.

He mumbled a prayer, "El Shaddai, you would not want to transform this camel into a stallion, would you? It might help your cause a bit."

El Shaddai did not tend to work that way and Uriel knew it, so he continued on with his pokey dromedary transport. He winced in pain and readjusted his dislocated shoulder.

Abram had a hard time hanging onto the carriage. It raced onward at full speed on a bumpy off-road path near the edge of the King's Highway, on a plateau with two hundred foot cliffs.

I am too old for this anymore, thought Abram. He remembered stories of his ancestor Methuselah wielding a battle-axe at nine hundred years old. Times were different then.

There was no time to complain. He had to save his nephew.

He looked in a window. Inside, Amraphel sat with the bound form of Lot.

Abram climbed up to the top of the carriage. The driver wildly whipped the horses to maintain their frenzied speed.

Abram needed to get to the driver to stop him.

Suddenly, from the side of the carriage, a boney, wraithlike creature climbed up and blocked his way.

It was Amraphel.

In his hand, a serpentine sword with a split-tongued tip, the edge glittering in the moonlight.

He looked a decomposed, deathly-looking shadow of what Abram remembered him as. But Abram knew his nemesis with certainty, when he looked in the king's eyes. That nemesis was still much taller and much stronger than Abram.

Amraphel finally spoke, "Godlicker, you have been the bane of my existence. And now, finally, I will be the bane of El Shaddai's."

Abram drew his sword and took his Karabu stance.

There was not much room to move on the rocking carriage top.

The carriage suddenly hit a rock. Both of them had to catch themselves to keep from falling off.

Abram looked down over the side. The carriage rode close to the edge of the plateau. In the darkness, he could not see the foot of the cliff. If he fell over that side, he knew he would not merely hit the ground, he would fall an additional several hundred feet down the side of the cliff to his death.

He gripped his sword.

Amraphel attacked like the madman he had become.

Abram barely kept up with the giant's onslaught, which was sloppy, but forceful and relentless.

Abram would not last long. Amraphel was stronger, a lifetime of fury and hatred pouring into his every move.

Abram was wearing down on the defensive.

In the carriage compartment below them, Lot struggled to free himself from his bonds. He heard what was happening above him. He hoped he would be able to join the fight.

But the bonds were not giving way. It did not help that he had two fewer fingers than usual to manage.

On the roof of the carriage, Amraphel continued his battery of blows. Finally, he made ringing contact. Abram's sword flew over the side of the carriage, down the cliff. Abram fell to his back.

Amraphel smiled in victory. Even in the poor light, Abram could see that his rotted teeth were full of grime.

Then, to Abram's surprise, Amraphel threw his own sword away. He took off his gloves and cast them over the side as well.

Abram knew why. Death by sword was too easy and unsatisfying for Amraphel. He wanted to strangle Abram with his own skeletal hands, to feel the life force leave him.

Abram steadied himself as the rocketing, speeding carriage hit another bump along the path.

Amraphel seethed with bile. "All my life has come down to this one moment. El Shaddai has taken everything from me. And now I can take everything from him."

Amraphel knelt down to reach Abram's throat. In his euphoria of triumph, he let down his guard.

Abram curled his legs up and placed his feet on Amraphel's gut.

Abram grabbed the edge of the carriage to steady himself. He heaved upward with all he had left in him.

Amraphel flew backward. He hit the carriage driver with such force that the man fell off his seat. He dropped through the horses' harness and was crushed beneath the wheels of the carriage.

Unfortunately, the driver did not let go of the reins until he was under the wheels. The horses were confused by the bizarre twisting of the reins. They jerked back and forth at odds with each other. It made the carriage rock back and forth.

Abram held on.

Amraphel was tangled up in the driver's gear, trying to hold on.

"ABRAM!" he croaked through his dry mouth. "Curse your god!"

The rocking increased. Abram knew the carriage could flip over any moment.

He saw his chance. He rolled off the side of the carriage, just as it almost tipped onto the flat ground.

But it did not land there. It rolled back to the other side. It flipped to the cliff side of the plateau with a big crash. It slid off the side of the precipice, pulling the horses and Amraphel with it, down into the rocky crags below.

With Lot.

Abram blacked out when he hit the ground and rolled. When he came to, he knew he had probably broken a few ribs. He coughed and tried to get up. It took him a couple of tries.

He limped to the edge of the plateau, murmuring to himself, "My nephew, my nephew."

He looked down. In the darkness, he could only just make out the shattered remains of the carriage, smashed to shreds four hundred feet below. Nothing survived that fall.

He could see the crumpled, broken corpse of Amraphel, the ghost who had haunted him for so long, finally and utterly dead. The giant who had become a monster, who had ruled the earth with a rod of iron, had finally met a most undignified ending, crushed at the bottom of a rocky plateau. Abram knew what awaited the giant at the Judgment would be far more painful and everlasting.

But there was no satisfaction for Abram, because he had not saved his nephew. He had failed.

"Lot, forgive me. I failed you."

Abram wept on his knees.

He heard a voice from behind him. "Uncle."

He turned. Lot stumbled toward him.

In the midst of the fight, Lot had managed to jump out the side door before the carriage careened off the ledge. Abram had been too occupied with his enemy to notice.

"Nephew!"

They hugged. Both groaned in pain because of the bruises from their falls. They shared a laugh together — which caused more pain in their bruised ribs.

"Let us find our way back to my forces," said Abram. "They will have slaughtered the enemy by now."

They turned from the precipice, but stopped short. Ten Gibborim of the east surrounded them on their mighty steeds.

"Uncle, it looks like we are the ones about to be slaughtered."

The lead warrior nudged his horse closer. It snorted, as if the horse itself was full of the same hatred as its rider.

Abram and Lot could not back up without falling four hundred feet to their deaths.

The lead warrior drew his sword. He wanted his prey to experience fear before he cut them down.

Abram sighed. "El Shaddai, this nameless, unimportant idolater is about to kill your seedline."

Almost as soon as he said the words, a lone, riderless camel trotted right across their paths, directly in front of the lead warrior. It gave a silly-sounding camel bellow that would have made Abram laugh if he were not facing death.

Such a simple, silly animal interrupting such a somber moment.

It was Uriel's silly camel.

The throat of the lead warrior burst open, pierced by an arrow from behind.

The other warriors whirled to face their intruder as he walked out from the darkness toward them. Uriel dropped his bow, whipped off his cloak loosing it into the wind, and drew his double swords.

The first two Gibborim attacked at once.

Their black steeds trampled toward him with fury.

Uriel dispatched them as they passed him by.

They fell from their horses, bodies cut in half.

The other warriors saw that this was one surly menace.

The seven of them got off their mounts and surrounded Uriel.

They waited for the right moment to strike.

Uriel called out, "Abram! Fear not!"

The warriors moved as one, all seven attacking simultaneously.

They were not about to give this angel the opportunity to fight one at a time.

Uriel was not interested in fighting one at a time. He stuck his swords out and spun around with supernatural speed. He cut them all down in seconds.

Uriel stopped, the seven of them at his feet.

He looked at Abram and said, "Now *that* is how you do *my* whirlwind move correctly."

Abram rolled his eyes. "That is very impressive, Uriel," he said. "I am sure you are the envy of all the archangels."

"A simple thank you would suffice," said Uriel.

Abram nodded. He did not want to be an ingrate for El Shaddai's help, regardless of how annoying that help was.

"Thank you for doing your job. Now, please help us get back to my men."

CHAPTER 52

Abram's coalition forces made their decisive victory complete by returning the captured men, women, and children, along with the plundered goods, back to the cities of Sodom and Gomorrah.

Abram left it to Chedorlaomer whether he would bother himself to chase his troublemakers all the way back into Canaan. After the long, drawn-out campaign, Abram doubted he would.

Abram reached the Valley of Shaveh, just outside the city of Salem a few miles north of the Oaks of Mamre. He had sent messengers to Sodom, to meet in this location for the return of the people and goods to Sodom and Gomorrah.

Lot stood next to Abram, Mamre, Eschol, and Aner in the small meeting tent. They watched the two kings approach them on the field. King Bera arrived with a pompous regal escort with horns and attendants, a leg of mutton in his right hand. When he entered the tent, his monstrous obesity almost did not fit through the entrance. The four attendants who usually helped him to move around waited outside as he sat now on a large carpet.

Bera disgusted Abram. He wondered what had gripped the soul of his nephew to desire such a decadent city and its debauched king, whose body odor alone was enough to make one gag.

The other king was the king of Salem, Melchizedek. He was a mysterious leader whose past was unknown to Abram. There was something very different about this ruler. He arrived with a simple escort, bringing bread and wine for their meeting. He wore a long robe with a hood rather than a crown. He had a well-groomed beard, and spoke as if he did not belong on earth.

Lot could not keep his eyes off the mysterious Melchizedek as he entered the tent, followed by a censor of incense. He offered the bread and wine as a symbolic meal of fellowship between the three leaders.

Before they sat down to the feast spread out before them, Melchizedek ordered one of his guards to bring forward several items; a set of cuneiform tablets, a compound bow, and a strange looking sword handle sticking out of a small leather pouch.

He handed them to Abram. "Blessed be Abram by El Elyon, God Most High, possessor of heaven and earth," he said. "And blessed be El Elyon who has delivered your enemies into your hand. I give these heirlooms to you."

"What are they?" asked Abram.

Melchizedek gestured to the weapons and said, "They are angelic weapons used by your ancestors. This is the Bow of Enoch and the whip sword of Lamech. They were both mighty giant slayers in their day."

Abram said, "How did you come by them?" Melchizedek looked familiar to him, but he still could not place him.

"That is not important," said the mysterious king. "All you need know is that they are yours for safekeeping, to pass down through your seedline. The bow is made of heavenly metal and strung with indestructible Cherubim hair. The sword is also heavenly metal that is both flexible like a whip and durable as the strongest sword. Your ancestor Lamech called it 'Rahab' after the sea dragon, because of its destructive capability."

Bera had already turned his interest to the food. He indulged his appetite as he listened.

Melchizedek picked up one of the clay tablets. "These are the toledoth tablets," he explained. "They contain the generations of your family, all the way back to Adam."

Abram looked at it. He already had some genealogy tablets he had received from Noah. But they were not as complete as these. He could see these tablets also contained stories of his forefathers that he would one day pass down to his posterity as well.

Abram stared into Melchizedek's eyes with intense curiosity. "How old are you?" he asked.

Melchizedek hesitated, as if not sure he should answer. "Too old to remember."

"Last of the old-timers," quipped Bera from his feasting.

Then Abram figured it out. His eyes widened. "Are you —?"

Melchizedek put his finger to his lips. "I am Melchizedek, king of Salem. I have no past. I am the servant of El Elyon, the most high God."

But Abram knew he was talking to Shem ben Noah, the blessed seedline, his great ancestor. It was why he was so old, and why he had the weapons that could only have been handed down from Noah. After the Tower of Babel debacle, Shem must have moved to Canaan and created a new identity for himself, wiping away his past, as the sons of Noah turned corrupt.

The gluttonous Bera had just stuffed the remainder of a loaf into his mouth. He still chewed it, grunting like a pig, when he spoke out, "What about me? Do I not get blessed?"

It took a moment for Abram to recall what Bera must have been ruminating over.

"You have the return of your people and spoils," said Melchizedek.

Abram butted in, "After a tenth of everything is given to the good king Melchizedek for his priestly services and mediation."

"Of course, of course," grunted Bera. He finished the wine, with some of it spilling down his beard. He ended with a rancid smelling belch. Then he turned sly.

"Abram, you can take the goods you have confiscated, just give me back the people stolen from me."

"I do not think you understand," said Abram. "I have lifted my hand to El Shaddai, God Almighty, who is El Elyon, possessor of heaven and earth, that I would not take a thread or sandal strap of anything that is yours, lest you should say that you had made me rich."

Bera's beady eyes narrowed, "No man is without his price."

Abram said, "I will take nothing but what we have eaten. As for Mamre, Eshcol, and Aner, let them take their shares, for they have been worthy allies."

"Indeed," said Bera. "And would your Amorite confederation consider a covenant with the Cities of Love, to build a wider alliance of defense?"

Abram stared at Bera with disgust. "I would sooner form an alliance with Sheol."

"Well," said Bera, "I guess you think you have purchased the right to insult me."

Their growing antagonism filled the air with tension.

Suddenly, messengers from Mamre's community entered the tent. They bowed before Abram and Mamre, winded from a speedy ride.

"My lords, Arba has attacked our clans."

CHAPTER 53

Abram and the three Amorite brothers raced their forces back to the Oaks of Mamre. Abram was horrified. That scheming miscreant giant had waited until all the best warriors left on their rescue mission to attack their unprotected villages. He did not have the honor to fight them like a giant. Abram knew exactly what Arba's motivation was: Sarai.

The leaders each found their villages in ruins. The few soldiers were all killed, but the women and children had not been taken captive.

Abram found Eliezer, who was bruised, but alive. He confirmed that the one captive taken was indeed Abram's beloved.

Abram met with Mamre, Eshcol, and Aner to assess their options.

He said to them, "My brothers, you have been more than hospitable all these years, and now your help in my rescue mission of Lot has brought this down upon our heads. I will take my forces against Arba to the last man, but your duty to me is done. You owe me no help in this matter."

Mamre stared at Abram with angry eyes.

"Nonsense, you dimwitted Mesopotamian. You would not have a chance against that giant clan. They are the finest Nephilim warriors of Canaan, and they devastated our lives just as much as your own."

Eshcol said, "Let us finish what Chedorlaomer started."

The four of them were suddenly aware of a presence with them. Three well-built paladins seemed to have slipped in out of nowhere, to stand amongst them in the shadows.

They were Uriel, Mikael, and Gabriel.

Mikael said, "We have little time. We must hurry."

Lot asked, "How are we going to assault Arba? He has a superior elevated position on the hill."

Mamre said with a smirk, "I have studied them for years, to figure out their weakness, just in case we might need it someday. Today is that day."

• • • • •

The stone palace of Arba was quite impressive in its display over the village of Kiriath-Arba. It rested near the top of the hill, overlooking the rest of the town. Arba had an eye toward expanding his kingdom's territory much farther in the future, so he enjoyed the view of distances the palace gave him. Its parapets hosted watch guards that could see for miles. A moat surrounded it. The stone walls, ten feet thick, were able to withstand just about anything that could be unleashed on them. It was a model of what was to come, for Arba planned to build a stone-walled, fortified city that would be impenetrable. He just needed more workers to be able to accomplish it. Since birth rate among his people was not as high as normal humans, he needed more time.

Inside those palace walls, a lonely and terrified Sarai wept on a huge bed. It was thirteen feet long, prepared with the finest silk sheets and down pillows. She had been placed in this "comfortable confinement" after she had been snatched from her tent in Mamre by the giant attack. She had seen Eliezer knocked out trying to defend her. When a giant had raised an ax to behead the faithful servant,

Sarai had screamed to stop. She would go willingly, if they promised not to kill any more of her people.

She hoped that Abram would have returned by now. He might already be negotiating ransom with the giant king Arba, in order to secure her return. But she could not stop weeping at the thought of how much pain she had put her husband through, by being captured like a petty slave.

"Oh, stop your blubbering, and dry up your tears, you old hag," came a voice behind her.

It was Naqiya, the queen of this clan. She bitterly resented Sarai's entire existence. She was jealous of Sarai's beauty and of her grace. And to make it all worse, Naqiya also felt very fat, with her large pregnant belly ready to give birth. But she knew the king's desires. Once King Arba wanted something, he would not stop till he got it. Anyone who stood in his way would be executed. It was why Arba had forced Naqiya to learn Abram's language, which she now spoke to Sarai.

Naqiya spit out, "You are the property of King Arba. And I have been cursed with the unenviable insult of preparing you."

"Preparing me?" said Sarai. "Has my husband returned in negotiation for my ransom?"

Naqiya looked at Sarai as one would a naïve child. "Are you really that stupid? Preparation for marriage, you moron. Arba is not going to 'ransom' you, he is going to mate with you."

Sarai's world fell in around her. She felt dizzy.

She *had* been foolish; foolish to believe in a world of honor and dignity amongst leaders, foolish to forget what she had seen in that monster years ago. She was helpless. Just the thought of Arba's massive six-fingered hands touching her made vomit rise in her throat.

All she could do was bow her head and pray to El Shaddai.

Naqiya had already walked over to the bath.

"Stop that nonsense," she barked. "Get into this bath *now* and clean yourself."

Sarai got off her bed and walked cautiously toward the bath and her giant, pregnant opponent. She slowly dropped her robe and felt vulnerable like a slave. She could feel the queen's eyes look her over with envy.

Naqiya barked, "We do not have all night."

Sarai got in the bath.

Suddenly, Naqiya felt a stabbing pain in her belly. She winced and made a slight moan.

"Is everything all right, Naqiya?" asked Sarai.

Naqiya looked at Sarai with an angry incredulity. Naqiya openly seethed with hatred for her, and yet this idiot bimbo seemed all concerned about Naqiya's welfare? It made her even more irritated.

Sarai washed herself, while Naqiya discharged her duty by explaining how to obey the king.

• • • • •

There was only one possible way to work a surprise attack on the fortified compound of Kiriath-Arba, by attacking it from its backside. But the backside was what made the hill almost inapproachable. It was a steep ravine of a thousand feet or so, that could only be scaled by experienced rock climbers. Certainly, a several thousand-soldier army had no chance.

The secret that made it *almost* inapproachable had been held tightly by Mamre, after his spies had discovered it years earlier. At the top of the hill stood the religious and astronomical megaliths set up for excarnation of their dead. After the bones had been picked clean by scavenger birds, they would be placed in ossuaries and brought below to a catacomb of tombs.

On his map, Mamre pointed out the approximate layout of the tunnels below the hillside town of Kiriath-Arba.

"That catacomb of tomb tunnels has a secret backside exit," said Mamre. "I know where that exit is."

Abram said, "I reckon it is a small one."

"One at a time," agreed Mamre. "We could not possibly get an army through it in time."

"We do not want to," said Abram. "The army will attack exactly where they would be expected to, the front of the town. The archangels and I will enter the tomb and engage in a behind-the-lines extraction, while everyone else is focused on you pummeling their forces out front."

"I want to go with you," said Lot.

"No," said Abram. "I will not lose you again, nephew."

"Uncle, before Sarai was yours, she raised me. I loved her as a sister, more dear than my own wife. I am going, whether you like it or not."

The angels were sympathetic.

But Abram was not, and Lot could see that.

Lot said, "I can do some fancy things with bitumen that you will not believe."

That drew a raised brow of interest from Abram. Lot was finally getting his headstrong uncle to listen to him. "Living in Sodom is not all bad, you know."

Gabriel added, "I think it is appropriate for me to reveal a few heavenly secrets about bitumen that just might add some kick to your earthly ones, if El Shaddai does not mind."

Abram said, "Get going. We have a village of giants to conquer."

CHAPTER 54

Arba had been ready for his attackers. He knew that the kidnapping of Sarai and the devastation he had inflicted on the Amorite villages would lead to war. So he had readied all his forces for battle while he prepared to satisfy his lusts on the woman who had driven him mad with desire. He really did not care what was going to happen outside. He had become completely obsessed with the blonde beauty of Mamre. His palace would be the last place in the town to be breached in an all-out war, only after all his forces had been wiped out. He knew that was not about to happen. His warriors were among the finest in the region. They could kill humans ten to one. He rested confident and prepared himself for his long-planned plowing of Abram's heifer.

Sarai finished her bath and dried herself with a towel. Naqiya continued her lecturing.

"And if you want to live, do not laugh at him."

"What do you mean?"

"Let us just say that he is not as big of a man as he appears to be."

Naqiya smiled to herself. In private, Arba lacked the self-confidence and manliness he paraded around in public. He seemed to drown in self-doubt and insecurities. It made him pathetic in her eyes and gave her some strength to withstand his childish outbursts of rage and violence against her.

Sarai anointed herself with oil and put on the perfume that had been chosen for her. She brushed a tear from her cheek. Where was her Abram? Where was El Shaddai?

• • • • •

Abram was below the city, crawling through the catacombs with Mikael and Uriel. El Shaddai was with them. The tunnels were tight and lined with ossuaries, the closer they got to the top of the hill.

When they finally exited the great mound, they left a large container full of pitch and other materials at the opening for their escape.

They wore servants' over-cloaks in order to blend in with the human element of the town.

They waited for their moment to move.

From the hillside below them, the sound of the call to war echoed throughout the town. The giants of Kiriath-Arba all turned to prepare for battle. It was the moment the team of three had been waiting for.

They slipped through the megaliths on their way to the palace walls near the top of the hill.

• • • • •

The Amorite brothers aligned their forces along the tree line just outside the town. They were not going to charge right away. They wheeled two catapults forward and began to fill them with special incendiary devices created by Lot and Gabriel.

They had been given access to the goods plundered from Sodom to create their new weapons. Lot gathered all the bitumen together, along with petroleum and sulfur. Gabriel called for saltpeter, linseed oil, tree resin, sheep fat, and quicklime.

Their Amorite helpers had no idea what they were making, but they gathered their ingredients for the angel. Gabriel used Lot to help craft the ammunition to be loaded in the catapults.

Lot showed the Amorites how to light the incendiary devices. The catapults began to barrage the town with their projectiles.

Due to their special creation, the projectiles did not just hit targets and demolish them; they erupted into huge explosions of fire that could not be put out with simple water brigades. Their explosive impact demolished an area with a hundred foot diameter. The impact zones would burn in an expanding ring of fire, consuming dozens of homes and their inhabitants. The assault struck fear into the hearts of the giant clan. Their fledgling city was going up in flames.

They did the only thing they could do in such a situation. They rushed the catapults with all their numbers.

They were met in the field by the Amorites with the clash of bronze, iron, and wood.

• • • • •

By the palace walls, Abram could see the fires throughout the town. The clashing line of combatants surged down the hillside like a flood.

The trio crossed the moat. Mikael threw a grappling hook high above them, to help them climb the walls.

"We have less time than you think," said Mikael.

Mikael and Uriel climbed up first with supernatural speed, and then they both yanked Abram up as if he were a mere cat tied to the rope.

Abram jumped down on the other side of the wall and looked around him. The place was empty. All the soldiers had assembled for the battle below, but surely Arba would require some of his giants to guard his palace? Had he secretly left? Were there other tunnels Abram was not aware of, to allow the king's escape?

Abram quickly got his answers. The three of them heard growls. They turned, to face the palace guards. A pack of five black dire wolves confronted them, twice the size of a human and full of muscle and claw.

The wolves leapt before the angels could even think of defense.

But these were archangels. They did not have to think. They moved with the fluidity of Karabu.

Mikael flipped in the air over the first wolf as it dove for him. Uriel then impaled its head in the ground with one swift downward plunge.

Mikael landed on the second one's back and cut its throat with lightning speed. The body tumbled to the ground.

A third one leapt for Mikael, jaws open with fangs bared. The angel swept around and beheaded it in midair.

The last two wolves pounced on Uriel. He ducked and the two of them knocked into each other, rolling to the ground in a pile of fur and fangs. Abram promptly disemboweled one as Uriel dispatched the other.

The gutted wolf gave out a howl that resounded throughout the palace. It brought another howl of response from the other side of the structure.

Mikael said, "We better keep moving. There are more coming."

• • • • •

Sarai sniffled a bit. She still feared her fate and prayed to El Shaddai every second she could.

Naqiya walked over to her with a small vial. "Here, take it."

"What is it?" asked Sarai.

"It is a drug. It will numb your senses, and you will not even remember what happened in the morning."

"Why would you offer me this?"

"It is my only chance of revenge on the slobbering pig."

Sarai thought it through. It would ruin Arba's pleasure for his object of lust to not experience the full pain of his perversion and worse yet to have no memory of it. For it was the victim's memory of being desecrated and abused that gave a monster the sweet aftertaste of power over his victim.

Only another victim could figure this out. And Naqiya was another victim — a vengeful one.

"No," said Sarai.

"What do you mean, 'no?'" barked Naqiya.

"You were right. I have been too ignorant for too long of the cruelty in this world. If I am to suffer, I will not retreat into ignorance and detachment from what El Shaddai has given me to suffer. It is too much a part of too many people's lives. I will not deaden my wits. I will not run like a coward."

Naqiya snorted, "You are one piece of work."

Sarai stared into the distance, her mind made up.

"Look at me when I talk to you!" yelled Naqiya. "Now, you listen to me. I am no coward either. I have suffered beatings, abuse, degradation and humiliation that you cannot even conceive of. But I now carry the royal seed in my womb."

"Naqiya, I did not call you a coward," whispered Sarai.

"Shut up! You call me Majesty!"

"I am sorry, your majesty. I meant no disrespect."

Naqiya could not find anything in Sarai's purity to feed her hatred, which made her even more frustrated. Sarai kept responding with graciousness.

Finally, Naqiya blurted out, "You are nothing but a shriveled up barren graveyard! But I will bring forth a giant king who will one day rule this entire land! I will birth a god!"

Sarai would not speak. She kept her head bowed in sadness and prayed for the giant queen before her.

CHAPTER 55

The battle for Kiriath-Arba quickly degenerated into a bloodbath of carnage and decimation. The giant clans were good warriors and fought valiantly, but the catapulted incendiary weapons had consumed their village and crushed their morale. The giants were desperate to stop the firebombing, so they lost their strategic edge. They were pushed back into the village until the thousands of Amorite forces wedging them in overcame them. Their homes were razed, and their families executed.

Mamre and Abram knew that to allow any to survive would only inspire that generation with the incentive to raise up and one day bring blood vengeance for their people. It would be endless war with endless bloodshed. This would have to be total annihilation. No slaves taken, no booty. These were children of Ashtart; they were the Seed of the Serpent.

• • • • •

From inside the stone palace walls, King Arba looked out and saw his hillside in flames and his people ravaged. He knew his time was short. He would take no more chances in waiting. He would take what was his, before he lost it again.

He crashed open the door to Sarai's chamber. Naqiya crouched in a corner, weeping. Sarai sat on the floor, praying, with the long satin sheet gathered over her head in useless protection.

He grunted pleasure to himself and strode over to Sarai. He grabbed the satin sheet and whipped it off of her.

It was not Sarai underneath. It was Abram.

He turned and threw a dagger at Arba, hitting him in the left eye. It buried deep. Arba bellowed with a howl so piercing it hurt Abram's eardrums.

Arba grabbed his wound and stumbled backward. With his good eye, he saw that Naqiya had been tied up. Her weeping was into a gag that had kept her from alerting him.

Two archangels stepped out of the shadows. Mikael and Uriel stood as shields before Sarai.

Arba screamed again with both pain and rage.

He pulled his sword from the scabbard at his belt and started slashing madly at Abram.

Abram was outmuscled. His sword flew from his hands, cracked in half by the sheer force of Arba's strength. But rather than stab him or slice him, Arba threw down his sword. He grabbed Abram by the throat, holding him up to the wall.

As he hung from the vise grip of Arba's large six-fingered hands, Abram could not help but wonder why these giants liked to kill with their bare hands so much. Abram's eyes darted to the angels. They did not move. He tried to scream for their help, but his voice was being choked out of him.

Abram could not understand why the angels were not coming to his rescue. It did not make sense.

The angels looked at each other. Uriel put out his hand to stop Mikael from moving.

Suddenly, Arba's grip went soft around Abram's neck.

Abram saw the giant's good eye roll upward. The monster suddenly stopped, dropped Abram, and then fell dead at Abram's feet.

Abram massaged his throat, trying to get his breath back. He snapped at the two angels, "Why did you just stand there?"

Uriel said matter-of-factly, "You want us to always save you, do you? We are here to help you, not make you lazy."

"But he could have killed me!" he protested.

"Not a chance. Your dagger pierced his brain. It just took a little longer for him to die than I thought it would. Sorry for the inconvenience."

Sarai ran to Abram and hugged him for all her life. They kissed. They could not stop kissing each other.

Uriel muttered, "It is not the end of the world yet."

Abram looked at Uriel's little smirk, then gestured toward Arba and Naqiya and said, "Hang them."

Mikael led Uriel, Abram, and Sarai through the courtyard. They meant to open the palace doors and allow the soldiers to enter and plunder. But before they could reach the door, they suddenly stopped. Twenty large black dire wolves surrounded them with snarling teeth. The four of them were in the middle of the courtyard and vulnerable. They gathered close to each other and drew their swords.

The angels assessed the situation. This would not be as easy as with the five wolves. They would be protecting two humans now. By the time they could kill half of the wolves, the other half would have overwhelmed Abram and Sarai and be licking their carcasses.

Uriel calculated that the door was too far. They would not be able to dash for it, to let all the soldiers inside.

He said to his companion, "I told you we should have done something about the rest of them, but you shrugged it off."

Mikael said, "Uriel, now is not the time to argue."

"It is never the time to argue. But I am right."

The wolves crouched to make their move.

The warriors readied their swords.

"Oh, very well! You are right," said Mikael.

Uriel smiled with satisfaction.

The head dire wolf pounced.

Suddenly, a storm of arrows rained down upon the dire wolves and filled them with wood and iron.

The animals howled in pain. Many died instantly, others were pinned to the ground with a dozen arrows.

The four looked up to the parapet. Abram's soldiers had scaled the walls. They waved to their patriarch, who waved back with relief.

Mikael commented, "Nice to be saved by humans once in a while."

The angels smiled at each other.

Uriel added, "But I was right, was I not, Mikael?"

Mikael rolled his eyes and sighed. "You are never going to let me live that down, are you?"

"Do not fret, Mikael," responded Uriel. "It is not half as bad as being teased about one's stature."

Mikael shrugged in deference. He could not deny that Uriel was teased too often about his size by the other archangels. Mikael himself was guilty of sometimes joining in.

Sarai said, "Let us go home."

Abram added, "I need a nap – with my beloved."

Sarai looked at him. His eyes narrowed purposefully at her. She knew what he really meant. It was amazing to her how the difference between good and evil men was not their universal desire, but rather where they directed it, to evil ends or to good ends.

She was thankful she loved a good man.

The king and queen were left hanging dead in their garden. They would be burned later in a bonfire with the bodies of the other dead. Carrion eaters already filled the sky, circling the massive dead.

One vulture swept down into the empty king's garden and landed on the king's head. It lowered its head to pick away at the flesh. It was shooed away by a bent-over, crooked old witch. She cawed and hit at the bird with a rock. It flew back up into the sky, to wait for a better moment.

The old witch had been beaten and left for dead, but had found her way up to the garden with singular intent.

She approached the swinging body of Queen Naqiya. She focused on the queen's pregnant belly, still carrying her royal seed, now dead along with her.

The witch chanted spells through mumbling lips. She pulled out a butcher blade from her cloak, and plunged it into Naqiya, ripping an opening across the queen's abdomen.

The hag reached up into the womb and pulled out the dead child.

She cut the umbilical cord and turned the large infant over. He had the signature long neck, strong musculature, and blonde hair of the giants. But he was blue with death.

She pulled some herbs out of a pouch and crushed them in her hand. She continued chanting as she rubbed the crushed leaves all over the little body. Then she slapped it several times.

Suddenly, the infant opened its eyes and yelped. It began to cry.

The witch picked up the infant and cuddled it in her arms. A demoniacal grin spread across her face. She said with pride, "The royal seed lives. Long live Anak, son of Arba. He shall be a mighty king and his sons shall rule this land, the sons of Anak. And he shall have his vengeance upon the sons of Abram. I vow this to the serpent god who rules Canaan."

CHAPTER 56

Time passed and Abram and Sarai rebuilt their lives. But there was still one thing they could not build: a family. Even though El Shaddai had promised them, those promises seemed farther and farther away with each year. Abram decided that his servant Eliezer, who had been adopted into their family, would be the heir of his family name. How else was El Shaddai going to accomplish such a task, with Sarai long past childbearing age and Lot moved back into the pentapolis of wickedness?

Sarai, on the other hand, could stand the impossible no longer. She loved El Shaddai, and believed in him. But it dawned on her that she would have to take things into her own hands if she was to fulfill God's promise of a family dynasty.

She did the only thing that made sense to her. She would offer Abram one of her servants as concubine to produce the promised seed. It was an acceptable custom in the land to do so, and she herself was old and useless anyway, so what did it matter?

Sarai barged into the tent one evening, pulling Hagar, an Egyptian maid, with her. Abram looked up, surprised. He had been praying for El Shaddai to give him some little sign of encouragement, after years of hearing nothing.

Sarai was irritated. She sputtered out the words, "El Shaddai has seen fit to prevent me from bearing children. Here is my servant Hagar. Give me children through her."

Abram was speechless.

Sarai was impatient. "Do you not find her pretty?"

"Sarai."

"Abram, if you love me, you will give me children through my servant."

It was clear to Abram she would not take no for an answer. After all, it was for the sake of the Promise, El Shaddai's own promise. Eliezer might be heir-worthy, but actual children made much more sense to Abram. At least, it was making much more sense to him as he looked at Hagar's beautiful young face.

Abram did not like the idea of having more than one wife. Variety was the herb of life, but Sarai was already enough to handle as it was. Though he loved her more than life itself, he could barely understand her emotional ways. Now, he imagined the stress of two women's impossible demands to please. He felt as if he was walking into a volcano and would regret it later.

As soon as Hagar told Abram she was with child, Sarai felt her world implode.

Sarai had come in from gathering some barley stalks for food, when she noticed Hagar in Abram and Sarai's private tent, holding her tummy protectively and watching Sarai with contempt.

Sarai stopped what she was doing and walked over to Hagar, glaring back at her.

A slight smirk crossed Hagar's lips. "*I* need to rest. *I* am with child."

Condescension oozed with every word from Hagar.

Sarai said, "How dare you."

Sarai turned on her heel. She headed out of the tent and straight out to the flocks, where Abram was taking a break with his shepherds.

She motioned to him, and he came to her.

She was steaming mad. Abram swallowed.

Sarai spoke with venom, "May the wrong done to me be upon your head."

Abram did not say anything. He did not know what he had done wrong now, and he did not want to add to the boiling cauldron.

"I gave Hagar for you to have your way, and as soon as she was pregnant, she looked upon me with contempt! May El Shaddai judge between me and you this awful wrong done to me!"

Abram was flustered. He would not let this go on. "Sarai, you speak to me as if it is my fault."

"It is your fault! You impregnated her."

"But you gave her to me against my better judgment."

"Now you are blaming me!" said Sarai.

"I am not blaming you."

"Well then, what is it when you say *against your better judgment*? That sounds accusational to me."

He knew he could not win. Nothing he said would change her mind. It only fueled the fire.

He decided to take control of the conversation.

"Sarai, she is *your* responsibility. She is *your* servant, to do with her as *you* please. So, go do what you must."

"All right, I will. I will do with her what I must."

Sarai stormed away.

Abram sighed, having dodged the arrow for just the moment.

Sarai stomped back to the tent, whipped back the curtain, and went right up to Hagar. She slapped her in the face and continued doing it. Hagar tried to cover up, but Sarai was relentless.

Hagar tried to cry out, "I am with child!"

Sarai said, "Yes, yes, we all know you are with child. You are endlessly reminding me you are with child. Fortunately, this is not going to hurt that child. This will only sting you for being insubordinate and disdainful of your mistress."

Finally, she stopped.

Hagar looked up at her. Sarai still saw that contemptuous look in her eyes, so she started to slap her again.

"I am going to wipe that silly little look of defiance right off your face, you ungrateful little minx!"

When Sarai picked up a small rug to use as a tool, Hagar could take no more of it. She ran out of the tent.

Sarai stopped. She could not believe what she had just done. She had become overwhelmed by her own emotions. Carried away, possessed by a spirit of rage.

She tried to catch her breath.

She walked outside to find Hagar, but she was nowhere to be found. She had run away.

Later that afternoon, Hagar had not returned for the lunch meal. Sarai began to be frightened for her. She could not take care of herself in the hill country. She wondered where Hagar might be, blaming herself for the outburst.

What was happening to me? she thought. The memory of the giant queen and her treatment of Sarai intruded in on her thoughts. *I have become the very monster I detest.*

Abram returned to the tent. He asked Sarai where Hagar was.

Sarai burst into tears, "I do not know, I do not know! I drove her away, and now she is somewhere in the desert or the hills and the wild animals will get her, and it is all my fault, and I am so sorry, Abram, please forgive me!"

She bawled into his arms. He held her tight.

"My precious, beautiful Sarai."

"What have I done?" She whimpered.

Abram patted her back reassuringly. "She will be back. I am sure she just wanted to give you time to cool off."

Sarai said through her tears, "I just want a family of our own."

"Sarai," he said with a hurt voice, "We are a family, you and I. We may not have children, but that does not make us any less a family in the eyes of El Shaddai."

He was right. She realized that by saying such a thing, she was reducing their marriage to a mere tool for having children. When El Shaddai created marriage in the Garden, he said the first priority was oneness. Procreation was second in importance to that union. She had made an idol out of children and negated her husband as her priority.

It only made her cry more in repentance.

"I am so sorry, my husband. You are my heart and soul. Please forgive me."

"There is nothing to forgive, my beauty pie. You are *my* heart and soul."

They kissed.

He said, "I did not tell you about the vision I had."

She looked at him curiously. "What vision?"

"Well, I was sitting by the Diviner's Oak of Moreh down by the river."

She interrupted, "What did you see?"

"El Shaddai appeared to me," he said.

"In what form?" she said. "Was he just a voice or did you see him?"

"Calm down," he chuckled. "I am trying to remember the details. He appeared in earthly form and told me — now what was it again? Something about — ah yes, he told me that my reward would be great, or something like that."

"Something like that?" She sighed. "Then what did you say?"

"Well, I told him that I still had no children and assumed Eliezer would be our inheritor."

Getting Abram to tell her the details was like getting a mule to talk. She said, "Then what did he say?"

"He said, Eliezer would not be my heir, but that we would have a child of our own."

He sat there, leaving the line lying there as if it were the climax of the story, without an ending. Sarai's eyes went wide with wonder. "Come, Abram, do not make me beg for the details." Men were terrible gossips. They just did not have a sense for the conversationally dramatic.

"I am trying to remember now," he said.

"You remember the number of our cattle, sheep, and goats, and the exact kinds of predators and prey in our area, down to the long haired jackrabbit. You can describe every possible variation of a shepherd staff or sickle sword. But you cannot remember what El Shaddai says to you?"

"I remember now. I just needed to jog my memory a bit."

"Well?" she said impatiently.

He grumbled, "Well, then he brought me out under the sky and showed me the stars of the heavens, and said, 'Number them if you can.' I laughed and he said, 'So shall your seed be.'"

Sarai said, "Then what did you say?"

"Nothing," he said. "I just believed him. And then he told me I was righteous."

"Why did you not tell me this, my beloved?" she said.

"I thought it would just drive you more into your sadness because it was just another hurry up and wait promise. I am sorry. I should have told you."

"You are probably right," she said. "It would have depressed me further. You know me so well." She held his face and kissed him.

"Ah, I almost forgot! Then he had me sacrifice a goat, a heifer, and ram, a turtledove and a pigeon."

"You almost forgot *that*?" she said incredulously.

"He made a covenant and passed between the halves of the sacrifices. And he told me once again that he gave this land to my seed, from the river of Egypt to the great river Euphrates."

Abram's face turned sober. "But then a great darkness fell over me and he said that my seed would be sojourners in a land not their own and that they would be slaves and be afflicted for four hundred years."

"Four hundred years?" she gasped. "That is forever."

"But he would judge that nation and bring them into this land in the fourth generation."

She was as confused as ever with El Shaddai's vague hinting. "So it will be four hundred years before your seed inherits this land?"

Abram added, "He said the iniquity of the Amorites was not yet complete."

Sarai was confused. "Whatever does that mean?"

"I do not know," said Abram. "But it does not sound good."

Just then, Hagar returned to the tent.

She looked to Sarai, to see if she was going to be punished. But Sarai was too exhausted, and she was genuinely sorry for her excess.

"Where did you go, Hagar?" said Sarai.

"The spring of water on the way to Shur," said Hagar.

"I am so sorry for raging out of control," said Sarai. "You did not deserve that. Please forgive me."

Hagar nodded her head. "I am sorry, mistress, for my arrogance."

Abram sighed with relief. And hoped their change of heart would result in a little evening affection.

Then Hagar said, "El Shaddai visited me at the spring."

Sarai was shocked that her lowly servant received such a royal presence. "What did he say?"

"He said I was to bear a son and to call his name Ishmael."

Sarai's eyes started to tear up. Everyone but her was getting a visit from El Shaddai. She held it back. She was not going to blow again. She was supposed to be more spiritually mature than that.

Hagar continued, "He said he would multiply my seed so that it would be a multitude."

Sarai and Abram looked askance at one another.

Abram said, "Hagar, did you just hear my discussion with Sarai?"

"No," she said.

They did not believe her.

Abram put his hands on his hips and asked, "Are you repeating El Shaddai's words to me as if he spoke to you?"

"I swear not, my lord," said Hagar. "He told me to return to my mistress and submit to her. And then he said that he had heard my affliction and that he was giving me a son, who would be a wild donkey of a man who would fight with everybody."

This was all very odd to Abram and Sarai, but then, El Shaddai was fond of doing odd things. They just dropped the subject.

Abram thought that this was the sign of a long, lasting regret for ever having listened to his wife and mating with Hagar.

CHAPTER 57

One day, Sarai and Hagar were cleaning the tent, when Abram came running in out of breath and rambling on like a madman.

"Where is a flint knife? Do we have a flint knife?"

"With the cooking things. What is wrong?" Sarai asked after him.

Abram let loose an uninterrupted stream as he raced around looking for the blade. "El Shaddai appeared to me again, and he told me to change my name to Abraham because he was making me a father of many nations. That he was establishing his covenant with me, and my seed after me, throughout their generations for an everlasting covenant. And that he was giving my seed the land of Canaan for an everlasting possession, and then he said to change your name to Sarah, and that he would bless you with a son, that kings would come from you!"

"Slow down, Abram!" she said.

"Abraham," he corrected her. "And El Shaddai said your new name is Sarah."

Sarai sighed. "Okay, master Abraham. We have been through all this before. He has told you nothing new."

"He gave us new covenant names."

"But did he give you any new information?"

"Where is that confounded flint knife?" he yelled impatiently.

She opened a box among the cooking gear and pulled out the flint knife. She handed it to him. "I guess it was not jumping out at you. What on earth do you want a flint knife so badly for?"

"Because El Shaddai told me to seal our covenant with circumcision. I have to circumcise every male in the household, as a sign of the everlasting covenant with El Shaddai."

Sarah was familiar with the procedure from their time in Egypt, where some of the Egyptians did it for ritual purposes. It was a bloody ritual, that entailed the removal of the fleshy foreskin sheath that covered the head of the male member. Done on male infants, it was virtually indistinguishable from any other pain an infant experiences in its newborn life, and it healed quickly. But for teenagers and adults, it was a very different and very painful matter.

Hagar had been listening to their exchange. "Ishmael too?" she asked.

"Every male — son, servant, and soldier."

Hagar fainted and fell to the ground. Sarah went to help her.

It was the heat of the day. The camp of Abraham was still. But the air was filled with the quiet moanings and groanings of male children and adults, tending the pain of their circumcision by the flint knife of Abraham.

Abraham himself sat in the door of his tent. If he did not move much, the pain was less. He turned his new name over and over in his thoughts, *Abraham. Abraham of Mamre.*

He thought about the meaning of circumcision, how it was a symbol of purification, through which the chosen seedline would come. It was part of his promise to El Shaddai that he and his offspring would not intermarry with the Canaanites of the land. They were to remain pure and untainted by the demonic religion and culture that enslaved these pagans.

He moved and groaned. "Sarah, would you please fetch me some water?"

She was already there with a goatskin for him. She whispered into his ear, "You men are so weak. Circumcision is nothing compared to childbirth."

"Nothing? This is worse than childbirth!" he yelped.

Hagar was nearby in the tent, cleaning up. She burst out laughing. She could not stop. She dropped her broom, laughing so hard. She had to gulp for breath.

"What is so funny?" complained Abraham.

"I am sorry, my lord," said Hagar between giggles. "It is just that you got a little cut across your private part." She looked at Sarah, and both of them belted out laughing.

"Why is that so funny?!" he bellowed. "You have no idea what it is like to have circumcision!"

Hagar barely got it out, "No. But you have no idea what it is like to give birth! And that is a much bigger pain in the bottom."

Abraham grumbled. He turned back around, to peer out the tent entrance. Sarah came up behind him and whispered to him, "All my empathy goes out to you, my lord and husband. Do you want me to kiss your boo boo?"

He winced, just thinking of the pain, "Owwwww! No! Get away!"

They moved on, smiling at one another.

"Heartless women," he muttered to himself.

His attention was caught by the sight of three men standing out by the Diviner's Oak, a short distance away.

He struggled off his chair to go meet them.

He limped, groaning with each step as he made his way to the large oak tree. Sarah and Hagar watched him curiously, wondering if the three men would come and introduce themselves.

When he got to the oak, he recognized all three of his visitors. One was El Shaddai, the Angel of Yahweh. The second was Mikael. The third was the huge, quiet, giant one he had met many years earlier, at the fall of the Tower of Babel: the Destroyer.

The monstrous angel's presence sent chills down Abraham's spine. This was the one who brought mass destruction and death to a population. What was he doing here?

Abraham bowed to the ground, grunting with pain.

El Shaddai chuckled. "I see you have responded with rapid obedience, regarding our covenant sign and seal."

"Yes, my Lord and God. I just hope recovery is as quick."

El Shaddai looked at Mikael and said, "Now *that* is faith."

Mikael playfully asked, "How is that Hagar situation working out for you, Abraham?"

"Please, do not ask," said Abraham. "I have reaped what I have sown. And I will never second guess my Lord again."

El Shaddai quipped back to Mikael, "I ask for faith, not perfection."

It was all in good-natured fun. Mikael would not question El Shaddai, but he liked to tease him about his odd choices of weak or flawed heroes for his seedline.

El Shaddai concluded with lightheartedness, "I think Mikael is spending too much time around Uriel. He is picking up Uriel's biting wit."

Mikael smiled.

The Destroyer did not. The Destroyer never smiled. He only sat and watched silently.

They helped Abraham stand up. He said, "If I have found favor in your sight, please do not pass me by. Allow me to wash your feet and prepare a meal for you, and after that, you can pass on."

El Shaddai said, "Go, do as you have said. But you do not have to run."

Abraham smiled and wagged his finger teasingly.

He hobbled his way back to the tent, yelling ahead of him, "Sarah! We need some bread cakes and milk! And get a calf from the herd! Hospitality! Hospitality for our guests!"

Abraham brought the meal that Sarah prepared with Hagar's help and stood with the visitors as they ate.

When they finished, they strolled with him back to the tent.

"Where is Sarah your wife?" asked El Shaddai.

"She is in the tent," said Abraham.

Sarah was hiding behind the flap, listening to every word the men spoke. She knew Abraham would probably only remember half of what they said, so it was her duty to listen in and get the full details.

El Shaddai said to Abraham, "I will return to you about this time next year, and Sarah shall have a son."

Sarah laughed to herself. Yeah, right. I am eighty-nine years old, a generation past menopause. We are a couple of worn out old goatskins.

El Shaddai said to Abraham, "Why did Sarah just laugh and tell herself that you are just a couple of old goatskins?"

Abraham's eyes went wide.

From behind the tent flap, Sarah's little voice peeped up, "I did not laugh."

"Oh, but you did," said El Shaddai, with a wink at Abraham. "Is anything too hard for El Shaddai? Come out here, my precious Sarah."

Sarah slowly revealed herself, like a child caught with her hand in the honey jar.

El Shaddai smiled at her.

"I did not laugh," she said again.

"Yes, you did."

"No, I did not."

"Did."

"Did not."

"Sarah," said El Shaddai, now sternly.

"Very well, I am sorry," she said, and bowed.

El Shaddai laughed. "I will return to you this time next year, and you shall have a son."

"Thank you, my Lord. It has been a long wait."

"Sarah!" scolded Abraham.

"No, it is all right," said El Shaddai. "You are right. It has been a long wait. I have not given you much to hold on to. And do you know why I waited so long?"

Sarah thought about it. She did not want to be irreverent or flip. But she could only think of one thing: "So it would be impossible?"

"Because I really like to hear you laugh," he replied and turned to leave with his two companions.

Sarah stood there with wonder.

And then, she laughed, but this time, with joy, and went back into the tent.

Abraham accompanied the three visitors up to the hilltop overlooking the valley.

El Shaddai stopped with Abraham as the two other angels continued onward to the east.

"Where are they going?" asked Abraham.

"I have thought to myself whether I should tell you or not," said El Shaddai. "The cities of the plain."

"Sodom," said Abraham, thinking of his nephew Lot. With the Destroyer going there, he knew it was serious. He knew Lot would not have a chance of surviving such an angel of mass destruction.

El Shaddai said, "The outcry against Sodom and Gomorrah is great and their sin is very grave."

"Is not this entire land full of such evil?" asked Abraham. "What makes Sodom and Gomorrah any different?"

"It is the source of the river, the hive of the hornets, the den of lions. Watchers are engaging in atrocities there that I sent the Deluge to stop. I am going down to see whether they have done according to the outcry that has come to me."

"Would you sweep away the righteous with the wicked?" challenged Abraham. "Suppose there are fifty righteous within the city? Would you not spare the city for those fifty righteous, or would you kill them all? I cannot imagine you putting to death the righteous along with the wicked as if they deserved the same judgment. Shall not the Judge of all the earth do what is just?"

El Shaddai continued to stare out at the two departing angels, now down in the valley on their journey. "If I find fifty righteous in the city of Sodom, I will spare the whole place for their sake."

The angels were crossing the plain and getting smaller in the distance.

Abraham broke the silence again, "My lord, I am but dust and ashes speaking to the very Creator of the heavens and earth."

"Say it, Abraham," said El Shaddai.

"What if there are only forty-five righteous people in the city? Would you destroy the whole city for lack of five?"

El Shaddai knew what Abraham was thinking. "I will not destroy Sodom if I find forty-five there. I will not destroy it if I find forty, or thirty, or even twenty righteous there."

Abraham winced a bit and said like a humble sheep, "Lord, please do not get angry, but…"

"For the sake of ten righteous, I will not destroy the city." El Shaddai had now grown distant in his look.

And with that, El Shaddai walked off in a northerly direction, away from Abraham and the other two angels who were already on their distant way to the southeast.

CHAPTER 58

Ba'al led Ashtart down the underground tunnel in a dog collar. It had been thirteen years since the battle of nine kings, where Marduk had defeated Ashtart and became Ba'al, the king of the gods of Canaan. Ashtart's plan had been set back generations with the devastation of her giant progeny throughout the land by Chedorlaomer's forces. But with the addition of Ba'al as the Most High God of Canaan, the two of them together could do what she could not do alone. Ashtart had revitalized the original program of miscegenation of the Watchers. The rest of the pantheon of gods were fearful of the consequences of such a pursuit, since El Shaddai had already flooded the earth the first time such a course of action had been undertaken. But with the two most powerful divinities united, the pantheon could do little but sit back and see what happened.

Ba'al and Ashtart entered a special caged room they called "the pit," where they had been pushing the envelope of their human experimentation.

"How is our little Blob?" said Ashtart. She grabbed a bucket of slop feed and threw it onto a bizarre, naked monstrosity that filled the cage floor before them. The sounds of one hundred different human beings fused together into a "blob" of human flesh filled the chamber. They had been surgically and magically amalgamated into one large biomass of humanity, a human unity of oneness with a hundred different bodies and a hundred different mouths.

The nearest of the humans tried to lick the slop up to fill their grumbling bellies. Others cried out in misery.

"Oh, keep your yaps shut!" yelled Ashtart. "You should learn to share more anyway! You are all part of the whole, so learn to suppress your selfish individualism!"

It was a physical embodiment of the gods' pursuit to dissolve distinctions in the created order. They had intermingled kinds such as human and divine, human and animal, male and female, and other chimerical hybrids. But this was the attempt to create a oneness of human beings that would elevate the collective above the individual. As individuals, they all pursued self-interest, which led to independent thinking and freedom of thought and division. But this would not do for a kingdom that sought to control the masses through dependency.

The Blob was an incarnation of the eradication of the individual. As an inseparable part of the collective, if one of them died, then that rotting corpse affected all those around them. This responsibility for one another ensured that everyone worked to keep the collective alive or suffer their own ultimate demise.

As a mass of fused beings, they had to help feed each other, keep each other healthy, clean each other's defecation, or they would all get diseased and die. No room for selfish individuals in this mass of flesh and bone, in this Blob of humanity.

But Ashtart was getting tired of this pet. She wanted more. She wanted to explore the limits of occultic possibilities. To her, there were no limits to the science of experimentation. If it *could* be done, it *ought* to be done. Humanity was a sacred shibboleth to be violated and the natural order, a creation of El Shaddai to be corrupted. She had been working on occultic spells that might make this Blob come alive as one giant creature of obedience to her. If all their minds could be melted into one mind, that mind would move with one accord as one creature. And that creature would do the bidding of Ashtart as her meat puppet.

She thought she had finally found the spell that would transform the blob into that solitary creature. But she had not had the opportunity to try it out yet because she was beholden to Ba'al's whims.

Ba'al was more interested in building his kingdom of power in Canaan. They were populating the land with the Nephilim seed, through their breeding of giants. They had sent them out to start new clans throughout the land. The other gods of Canaan; Molech, Dagon, Asherah, and Resheph and Qeteb were helping to secure the region with varieties of cult practices to ensure that the god of this land would not be El Shaddai, but the Serpent. The five cities of the plain, headed by Sodom and Gomorrah, had been a dream come true for their scheme.

But it had been too excessive. Ashtart and Ba'al had become addicted to the forbidden union with the daughters of men. They had been warned by Mastema himself that the outcry of Sodom and Gomorrah had reached heaven. Ba'al and Ashtart were just arrogant enough to count on the fact that El Shaddai would never flood the earth again.

But a flood was not the only means of cleansing corruption.

Lot had eaten lunch with his family. He prepared to return to the gate for more adjudication. In fact, he could not wait to get away. His family had become intolerable for him. He had lost control of his headship years ago. The city was a hive of centralized thought. It had much more control over its citizens than individual families did. His twin daughters were educated by the government of the city in order to secure a unified way of thinking. They were but fourteen years old, and were convinced that the world revolved around their greatness. They were called "Ba'al Youth," as were all children of the city. They had become so thoroughly indoctrinated in the religion of Ba'al and Ashtart that they would even inform on their own parents, if they expressed thoughts that went against the state or the gods. Lot cringed every time he heard them singing around the house their songs of indoctrination about Ba'al's new world. *He is gonna change it, rearrange it. Ba'al's gonna change the world.* Lot had lost control of them long ago. They had become little monsters of chaos.

Those two little monsters had been betrothed to young men of the city by the Ministry of Love, a government department that was responsible for taking over the matchmaking of marriages in order to ensure the continuity of the city-state. Though marriage had been spurned, even castigated, procreation was still necessary or the society would die out. Thus the Ministry of Love required all youth to engage in breeding by issuing "propagation licenses" for a period of time, in order to maintain population replenishment. Of course, this was not allowed to interfere with their cult of free love with any and all beings, human, animal, or god.

Lot's wife, Ado, did not make life any easier for him. She had been an orphan of Sodom, so from birth had been groomed to be a dependent slave upon the "good welfare" of the city. She let the children rule their lives. She let the city define her. Sodom was her true home, and the government, her true family. She had submerged her identity into the whole and found her identity as a child of Sodom.

Lot had been emasculated, as had all men of the Cities of Love. Patriarchy, or male headship in the family, had been stamped out long ago, by reducing men to workers of the collective without individual initiative. The collective of mediocrity suppressed leaders, in order to keep others from looking bad. Everyone was equal, so no one was exceptional — and therefore everyone was manageable. When the state controls the family, it becomes the true god of the people, and only one god may rule at the top: Ba'al.

Lot trudged his way to the gates of the city. He had a deadness in his eyes. He had given up. He felt helpless, a victim without the ability to make a difference. So he survived. He became a cog in the wheel of the machine of madness. He became a bureaucrat.

He made it through another mindless day, with barely a memory of what he had said or done. And now, he was going to go drinking. He wanted his family to be asleep when he arrived home, so he could avoid the nagging of his wife and the selfish demands of his daughters. He just wanted to sleep. He wished he could sleep the rest of his life.

As he prepared to leave the gates, he noticed something that woke him from his slumber. Two visitors approached the city entrance. They did not have beasts of burden, and appeared to be all alone. One was huge and both walked with a confidence he had not seen in a long while.

When they approached him, he knew exactly who they were: angels. They stopped before him. He bowed low to the ground and said, "Please, turn aside to your humble servant's house and wash your feet, and you may rise early and be on your way out of Sodom."

Mikael said, "We will spend the night in the town square."

Lot's blood ran cold.

"Trust me, please, dear sir. You do not want to do that. Sodom is not a place of hospitality for strangers — or angels."

Mikael raised his brow in curiosity. This Lot was quite observant.

Sodom's inhabitants had become so experienced in copulation with strange flesh, they could smell an angel a mile away. Some had already done so at the gate. Lot looked around nervously. Some of the more surly elements began to congregate nearby, observing the strangers' interaction with Lot.

Lot did not bother to tell his visitors that the town square was where the citizens would take visitors, strangers, and other unwary traveling merchants, to gang rape them before sending them on their way. Their depravity had reached such depths of obscenity that they had become like unthinking animals, creatures of malevolent instinct, born to be caught and destroyed, waterless clouds driven by a storm. They kept seeking deeper and deeper thrills of the forbidden. And the ultimate forbidden experience of lustful indulgence was the pursuit of unnatural flesh, sexual union with an angel.

The gathering men watched the large angel with particular desire. Yes, he would be a more difficult catch, but it made the trophy that much more thrilling to them.

"Please, please," said Lot to the visitors. "Come with me now. It is already getting dark, and this is no place to be at night."

Mikael said, "Very well. Lead the way, elder Lot."

Lot look surprised at him. "How did you know my name?"

Mikael said, "We *are* angels after all."

Lot shrugged and led them quickly to his home in the heart of the city.

CHAPTER 59

Lot's wife Ado made a meal for the angels. The entire family sat with them as they ate.

She watched them with a wary eye. She said to Lot. "You know we are breaking several laws by housing these men here for the night."

His eldest daughter, Ishtar said, "Father, we are duty bound to report this to the Ministry of Hospitality."

"I know, I know," said Lot. He was scrambling, trying to figure out how he could possibly get out of this mess he had gotten himself into.

Mikael watched the nervous Lot with sadness. "You have done what the Creator requires. Be strong and courageous, man of faith. El Shaddai is your strength."

Now Gaia, the youngest daughter piped up, "Blasphemy! You two are going to be in real trouble now."

Mikael kept his eyes on Lot. "You need to take back authority over your family, Lot."

"How dare you!" yelped Ishtar. "Ba'al Youth are the future of this world! We are the sons and daughters of Ashtart."

Gaia added, "King Bera loves us, and you are the son of a mongrel!"

Suddenly, Lot banged his fist on the table and yelled as if he had never yelled before at his family. "ISHTAR AND GAIA, SHUT YOUR MOUTHS OR I WILL SHUT THEM FOR YOU!"

Ishtar and Gaia stared with fear at their father. But they shut their mouths.

A loud crash outside broke the silence. Then came a pounding on the door. Ado jumped. The girls shrieked.

Lot sighed with resignation. "They followed us."

He looked at Mikael and said, "This is not good, my friend. You may be angels. But these miscreants have savaged worse."

Mikael looked at the Destroyer, who only gave a slight smile.

Lot said, "Let me see what I can do."

He got out of his chair and went to the door. He lifted the bar across the heavy oak door, turned and said, "Lock the door behind me."

Ado obeyed.

Lot stepped out into the night.

All around his house were a thousand shadows of the night. Riff raff, gangs, and the darkest elements of Sodom, both young and old. They had come for flesh, angel flesh — male angel flesh.

The leader, Belus, a giant of a man, with large muscles from mining, stepped out. "Where are the men who came to you tonight?" he said. "Bring them out, Lot. It is our right by law to penetrate them!"

The crowd around the house cheered. City legislation protected the citizens who engaged in immoral atrocities with strangers and merchants who visited the city.

Lot yelled back, "I beg you, my brothers, do not act so wickedly!"

The crowd jeered him.

Belus was offended. "I am outraged! How dare you spew your hatred and intolerance, calling *us* 'wicked!' You should be hanged for such criminal hatred!"

The criminal element cheered again.

Lot was undeterred. He knew that Mikael and the big one were angels, and he still maintained his shred of faith in El Shaddai. Still, he was sweating now, imagining his own torture and abuse along with the angels.

He approached Belus with a conciliatory tone, "Belus, listen to me. I have two virgin daughters who have not known a man. They are of age for knowing. Please, let me bring them to you to do as you please. But do nothing to these men, for they are under my care."

Belus burned with anger now. He turned to the others with a prophet's oratory. "This man, Lot, came to sojourn in our good City of Love! Now, he sits in judgment over us?"

The shadows of Sodomites came out into the firelight of the torches carried by the bolder ones. There were at least a thousand in the open square alone, and God only knew how many more still hid in the shadows.

Lot backed up to his door.

Belus pronounced like a judge, "I say we will deal worse with you than with those angels!"

The crowd yelled again. But they were becoming more agitated and less in unison. Belus ignited them, but there would come a moment when he had no more control over them. Then they would simply sweep over Lot and take what they wanted.

Suddenly, a large pair of hands reached from behind the door and pulled Lot into the house.

It was the Destroyer.

Mikael stepped out front, just as some of the men had decided to move and break down the door.

A group of ten of them jogged toward Mikael and riled the crowd forward.

Mikael then held his hand out. A bright ball of light seemed to appear from his hand. It burst outward like an arc of lightning that blinded everyone in the open square.

The ten running men tripped over each other and fell to the ground. Others rubbed their eyes, trying to get their vision back. But it was not going to come back. All thousand pairs of eyes had had their retinas permanently burned out. They groped for the doorway, but fell all over each other, trying to find their way. Fights broke out over their stumbling and they started brutalizing each other.

Inside, Mikael told Lot, "Have you any other family here?"

Lot said, "Just my sons-in-law betrothed to my daughters."

"Go out the back and get them now. We are leaving."

Lot obeyed and went out the back door.

Ado said, "What do you mean, we are leaving?"

Mikael said, "The outcry against the pentapolis and its people has become so great before El Shaddai that he has sent us to destroy it."

Ishtar blurted out, "I am going to tell Ashtart about this! You have no right!"

Gaia shook her little fists and ranted in a tantrum. "I am not going! I am not going!"

The noise of the commotion outside became riotous. The blindness had infuriated the men, but they were taking it out on each other in a riot of rage which would soon find Lot's home.

After a short time, Lot returned through the back door. No one was with him.

He saw his two girls in a mutual tantrum, holding their eyes shut and crying, "I am not leaving! I am not leaving!"

He walked up and slapped both of them, until they stopped wailing in fear of the gall of their father.

He was taking charge.

Mikael asked Lot, "Where are your sons-in-law?"

Lot shrugged. "They did not believe me. They thought I was joking."

He did not say so, but he felt it was a good thing. Lot did not care for the two juvenile delinquents. They were disrespectful Ba'al Youth who had no shred of moral integrity.

Mikael said, "Leave now, lest you be swept away with the damned in punishment."

Lot hesitated, "Is there not any other way of doing this? Can you not find the leaders and punish them? Do you have to kill the innocent with the guilty?"

"We are not killing the innocent," said Mikael.

It struck Lot that Mikael just implied that there was not a single other righteous person in the city but him and his family. And he was not even sure of his family.

"You have wasted too much time," said Mikael. "Destroyer, grab them."

The Destroyer picked up Lot and Ado. Mikael picked up Ishtar and Gaia, and went for the door.

The girls started kicking and screaming. Mikael squeezed them so tight, they passed out.

Lot saw it and could not help but give a smile of approval.

Mikael backed up. The Destroyer gave a swift kick. The door exploded outward with a blast that slew the ten closest blind criminals and laid a dozen others out flat on their backs.

The angels led the family through the confused blind crowd and out of the city.

The morning was dawning over the mountains.

Someone had informed the gods about the commotion at Lot's home, and that there were angels in the city.

Ba'al and Ashtart were raving mad that angels had sought such subterfuge. They were on their way to capture the offenders, when they saw the angels carrying Lot's family toward the gates.

Ba'al stopped in his tracks and held back Ashtart.

"What are you doing?" complained Ashtart. "They are getting away."

Ba'al's skin went pale as the blood left his scales. He knew who that huge, angelic hulk was.

"The Destroyer," said Ba'al.

Ashtart knew as well. She knew they would not stand a chance against the Destroyer. No one stood a chance against that holy one of heaven's host.

"We need to leave now," said Ba'al.

They turned tails and ran back to their temple.

But Ashtart had one last punch she wanted to throw.

Outside the gates of the city, Mikael told Lot, "Do not look back or stop anywhere in the valley. Escape to the hills, lest you be swept away."

Lot stopped him, "My lords, you have shown me great kindness in saving my life, but I cannot make it to the hills in time. I will be overtaken. May I flee to Zoar? Would that be far enough?"

Mikael looked at the Destroyer, who nodded. Mikael turned back to him, "Very well, I will grant you this favor. Go to Zoar, but do not stop until you get there. I will hold off until you arrive."

Lot, his wife, and their two daughters then set off on their horses, toward Zoar a few miles away.

Mikael and the Destroyer reentered the city.

As they stepped through the gates, they heard a heinous screeching bellow come from the main street leading to the temple. It was not human; it was more like the sound of many humans full of furious rage.

The ground trembled beneath their feet. They saw the thing come at them from the street.

It was the Meat Puppet blob, the creature from the Pit of Ashtart's experimentation. It was about twenty feet tall, a mass of muscle and flesh and bone coming at them. It had appendages that worked as two arms and two legs, but they were not very human looking. It was made of humans that had become melded together in a singular consolidated creature of fury. Ashtart's spell had worked. It had united the minds of the individuals who made it up into one hive mind, in service to Ashtart. That mind was inhabited by Nephilim demons. And Ashtart had commanded it to kill.

It ran full speed at the angels. It had no pair of eyes, for it had two hundred eyes all over its body, the eyes of its composite human bodies merged into one.

It was grotesque. Hideous.

It swiped one of its mutant hands and hit the angels, launching them a hundred feet. They slammed into the wall of the city. The rock dissolved into a pile of rubble.

Mikael had the wind knocked out of him, but the Destroyer was only angry. He stood up and brushed himself off.

The Meat Puppet reached them. It tried to crush Mikael with a pummeling fist of flesh and bone. Mikael rolled out of the way.

The Destroyer grabbed one of the legs and ripped it off. The Blob shrieked in pain and it fell to the ground in a bloody mess.

But then it reshaped itself with a new leg, like a mutating organism.

"This is not going to be easy," said Mikael.

The Meat Puppet swung and hit Mikael again. He slammed into another wall and this time stayed down.

The Destroyer would not go down so easily though. He drew a sword from his sheath. The hefty sword matched the angel's powerful arms and large size. He wielded it with a mighty arc, and cut off the Meat Puppet's left hand.

The titan screamed again, all ninety of its voices in painful unison, as it reshaped its hand. The Destroyer promptly cut it off again, bringing the thing down in size with each chop.

The Meat Puppet backed off.

Mikael had feigned unconsciousness. He snuck up behind the creature and jumped on its back. He plunged his own sword deep and ripped out a dozen of the human bodies.

The Blob fell to the ground. Mikael rolled off.

Mikael and the Destroyer ran into the midst of the city, to lose the thing in the labyrinth of streets. The Meat Puppet followed them, limping with its bloody mass of seventy bodies, still held together by magic and villainy.

· · · · ·

By the time, Lot and his family made it to Zoar, they were exhausted. He found a place to stay and he dropped off to sleep.

Ado could not sleep. She had been upset by the way things had gone. Her soul was in Sodom. She had never left the city her entire life, and now she was forced to leave by a pair of mean-spirited angels, who had no compassion for the people of her city who had become her family. She thought of being alone with Lot and her girls and how they would have to start a new life together in a cruel world of frightening uncertainty.

She could not stand it. She could not stand to follow this vindictive and capricious god El Shaddai who put them through so

Brian Godawa

much pain and misery. At least Ba'al had cared for them. He provided them with everything they needed to live and thrive in the city. He brought rain for the crops, and bitumen from the fields, and copper from the mines.

The city was her heart.

After Lot and their daughters were fast asleep, Ado got on one of the horses and made her way back to Sodom. She was not going anywhere. She would stay with her city, come hell or high water.

It was hell that came.

CHAPTER 60

Mikael and the Destroyer led the Meat Puppet monstrosity into the center of the city, where the riot of blinded Sodomites had occurred.

The occult spell that Ashtart had used was loosening its grip on the creature as it stumbled into the open square near Lot's old home.

But the angels were not running away. They were drawing everyone to the epicenter of their plan.

When they reached their destination, they turned and faced the Meat Puppet and the few stragglers still stumbling around in the aftermath of the blinding. The stragglers cried for mercy. Their eyes had been burned out of their sockets. They flailed for anything to grab onto for security.

Mikael and the Destroyer stood in the center of the square. Mikael looked up and prayed, "El Shaddai, God Almighty, the Most High God, El Elyon, possessor of the heavens and earth, bring down your wrath!"

With that prayer, the Destroyer lifted his massive sword and plunged it into the ground all the way up to the hilt.

The earth trembled and shook.

The Meat Puppet lost its footing and fell to the ground.

Up above, a large storm cloud gathered. Thunder cracked the sky.

The Sodomites circled the angels.

Suddenly, a light from heaven burned down upon the two angels and they were gone, translated up to heaven.

• • • • •

All along the Valley of Siddim, the long, gigantic rift began to spasm. Large fractures opened in the crust. Massive amounts of heat and gas escaped into the air.

The land rolled like a tsunami wave of earth.

Up above, lightning joined the thunder in the black heap of cumulus storm clouds.

Sodom, Gomorrah, Admah, and Zeboiim were at the very epicenter of the catastrophic conflagration. Their buildings crumbled in the wake of the shaking. The sounds of a population in chaos could be heard in each city as their citizens sought refuge and found none.

The storm front created a pressurized system that caused a huge uprush of wind from the ground to the sky.

Outside the city, the bitumen pits exploded with black pitch spewing out like a field of small, gushing volcanoes of black vomit. The earth was in upheaval. It belched forth gasses, solids, and liquids into the sky. The hurricane-like winds sucked the volatile materials up into the whirlwinds high above the entire valley.

Then the lightning struck.

A massive display of multiple lightning strikes painted the sky with a frightening brush. It lit the combustible elements in the whirlwind.

A rainstorm of fire and brimstone from heaven engulfed the four cities of the plain in a furnace of sulfurous flames.

Nothing survived.

Ado had made it back to the city gates by the time the destruction had started. She was turned into a pillar of salt. Everything was turned to salt and embers.

But the finale was yet to come.

Huge geysers of salt water burst out in locations all about the Jordan Sea. They had been released like vents from Sheol. The salt water would kill all sea life in its wake as it spread through the fresh waters. One last seismic convulsion ripped through the plain. The entire valley dropped three hundred feet in five seconds. It was as if the earth had been sucked downward.

In the sudden surface change, a runoff of the Jordan Sea rushed in, to fill the newly lowered plain. A wall of salt water washed over the cities of the plain, putting out the fires. It buried the inhabitants and their ruins under a blanket of salt water. A new shoreline washed up all the way to the town of Zoar, where Lot had fled to.

Black steam billowed and mixed with the smoke of the burning bitumen.

The plans of Ba'al and Ashtart had been thwarted. Sodom and Gomorrah, Admah and Zeboiim, were now under the deadly brine waters of what would now be called the Dead Sea.

· · · · ·

Thirty miles away at Mamre, Abraham stood in awe of the huge black pillars of ash that poured into the sky like the smoke of a furnace. The cities of the plain were gone from the face of the earth, buried in the judgment of El Shaddai.

EPILOGUE

Lot had been so traumatized by the devastation of Sodom and Gomorrah that he took his daughters up, out of Zoar. He lived in a cave in the hills, away from all human contact.

His daughters fretted that they would never be in the presence of civilization again, and would become two old, unmarried maids. So they acted out of desperation to preserve their family seed in honor of their mother.

One evening, they got their father drunk, which was not hard to do. He had lapsed into depression from his lifetime of failure to honor his god El Shaddai.

The eldest, Ishtar, then slept with him to get pregnant. Because Lot had been so inebriated, he had no recollection of the incestuous deed, just a phantom memory of having a shameful dream that made him even more depressed.

The second evening, the daughters got him drunk again and Gaia, the youngest, slept with him and got pregnant as well.

The fruit of their incestuous intercourse would one day prove to be a thorn in the side of Abraham's seed to come. The firstborn bore a son and called him Moab. The younger one bore a son and called him Ben-ammi. These two would be the fathers of the Moabites and the Ammonites.

• • • • •

True to his word, El Shaddai did visit Sarah one year after the incident of laughing. This time, it was to oversee a birth. Sarah did conceive as El Shaddai promised and she bore a son for Abraham, whose name was Isaac. This time Sarah laughed with happiness instead of doubt and said, "God has made laughter for me. I have borne a son for Abraham in his old age."

• • • • •

Somewhere out in the Negeb desert, not too far from the ruins of Kiriath-Arba, a young fifteen year old giant named Anak finished his fighting practice for the day. He sat before a fire. His long, muscular neck pulsated with rage, as he listened to an old witch tell him again the story of his birth and the annihilation of his entire giant clan by the armies of Abraham, who came from the oaks of Mamre.

One day, he thought, *I will spawn a people and destroy the entire seed of this Abraham. And my seed will rule Canaan.*

For the next book in this story timeline get *Moses: Against the Gods of Egypt*. Though it is in the Chronicles of the Watchers series, it is the next one you want to get. This is because Chronicles of the Watchers is interwoven with Chronicles of the Nephilim to fill in the gaps of the storyline of the Nephilim series.

If you liked this book, then please help me out by writing an honest review of it on Amazon. That is one of the best ways to say thank you to me as an author. It really does help my exposure and status as an author. It's really easy. In the Customer Reviews section, there is a little box that says "Write a customer review." They guide you easily through the process. Thanks! — *Brian Godawa*

APPENDIX
BETWEEN THE LINES: IN DEFENSE OF ANCIENT TRADITIONS

There is a danger for any author who shares the research behind his fictionalized storytelling. If he reveals "what really happened" as different from his story, then readers may have their story spoiled much like a child who is told the true story behind Santa Claus. If he shares the choices he makes of which evidence he chose over others, then the magic and mystery is ruined for those who prefer their imagination to the "historic details." But since I have established a kind of tradition by providing appendices in each of the books of the *Chronicles of the Nephilim*, I have decided to continue that dangerous tradition with the hopes of inspiring readers to go deeper in their study of the Bible than daily devotions and inspirational readings.

Retelling the story of the Tower of Babel and the life of Abraham is a particularly difficult task. The problem is that the further back in history one goes, the murkier are the waters, and anything in the fourth millennium B.C. Mesopotamia is complete guesswork. Biblically speaking, anything before the Davidic monarchy around 1000 B.C. is being increasingly contested by archaeological interpretations of the Near East.

The Biblical scholarly consensus is that Abraham lived around 2000 B.C. in Mesopotamia. But the evidence for this is thin and largely anecdotal. The best that can be offered is that there are some customs discovered in second millennium archives like Ebla and Mari that are similar to some customs in the Patriarchal narratives. Famous Egyptologist Kenneth Kitchen elucidates these similar customs such as treaty types, patriarchal proper names, patriarchal religion, slave prices, the use of camels, and other cultural customs.[1]

But David Noel Freedman points out that such cultural connections are not very reliable in establishing dates because "The Middle Bronze pattern of social custom and practice survived basically unchanged for centuries in certain localities in the Near East."[2]

Of all the events that occur in the Abraham narrative, none of them correspond with any known external historical or archaeological sources we have. This is not to say Abraham was made up, but merely to point out that scholars simply do not know for sure when Abraham's story took place in history because they do not have corroboration.

With the release of *Centuries of Darkness* in 1991 by Peter James, a dirty little secret of historiography was let out of the bag: There is a period of several centuries of historical "darkness" at the end of the Late Bronze Age in the received historical chronology of the ancient world. James argued that this period of darkness was an artifact of improper chronological accounting of the texts. A

---

[1] Kenneth A. Kitchen, *On the Reliability of the Old Testament* (Grand Rapids, MI: Eerdmans, 2003), 353-355.
[2] David Noel Freedman. "The chronology of Israel and the Ancient Near East," *The Bible and the Ancient Near East* (Winona Lake, IN: Eisenbrauns, 1961) 208.

chronological revolution was established that began to rewrite ancient world chronology with a three hundred year shift.

Much of ancient history is anchored in Egyptian chronology that is notoriously ambiguous and imprecise and creates problems for all kinds of historical anchoring of events. Donovan Courville in the 1970s, and more recently David Rohl, has explored the Egyptian problems to offer a "New Chronology" of the ancient world that roots Biblical history in new contexts significantly different from the conventional chronology.[3] They too have shaken up the establishment by uncovering the significant chronological problems of the conventional view.

In more recent years, Gerald Aardsma, has offered the Biblical theory that the Exodus occurred in 2450 B.C., *nearly one thousand years earlier* than the conventional dates of 1445 B.C. or 1225 B.C.[4] This would place Abraham in Mesopotamia around 3000 B.C. instead of 2000 B.C. A radical reconsideration.

But the reason why this is all so important is because the standard interpretation of Biblical archaeology is increasingly that the events of the Bible did not happen because they do not line up with the artifactual evidence of archaeology. There is simply no current evidence of a crushing defeat of Egypt or the resultant wandering of the Jews in the desert around the critical late date of 1275 B.C. There is no current evidence of the cities of Ai or Jericho being inhabited, much less destroyed around the dates that critical Biblical scholars say they must have happened. Rohl and the New Chronology shows that there is however archaeological evidence of

---

[3] Donovan Courville, *The Exodus Problem and Its Ramifications: A Critical Examination of the Chronological Relationships Between Israel and the Contemporary Peoples of Antiquity* (Loma Linda, CA: Challenge Books, 1971); David Rohl, *A Test of Time* (London, Random House, 1995); *From Eden to Exile: The Five Thousand Year History of the People of the Bible* (Lebanon, TN: Greenlead Press, 2003).

[4] Gerald E. Aardsma, Ph.D., *A New Approach to the Chronology of Biblical History from Abraham to Samuel* (Loda, IL: Aardsma Publishing, 2003, 2005); Aardsma, *The Exodus Happened 2450 B.C.* (Loda, IL: Aardsma Publishing, 2008).

all of the above occurring hundreds of years earlier in the fifteenth century B.C. With a few centuries shift backwards, all the Biblical history falls into place with known external evidence.

I write this because in my fictionalized novel, *Abraham Allegiant*, I used the interpretation of ancient Jewish texts and legends as my paradigm to place Abraham back during the time of the Tower of Babel, an event that would be considered about a thousand years before Abraham under the conventional chronology. While this supposition is largely rejected now, it has a long venerable tradition in 2nd Temple Jewish literature and Talmudic interpretation and shows up in Ginzberg's famous *Legends of the Jews*.[5] It is that interpretation that I found interesting enough to present within the pages of the novel because I have used these ancient Jewish sources throughout the entire series of *Chronicles of the Nephilim* to bring to life such characters as Enoch, Noah, Adam, Cain, the archangels Mikael, Gabriel and Uriel, and others.

The Book of Jasher

One of the dominant references I used in retelling this tale of Abraham and the Tower of Babel was the ancient *Book of Jasher*. *Jasher* is said to be one of the historical sources used by the Bible writers for their own texts (Josh. 10:13; 2Sam. 1:18). The only copy we have of this text is a medieval manuscript that most believe is a forgery. But Bible researcher Ken Johnson has argued for its authenticity based on the caliber of its writing, its possible transmission, its inclusion of the Biblically quoted material, as well as other missing details. Johnson fearlessly confronts some of the strange things in the book as indications of why it is not Scripture, while maintaining it as a solid historical reference used by the Bible

---

[5] Louis Ginzberg; trans. Henrietta Szold, (2011-01-13). *Legends of the Jews*, all four volumes in a single file, improved 1/13/2011 B&R Samizdat Express. Kindle Edition.

writers. He argues that it was one of the texts brought from Jerusalem to Spain at the fall of Jerusalem in A.D. 70.[6]

In the *Book of Jasher*, we read about the story of Nimrod building the Tower of Babel and hearing an astrological prophecy about the birth of Abram whose seed would rule over kings. Nimrod confronts Abram by throwing him in a furnace of fire, and Abram survives it by a miracle. It is also in this text that Amraphel, the king of Shinar who joined the four-nation confederation of Chedorlaomer that invaded Canaan, is explained as Nimrod under a new name.

What's in a Name

The idea of individuals changing their names is nothing new in the ancient world. We know that Abram's name which meant "exalted father" was changed to Abraham to mean "father of many nations" (Gen 17:5) based on the historical events of God's covenant with him. Later in the Bible, Jacob ("usurper") was changed to Israel ("struggles with God") as the ancestor of the people of God. Even ancient gods changed names based on locales. Inanna of Sumer became Ishtar of Babylonia, and then Ashtart of Canaan. Ninurta of Sumer was probably the basis for Marduk of Babylon, and then Ba'al of Canaan.

While it is a cardinal rule not to change a character's names in a modern story in order to avoid confusion, I have utilized this technique of changing names and identities as a foundational element in the *Chronicles of the Nephilim* storyline in order to incarnate the living cultural zeitgeist of the ancient world. Names were more than mere shallow title references to a person; they were believed to incarnate the person's very essence or identity, as well as mark significant moments in their lives.

---

[6] Ken Johnson, *The Ancient Book of Jasher: Referenced in Joshua 10:13, 2 Samuel 1:18, and 2 Timothy 3:8* (Biblefacts Ministries, 2008) 4-6, 188-190.

Yahweh

Even God himself is referred to by many different names in Scripture. Critical scholars use this fact to concoct a conspiracy theory that these different names were different gods that Israel worshipped in their own pantheon. As years went by elitist Jewish religious leaders became more intolerant. They finally recorded their zealous monotheist demands to worship one God instead of the others, but somehow foolishly left the residue of polytheism in the text of the Bible by neglecting to edit out the names from their source texts.

Apart from the fact that there is not a single scrap of actual historical or archeological evidence for this theorizing, it also reeks of modern imperialism by projecting stupidity onto the writers of some of the most intelligent and poetic literature in history. Such arrogance is easily dismissed when one studies the ancient cultural context of divine names as expressing character traits related to specific situations.

The text that illustrates this most suitably is Exodus 6:3-4 where God speaking to Moses says, "I am Yahweh. I appeared to Abraham, to Isaac, and to Jacob, as El Shaddai, but by my name Yahweh I did not make myself known to them."

Unfortunately, English translations obscure the meaning of the text by painting over the Hebrew names with bastardized generic terms. Thus, Yahweh is translated as "the LORD," and El Shaddai, as "God Almighty," which drains them of their rich cultural context and meaning. They further this offensive activity by translating El Elyon as "God Most High," and Elohim as "God," and on and on. We have reduced the names of the living God to nameless generic references to a "supreme being." This *de-naming* of Yahweh Elohim is more a reflection of the Greek impersonal "Prime Mover" than the Hebrew personal "Named One."

But when one researches the meaning behind the original Hebrew words, their truer fuller meaning comes to light. Elohim is revealed as a more generic plural reference to the Creator as all humankind can know through general revelation.[7] El Elyon has a linguistic affinity to the Ugaritic "Elyon Ba'al" a name for the Most High God of Canaan, and therefore a polemical stance against him. Ba'al is not the Most High, the God of Israel is.[8] El Shaddai, carries with it a possible derivation of "God of the mountain," a common understanding of deities in the ancient Near East as revealed in power on mountains (Mount Sinai and Mount Zion are God's locations of self-disclosure).[9] Finally, Yahweh is the "eternally self-existent one" who is the unique covenantal name of Israel's deity in opposition to the nations.[10]

When Yahweh told Moses he revealed himself to the forefathers as El Shaddai, but not as Yahweh, he was saying that they only knew him in a limited sense that was not as full as he was about to reveal. The Mosaic revelation of Yahweh on Sinai would be a dramatic world changing self-disclosure of God's unique character through his Law, a new revelation of God. This is what would separate them from the nations as a holy people of God's own choosing.

In the section below on Babel Inheritance, Deuteronomy 32:9 is shown to describe Yahweh as dividing the nations up at Babel and allotting the peoples under the authority of other gods, while keeping

[7] Names of God: Elohim, vol. 2, *The International Standard Bible Encyclopedia, Revised*, ed. Geoffrey W. Bromiley, 505 (Wm. B. Eerdmans, 1988).
[8] E. E. Elnes and P. D. Miller, "Elyon", in *Dictionary of Deities and Demons in the Bible*, ed. Karel van der Toorn, Bob Becking and Pieter W. van der Horst, 2nd extensively rev. ed., 295 (Leiden; Boston; Köln; Grand Rapids, MI; Cambridge: Brill; Eerdmans, 1999).
[9] Gordon J. Wenham, "The Religion of the Patriarchs," A.R. Millard & D.J. Wiseman, eds., *Essays on the Patriarchal Narratives*. Leicester: IVP, 1980, pp.157-188.
[10] Names of God: Yahweh, vol. 2, *The International Standard Bible Encyclopedia, Revised*, ed. Geoffrey W. Bromiley, 507 (Wm. B. Eerdmans, 1988).

Israel as his own people. Yahweh would be the name he would use to mark the strong demarcation between his people and the people in slavery to other gods.

Gilgamesh

This ancient Near Eastern obsession with changing names was also why I made Gilgamesh change his name and identity into Nimrod. This was not mere fancy or fabrication. There are some scholars who believe that Gilgamesh was the person behind the Nimrod of the Bible. But again, because of its antiquity, there are as many theories of who Nimrod really was as there are scholars.

W.H. Gispen listed just a few options of theories for the true historical identity of Nimrod by other scholars:

1. Gilgamesh, king of Uruk (2750 – 2600 B.C.)
2. Ninurta, the Sumerian deity
3. Marduk, the Babylonian deity
4. Tikulti-Ninurta, king of Assyria (1242-1206 B.C.)
5. Naram-Sin, king of Akkad (approx. 2300 B.C.)
6. Sargon, king of Akkad (2350 – 2294 B.C.)[11]
7. Enmerkar, king of Eridu in Sumer (approx. 2850 B.C.)[12]

As the reader can see, the theories are as widespread and diverse in their possibilities as a deity or a king, with a space of about one thousand years difference of possible fulfillment. The conclusion is pretty clear: Nobody really knows who Nimrod *really was*, but the name of Nimrod was most likely a Hebrew play on words that demonized the leader, because Nimrod in Hebrew means "to revolt." One hardly thinks a person would make his name with such negative

[11] W. H. Gispen, "Who Was Nimrod," in *The Law and the Prophets*, ed. J. H. Skilton (Philadelphia: Presbyterian & Reformed, 1974), 207–14.
[12] Rohl, *From Eden to Exile*, 58-77.

connotations, since such kings often considered themselves like the gods — Unless a king did so as a defiant gesture "in the face of" a deity he hated. Thus the motivation behind the Nimrod of the *Chronicles*.

Scholars van der Toorn and van der Horst suggest that Nimrod was most likely a deliberately distorted Hebrew version of Ninurta as the hunter god of Mesopotamia. They argue that the reign of Nimrod was most likely a symbolic synopsis of the history of Mesopotamia embodied in one character, a deity deliberately dethroned by the Jewish writer to a hunter king.

> The cities [of Nimrod] mentioned in Gen 10:9-12 are given in a more or less chronological sequence. The list reads as a condensed resume of Mesopotamian history. Akkad, though still in use as a cult-center in the first millennium, had its *floruit* under the Sargonic dynasty. Kalhu had its heyday in the first half of the first millennium BCE, some fifteen hundred years later. If Nimrod is not a god, he must at least have enjoyed a divine longevity, his reign embracing both cities.[13]

Babel

The Tower of Babel incident is also an event that has a long history of as many interpretive possibilities as there are scholars. The standard ancient interpretation was that Babel and its tower were simply the city of Babylon in mid-Mesopotamia that had been started, then stopped by the confusion of tongues, only to be reborn a thousand years later under Hammurabi's predecessors.

---

[13] K. van der Toorn and P. W. van der Horst, "Nimrod before and after the Bible," *Harvard Theological Review* 83 (1990): 1–29.

Contrarily, Anne Habermehl has argued that it was in the far northeastern part of Syria;[14] David Rohl argued that Babel was actually the oldest known city of Eridu in the southernmost region of Sumeria on the gulf, and its tower was the famous ziggurat called *Nunki*.[15]

Again, with so many different interpretations possible, spanning thousands of miles of geography, no one really knows. But I went with the traditional interpretation on this one because it was still a sensible option. Unfortunately, because the water table is so high in the modern region of the ruins of Babylon, we will never be able to excavate any layers of sediment below to discover its more ancient past.

Abraham and the Giants

The picture of Abraham as a warrior fits very well with the warrior motif of *Chronicles of the Nephilim*. But even this is not as much fiction as it is Biblical fact because in Genesis 14 we read about Abram leading 318 warriors trained in his household on a rescue mission of his nephew Lot. Not only did he and his men, along with an unspecified group of allies from three friendly Amorite tribes, bring back the Sodomite captives and their booty, but they overtook a four-city coalition army that had just swept through Canaan. Abraham and his men were no mere pastoral shepherds. They were warriors.

But Genesis 14 is a particularly peculiar Biblical passage because it speaks of that four-city coalition, led by Chedorlaomer, as specifically coming to Canaan to punish Sodom and Gomorrah and the five cities of the Plain for rebelling against them as their vassals

---

[14] Anne Habermehl, "Where in the World Is the Tower of Babel?" *Answers Research Journal* 4 (2011) 25–53.
[15] Rohl, *From Eden to Exile*, 65.

(v. 4). But before Chedorlaomer goes to Sodom and Gomorrah, he goes out of his way to wipe out giant clans throughout Canaan.

> Genesis 14:5–7
> Chedorlaomer and the kings who were with him came and defeated the Rephaim in Ashteroth-karnaim, the Zuzim in Ham, the Emim in Shaveh-kiriathaim, [6] and the Horites in their hill country of Seir...[7] Then they turned back and came to En-mishpat (that is, Kadesh) and defeated all the country of the Amalekites, and also the Amorites who were dwelling in Hazazon-tamar.

All these named tribes are elsewhere in the Bible described as giant clans as listed below.

> Rephaim (Deut. 2:10-11, 20; 3:11)
> Zuzim, short for "Zamzummim" (Deut. 2:20)
> Emim (Deut. 2:10-11)
> Horites/Horim (Deut. 2:21-22)
> Amalekites (Numbers 13:28-29)
> Amorites (Amos 2:9-10)

Chedorlaomer and his armies were targeting the giant clans before returning home to Mesopotamia. After this genocide, we do not hear much at all about the giants again until over 400 years later when the Israelites are entering Canaan. So the remnant of giants must have taken all that time to rebuild their population numbers.

Semiramis

Another tradition that shows up in ancient legends surrounding Nimrod and Babylon is that of Queen Semiramis. The most well known ancient reference to this queen of Babylon comes from the Greek historian Diodorus Siculus who wrote of the mythical romance of Semiramis with King Ninus, around 2189 B.C.[16] Since Ninus was the reputed founder of Nineveh, it was a simple connection to be made with Nimrod who was the founder of Nineveh in the Bible.

Later in 1853, Protestant minister Alexander Hislop expanded on the relationship of Nimrod and Semiramis in *The Two Babylons*. Hislop's mythmaking became very influential though it was entirely fabricated by the writer to serve his anti-Catholic polemic.[17]

The closest historical personage that can be said to be the source of the Semiramis legends was Queen Shammuramat of Assyria, who reigned with King Shamshi-Adad V around 824-811 B.C., and whose Neo-Assyrian empire included Babylonia. There was a legend that she had once been a brothel keeper in Uruk, thus her connection with Shamhat the harlot from *Gilgamesh Immortal*.

Arba

The giant king Arba makes his appearance in *Abraham Allegiant*. But this is not a character of the author's imagination. There was a giant named Arba after whose name the city of Kiriath-Arba (later called Hebron) was named. He was of such significance to the author of Joshua, that he wrote of him, "Arba was the greatest man among the Anakim" (Joshua 14:15), and that "he was the father

---

[16] Diodorus Siculus, Library of History, Book II, (Loeb Classical Library Edition, 1933) Online: <
http://penelope.uchicago.edu/Thayer/E/Roman/Texts/Diodorus_Siculus/2A*.html>
[17] Ralph Woodrow, *The Babylon Connection?* (Ralph Woodrow Evangelistic Association, 1997, 2004).

of Anak" (15:13). The Anakim were the giant descendants of the Nephilim who seemed to dominate southern Canaan when Israel arrived for conquest. Joshua's campaign in the hill country was focused on eliminating these Anakim as mortal enemies (Joshua 11:21-22).

Since Arba was the father of the giant Anak who birthed the people devoted to destruction much later in history, and since Abraham was said to live only two miles from the city founded by Arba (Gen 13:18; 23:2), it is not too much to speculate that Arba may have met Abraham, foreshadowing the providential rivalry these two people groups would have over that territory.

The Destroyer

"The Destroyer" is a translation of the Hebrew word used of the angel who entered the houses of the Egyptians and killed their first born as God's last plague on the Hebrews' oppressors (Ex 12:23). The *Dictionary of Deities and Demons in the Bible* says of this peculiar angel,

> "'Destroyer' is the designation of a supernatural envoy from God assigned the task of annihilating large numbers of people, typically by means of a plague... there was originally a distinction between the angel of death who comes to an individual at the time appointed for him to die and the Destroyer who massacres entire populations with premature and violent deaths. Later traditions, however, fuse the two conceptions.[18]

---

[18] S. A. Meier, "Destroyer", in *Dictionary of Deities and Demons in the Bible*, ed. Karel van der Toorn, Bob Becking and Pieter W. van der Horst, 2nd extensively rev. ed., 240 (Leiden; Boston; Köln; Grand Rapids, MI; Cambridge: Brill; Eerdmans, 1999).

In 1 Chronicles 21:14-16 we see a poignant picture of God sending the Destroyer to wipe out Jerusalem with a plague, but changing his mind from the calamity. One wonders if this is not also what happened at Babel.

Babel Inheritance

Another key element of the storyline of *Chronicles of the Nephilim* is the allotment of nations to the sons of God as punishment for humanity's rebellion. While I wrote a bit about this in the appendices of *Noah Primeval*, *Abraham Allegiant* is where this fascinating Biblical theological legal concept takes place at the Tower of Babel incident.

A brief look at the original full text of the Tower of Babel pericope in the Bible will help set the stage for a closer look at the theological ramifications of what it was all about.

> Genesis 11:1–9
> [1] Now the whole earth had one language and the same words. [2] And as people migrated from the east, they found a plain in the land of Shinar and settled there. [3] And they said to one another, "Come, let us make bricks, and burn them thoroughly." And they had brick for stone, and bitumen for mortar. [4] Then they said, "Come, let us build ourselves a city and a tower with its top in the heavens, and let us make a name for ourselves, lest we be dispersed over the face of the whole earth." [5] And the LORD came down to see the city and the tower, which the children of man had built. [6] And the LORD said, "Behold, they are one people, and they have all one language, and this is

only the beginning of what they will do. And nothing that they propose to do will now be impossible for them. [7] Come, let us go down and there confuse their language, so that they may not understand one another's speech." [8] So the LORD dispersed them from there over the face of all the earth, and they left off building the city. [9] Therefore its name was called Babel, because there the LORD confused the language of all the earth. And from there the LORD dispersed them over the face of all the earth.

So we see that within a short time after the Flood, mankind had proven to be corrupt once again in seeking to unite in a headlong pursuit of self-deification. They decidedly used kiln-burned brick with bitumen for mortar most likely because of their memory of the Flood wiping away their mud brick buildings and temples. This waterproofing technique was the first expression of their devious attempt to circumvent God's future judgment.

Then they seek to build a city and a tower "with its top in the heavens." The Hebrew word for tower no doubt referred to the ziggurat temple-tower at the heart of every Mesopotamian city. To discover the idolatrous meaning of this reference, John Walton explains that the function of the ziggurats came from the names given to them:

> For instance, the name of the ziggurat at Babylon, *Etemenanki*, means "temple of the foundation of heaven and earth." One at Larsa means "temple that links heaven and earth." Most significant is the name of the ziggurat at Sippar, "temple of the stairway to pure heaven." The word translated "stairway" in this

last example is used in the mythology as the means by which the messenger of the gods moved between heaven, earth, and the netherworld.[19]

So the temple-tower of Babylon was a religious incarnation of their attempt to create a forbidden link between heaven and earth by building their own stairway to heaven for the gods, a violation of God's monarchic authority.

Then they seek to "make a name for themselves," which is a common Biblical and ancient Near Eastern idiom for greatness. By uniting together, their pride was so great that there would be no limit to their hubris. This blasphemous self-deification would be a real threat because, remember, mankind was God's image, his representative ruler over creation. So, if man would unite in this kind of rebellion, imagine the evil that would result, an evil that might rival what happened before the Flood.

So the confusion of tongues and dispersion of mankind breaks apart the tyrannical potential of this global one world government.

We are told twice that God "dispersed them over the face of the earth" in order to stop the megalomaniacal and totalitarian potential of mankind unified in rebellion against God.

The seventy nations described in Genesis 10 are the resultant new boundaries allotted to mankind that came from this Dispersion.

But this Dispersion is not the whole picture. There is something else that happens at this dividing of mankind, something spiritual and legal in the heavenly courtroom of God. God actually divides up the seventy nations and apportions them under the authority of the

---

[19] John H Walton, *Zondervan Illustrated Bible Backgrounds Commentary (Old Testament) Volume 1: Genesis, Exodus, Leviticus, Numbers, Deuteronomy*, (Grand Rapids, MI: Zondervan, 2009) 62.

Bene ha Elohim, the sons of God, those divine beings that surround his heavenly throne.

Let's take a look at some of the Biblical passages that reveal this allotment of nations.

> Deut. 32:8–9
> When the Most High gave to the nations their inheritance, when he divided mankind, he fixed the borders of the peoples according to the number of the sons of God. But the LORD's portion is his people, Jacob his allotted heritage.

In this passage, the Scripture refers to the "dividing of mankind," which happened in the Dispersion at the Tower of Babel that we already looked at. God separated the nations by giving them different languages so they can no longer unite in blasphemous self-deification. And he divides up the borders of their dwelling. But he does so *according to the number of the sons of God.*

God put the seventy divided nations under the authority of these sons of God to whom they were "allotted." But he allotted the people of Jacob to himself as his heritage. The question then arises, what kind of authority do these sons of God have over the nations? Are they good or evil host of heaven? A look at other Biblical passages reveals that these sons of God are fallen beings and they are to become the false deities that own and rule over the pagan nations as Yahweh owns and rules over his people.

> Deut. 4:19-20
> And beware lest you raise your eyes to heaven, and when you see the sun and the moon and the stars, all the host of heaven, you be drawn away and bow

down to them and serve them, things that the LORD your God has allotted to all the peoples under the whole heaven. But the LORD has taken you and brought you out of the iron furnace, out of Egypt, to be a people of his own inheritance, as you are this day.

Deut. 29:24-26
Then men will say, 'Because they forsook the covenant of the LORD, the God of their fathers, which He made with them when He brought them out of the land of Egypt. They went and served other gods and worshiped them, gods whom they have not known and whom He had not allotted to them.

Here again, we see a description of the "allotment" of the host of heaven to the pagan nations along with the allotment of Israel to Yahweh as his inheritance. The gentile nations are allotted to the sons of God/heavenly host/false gods of the land, while Israel is allotted to Yahweh and Yahweh allotted to Israel.

But notice in this passage, there is an equivalency of the sun, moon and stars with the host of heaven, a term used interchangeably with the Sons of God.[20] The sun, moon, and stars were worshipped as gods, and Yahweh is saying that these gods are the ones allotted to the nations. So, this is not a holy host of heaven, but an unholy host of heaven. These sons of God are not in God's heavenly court, they are evil fallen beings from that divine council.

---

[20] H. Niehr, "Host of Heaven," Toorn, K. van der, Bob Becking, and Pieter Willem van der Horst. *Dictionary of Deities and Demons in the Bible DDD.* 2nd extensively rev. ed. Leiden; Boston; Grand Rapids, Mich.: Brill; Eerdmans, 1999., 428-29; I. Zatelli, "Astrology and the Worship of the Stars in the Bible," *ZAW* 103 (1991): 86-99.

The demonic reality of pagan gods is expressed further down in the same Deuteronomy chapter 32. The false gods were demons, real spiritual beings that had fallen from God's divine council:

> Deut. 32:16-17
> They stirred him to jealousy with strange gods; with abominations they provoked him to anger. <u>They sacrificed to demons</u> that were no gods, <u>to gods</u> they had never known, <u>to new gods that had come recently</u>, whom your fathers had never dreaded.

Second Temple Jewish literature and legend is not Scripture, but it certainly shows a paradigm that lines up with this Biblical notion of God allotting pagan nations to geographical territories ruled over by Sons of God as their deities. A perusal of some of these passages sheds more light on this paradigm:

> Ginzberg's Legends of the Jews
> It was on this occasion that God and the seventy angels that surround His throne cast lots concerning the various nations. Each angel received a nation, and Israel fell to the lot of God. To every nation a peculiar language was assigned, Hebrew being reserved for Israel.[21]

> Jubilees 15:30-32
> (There are) many nations and many people, and they all belong to him, but <u>over all of them he caused spirits to rule so that they might lead them astray from</u>

---

[21] Ginzberg, Louis; Szold, Henrietta (2011-01-13). Legends of the Jews, all four volumes in a single file, improved 1/13/2011 (Kindle Locations 2586-2588). B&R Samizdat Express. Kindle Edition.

following him. But over Israel he did not cause any angel or spirit to rule because he alone is their ruler and he will protect them and he will seek for them at the hand of his angels and at the hand of his spirits and at the hand of all of his authorities so that he might guard them and bless them and they might be his and he might be theirs henceforth and forever.[22]

Targum Jonathan, Deuteronomy 32, Section LIII
When the Most High made allotment of the world unto the nations which proceeded from the sons of Noach [Noah], in the separation of the writings and languages of the children of men at the time of the division, He cast the lot among the seventy angels, the princes of the nations with whom is the revelation to oversee the city.[23]

Philo, On the Posterity of Cain and His Exile 25.89
The Most High, when he divided the nations, dispersed the sons of Adam, and fixed the boundaries of the nations according to the number of the angels of God. And the portion of the Lord was his people Jacob, the limitation of the inheritance of Israel."[24]

---

[22] James H. Charlesworth, *vol. 2, The Old Testament Pseudepigrapha and the New Testament, Volume 2: Expansions of the "Old Testament" and Legends, Wisdom, and Philosophical Literature, Prayers, Psalms and Odes, Fragments of Lost Judeo-Hellenistic Works*, (New Haven; London: Yale University Press, 1985) 87.

[23] See also *Targum Jonathan, Genesis 11*, Section II; *Concerning Noah's Work as a Planter* 14.59; *On the Migration of Abraham* 36.202; *1 Clement 29*; Origen, *First Principles* 1.5.1. Thanks to Don Enevoldsen for some of these passages.

[24] Philo of Alexandria and Charles Duke Yonge, *The Works of Philo: Complete and Unabridged*, 140 (Peabody, MA: Hendrickson, 1995).

Now, when we take a look at Psalm 82, an otherwise confusing passage becomes crystal clear in its context of the Tower of Babel, the Dispersion, and the Allotment of gods and nations.

> Psalm 82:1–8
> [1] God has taken his place in the divine council;
> in the midst of the gods he holds judgment:
> [2] "How long will you judge unjustly
> and show partiality to the wicked? Selah
> [3] Give justice to the weak and the fatherless;
> maintain the right of the afflicted and the destitute.
> [4] Rescue the weak and the needy;
> deliver them from the hand of the wicked."
>
> [5] They have neither knowledge nor understanding,
> they walk about in darkness;
> all the foundations of the earth are shaken.
>
> [6] I said, "You are gods,
> sons of the Most High, all of you;
> [7] nevertheless, like men you shall die,
> and fall like any prince."
>
> [8] Arise, O God, judge the earth;
> for you shall inherit all the nations!

Many Christians try to interpret this passage as if it were talking about human judges over Israel being punished for not meting out justice. But in its ancient Near Eastern context we can see that God is talking to the supernatural Sons of God ("sons of the Most High"), who were allotted the gentile nations to rule over them being judged for their failure to rule justly. And then the writer says that Yahweh will inherit those nations, a reference to the Gospel where all the pagan nations would be allowed to come under God's rule through faith in Jesus Christ.

In a very real sense, the Gospel breaks the power of false gods over the gentile nations and brings them into the fold of God's people along with believing Jews. God will inherit the nations who were once under the allotment and inheritance of the pagan gods.

The event of Pentecost that occurs in Acts 2, where a diversity of gentile tongues proclaimed "the mighty works of God," is a theological reversal of Babel by the Holy Spirit. At Babel, God confused their languages, and dispersed the peoples, placing them under the authority of Sons of God as their deities. God "gave them over" to their wickedness. With the arrival of Messiah, the Gospel liberates those gentile nations from their bondage to be drawn back and become united as one in Christ through faith. The power of the false gods over the gentile nations is broken.

Thus the apostle Paul can preach to his gentile pagans,

> Acts 17:26–31
> "And he made from one man every nation of mankind to live on all the face of the earth, having determined allotted periods and the boundaries of their dwelling place, that they should seek God, and perhaps feel their way toward him and find him. Yet he is actually not far from each one of us...
> The times of ignorance God overlooked, but now he commands all people everywhere to repent, because he has fixed a day on which he will judge the world in righteousness by a man whom he has appointed; and

of this he has given assurance to all by raising him from the dead."

For additional Biblical, historical and mythical research related to this novel, go to www.ChroniclesoftheNephilim.com under the menu listing, "Scholarly Research."

If you liked this book, then please help me out by writing an honest review of it on Amazon. That is one of the best ways to say thank you to me as an author. It really does help my exposure and status as an author. It's really easy. In the Customer Reviews section, there is a little box that says "Write a customer review." They guide you easily through the process. Thanks! — *Brian Godawa*

GREAT OFFERS BY BRIAN GODAWA

Get More
Biblical Imagination

Sign up Online For
The Godawa Chronicles

www.Godawa.com

Updates and Freebies
of the Books of Brian Godawa
Special Discounts,
Weird Bible Facts!

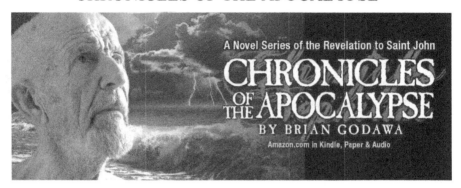

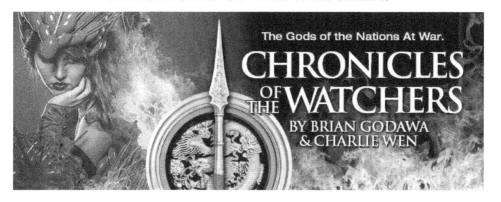

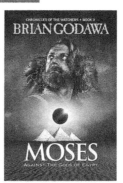
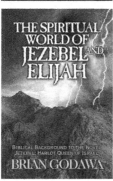
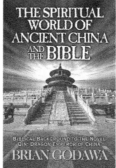
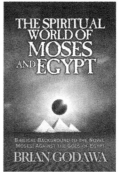

VIDEO LECTURES

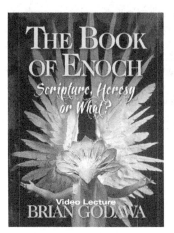

The Book of Enoch: Scripture, Heresy or What?

This lecture by Brian Godawa will be an introduction to the ancient book of 1Enoch, its content, its history, its affirmation in the New Testament, and its acceptance and rejection by the Christian Church. What is the Book of Enoch? Where did it come from? Why isn't it in the Bible? How does the Book of Enoch compare with the Bible?

Available on video.

Chronicles of the Nephilim: The Ancient Biblical Story

Watchers, Nephilim, and the Divine Council of the Sons of God. In this dvd video lecture, Brian Godawa explores the Scriptures behind this transformative storyline that inspired his best-selling Biblical novel series Chronicles of the Nephilim.

Available on video.

To download these lectures and other books and products by Brian Godawa, just go to the STORE at:

www.Godawa.com

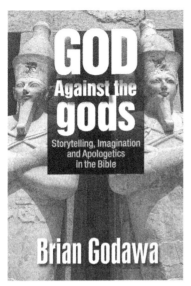

How God Captures the Imagination

This book was previously titled *Myth Became Fact: Storytelling, Imagination & Apologetics in the Bible*.

Brian Godawa, Hollywood screenwriter and best-selling novelist, explores the nature of imagination in the Bible. You will learn how God subverts pagan religions by appropriating their imagery and creativity, and redeeming them within a Biblical worldview. Improve your imagination in your approach to glorifying God and defending the faith.

Demonizing the Pagan Gods
God verbally attacked his opponents, pagans and their gods, using sarcasm, mockery, name-calling.

Old Testament Storytelling Apologetics
Israel shared creative images with their pagan neighbors: The sea dragon of chaos and the storm god. The Bible invests them with new meaning.

Biblical Creation and Storytelling
Creation stories in the ancient Near East and the Bible both express a primeval battle of deity to create order out of chaos. But how do they differ?

The Universe in Ancient Imagination
A detailed comparison and contrast of the Biblical picture of the universe with the ancient pagan one. What's the difference?

New Testament Storytelling Apologetics
Paul's sermon to the pagans on Mars Hill is an example of subversion: Communicating the Gospel in terms of a pagan narrative with a view toward replacing their worldview.

Imagination in Prophecy & Apocalypse
God uses imaginative descriptions of future events to deliberately obscure his message while simultaneously showing the true meaning and purpose behind history.

An Apologetic of Biblical Horror
Learn how God uses horror in the Bible as a tool to communicate spiritual, moral and social truth in the context of repentance from sin and redemptive victory over evil.

For More Info
www.Godawa.com

Art, Creativity and Truth in the Bible

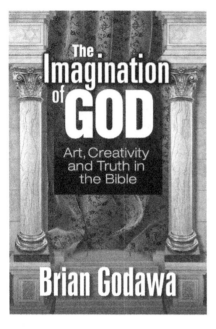

In his refreshing and challenging book, Godawa helps you break free from the spiritual suffocation of heady faith. Without negating the importance of reason and doctrine, Godawa challenges you to move from understanding the Bible "literally" to "literarily" by exploring the poetry, parables and metaphors found in God's Word. Weaving historical insight, pop culture and personal narrative throughout, Godawa reveals the importance God places on imagination and creativity in the Scriptures, and provides a Biblical foundation for Christians to pursue imagination, beauty, wonder and mystery in their faith.

This book was previously released with the title, *Word Pictures: Knowing God Through Story and Imagination.*

Endorsements:

"Brian Godawa is that rare breed—a philosopher/artist—who opens our eyes to the aesthetic dimension of spirituality. Cogently argued and fun to read, Godawa shows convincingly that God interacts with us as whole persons, not only through didactic teaching but also through metaphor, symbol, and sacrament."

— Nancy R. Pearcey,
Author, *Total Truth: Liberating Christianity from its Cultural Captivity*

"A spirited and balanced defense of the imagination as a potential conveyer of truth. There is a lot of good literary theory in the book, as well as an autobiographical story line. The thoroughness of research makes the book a triumph of scholarship as well."

— Leland Ryken, Clyde S. Kilby Professor of English, Wheaton College, Illinois
Author, *The Christian Imagination: The Practice of Faith in Literature & Writing.*

For More Info
www.Godawa.com

ABOUT THE AUTHOR

Brian Godawa is the screenwriter for the award-winning feature film, *To End All Wars,* starring Kiefer Sutherland. It was awarded the Commander in Chief Medal of Service, Honor and Pride by the Veterans of Foreign Wars, won the first Heartland Film Festival by storm, and showcased the Cannes Film Festival Cinema for Peace.

He also co-wrote *Alleged*, starring Brian Dennehy as Clarence Darrow and Fred Thompson as William Jennings Bryan. He previously adapted to film the best-selling supernatural thriller novel *The Visitation* by author Frank Peretti for Ralph Winter (*X-Men, Wolverine*), and wrote and directed *Wall of Separation,* a PBS documentary, and *Lines That Divide*, a documentary on stem cell research.

Mr. Godawa's scripts have won multiple awards in respected screenplay competitions, and his articles on movies and philosophy have been published around the world. He has traveled around the United States teaching on movies, worldviews, and culture to colleges, churches and community groups.

His popular book, *Hollywood Worldviews: Watching Films with Wisdom and Discernment* (InterVarsity Press) is used as a textbook in schools around the country. His novel series, the saga *Chronicles of the Nephilim* is in the Top 10 of Biblical Fiction on Amazon and is an imaginative retelling of Biblical stories of the Nephilim giants, the secret plan of the fallen Watchers, and the War of the Seed of the Serpent with the Seed of Eve. The sequel series, *Chronicles of the Apocalypse* tells the story of the Apostle John's book of Revelation, and *Chronicles of the Watchers* recounts true history through the Watcher paradigm.

Find out more about his other books, lecture tapes and dvds for sale at his website www.godawa.com.

BLANK PAGE

BLANK PAGE

BLANK PAGE

Made in the USA
Coppell, TX
13 January 2024

27660116R00226